THE GLASS BARRIER

Growing up together in close intimacy, exchanging hopes and confidences, then discovering that there is a barrier between them, transparent but impermeable . . . that is the situation between the young people in this book. The situation occurs everywhere, but here there are special tensions, because this is a book about young South Africans.

In the beginning there is the discovery of two young girls "brought up in the same puppy basket" that they want the same man. Maxie Lamotte, impulsive and vulnerable, is afraid of her own feelings; Rima Antrobus has no misgivings. She is a vital, determined girl, whose artistic talent is already remarkable. She wants Simon, her adopted brother, and means to ward Maxie off. Maxie's brother Claude wants a girl too, but here the barrier is something tougher than glass, for Claude is White and Fara is Coloured.

It is in 1960 that the personal tensions merge into the national tragedy. Simon and Maxie, driving to the airport to meet Claude, who is bringing news that they alone know and fear, see flames on the horizon above the native location of Langa. They hear the uproar of rioting and shooting and try to turn aside; on the road ahead they see a police van stopped by a car which has been stoned and set on fire. It is Maxie's father's car and he was in it.

A state of emergency is declared; superstitious fears mount and no one, black or white, is immune.

THE
GLASS BARRIER

A NOVEL BY

JOY PACKER

1961
EYRE & SPOTTISWOODE
LONDON

FIRST PUBLISHED 1961
© 1961 JOY PACKER
PRINTED IN GREAT BRITAIN
BY BILLING & SONS LTD
GUILDFORD & LONDON
CAT. NO. 6/4247/2

CONTENTS

Part 1. Growing Pains

Part 2. New Horizons

Part 3. *Year of Fate*

Part I

GROWING PAINS

I

THE SECRET

I WILL NEVER FORGET the shock of my cousin, Rima's, secret.

We were thirteen. Over seven years have passed since then, and they say that every seven years you are a new person. I can believe that. I am by no means the same person I was then. But that particular shock is with me still. It is in my mind and my heart and every physical bit of me – a small individual earthtremor that warned of greater quakes to come.

It was so often that way. A state of affairs would exist – dormant, tranquil, pleasant or unpleasant, as the case might be – and then suddenly Rima'd stir it up, and after that there'd be no more peace.

We four – Simon and Rima Antrobus and my brother, Claude, and I – were more like one family than two separate units. Simon and Rima belonged to Cape Town, whereas Claude and I were children of the beautiful fertile Paarl Valley. They were of the city; we were country cousins. But we were all interchangeable. We shared their background and they shared ours.

In term time Claude and I lived in Cape Town with the Antrobus family, and in the holidays Simon and Rima came to our farm, Loire. It was part of the interlocking mesh of our lives. From time to time we escaped each other, but we were always drawn together again as if magnetised.

Rima's mother and mine were sisters, devoted but unalike, and we cousins were devoted too, after our own fashion. But from time to time we got at each other's throats with a cruel instinctive ferocity that knew well how to inflict the deadliest wounds. It was like that on the hot summer day when Rima told me her secret in the lofty raftered bedroom we used to share at Loire.

Everything in that room was old and seasoned, from the yellow-wood floor and ceiling to the stinkwood tallboy and the huge four-poster bed. Everything except us. We were those creatures of no-man's-land that

A*   9

grown-ups calls adolescents with a note of irritation and pity in their voices. Thirteen. The sap is rising and spring has a meaning – a real meaning. It is no longer just a season of the year, it is a season within your own body; and the languor of summer is a sensuous ache. It ached in both of us that January afternoon. Our room, which always smelt slightly of lavender and beeswax, was reasonably cool, but outside it was cooking. Heavens, how it can steam up in our valley! The violet mountains, enfolding the many morgen of Loire, grow pale and ethereal; lakes of mirage shimmer in the parched bush; the vineyards and wheatfields dance to the high feverish music of cicadas; and only the oaks are cool, standing in their private pools of shade, gently filtering the glare through green foliage, their life of dove and squirrel drowsy in the heat.

We could see the dense design of leaves framed by the tall sash window with its wide teak sill and small panes. I loved that rich green summer picture, but Rima liked it best in winter when it became an etching with only a few golden tatters clinging to the boughs. "Then it's revealed – the whole delicate system," she'd say, precociously artistic.

We had just come up to the house from the dam, where we'd been swimming with the boys – Simon, Claude, and Jamie Vermeulen, who was the son of our Afrikaans neighbour at Bergplaas. Jamie was the fifth wheel to our youthful wagon in the holidays. He was always around, more one of us than my brother, Claude, in some ways. He "spoke our language" – though literally his home language was Afrikaans and ours was English – whereas Claude often seemed to us to be existing on some other plane and in some other age.

Rima slammed the door, not because she was cross but because it was the way we treated doors, and then she stared at herself in the cheval mirror, tipping it to suit her height. She leaned forward to study herself, as if this were a moment on the wing which must be caught, or lost for ever. We did that sort of thing a good deal about then, because we were constantly astonishing ourselves. We were a little different every day. We were turning into women. Every stage of our development fascinated, and sometimes alarmed, us.

"I'm a fox," said Rima. "Pointed nose, pointed chin, yellow-brown eyes and fluffy rufous hair—"

"Rufous?"

"With humans they call it auburn. The bird book calls it rufous. I'm a fox with the hounds on my scent! I have a persecuted face – a face carved

for betrayal and death. It's the Jewess in me – the long ago pogroms and
the wailing at the wall."

She often said things that stuck in one's mind like swear words or frag-
ments of poetry. They made me want to argue.

"One Jewess way back in your family doesn't make an Israelite of
you."

"She was my namesake, and I have a special affinity with her."

That other Rima – a refugee and a famous pianist – had alighted, like a
weary, exotic bird, on the Anglican family tree of Antrobus. To my cousin
she stood for glamour, the arts, and the phoenix quality of the Jewish
nation.

Rima swung round and studied me critically.

"Yours is an Aryan face, Maxie. I hardly know what animal you'd be.
Something supple and domestic, but independent, with a touch of wild-
ness. Blunt nose, pale silky fur, blue eyes tilted just a trifle—"

"Freckles—"

"A leopard has freckles – huge ones – but you aren't savage enough to be
a leopard. Except when you get in one of your tempers. You could be a
cat – a Siamese – yet you aren't really feline. You mind about people. They
can hurt your feelings. If somebody says something mean to you, tears
jump into your eyes. You cry easily. That's a dog trait. Dogs care about
people."

I was sensitive about that. "Dogs don't cry tears. They yowl."

"Their eyes tell all. Sadness, loving, fierceness. Everything is in their
eyes – like it's in yours." She was laughing. "This minute you look quite
furious! I think you could be a cheetah, though. Wild and swift but can
be tamed. They say cheetahs make sweet pets."

She peeled off her swim-suit. She was shorter than I was, but already
more mature. I envied her that. I flung a towel round my naked body, too
boyish still for my liking, and perched on the wide wooden window-sill
in the pink glow of the sunset. I could see the three lads, Simon, Claude
and Jamie Vermeulen, crossing the lawn from the direction of the dam as
they strolled up to the house to go to my brother's room.

"Here they come, Rima. What animal would you say Jamie was?"

She hitched herself up onto the sill, her striped towel about her slim
sloping shoulders. She watched them drawing nearer, Jamie and Claude
on either side of Simon; Jamie tough and sturdy, Claude's glasses catching
the light – a shame he had to wear them all the time, even for sport – and

I could just glimpse the top of Simon's head, high and mettlesome, the damp brown curls matted.

"Well?" I said.

"Jamie? Oh, I guess he's one of the big antelopes. Strong and rather splendid. A herd animal. He'd be the hell of a fighter in the mating season!"

The thought of Jamie in the mating season, fighting to the death, was rather exciting.

I flexed my toes along the sill, and they met Rima's and began to quarrel. We giggled. Our hands were locked about our knees; our heads were turned to the lawn outside the window, to the boys who were young men already – seventeen, and shaving.

"Back to back we'd make a good pair of book-ends," said Rima. "In sandal-wood."

She was always conscious of form and balance. It encroached on her mind at every point. She never had to seek her art. It lived inside her. She would have written history as the ancients did – in architectural frescoes – while I would have expressed it in human stories.

They were coming abreast now. Rima said:

"There's a real cat-man – your brother, Claude. Aloof and alone, a black hunting-cat, with a dusty coat and eyes that don't give a damn for anybody, not caring for a thing except his purpose."

He moved, lithe and shadow-like, on the far side of Simon, the slightest of the three. He was dark and reticent, more Beeford than Lamotte. I was the one who followed my father's family, the passionate, unpractical, high-handed Lamottes.

"And Simon – what about Simon?"

Rima had her answer pat. She didn't have to think. She'd done her thinking about Simon. He was known to her. Heavens, how well he was known! Not just the look and smell and feel of him, but the pace of him, his life-rhythm, the beat of his heart, staccato as the clip of hoof-beats. Or am I talking now of *my* knowledge of Simon? Am I lending her, in retrospect, what is essentially my own? It could be. But Rima saw him very clearly, all the young fiery male quality of him that could take our breath away and leave us faint with wanting something that still lay beyond our experience.

"Simon is the bible horse," she said. "The warrior horse. 'Canst thou make him afraid as the grasshopper? The glory of his nostrils is terrible.' "

"Simon blows out his nostrils," I said. "He snorts!"

" 'He paweth in the valley and rejoiceth in his strength . . .' How does it go on, Maxie?"

" 'He saith among the trumpets, Ha, ha, and he smelleth the battle from afar . . .' Something like that."

"When he's in a rage he rolls his eyes and tosses his head."

We chortled with delight. We said "Ha, ha!" and imagined Simon cantering along the foothill fences like our own wild unbroken Loire foals with spirited eyes and flying manes. Then we whispered "*Hush!*" as the three lads passed under our window to cross the courtyard. They didn't see us, they were absorbed in their talk. We heard their voices, but not their words. Claude's was mellow, warmer than you'd expect; Jamie's was deep and furry, with its Afrikaans inflection; and Simon's was vibrant, with laughter near the surface. That was the way we heard it oftenest – laughing at us and teasing us. However conscious we might be of our growing pains, to the lads Rima and I were still just kids.

They had disappeared. They were out of hearing. Rima leaned forward to bring her head closer to mine. We were a frieze on the wide teak sill, confidential and immature. The towel had slipped from her shoulders; her small half formed breasts were bare, chequered with rosy light. Her eyes were agate, neither gold nor brown, her reddish hair was wild and tangled, ball-shaped to frame the sharp pale wedge of her face.

"Shall I tell you a secret, Maxie?"

I was silent, biting my lip, consumed with curiosity but suspicious. Swapping secrets was one of our things. Some weren't worth the name, others were terrific, but the anticipation of being let into a secret was always a thrill. Yet suddenly the danger signals were chasing round my nerves saying "No! No! Don't listen to this one!" Perhaps her expression warned me. It was intent and greedy. She was not the hunted now but the huntress – the fox, cunning and remorseless, at the door of the fowl-run. I ought to have jumped down and run away, but her eyes held me. I was tingling all over and the goose-pimples bumped up on my arms as they do when there's something to be frightened about. My mouth was dry and I didn't want this secret.

"Maxie! My secret is to do with Simon."

"Simon? What about Simon?"

"I'm in love with Simon."

I stared at her, incredulous, with a sense of injury and outrage.

"You're shocked?" Her expression was challenging.

When you are shocked through and through you don't answer back. Not at once. It's like flying along smoothly and dropping into an air-pocket—a sick moment of emptiness and lost control, of impending crash. I recovered myself with a blinding flash of anger.

"You can't be in love with Simon! You can't!"

Her eyes narrowed. "Why not?"

"He's your *brother!*"

"*Oh, no; he's not!*"

"He's your father's stepson. Adopted too. He's part of your family – Antrobus—"

Her pointed chin shot forward and her eyes flashed. "He's Trevor! He only took the name Antrobus to please Daddy. Claude is closer to me than Simon. Claude is my cousin. Simon's no blood relation whatsoever. Don't dare forget it!"

In love with Simon – *Simon!* In love at thirteen years old! Admitting it . . . telling me . . . as a secret. This was one of her quick sly cheats. Spotting something, getting in first, throwing me an uninvited confidence that would disarm me and make me an ally before I could become a rival. I have put it into words now, but it wasn't neat in my mind then. It was just a tide of rage, a conviction of treachery.

I didn't let go. "You've been brought up as brother and sister – you and Simon. Brother—"

"Shut up!"

Her hands darted out like snakes and closed round my wrists. Her nails dug into my flesh. I can feel them now. My skin remembers things. It has a memory of its own.

"Never say that again! Never even think it! *Never!*"

She let me go. She slid down from the sill and began to pull on her clothes.

The red glow had faded from the sky and my anger with it. The cool grey dusk seeped into the room. I held my hands palm upwards and looked at my wrists, thin and blue veined. I could see the little pulses beating and the marks of Rima's nails. There was an ache in my chest as if some animal I loved had been maimed. Something simple had been spoilt. It would all be different now – between Rima and Simon and me.

2

WE FIVE

IT WAS DIFFERENT, but not all the time. There were long equable stretches when nothing seemed changed at all.

Rima and I, temperamentally so opposed, were as necessary to each other as the air we breathed. The same things made us laugh. But, while I was easily moved to tears or anger, Rima seldom cried. Her temper was as cold and intense as mine was quick. Once roused it lasted for a long time. Mine was a sudden storm, hers was a whole winter. But we understood and put up with each other's moods, just as we accepted Claude's withdrawals, Simon's undisputed leadership, and Jamie's infuriating habit of hanging onto a point of view as if his life depended on it.

"Even if he *has* to throw it up, he comes back to it," said Rima. "Dog to its vomit."

When she said things like that she'd glance at me inquisitively to see if I'd spring to Jamie's defence. She'd play him down – but not too much – and build him up the same way. She wanted to make me go for Jamie.

Claude wasn't keen on horse-riding but Rima and I used to ride for miles with Simon and Jamie, inspecting the jackal-proof fences of both Loire and Bergplaas – strong wire-mesh fences aproned to the ground by heavy stones. Towards sunset we'd go up into the foothills, because we loved to watch the buck coming to drink at the upper dam with the cattle and sheep – grysbok, duikers, rhebok and occasionally a pretty little klipspringer. There'd be meerkats too, sitting up and praying with their tiny paws upraised, and maybe a black and white skunk. The baboon troops came too, so human in their behaviour and appearance, picking up their children to give them a ride, or smacking down the cheeky ones. There are farmers who shoot baboons because they are so destructive to root and vegetable crops and steal eggs and generally make a nuisance of themselves, but Daddy never would. He said it would be like mowing down your neighbours. And they'd surely haunt you afterwards.

Flamingos or herons waded in the dam or stood reflectively on one leg in the marshes; skeins of wild geese or duck circled overhead, and the swaying reeds and bulrushes were tremulous with twittering birds every evening. The swallows came and went in their seasons, and at times we'd see the predatory hawks and eagles wheeling slowly against the sky – *lammervangers*, lamb-catchers, waiting to pounce on the new-born lambs.

"Man," said Jamie once, as he reined in his horse and looked across the wide lovely valley flaunting its orchards and grainlands, its vineyards, hamlets and homesteads, "doesn't it do something to you – just to see it? Me, I'd fight for it and die for it! I'd rather be ploughed into Bergplaas earth and fertilise it with my own blood and bones than give up one inch of it!"

He meant it too.

The boys often drove the tractors and the harvesters. Even Claude. They liked the mechanised aspect of farming; but I preferred the timeless activities, mules or oxen ploughing along the contours of a hillside or the *click-clack* of the shears in the big cool shearing-sheds.

Oom Gert Vermeulen, Jamie's father, had a first rate team of Coloured sheep shearers, who came to us every spring. They held their victims in a jujitsu grip, sitting on the floor, and snipped off the pelt, neat and quick as lightning. Then the shron sheep, free of their winter coats, frisked out into the September sunshine, probably feeling much as we did when we stripped off our school uniforms and ran down to the dam in our brief swim-suits. Old Abel, who was nearly blind, separated the pelts on the long slatted table, his deft experienced fingers sorting the greasy burr-tangled neck and back wool from the soft fine belly wool, and flinging the graded portions into their different compartments on the shelves along the walls.

I remember Claude standing next to me, his hands running over the curiously gossamer texture of a newly shorn pelt, testing the strands of wool, the differences between them.

"The coarse and the fine, the dark and the light ... we separate them for our profit. Nature doesn't. They are all part of one animal."

He had this habit of thinking aloud sometimes, developing the theories and ideas that were to pervade everything he saw and did. Claude's creeds shaped his life just as Rima's art drew us all into the strange web from which there was no escape.

In summer Rima'd take her sketch-book down to the vineyards where the *volkies*, men, women and older children, were picking the grapes and piling them into the deep baskets made by the blind. They have done it for generations, families born and bred on Loire land. Our grapes were not for export, nor did we make our own wine, for ours was really a mixed farm. We sold our harvest to the government distilleries. But to Rima the vintage was the season of grace. She caught it in her swift simple line drawings – the whole Bacchanalian spirit of it. Every now and again her imagination broke out in embellishments that included us. Centaurs appeared among the vines with saucy Bacchantes.

"That's you and me, Rima!" said Simon with a wide grin.

He was looking over her shoulder as she sat under a tall blue gum on the edge of a vineyard. The trunk of the gum was pealing; it was mottled, dark and pale. She glanced at Simon with dancing eyes, and then, knowingly, at me.

" 'The glory of his nostrils is terrible . . . he paweth in the valley and rejoiceth in his strength!' "

We giggled, and Simon said, "What are you nattering about?"

But she had caught it – his look of a young stallion. And the bare breasts of the Bacchante were hers, firm, provocative, not yet a woman's.

She was so clever, my cousin Rima. Somehow she was turning the tables on me. It was I Simon treated as his kid sister. The quarrels and the horse-play were between him and me. She had already put herself upon some other level, deliberately investing herself with a quality of the unexplored and tempting. I was the one he took as a matter of course. He ducked me in the dam, or spanked me when I tormented him, as I often did. Anything to capture his attention!

But the horseplay and the quarrelling meant touching, and every time he touched me I felt a wild exultant thrill. Once, in the dam, I swam far out from the bank and pretended to be in difficulties. He came to my rescue with powerful fast strokes and scissor kicks. I clung to him, gasping.

"Take it easy!" he said. "Just rest your hands on my shoulders and leave it to me."

I floated, face-down, above his body as he did the breast stroke. The smooth feel of his skin, cold in the water, the ripple and movement of his muscular shoulder-blades was grafted into my palms, never to be forgotten, never to be totally lost.

In spite of the heat Claude loved the summer. There was less sport then and more time for him to laze and read and study. I liked the spring best.

Autumn and winter made me sad without knowing why. But Jamie Vermeulen and Simon didn't feel that way. Each had his own reason for preferring the winter. Jamie, because of the rugger – he was a wing-three-quarter, and playing for South Africa at seventeen – and Simon, because of the hunt.

Oom Gert Vermeulen owned a pack of Irish hounds that was the pride and joy of his heart, and we used to go after the sheep-killers – jackals, leopards and *rooikatte* – and the wild pigs who got into our vineyards and devoured the black grapes. *Oom* Gert, who was the Master of this Farm Hunt, always carried a gun, and so did my father, who cut a dashing figure on his big roan.

Hunting wasn't really a blood sport to us. It was a necessity. The beasts we hunted were the marauders who destroyed flocks and crops. There were no pink coats among us, no atmosphere of John Peel, but we had quite a cosmopolitan turn out at times, for, since the war, new German, Polish, Hungarian, Dutch and English settlers had come to our valley, and all the farms were plagued by the same wild beasts, especially in winter when hunger drove them from the mountains into the grazing lands. *Oom* Gert's hounds, like Daddy's springer spaniels, were trained never to worry buck or birds. They only followed the scent of vermin. And, when they had led us to our quarry, they set up a great baying, but they knew better than to tackle a lynx or a leopard on their own. They tree-ed the creature or cornered it, and then a shot put a quick end to the business.

Rima and I were allowed to go out with the Hunt, for, young as we were, we were both experienced riders. I was the better of the two, and knew it. My long limbs were moulded to my horse's flanks, and my hands felt his mouth sensitively. Rima's hands were surprisingly strong, but there was less give in them. Jamie rode with a long stirrup and a slack rein, while Simon was part of his mount which was usually Snow, my father's white stallion, bred and broken on Loire.

Our Cape winter is stormy, but the sun is never far away, and every now and again we get glorious bright days that make your blood sparkle in your veins.

It was on such a day, with the ploughed lands all lion-coloured and the mountains purple and bony against a high sky, that we went after a *rooikat* which had torn out the throats of fifteen of *Oom* Gert's pedigree merino ewes the night before. It was an exciting and successful chase, for we got not only the killer but her mate.

"That's one bloody massacre revenged," said *Oom* Gert, with satisfaction.

On the way home I decided to take my own line back to Bergplaas, and suddenly I heard Simon thunder up behind me on Snow.

"What's the idea? Why break away on your own? You're always doing that, Maxie! Who the hell d'you think you are?"

"This horse is tired," I said. "I borrowed him from *Oom* Gert, and, though he's a rocking-horse, I don't trust him. I'm getting him back by the short cut."

"Over the widest, deepest *donga*?"

"He's a good jumper."

"All right." Simon's tone was resigned. "But, if it's the horse you're considering, let's give him a blow first."

He dismounted and loosened the girths of both animals, and we rested for a few minutes. We could see the others taking the longer circuit, and Daddy waved to us, as if to say, "That's all right, we won't bother about you."

Simon stood with his hand on the powerful arched neck of his mount. "God, he's a beauty! How I love this fellow!"

I thought they had a look of each other – a gentle racy splendour. We went on, presently, at an even canter, with me a little in the lead. The *donga* cut the upper part of the field, a deep erosion cleft that had widened since the last rains. I dug my heels into my horse's flanks and gave him his head. He cleared it well. Then I felt him rise under me again in a terrible spasmodic leap. I heard Simon's yell. "Jump for your life!"

I obeyed instinctively, throwing myself clear just as the wretched animal fell with thrashing legs, and died where he lay.

I scrambled up, trembling and shaken.

"He's dead! Simon, he's dead!"

Simon was off Snow's back in a flash. With the rein looped over his arm he held me against him.

"I've seen it happen before – a heart attack. But you – are you hurt, Chick?"

"No, no, I'm all right. Was it my fault? Poor animal . . . *Oom* Gert'll never forgive me . . ."

"You couldn't help it. It was bound to happen some time. The jump was too much for him. You couldn't be expected to know."

My eyes were smarting and my throat was all in knots. Simon looked at me and pretended not to see the brimming tears. He lifted me onto Snow's back and sprang up behind me.

"We'll get right over to Bergplaas, and they can send out the Landrover. Lucky you're a lightweight!"

Snow carried us both for the five miles we still had to go. Simon's right arm held me pressed against him, melted into his warm strength. We three were one animal – he, Snow and I – one rhythm. The afternoon was amber and gusty; it smelt of earth and stubble and old leather. The dead horse no longer mattered. He was finished and a stranger, his time had come, and he was nobody I loved. To be part of Snow and Simon was the core of life.

The wind was rising, and when we got to the oak avenue leading to Bergplaas, the loose scattered leaves swirled about us, funnelling here, there and everywhere in their frenzied dance of death.

Snow hated the leaves. He snorted and tossed his head, and pranced nervously till we came to the rambling old house where Jamie's mother, plump, fresh-faced and German, and known to all the valley as *Mutti* Vermeulen, was standing with Rima on the stoep. We realised that they were waiting for us.

"What happened?" they called out together, and then *Mutti* said, "Everybody's nearly finished tea; we were getting anxious about you."

"Not anxious enough to spoil their appetites for your wonderful tea, I'll bet," grinned Simon.

Briefly he told them of the horse's death. "The staggers, poor brute. *Oom* Gert'll be upset. After the business with the sheep – this!"

A groom came and took Snow's reins and Simon dismounted and put out his arms for me. I slid through them onto the ground. Even then he didn't let me go.

"Sure you're all right, Maxie? Steady on your feet?"

"She looks very pale," said *Mutti*, taking my arm in hers. "No wonder we were worried." The words "very" and "worried" were softly guttural. After thirty years in South Africa *Mutti* had learned to speak Afrikaans and English, but she had never lost her German accent.

"You had something to worry about," admitted Simon.

"A dead horse!" Rima's clear bird-like voice rang out sharply.

Simon wheeled at her tone. The wings of his nostrils whitened.

"A live little girl, who might have been badly hurt! If that animal had rolled on her—"

"She'd have been flattened even flatter than she is!"

Simon had no smile for her. For a moment I thought he would smack her. But she said quickly, "Well, it *didn't* roll on her. So that's that."

He turned and sprang up the steps to meet *Oom* Gert and my father.

"Lucky Simon followed you – when you separated from the rest of us! Why must you always go your own way – a different way?"

Rima threw the words at me like an accusation. Her eyes were dangerous, hot with jealousy, a hint of fear in them. They reminded me of the lynx this afternoon, up in the hills, its back to the rock, the hounds closing in on it, and *Oom* Gert's gun levelled. For a moment Rima had become my enemy, fierce and defensive, her possession of Simon threatened. And by me. Of all people – *me*.

3

LOIRE

I T WASN'T ONLY RIMA who was upset. Mummie was too.

She called me into her bedroom as I was passing her door to go and get tidy for supper. I was still in my jodhpurs and turtle-necked yellow sweater, and, as I caught a glimpse of myself in the long wardrobe mirror, I realised that Rima's crack was justified. I looked no more than I was – an early teenager, with a long way to go before any boy would glance twice at me. Simon had called me a "little girl" and that was the way he saw me. The pullover was nice with my hair, but it took all the usually fresh colour out of my cheeks, or maybe the fright had done that. I sat on the edge of my mother's bed.

"What's up?" I was on guard.

She was at her dressing-table, brushing her short dark hair already lavishly sprinkled with grey. It was as springy as a horse's tail. Her sharp clear-cut features were stern and her deepset eyes had their "won't stand any nonsense" expression. When she looked like that you could see the sort of determination that had made it possible for her to run Loire during those difficult years when Daddy was at the war and all the home responsibilities were hers.

"Listen," she said. "I'm the last person to check initiative in anyone, but you take it too far, Maxie."

"How d'you mean?"

"If your father hadn't told Simon to chase after you this afternoon when you saw fit to go off on your own—"

"Did Daddy *tell* Simon to chase after me?" My heart sank.

"Of course. Daddy tries to keep an eye on you girls, but you don't make it easy, Maxie. If Simon hadn't followed you and shouted to you to jump clear, you might have been badly injured. Or killed."

"It wasn't my fault. Simon said so."

"Don't argue. Listen, for once! You're always acting on impulse. You

22

think you can take snap decisions without referring to anyone, and it won't do. If you join the Hunt you must stay with it – or stay at home."

"Daddy didn't give me a rocket—"

"Your father spoils you, just as Rima's father spoils her. And you both take full advantage. What's more, I don't like your habit of going up into the berg alone. And your Aunt Kate likes it still less when you walk up Table Mountain by yourself. There are many reasons why that sort of thing isn't safe for a young girl."

"Mummie," I said desperately. "Sometimes I need to be alone – to get off by myself. Sometimes I just *have* to!"

"Then you can find a place to be alone in the garden – either here or at Rosevale."

"It's not the same."

"I can't help that." Her mouth was a thin line and I could see the down on her stretched upper lip. Suddenly I hated the way she'd made her face look by folding in her lips like that.

"It's a new departure – this mooching off alone, whether on foot or on horseback."

"I take the dogs." It was all I could think of to say. I couldn't explain the inexplicable – the deep-down need to get away by myself and just sit and listen to the birds, and the wind in the trees, and watch the sea breaking on the rocks, and the clouds shepherded across the sky by the wind; and the way these things smoothed out all the ridges that made me feel rough and miserable without knowing why. Those things – the sky and the sea and the mountain – are forever, we are for now, and the forever things make us part of them when we just sit quietly in a place of grandeur and beauty which hasn't been touched by the hand of any gardener except God. How could I say such things to my mother?

"The dogs couldn't help you if you fell and broke your ankle," Mummie said. "You remember what happened to Simon's mother?"

I shivered. Simon's mother had been headstrong too. She had loved climbing Table Mountain, often by herself. She had gone out alone on a misty day and fallen seventy feet to her death. She had only been married to Uncle Gideon for six months when she was killed, leaving him with a handful of poignant memories – and her little son, Simon, aged three. Yet, if she hadn't been killed, Uncle Gideon wouldn't have married Aunt Kate, my mother's sister; my cousin, Rima, wouldn't have been born;

Claude and I wouldn't have spent our schooldays at the Antrobus' home, Rosevale; and everything in our whole lives would have been quite different. So perhaps it was meant that she should lose her way in the mist and plunge to a violent end in order to accomplish some other purpose in the story of human lives.

"Now you've gone off into a daydream!" My mother spoke with irritation. "You escape mentally as well as physically. It's impossible to nail you down."

Mummie liked to "nail" people down. To her, it meant knowing where she was with them. To me it sounded terrible – like the coffin or the Cross.

"Don't look like that, Maxie! Just try to be sensible. And, if it's any comfort to you – it's none to me! – your brother is no better than you are. Claude's a real cat who walks by himself."

"How funny you should say that! It's what Rima calls him. A cat man."

"Rima sees a long way into people – into their fundamental nature. What's more, she catches it in her sketches – to a remarkable degree. She's very old for her age – several thousand years old."

I stared at my mother, amazed that she should know such a thing.

"Buzz off, now!" She was smiling. "Or you'll be late for supper."

The lovely day had turned stormy. The rain-wind whined round the house and rattled the teak shutters. Rima wedged our windows before we went to bed, and that night we snuggled up to each other in the big four-poster, our blankets drawn up to our chins. I expected Rima to be in one of her sulks. But she wasn't. She was alight with a secret elation.

"Simon was furious with me today," she whispered. "We quarrelled."

"No wonder. You were horrible."

"After *Mutti* Vermeulen had fed you tea and made a fuss of you, I was alone with Simon. We went round the back to get Snow. He ticked me off for being a cad to you, and I stood up to him. He shook me. Like Spot with a rat."

"Then you deserved it."

"Possibly. It was worth it, though. Suddenly he stopped shaking me – in that oleander shrubbery behind the stables – and he said, 'Oh, my God, what a brute I am! And you – only a kid!' "

"What did you do?"

"Looked at him – just looked, Maxie. And he stared down at me as if he'd never seen me before, and his eyes were puzzled – and sort of different.

He said, '*Rima*...?' Like that, as if he were asking a whole lot of questions rolled into one. And he ran his fingers through his hair the way he does."

"So what?"

"So now he's wondering."

"Wondering what?"

"If I *am* only a kid."

I drew away from her warmth, from the small rounded body so fast becoming aware of its own seductive charm. I made up my mind to ask Mummie to give us separate beds next holidays. I'd explain that I fidgeted and had nightmares. And that was true. Rima always grumbled about my nightmares, because they woke her. She said I made noises like an animal caught in a trap. She used to wake me and get cross, but I was grateful to be wakened, however cross she might be. That was the queer thing about us – the way we made each other wild and the way we put up with each other. It was more than putting up. It was as if our souls were handcuffed without their knowing it. That night I hated her, as she had hated me earlier the same day. I couldn't bear to be so intimately near her. But next morning I couldn't hate her any more. She went off with her sketch book and her paintbox, and she painted a picture. An impression mostly, a few strokes and touches of colour.

"For you," she said, when it was done.

I took it from her, and for a while I couldn't speak because the picture was so exciting and so beautiful.

A white charger plunged through a whirlpool of golden leaves, his tail streaming, his eye wild, a knight and a fair damsel on his back. The knight had Simon's brown curls and proud nose, and the damsel was me – very small and virginal, slim as a new moon, curved into the shape of his body. And all round us was the windy weather and storms past and yet to come.

"He smelleth the battle from afar ..." I said. "Oh, Rima, this is a wonderful picture! And there's a white dove too—"

"Dove of peace." She was laughing. But her eyes were full of wisdom – ancient feminine wisdom like the witch-wisdom of old Lizzie, the midwife of Bergplaas – and suddenly I remembered my mother's words. "Rima is old for her age – several thousand years."

My father hadn't been annoyed with me for taking the short cut on my own, although he had felt it necessary to back Mummie up. He'd put it very mildly and briefly in four words. "It was bad manners." Which made me feel small and ashamed.

Daddy and I understood each other well, but there was more to it than that. In many ways he loved me at the expense of my brother. I had the physical boldness he would have wished to see in his son. He was never able to appreciate that Claude's intellectual boldness and moral courage were infinitely superior qualities. He judged Claude by the standards of a countryman and found him wanting. He'd have liked his son to be more like Jamie Vermeulen, a good scholar and a better sport, with a true feeling for the land, and for the *volkies* who worked it. Jamie knew the Coloured people with his instinct, their moods, sullen and gay, their loyalties and ready humour, their limitations. He joked with them and made them laugh, and their dark faces lit up when he came by. Already they accepted "*baas* Jamie" as their friend, their young master, and their adviser. He expected no more of them than they were able to give.

Claude only knew them with his mind. He deplored their drunkenness and unreliability, "cause and effect" he said, and blamed both on the farmer.

"We corrupt them with the tot system – giving them part of their pay in wine – a habit-forming stimulant. It should be abolished, like so much else."

We were standing under the old fig-tree in the wintry sunshine – Daddy, Claude, Jamie and I – watching the Coloured foreman as he whacked out the tots from a barrel of red wine in the floor-level cellar-room. The labourers filed past the open door to have their mugs filled, but those who had to go to work in the far fields, or the shepherds, produced bottles instead of mugs and received a double tot.

Jmaie laughed at Claude's solemn face. "*Og*, man, it's a traditional custom. You can't break custom. There are pussy-foot farmers who've tried to cut out the tot system. What happens? They can't get labour. You know it."

"A sailor gets his tot of rum – or *brandywyn* – and is the better for it," added Daddy. "You can't reform men of the earth or the sea, and turn them into little angels. Take them as they are, for God's sake!"

But Claude wasn't one who could easily take people or conditions as they were. He saw them as they might be. Even as they ought to be.

"Your trouble," continued Daddy, "is that you want everything fancy. Artificial. Where Jamie and I find horse and cow manure as sweet in our nostrils as attar of roses, you twitch your nose in the direction of some bloody chemist's fertiliser!" He smiled, so that the pale sunlight glinted on the little gold filling in a front tooth. There was such charm in his smile that you had to respond. Claude certainly wasn't proof against it.

"Be fair!" he grinned. "Admit the chemists have done something for agriculture! You don't turn up your nose at sprays for your fruit trees."

"Not my nose," agreed Daddy. "But there've been farmers who've turned up their toes at your damned lethal sprays. Consider that, my boy!"

"Man," said Jamie. "Accidents can happen. Maybe those farmers don't know how to read instructions."

Claude laughed. Science and chemistry were his subjects, and he knew that Jamie envied him his grasp of them. But Daddy was on the attack again.

"The trouble with you, Claude, is that you love the land like a vivisectionist loves his experimental dog. It's the wrong attitude. No heart in it."

He did this sometimes, took sides for Loire against Claude, as if he feared that the future "marriage" between them might fail because Claude's affection for the Lamotte heritage was of the wrong calibre. I think he often regretted that it was Claude, and not I, who should one day be wedded to this corner of the valley so precious to him. But he was always sorry when he nagged Claude. He blamed himself and tried to make amends.

"You're a brilliant throw-back, my boy," he said. "We've had these queer analytical Lamottes in the family before today – the scientific types. Well, sometime we'll harness your talents to the farm." He turned to me. "As for you, Maxie, you're one of the scribbling Lamottes. We breed them too. There's even a poet in your pedigree."

Claude gave his soft infectious chuckle. "Has it struck you, Dad, that we're Mother's children too? Fifty per cent Beeford."

Daddy made a gracious expansive gesture. "Sure! Beefords were the pioneers of commerce in South Africa. Like their partners, the tribe of Antrobus. Antrobus and Beeford – A. & B. – the best department store in the Southern Hemisphere, with branches in all the major cities from Cape Town to the Copper Belt. See, I've got the patter and I recognise the achievement. But don't ask me to get excited about it!"

My father had the peculiar arrogance of the landowner. He patronised all townsmen, and most of the professions, and only really admired the merits of the Fighting Services. But he treated doctors and clergymen with wary respect.

"They dabble in magic," he told me once, rubbing my hair with the flat of his hand as if I were a dog or a cat. "And I'm not one to despise sorcery. All the same, I'd just as soon ask the advice of Lizzie, the Wise Woman of Bergplaas, as of a country practitioner; and, when the churchmen claim to interpret the will of the Almighty, I reckon they're pinning medals on themselves. My experience of interpreters is that they can cook the original word into an indigestible hash, whether on purpose or through ignorance. Any farmer has seen the wonders of the Lord, His bounty, and His wrath. We watch the flowering of the land and fight its plagues; we give thanks for the fat years, and, in the same breath, we plan against the lean ones. I don't need any sanctimonious buzzard to tell me that my Creator breathes in a field of wheat or a skipping lamb. God has never talked to me from a pulpit Maxie. He is the Voice that walks in the garden in the cool of the day. And I mean no irreverence when I talk this way."

"I know," I said.

That was why I so often wanted to be alone among growing things, or on the seashore.

4

ROSEVALE

LOIRE WAS THE HOLIDAY side of our lives. But we never minded going back to school because that meant living at Rosevale, the spacious pink villa Uncle Gideon Antrobus had built for Simon's mother on the western buttress of Table Mountain. Although she had only enjoyed it for one summer before her fatal accident there was no sadness or mourning in the atmosphere of Rosevale, and Claude and I were as much at home there as we were at Loire, which says a great deal for Aunt Kate, who never allowed us to feel out of it. Like Simon, we were part of her family.

Both Mummie and Aunt Kate disapproved of boarding schools for boys and girls who had no need to go to them. But many of our friends were boarders at schools only a few miles from their homes. Their parents contended that boarders got fuller value out of school – the benefits of communal life, learning how to fit into a group, and developing what they called the "team spirit".

We didn't agree. Jamie Vermeulen had plenty of team spirit, but he went to a day-school at Stellenbosch, where he lived with one of his married sisters during the term. As for ourselves, we were well content to do without the joys and blessings of an unbroken herd existence.

"It's all hooey," I scoffed. "Parents only make their children boarders when they can't be bothered to have them at home."

"Just imagine Claude as a boarder!" said Rima. "He's rotten at games and he'd be utterly miserable trying to fit into a communal life."

"Simon would be all right."

"Oh, yes. Simon's adaptable. He's quite a chameleon. He changes his colour to match the shrub on which he finds himself."

"He does not! He stands out anywhere. There's no camouflage about Simon."

"He remains himself, if that's what you mean. When I say he changes like the chameleon I simply mean that he's able to blend and make himself part of the whole, instead of sticking out like a sore thumb the way Claude does. You're silly about colour, Maxie. You let it bluff you. You should look right through it to the essential shape, the true values."

Claude would have shouted "Hear! Hear!" if he'd been with us. But then my brother would have given Rima's words a much wider implication than she intended. Colour, to Claude, suggested the whole set-up of the multi-racial society in which we lived. Shades of human pigmentation. White. What a vague term! Coloured. Even vaguer. Asiatic, the parchment and vellum of Malay and Chinese, or the dusky Indian. Bantu, the gleam of bronze or the bloom of indigo.

We had quite a selection in Aunt Kate's household alone, from Fatima, the Malay laundress who came to do the weekly wash, to Rocky, the Shangaan butler. One look at Rocky's complexion, smooth as a purple grape, his portly figure and air of authority, proved him to be a man of substance. A king-pin. His cheerful gurgling voice matched the twinkle in his eye, and, when he decorated his tunic with an emerald green silk sash, with a badge like a royal order across his chest, and wore his tasselled turban to match, he was magnificent, and played up to his appearance. But, when he went out, he dressed in a sober suit and overcoat, grey gloves and hat, and a dog-collar. For Rocky was an ordained parson.

"It's his hobby," said Rima. "He wouldn't want to be a full-time parson. He's too keen on the social side of life."

"He's a terrific snob," grinned Simon. "Dad's guests can assess their social status by the size of the whiskey Rocky pours for them."

Rocky's influence pervaded Rosevale, inside and out. Goodwin, the cook, in his high chef's hat, came from the same part of the Northern Transvaal. So did Leslie, the gardener, and both had been introduced and vouched for by Rocky. "Reference enough!" said Uncle Gideon, who was always amused at his butler's self-importance.

Rocky was an established urban Bantu with a wife and five children in the Native location of Langa a few miles out of Cape Town. But the other Rosevale Natives returned to their country every two years for several months to attend to such personal matters as building a new hut, marrying a new wife, or laying the keel of a new piccaninny, as Simon put it.

Annie, the Coloured housemaid, who did the bedrooms and looked after Aunt Kate's clothes, had been bequeathed to Rosevale by our late grandmother Beeford. There was a permanent cold war between her and Rocky. Each looked down upon the other, and their habits and ideas seldom coincided. For instance, the Bantu staff was supplied with meat and cereal, which Goodwin prepared according to Native taste, whereas Annie ate from "the mistress's table", and carried her meals into her own bedsitting-room. Even with a parson at the head of the kitchen table, she could not bring herself to "sit down with Natives". And that suited them. When Fatima was there, she ate with Annie, but she brought her own Moslem food with her, except during the Fast of Ramadan, when not even water crossed her lips between sunrise and sunset. This complex arrangement followed the traditional way of life of the Cape, where, for over three centuries, racial distinctions have been respected. But no one ever thought about them until they became enforced.

Rima and I loved to talk to Leslie, the gardener, who knew everything in the world about wild life, and quite a lot about magic. Once, when we saw Rocky going out in his clerical garb, we asked Leslie if he, too, was a Christian. His eyes, with their saffron whites, rolled thoughtfully. He leaned on his rake as he answered: "Sometimes I am littie-bittie Christian." He had a sonorous gentle voice and a ready laugh, except when he had been smoking *dagga* which reddened his eyes and made him sulky and belligerent.

"Not all the time?" Rima's eyes sparkled with interest.

"Not all the time." He smiled, and his big teeth shone in his soot-black face.

Leslie had many reservations about Christianity. His people were polygamous by tribal custom and they believed strongly in witchcraft and the Old Gods of Africa, and the power of men to change into animals, and of animals and reptiles to assume the masks of men. Sometimes we could persuade him to tell us about these things, and we would listen enthralled. But we had to get him in the right mood.

Leslie, unlike Rocky, lacked the sophistication of the townsman. He was still a man of his own country, where the rivers teemed with crocs and hippos, elephant and giraffe roamed the forests, and the bush was alive with buck, zebra and lion. His long limp hands were as deft as they were strong, for his people made their reed huts with all the skill and ingenuity of weaver-birds. He was a hunter and herdsman by nature, and, although the pull of civilisation had drawn him far from his beginnings, the old roots were still deep.

Because he believed all that he told us, however fantastic, we believed it too.

"That's faith," said Claude, when we passed on Leslie's stories later, our eyes wide with wonder and credulity. "The ability to believe the unbelievable. And it's infectious. You're a pair of Pagans, Maxie and Rima."

We didn't see much of Claude and Simon those last six months of their schooldays. Both were working hard for the matric, which loomed at the end of the year.

September was stormy, with torrential rains, and the Twelve Apostles were particularly vicious. They rolled avalanches of rock and earth down their steep slopes, blocking the coast road and threatening the pretty chalet settlements that clung precariously to the cliffs above the coves and beaches. Occasionally somebody's home was engulfed. Even Rosevale was often shrouded in mist, and down in Table Bay the fog-horns *mooed* dismally.

One afternoon, when I was doing my homework in the old playroom that was our all-purposes room nowadays, Simon came in, rubbing his fingers through his dishevelled hair.

"I can't take in another word of the stuff I'm swotting. Want to come for a walk, Chick? The rain's let up for an hour or so."

I sprang up. "Let's go!"

"Where's Rima?"

"It's her art class today."

"We'll be off then. Bring your mac."

I pulled my raincoat over my gym-tunic and changed into old climbing shoes, and we set off briskly, up to Kloof Nek and along the western trail high above the sea.

Perhaps because we'd had three days of storm, with the threat of more to come, the brief golden break in the weather lifted my heart and sent a singing happiness through me. Or maybe it was just being with Simon.

It was misty still, but the evening sun came warmly through the haze, and the spring scents of the soaked earth steamed up through beds of leaves and pine-needles, resinous and intoxicating. The sea was still angry, with the surf thundering onto the beaches or bursting over the rocks and exploding against the towering cliffs. Simon took great gulps of the strong clear air.

"This clears the head! Your brother takes to brain work better than I do."

"You'll pass the matric all right."

"Dad'll be mad if I don't get a first."

"What's it matter, so long as you scrape through?"

"For heaven's sake, what scandalous talk! You should know that the best isn't good enough for Gideon Antrobus. Especially for anyone who hopes to be employed in A. & B."

"I can't see you in an office. Or behind a counter."

"Where can you see me?"

"In the Air Force or the Navy – or on a ranch."

"Glamour boy. Sorry. It'll be the counter and the office for a bit, to get experience. Though Dad's planning to send me to a University in America where they run a special course in retail trade. And then, if I make the grade, the world's my oyster. A. & B. has contacts in Europe, America, Australasia, the Far East, and even Russia, to say nothing of the African Continent. If I can get as far as being the Chairman's representative – Dad's right hand – I can really travel."

"You make it sound exciting."

"It is. Dad says trade's the key to the wide world. Maybe one of these days we'll be opening a branch of A. & B. on the Moon."

I laughed, and took skipping steps to keep up with his long stride. I'd like to have weaved wildly back and forth like the dogs. Sambo, the black Labrador, and Pim, the Poodle, were ahead of us, exploring every bush, checking on every tree, going frantic with delight at being taken for a walk after the abysmal boredom of the rainy days.

"Or on Mars. Wouldn't that be wonderful! Finest quality earth goods obtained at Antrobus & Beeford, Mars branch, at incredibly reasonable prices."

"And don't forget it's a two-way street. We'd have our Moon and Mars departments in Adderley Street."

"Oh, and among all the foreign visitors who come to Rosevale with A. & B. connections, there'd be people from the Moon and Mars. That'd shake Rocky!"

"It would indeed. Goodwin too. They probably have very curious eating habits. Claude's the one who'd have to be our space behaviour advisor in chief. Claude's a man of the Universe. He'd soon have them taped."

"If not, he'd go back with them on the next flying saucer, and find out. He's the most inquisitive man I've ever met."

"He has the scientific mind. It needs to know all the answers."

Simon tweaked my bouncing pony-tail of thick fair hair.

"What'll you do when you grow up, Chick?"

"I'll be a buyer for A. & B."

"Why not? We thrive on nepotism, and you're half Beeford. But Dad always expects the members of the family to make good in some other firm first. He also demands that they work."

"I'll work. And I'll make good. I mean to learn Italian next year – maybe French and German too."

"Why Italian?"

"Daddy wants to go back to Italy for a holiday. He says when we have a boom year he's going to take Mummie and me up into the Italian mountains where the peasants hid him all the last winter of the war. It's a sort of pilgrimage he's planning."

"It's a nice idea. And Italian could be useful to you in A. & B. one of these days. We buy a good deal from Italy. From France and Switzerland too."

"P'haps I can get a job in Rome and live in an Italian family, and really get good at the language, and then I could go to London and work in a big store there, before coming home and asking Uncle Gideon for a job."

"If you bring all that off, I should think he'd welcome you with open arms. When did you dream up this plan?"

"Most of it came into my head now – when you made A. & B. sound exciting."

He threw back his head and laughed, and I saw the length of his neck and the proud way it grew up out of his shoulders, with the soft open khaki shirt revealing its strength. Jamie's neck was shorter than Simon's, and Claude's was thinner, with too much Adam's apple.

"Everything bubbles up in you, Maxie. Someone says something, and in a flash you've taken fire from it."

"What's wrong with that?"

"You can let me know in the years to come. People like you rocket off into bad things as well as good ones."

"You're that sort of person yourself."

"I'm not so sure. I'm the product of Dad's upbringing. He takes risks – big financial risks – but they're calculated. You can't jockey him into wild-cat schemes. And he looks ahead. He's the best chairman A. & B. have ever had."

"Are you a product of your upbringing in the long run? Or of your blood?"

He smiled. "Environment versus heredity. I don't know. Come to that, I don't know much about my own heredity."

The sun was bright now, warming us through, making a dazzle of the wide expanse of sea. Far out a tramp steamer heaved on the swell. The fishing boats were still safe in harbour. Cloud banners streamed across the sky, driven by winds we could not feel.

"Want a rest?"

He spread his waterproof lumber-jacket on the sparkling damp grass. The air was sweet with the fragrance of the pale yellow mountain mimosa and quivering with the busy wings of small twittering birds. We could hear the waterfall cascading down the kloof in the dense shade of wild cherry trees, giant ferns and flowering bushes. Clumps of creamy arums starred the grass at our feet.

"Do you often think about your mother?" I asked.

"No," he said. "Hardly ever, to be honest. I was so small when it happened ... too small to remember anything about her. I never knew my father either. Rima's parents are the only father and mother I've ever known."

"Daddy says your father was a wonderful fighter pilot, and a born leader of men – very brave and daring. But not the marrying type. He couldn't stick to one woman. Daddy says your mother couldn't take it ... the others ..."

"No. They divorced when I was only a baby. But I think my mother must have cared about him right to the end. The day she had her accident was the day she heard he'd been killed in action over the Western Desert."

"Oh, Simon! But I can understand that so well. She must have gone off by herself to get used to the sad thought. I'd have done the same – gone up the mountain to think, and try to take it in."

He looked at me, and suddenly he put his arm round my shoulders and gave them a squeeze.

"That's just what you would have done, you funny little thing. But the mountain's a dangerous friend, Maxie. You have to think what you're doing when you're climbing – specially when it's misty ... as it was that day."

I could see Simon's mother – Starr was her name and she was young and very pretty – climbing alone on the perilous bastion above Rosevale, her eyes filled with tears, her heart in a turmoil about Simon's father, who must surely have been the real love of her life rather than Uncle Gideon, who was so much more successful than lovable. So easy to be careless. To slip. So disastrous. I closed my eyes tight against the picture that formed of someone tremendously alive one minute and the next – nothing. Like the horse that had jumped the *donga* and fallen dead. Death should surely come gently, in the night, as it had done to Grannie Beeford, who had been ill a long while before she slept without waking. But for Starr it had come suddenly at noonday, in the prime of life. And a little boy had been orphaned.

"Snap out of it!" said Simon.

I nodded. Although I had tried to visualise sudden death it had no true meaning for me. No reality. It had never touched me then, or shown me its face. I hadn't cared about the horse.

A golden fleece of cloud hung above the horizon. Fingers of radiance reached up from the setting sun to pierce and separate it, and, wherever they probed, the ragged edges flamed with glory. We watched the sun slide between the rim of the sky and the sea; and the mystery of its passing lingered a while in a blaze of scarlet and gold.

"Why should it hurt, Simon? So much beauty shouldn't hurt."

"It hurts because you can't keep it. You know it'll never come again – not quite like that. It hurts because it's the end of the day. And time we went back to our homework."

5

BUSH FIRE

THAT SUMMER THE COLOURS of the interwoven pattern of our lives began to stand out bright and bold. Like the fires that devastated the countryside.

It had been particularly hot and dry, and, from Rosevale, we could look down almost daily and see the blue smoke of a veld fire somewhere on the Flats. The slopes of Table Mountain suffered their inevitable outbreaks too and at night snakes and ladders of flame blazed spectacular trails across the peaks, and menaced houses on the high levels all round the Peninsula.

But it was at Loire that things hit us. Good and bad.

The atmosphere that vacation was charged with growth and the promise of change. Simon, Claude and Jamie were in suspense about the results of their school-leaving examinations. Jamie had an outside chance of a Rhodes Scholarship, but, though he was a good all-rounder and a superb athlete, it was by no means certain that his work was up to the necessary high standard. Claude hoped for a Science Bursary at the Witwatersrand University; and Simon expected to go to America in the New Year.

Rima and I were very conscious of the widening gap between ourselves and the boys. In Cape Town they sought girl-friends of their own age or older and we felt relegated to the nursery. But at Loire we still did things together, riding, swimming and playing tennis. And on Saturday nights they took us to the pictures at Wellington.

It was on a Saturday night that the bush-fire broke out on Bergplaas land, which could hardly have been more awkward, because most farm *volkies* get drunk on the weekend after receiving their pay, and, as they drink for oblivion, nothing less than the crack of doom is likely to wake them.

We returned near midnight to find the bush ablaze all along the foothills with a high, but capricious, berg-wind blowing the flames down towards the Bergplaas homestead and Loire.

Oom Gert and Daddy had already got the fire drill under way, and, by the time we arrived on the scene, every available beater had been doused and roused and put on the job. Fortunately they were so used to fire-fighting throughout the summer that they could do it, drunk or sober, or in their sleep, and some sixth sense kept them from making the dangerous mistakes that can cost a man his life.

As fires go, this wasn't really a bad one. Much of the land in the foothills is marshy at that point and wide fire-breaks protect the plantations. It had not yet got a real grip when we tackled it, and the only trouble was the wind.

But I made a fool of myself. I ought to have known better than to get myself into the fix I did. Things stand out in my memory erratically, illumined by the glare of the crackling flames devouring the parched bush above the marsh. Funny irrelevant things, and others not funny at all.

The baboons, burned out of their sleeping place on the berg, came bounding down the dark hillside, and Daddy, looking up and seeing their silhouettes, shouted, "More beaters, thank heaven!" He cursed them mightily as they fled.

My mother and *Mutti* Vermeulen were organising coffee and sand-wiches at Bergplaas and Loire, as all our people, capable of wielding a branch or a spade, were beating and would need food later.

Rima was beating side by side with Simon. Jamie was between them and me. I was right out on the flank. I had flung on my jeans and a shirt and head-scarf, and pushed my feet into gum-boots, but I hadn't been able to lay hands on my lumber-jacket and I hadn't wasted time looking for it. That was stupid. And I'd allowed myself to get too far from the others.

Beyond me a high wall of flame was hooking down towards the marsh-land when suddenly the wind changed and blew gustily back at us. A shower of sparks flew over my head onto a patch of dry grass between Jamie and me, and within seconds I found myself cut off from him, en-circled by a barrier of flame fanned by the wind. To be surrounded is the dread of anyone who has ever been in a bush or forest fire, and I stood paralysed, thinking, "This is it!" I screamed, but it was like a nightmare when one cannot cry out or move. Maybe I produced some horrible sound of terror, but it was lost in the roar and crackle of fire closing in on me. I covered my face with my hands and felt the appalling heat on my back and the scorching lick of flame catch my thin shirt. Then suddenly arms and a jacket were flung round me and I was lifted bodily and borne through the red glare into the night.

Jamie said afterwards: "Man, I've never run so fast in my life – not even with a rugger ball in my hands and a Springbok badge on my vest!"

He touched me down without ceremony in a marshy pool and rolled me over and over till we were both covered with muddy water.

My shirt had been scorched off my back; Jamie's hands and arms had been badly burned, for they had been left bare when he had stripped off his jacket and covered me with it, but he slung me over his shoulder with a fireman's hitch and carried me to the nearest farm lorry, where I lost consciousness.

Jamie, in great pain, acted by instinct. He drove me straight to old Lizzie's hut. Lizzie was the Coloured herbalist and midwife of Bergplaas, a Wise Woman who could brew a love-philtre or put the evil eye on you if you were her enemy. She was a legend among the *volkies*, and it was said that she had saved *Mutti* Vermeulen's life when Jamie came into the world on a stormy night six weeks before his time. Without Lizzie to help her, Jamie's mother would have bled to death before the doctor could get to Bergplaas.

When I came to, I was in Lizzie's little white-washed house, lying across a big double bed which took up most of the dingy room lit only by a candle stuck into an empty wine-bottle. The old woman's gentle dark fingers were spreading some sort of soothing balm over my burned back.

"I've sent a *kleintjie* for your pa, Miss Maxie. Dis yelly made from tea-leaves an' herbs'll put you right, but *baas* Jamie mus' git his han's to a proper doctor . . ."

I sat up dizzily, clutching a tattered but clean towel to my breast. Jamie was perched on the edge of the bed waiting his turn for her attention. His face was grimed and ghastly, his bright hair grey with ash. He tried to grin at me, not very successfully. He was in agony.

A young girl of about fourteen was standing beside the fat-rumped figure of old Lizzie. She held the pot of balm between her small brown hands. I recalled her vaguely as one of the many farm children who hung around the clumsy collapsible wire gates between the different camps, opening them for cars and scrambling gaily for the reward of a shower of sweets or coins. But lately I had not seen her. She was too big now to haunt the gates. She was a schoolgirl. She was dark for a Coloured girl

with huge eyes and full lips. She was memorable – a symbol of pain and
fear and of Jamie's suffering as well as my own.

"Corinne, dat ointment! Make quick, Corinne!"

The girl moved obediently into the circle of candlelight, and Jamie held
out his poor blistered hands to old Lizzie. It was all part of a nightmare. I
was badly shocked and the shivering had begun.

There were hurried footsteps outside, and a child's voice called,
"*Hierdie's Lizzie s' huis, baas!*"

Then my father was in the open doorway with the Coloured women
and children crowding round him, trying to peer inside.

"Maxie! You're safe, child! Jamie, you saved her life—"

His voice broke, and he brushed his hand across his eyes.

I heard Simon's little second-hand car at full throttle, the cut-out open,
and, within seconds, somebody was saying, "Here's the doctor." The rest
was darkness and a dream.

After that night I formed the habit of sleeping face-down, with my arms
crossed under my body and my cheek sideways on the pillow. It was the
beginning of the terror of fire that is with me still.

Jamie's burns took longer to heal than mine. But the berg itself took
longest of all. I hated to see it scarred and shorn of its natural vegetation.
Without its flowering shrubs and its varied heaths and proteas, the rocky
ledges and chasms appeared crude and bleak, and the sandy soil, no longer
bound by bush, had the arctic pallor of a snow scene.

"The skeleton shows," I said. It was a death-thought and made me
shudder. But Rima saw it differently.

"Barren and stripped to the bone, this berg has a strange beauty—"

"Like Yul Brynner's head," put in Simon, who knew that she was mad
about Yul Brynner.

"Yes! The naked shape. Heaven!"

"Oh, you artists! What a line you shoot!"

But she wasn't shooting a line. Pure form meant a great deal to Rima.
Colour never touched or thrilled her as it did me. Light and shade, yes.
That was important, accentuating angles, curves, the three dimensions,
suggesting weight and atmosphere. She did instinctively what she had
once told me to do. She looked right through the disguise of colour to the
truth beneath it. She saw life very clearly always.

One afternoon, when Jamie's hands were still in bandages, *Oom* Gert
drove him over to Loire specially to see me. Jamie found me alone in my

favourite place in the glade of oaks round the side of the house. I was sitting on a fallen tree-trunk, reading a book. I was wearing very brief shorts and a backless suntop. My shoulders and the upper part of my back were still tender. I heard his step and looked up. His face was transfigured with pride and joy.

"Maxie, I've got it – the Rhodes Scholarship! I've just heard. I had to come and tell you at once."

He held out his arms. I dropped my book and rose and went to him. I could hardly speak for gladness and pride that he should have come to me before anyone else.

"Jamie, how wonderful! I'm so happy for you!"

Rima found us standing in a curiously formal embrace. His bandaged hands were joined across the small of my back and my own arms were linked round his waist. Our heads were inclined forward, my chin resting on his shoulder, his cheek against my hair.

"Hold it!" she said. "That's beautiful!" But her voice and her presence broke the spell and we came apart – "like twin peanuts when the shell is cracked," she complained crossly.

"Listen," I cried. "Listen, Rima! Jamie's won a Rhodes Scholarship!"

"Oh . . ." she gasped. "Oh, Jamie, congrats . . . how grand!" Then she added. "But now we'll lose you. You'll go to Oxford."

"Only for three years. What's three years between friends?"

"Time enough for Maxie to grow up," she said, wickedly.

"Must she? I like her as she is."

"She must," said Rima. "She's doing it fast. Haven't you noticed?"

Jamie laughed, his eyes still glowing with the excitement of his achievement, the promise of the future, his parents' pride in him. "Maybe I have noticed. But don't change too much, Maxie."

After he had gone Rima fetched a hunk of plasticine and busied herself with it.

"What are you doing?" I asked.

"This."

"What is it?"

"Oneness," she said.

The two figures with arms entwined were as one, locked in a guiltless embrace. Tears sprang into my eyes.

"What's wrong?"

"It's so sad," I said.

B*

I had been very much at the mercy of my emotions since the fire. Rima threw me an odd inquisitive glance. She looked from me to the model.

"*Sad?* Why sad, Maxie?"

I shook my head, speechless. I could think of no real reason. Jamie and me, I thought. That's how she saw us!

She had captured a singularly stylised attitude born of the circumstances – my back, his hands, still tender from an agonising shared experience. But there had been no melancholy in that brief embrace. Yet, years later, when she had carved "Oneness" out of cedarwood in a perfect flowing primitive sculpture, my brother perceived the truth. He said, "Those lovers have passed beyond passion into pure togetherness." And I felt once more a poignant stab of pity. To pass beyond passion you must know passion with all its torment and bliss. There can be no aftermath without the storm. The faces of Rima's formal design were anonymous. But the bodies were young – too young for so great a peace.

But, that day, under the oaks, my cousin only laughed at me as she crushed the putty into a shapeless mass between her strong creative fingers.

"There," she said. "Nothingness – if you prefer it."

"You know something," she added. "I was reading, in a book about China, that if you saved a Chinaman's life he was your responsibility for keeps. You've cheated fate, so he has the right to sit on your doorstep and say, 'Feed me and house me. We belong together for evermore – till one of us dies.'"

"It's the wrong way round. The obligation is upside down."

"So are most things in China, according to this book."

We heard the clatter of hooves on the gravel and looked up to see Simon on Snow. The white stallion tossed his head and the pink silk lining of his nostrils palpitated as he stamped and fretted. Simon's face was flushed, his hair was wild and curly, and he was bursting with the good news he had to tell us. Beads of perspiration stood on his upper lip.

"Have you heard about Jamie?"

"About the Rhodes? Yes we have," said Rima. "It's splendid, isn't it?"

"He deserves it. Proud of your rescuer, Maxie?"

I nodded, and smiled, but there was a salty taste at the back of my throat. Why hadn't Simon been the one to save my life? If only it could have been Simon!

6

WE THREE

SOON AFTER THAT the young men scattered.
Jamie went to Oxford in the new year. Claude left for the
Witwatersrand University in Johannesburg. Simon sailed for the
United States.

Rima said, "There'll be other girls in their lives. We'll have to put up
with that – till we catch them up."

"Maybe there'll be other boys in ours."

A gleam lit my cousin's eye. "That's the talk!"

We went on board Simon's ship to see him off. Uncle Gideon and Aunt
Kate came too. But Rima and I were the very last to go ashore. We stood
at the top of the gangway, hesitant and hating this parting. Suddenly
Simon seized me and gave me a rib-breaking hug. I gasped. My skin was
still sensitive. I may have turned pale, because he said: "Chick, I've hurt
you! I forgot."

I didn't care. I think that was when I first accepted the fact that everything to do with Simon and me was going to be laced with pain – for one
of us, at all events.

Rima was waiting her turn to bid him goodbye. She was hatless, flame-
vivid in her yellow summer dress with her copper hair burning in the high
mid-morning sun. They stood staring at each other, those two, as if they
didn't know how to tear themselves apart. I realised suddenly that it was
ages since Simon had treated her as a little sister. I saw him reach for her
hands and draw her towards him. She raised her face and arched her body
against his, and I knew that the way he kissed her then was not the way he
had kissed me. I turned and ran blindly down the ladder. Uncle Gideon
caught me.

"Hey, Maxie – look where you're going!"

"I'm sorry." I turned my head away. I had no hat and no dark glasses
and I couldn't bear that he should see my face at that moment.

43

He is all long limbs and sharp angles, like the wiry inhuman figures Rima went through a phase of modelling out of *ciment fondu*. A grey unyielding man. He stepped past me and as good as lifted Rima off the bottom rung of the gangway.

"Were you trying to sail with Simon, my girl?"

"Perhaps I was," she said, taut, biting her lip, holding onto her self control. He had her arm tucked against his side, and he must have felt her vibrate. They were akin in so many ways – strong, ruthless people, both of them.

Aunt Kate was next to them, waving her little green parasol at Simon as the last ropes were flung clear and the ship began to move. She said to Rima, over her shoulder: "I can't bear to think of Rosevale without Simon. You're going to miss your brother very much, darling. We all are."

Rima whipped round on her mother.

"Simon's *not* my brother! Never call him that again! *Never!*"

In the pitiless sunlight I saw the shock in Aunt Kate's dark eyes, and suddenly I remembered the day Rima had lashed out at me for the same reason.

In the midst of the general murmur on the wharf we stood together in a pool of silence. Uncle Gideon was staring down at his daughter, whose small white teeth gripped her quivering lower lip. There was a crinkle in her chin and I thought, How strange, Rima's going to cry! But she mastered herself, and I heard Uncle Gideon say quietly and deliberately, "Rima's quite right, Kate. Simon isn't her brother. Why should we make believe he is? He belongs to our family by adoption."

Rima glanced at him quickly and a look of absolute understanding – almost conspiracy – passed between them. She gave his arm a grateful squeeze. And in that moment – with so little said and so much implied – my cousin and her father became firm allies in a matter of vital importance to all of us.

The strip of water between the ship and the shore widened. The propellers churned, and the liner, guided by her tugs, set course for the open sea.

Rima was seventeen when she persuaded Uncle Gideon to give her her very own studio. She was to begin her course in Fine Arts at the University of Cape Town in the following year, and all that spring we were both in a ferment of excitement about the studio. We pored over the plans together.

She had drawn them out herself in detail and she submitted them to me for criticism and suggestions. She was astonishingly open to either, giving my ideas quick comprehensive consideration, tossing them on one side in her curt way or incorporating them with enthusiasm. But, when she did adopt them, they changed their character. In their final interpretation they reflected Rima.

"A skylight?" I said tentatively.

"No. I don't ever want to be a painter. I'm going to be a sculptor. Besides, skylights leak."

She was practical and immensely persuasive.

"Look," said Uncle Gideon. "There's a limit to what I'm allowing you to spend."

"Don't tell me!" she implored. "Let me run wild at this stage! When you get the estimate, you can cut me down."

As usual, he found her impossible to resist.

She was very highly charged with something more than ordinary life. A concentrated energy seemed to have built up in her for much longer than her material existence, how long, heaven knows, but it must have been there in the ether – a nucleus of tremendous magnetism – long before flesh and bone caged it in the slight frame known to us as Rima Antrobus.

We chose the site together, in the upper part of the grounds behind Rosevale, which we always called "Antbus Rez", out of deference to Rocky, who, whenever he answered the telephone, picked up the receiver and said in his fat rumbling voice, "Mizz Antbus rezzidence". The words buzzed over the line in a resonant chant. We found "Antbus" a delightful version of Antrobus, and Rima sketched a hilarious little bus full of spiky black ants with comical faces, and included it in one of her many illustrated letters to Simon.

Aunt Kate wasn't keen on the studio scheme, and the place we had chosen for it was too lonely for her liking, too far from the main house. But Rima had her way. She and I paced out the ground, which was still rough bush on the highest section of the Antrobus property.

"It should be right here," said Rima. "Just below the rock wall. There's plenty of room, and these trees'll shade it."

The trees were silvery *keurbome* – the wild mountain cherry which bears no fruit, but is covered twice a year with sweet-scented flowers like a cloud of mauve butterflies. *Keurbome* attract swarms of charming little birds from time to time, and Rima loved birds.

"Leslie can make a rock garden," she added. "It'll all help to hold the soil and bring more birds."

"Antbus Rezz'll block your view," I said.

"Only of Cape Town. I'll have the kloof and the mountain above me, and Devil's Peak to the east, and dear old Lion's head on the Sea Point side. Those are what matter – the high things standing up against the sky."

She added a sunporch with an aviary for her budgerigars, and a washroom with a small refrigerator and an electric kettle. The studio was to be painted candy-pink like the big house.

"It's got to be ready by the time Simon comes back," said Rima. "That's March – the end of the summer."

"It's for you," I pointed out. "Not for Simon."

"It's for me. But it'll be a focal point for all of us."

She had her sly smiling look, as if she were hatching plots and enjoying it. Suddenly I saw how much she had grown up in the past two years, since the day we had stood on Cape Town docks and waved Simon farewell. She was taller and slimmer, yet more feminine, her wide-set yellow eyes seemed larger and more jewel-like in her face, so far removed from beauty, but arresting by virtue of its strangeness. What'll Simon think when he sees her again? I wondered. This new grown-up Rima, an artist with a studio of her own.

By the end of March the curtains were up, the rush mats were on the floor, cushions were scattered over the divan, and the love-birds were in their aviary on the glassed-in porch. You could slide the windows of that suntrap open, so that the dwarf trees in the huge cage rustled softly in the draught. Wire netting kept the birds in, but they wouldn't have flown away anyhow. There were always others wanting to join them.

But Simon didn't return till April, and by then I was back at Loire for the Easter vacation, restless, longing to see him, yet dreading it in some contrary way. I began to work hard on my appearance, struggling to get rid of the freckles across the bridge of my nose; trying to burn evenly, and not succeeding very well because my fair skin didn't take a good tan; and brushing my hair till it gleamed. I no longer wore it in a pony-tail, but loose, so that I could feel its warm silky weight toss on my shoulders when I flung my head back. I studied the curve of my neck and chin in profile and found it pleasant, but my ears were not as nice as Rima's. Rima tied her fluffy hair back to show those small beautifully convoluted ears, and it hung on her neck like a fox's brush, soft and bright auburn.

Mother had house-guests over Easter, and Corinne, the grand-daughter of old Lizzie, the Bergplaas Wise Woman, came in to help and stayed on till after the holidays. She too was growing up, but faster, in the tropical hothouse of her dark skin.

On Easter Monday Rima and Simon drove out from Cape Town in Uncle Gideon's big American car. They were to spend the day at Loire and take me home with them after supper, ready to begin the new term next day.

I could scarcely breathe for excitement when I ran down the steps to meet them. It was two years since last I had seen Simon. An eternity. He sprang out of the car and literally swept me off my feet.

"Wonderful to be home! Rosevale and Loire. Nowhere to touch them!"

The full sunshine was on my face as he stared at me with his laughing, penetrating, well-remembered eyes.

"You've grown up! Or have you?" His finger traced the freckles across my nose. "Same little constellation of golden stars – same old Maxie."

Mummie and Daddy came out of the house, and we were all caught up in greetings and talk and laughter.

"You've broadened out," said Daddy. "Good heavens, man, you're as tall as I am! And is that a Savile Row sports jacket you're wearing?"

"Off the peg in Piccadilly, Uncle Etienne."

Simon was the centre of attention, but all the time I was conscious of Rima, her furtive watchfulness; not the fugitive fox today, but the cunning little vixen.

During his two years away Simon had worked in department stores in New York and London, he had learned a lot, and his confidence and enthusiasm for the future of A. & B. were catching.

Mummie smiled. "I s'pose you mean to revolutionise our staid old family firm – give it a dose of monkey gland?"

"I've plans and ideas," he admitted. "How many of them go into operation depends on Dad."

Rima laughed. "Dad sent you away to get ideas and bring us up to date. He won't hamstring your inspirations."

After lunch we went for a long cross-country ride, and Simon said: "Remember *Oom* Gert's dead horse, Maxie?"

"The one I killed. I can never forget it."

He was riding Snow. Everything was the same. Yet different.

"It's funny being here without Claude or Jamie. What gives? They don't write letters. At least, not to me."

Rima said: "Jamie writes to Maxie."

"He loves Oxford," I said quickly. "And he spends most of his vacs going around studying different sorts of farming in a practical way. He wants to start a Jersey herd when he gets home, and concentrate on dairy produce."

As I spoke, I thought how well they fitted into the pre-ordained pattern of their lives – Jamie, a born farmer, and Simon keen as mustard on all that the world of commerce would ultimately offer him.

"What about Claude?" he asked.

"He only comes home once a year. He's made friends in the Federation and the Protectorates and South West Africa – and he gets around."

Of the three of them, only Claude showed signs of deviating from the planned future. Whereas all Jamie's letters breathed Bergplaas, the pull of Loire seemed curiously light on my brother.

Corinne waited on us at supper that evening, and Rima's eyes followed her intently. Was she interested in the girl, or in her features? I knew my cousin's passion for a possible model. She turned to my mother.

"That girl's new, Aunt Clare. Where does she come from?"

"Corinne? She's a farm girl from Bergplaas, one of old Lizzie's grandchildren. She gives us a hand from time to time."

"She has a head worth sculpting."

"You must get her to sit for you one of these days," suggested Daddy.

After supper we went out onto the loggia for coffee. It was very peaceful there, with the tinkle of the little fountain in the centre of the enclosed courtyard. Honeysuckle and jasmine tumbled over the low parapet and a wistaria pergola, leafless now, left it open to the stars.

Later, when Corinne had fetched the coffee tray, Rima said: "Our old Annie's getting past it. She wants to retire and Mom's quite willing to pension her off as soon as she finds a suitable replacement. Mom can't manage without somebody to maid her and take care of her clothes."

Mummie smiled. "Yes, even Rocky has his limitations. You're thinking of Corinne, I expect. She'd be easy to train. She's quick and clever, and reasonably well educated."

"Her generation usually prefers industry to domestic service." As he spoke, Daddy lit his pipe and drew on it. The small red glow showed up the deep crevices on either side of his wide generous mouth. "I'll bet you Corinne would go to Cape Town eagerly enough, but, in her own mind, a situation at Rosevale would only be a stepping-stone to work in a factory or a restaurant. It's one of the many signs of the industrial revolution that we're passing through in this country."

"You can't blame her – or any of them," said Simon. "Who wouldn't prefer the independence of an industrial job? So many hours on duty and the rest of your time your own. Living day and night in the atmosphere of your work must be real drudgery."

Rima shot him a quick glance. But Mummie only smiled at his vehemence.

"Oh, come now. It's not as bad as all that! A good home has its advantages, and a considerate mistress will see that her maids get plenty of time off."

"If you don't want Corinne for Loire, Aunt Clare, I'll mention her to Mom," said Rima. "I'm sure she'd fill the bill."

"I'd be glad to see her in a good job."

The full moon of Ramadan was high already, bleaching the white walls, etching the ghostly tracery of oak leaf and creeper upon them. I found myself shivering, the skin on my shoulders and back crawling.

"I don't think Corinne should go to Rosevale."

They all looked at me in surprise, and, just for a moment, I wondered what I had said, and why I had said it.

"Why ever not, Maxie?" Rima's tone was gentle.

I couldn't answer. An old memory had risen to haunt me. Lizzie's dark little house, a candle stuck in an empty wine-bottle, Jamie's blistered hands held out to the Wise Woman; and her sharp words. "Corinne, make quick!" My back was aching with burns long since healed; my eyes smarted; and a host of forgotten fears flew in and flocked about me like birds of doom.

"She's cold," said Simon. "It's turned chilly. And anyway, we ought to be on our way. Tomorrow's a working day."

He rose, and flung his arm lightly round my shoulders with a familiar gesture. I flinched, my flesh twitching like a horse's hide when a blind-fly nips.

Corinne was waiting for us at the car. She stepped out of the shadows as we were about to get in.

"Miss Maxie—"

"Corinne! What is it?"

" '*skuus*, Miss Maxie, but I want to work in Cape Town. If you could hear of a place for me, please to remember."

It was Rima who replied.

"I'm sure we can find a place for you. When do you want to come?"

"Any time, Miss Rima."

"I'll let you know. Goodnight, Corinne."

"We'll all sit in front," said Simon. "More sociable. Come on, Maxie, you be the jam in the sandwich."

I sat between them. We generated our own warmth. Simon drove fast along the country tracks, and faster still when we hit the broad National Road from the north. The ploughed fields were rough-cast under the moon; the mountains, silvered and remote, held their rich invisible life of bird and beast and reptile in their eternal laps.

"Why do you kick at the idea of Corinne coming to Rosevale?" asked Rima suddenly.

I frowned. "Honestly, I don't know. There's no sense in it."

"Have you anything particular against her?"

"Not a thing. Lizzie's family have been at Bergplaas for generations. They're descendants of the old Bergplaas slaves. Good people."

"I've seen that girl somewhere," Simon's voice was puzzled, trying to place her. "As a kid, perhaps, hanging around the farm gates . . ."

"Yes, there – and on the night of the fire too. Didn't you come to Lizzie's house that night, after Jamie took me there?"

I felt him start. We were sitting close, touching each other. Thigh to knee, my leg rested against Simon's; and Rima's arm, along the back of the seat, brought her body into warm contact with mine. Every now and again I was aware of strong vibrations coursing through the three of us, threading the steady impersonal purr of the car with individual human notes.

"That's it, Maxie! She was there that night. I remember now – coming into the room; you, huddled on the edge of the big bed, your arms folded across your chest, looking so sick and scared and hurt; Jamie with his hands held out to Lizzie; and Corinne in the background, with that dark little face, half frightened, half fascinated."

"One wouldn't forget Corinne's face," said Rima thoughtfully. "But now I know why Maxie gets in a state at the notion of having her around.

She reminds you of something bad and painful in your past, Maxie. Something you want to forget."

I didn't say anything. I appeared to accept Rima's assumption. But every woman has her own particular well of intuition, harbouring its dark mysterious presentiments of good and evil; and, somewhere in those intangible depths, I sensed that it was *not* the past I feared.

7

THE STUDIO

THERE WERE TIMES when I envied Rima her studio quite fiercely. To have a bright airy workroom of your very own, somewhere you could go and hide, or entertain your friends, was almost like owning a flat. It lent her great prestige.

But Simon said, "It makes Rosevale lopsided, like a pink elephant with only one ear."

He prowled round the studio, interested and impressed as he riffled through the pages of her sketch-books and examined the models she'd carved or worked in clay and plaster. Her chisels lay in the slots of their folding canvas case on her big work-table, and there was usually some hunk of wood, standing against a wall, waiting to come to life.

"What's this old log?" he asked. "It's so hard it's practically fossilised."

"Raw stinkwood," she said. "Very exciting."

"It may be when you've finished with it, but it's just a bit of dead wood now."

She fired up at once. "Wood is never dead!" Her strong supple fingers, with the square unvarnished nails, touched it lovingly, as if the sap still ran under the dry bark, as if the nodules might burst into leaf next spring.

"It's waiting," she said.

"What'll you make of it?"

"It hasn't told me yet. We have to live together – weeks, months, maybe even years – till we understand each other. Then suddenly, one day, I'll know."

Simon laughed. "I'll take your word for it."

"I don't expect you to understand." Her tone was magnanimous.

"It's your own sorcery. Inside that dirty old log there's something – a crocodile or a dryad – and, when the time is ripe, you propose to let the creature out. Fair enough."

For several weeks the log stood passively against the wall to the right of the door, biding its time. Then, one day, we saw that it had changed its position. It was Simon who noticed.

"You've turned it round. New carbuncles and notches are showing."

Rima shrugged her shoulders. But I could sense the suppressed energy and excitement inside her. She looked up at him, mischief in her bright eyes.

"Well?" His head was thrown back, eyebrows raised.

"It's quickened," she said.

Soon she began to work on it in her spare time. We were forbidden to come into the studio uninvited. If we passed near the open windows we'd hear the flirtatious twittering of her love-birds and Rima humming softly under her breath as, bit by bit, she delivered the stern stinkwood of its burden.

Simon and I strolled up to the studio one summer's evening after the heat of the day had begun to wane. We meant to call her out for a walk or a swim. But we found her outside, sitting on a rough bench under the feathery *keurboom*. She was dressed in her working jeans and smock. Her feet were bare, her hands hung limp between her knees, her perspiring face looked small and exhausted. She glanced up at us and smiled without shifting her position. Simon dropped down on his haunches beside her; he lifted her right hand in his and looked at the callouses. She let it lie quietly in his big palm as if she had no further interest in it. For the time being its task was done.

"How's the child of your inspiration?" he asked.

"Born," she said.

I was consumed with curiosity. She had never allowed us to watch her at work, and we had only seen the unfinished sculpture modestly draped with an old sheet all torn at the edges where she had ripped off bits to use as paint rags.

"Can we go and look at it?"

She jerked her head over her shoulder towards the studio door.

"If you like, Maxie."

She didn't go in with us. She stayed out in the cool of the evening, just as we had found her, relaxed, tired, contented. But I knew her contentment wouldn't last. She was never satisfied with her work, except in the hour of completion. After that she would turn against it.

The sculpture stood on her work-table. The dark handsome wood, so resistant to the chisel, so cruel on her hands, was in glowing contrast to the pale paint-stained surface on which it rested. From the body of the log Rima had dragged her own conception of Genesis, a Negro mother suckling her infant. We stared at the massive study; naked, faceless, symbolic. It had been oiled, polished, and oiled again. The swollen belly and breasts, the rolling buttocks and thighs, the round head of the child and its groping hands shone as if with tropical sweat.

Simon drew in his breath sharply. Minutes passed before either of us spoke. Then he said in a low voice. "It's terrific. But nothing like what I'd expected."

"What did you expect?"

"Something . . . attractive."

"You should know Rima better than that! *This* was in the wood. This was what she had to bring out of it."

He glanced at me, surprised that it was I, not he, who had grasped the nature of her achievement.

"You're right. She's a fearless artist – prepared, if necessary, to be midwife to a monster!"

"This isn't a monster."

"Near enough. When Mom sees it she'll say it's shocking."

I touched the oiled wood and felt the warm, heavy texture of its life – its strength and durability.

"It'll talk back. This has a lot to say."

We heard Rima come in. She leaned against the wall where the log had stood inanimate for so long. She was spent of her usual energy.

"What does it say to *you*, Maxie?" she asked.

"Africa."

"Just that?"

"The birth and the beginning. The nourishing, the growing and the continuing."

She turned her head away and closed her eyes. Tears glistened on her thick brown lashes and spilled down her cheeks. They splashed onto her smock. Her lips trembled, but they were smiling, and I saw for the first time that her mouth was beautiful. Simon saw it too. I went out into the gathering dusk and left them alone with the dark atavistic mother and child.

The studio wasn't merely Rima's workroom. It soon became what she had originally intended – a focal point for her friends, for entertainment or discussion.

She was taking her Fine Arts Course at the University, while I was learning shorthand, typing and business routine at the Technical College, with lessons in Italian and German on the side. Simon was in the saddle at A. & B., and enjoying it. Often, after dinner, we gathered in the studio with our young friends, and, over beer and buns, we talked endlessly about our own problems and those of our country. We all held different views, but, in the main, we were agreed that the Union was a century behind the times. And many of the laws calculated to protect the Whites in South Africa infuriated us with their injustice. Simon came up against aspects of this time and again in the course of his work at A. & B., where certain types of employment were, by law, limited to Europeans.

"It's so damned unfair!" he'd complain. "A White person holds down a job at A. & B. that a Non-European could do just as well, if not better. Merit doesn't come into it. It's entirely a matter of complexion. It's bad for everybody – the White who sits pretty, the non-White whose ambition is still-born, and the firm which is hamstrung by job-reservation."

"To deny anyone the right to give of his best – and be paid for it – is a sin," said Rima. "It stunts the growth of the soul."

"Never mind the high-falutin' spiritual angle. It'll undermine the economy of the country sooner or later."

"But I do mind the spiritual angle," persisted Rima.

We all did. Like many thousands of our fellow citizens, we were in sympathy with the dark underdog. The more we saw him smacked down, the more we took his part. We joined mass protests against every new law designed to whittle down his individual freedom and keep him in subjection. We stood outside Parliament or the City Hall or the University with placards round our necks; and paraded the streets of Cape Town in processions against the infringement of Human Rights, as countless numbers of citizens were doing in other parts of the Union. But in the *platteland* – the wide country districts – the political turmoil of the towns passed unheeded. There the European conscience still dozed – if a trifle uneasily – and there the old concept of a White ruling minority and an immense Black labour force remained unaltered, accepted quite literally as gospel – the convenient Will of God proclaimed and imposed by "divinely appointed" leaders.

Claude came home for the Christmas vacation. Simon, Rima and I met him at the station and took him to Rosevale, where he was to spend a couple of days before going out to Loire. In the new year he was due to specialise in agriculture at Stellenbosch University. But this plan, we soon discovered, was to be abandoned. My brother had won a valuable science bursary to London University. It was sponsored by a famous English firm of manufacturing chemists. "And, if I don't blot my copy-book," explained Claude, "I can count on getting a good job in their laboratories later on."

"You didn't tell us you were trying for this bursary," I said.

Claude grinned. "I prefer to keep my failures to myself."

"You didn't fail."

"I was lucky. There's plenty of competition in my field these days."

When we arrived at Rosevale Claude telephoned Daddy, who was as proud and pleased as he was astonished. We heard Claude say:

"We'll thrash it all out from A to Z when I get home the day after tomorrow ... Yes, Stellenbosch have been informed ... I'm going back to Wits. For one more term, and in July I hope to sail for England. I'll see about a passage tomorrow."

That night we four young ones talked till long after midnight, sitting on the lawn outside Rima's studio in the soft summer moonlight. Through the woods we could see the lights of the city and the bay far below, and the jewelled ribbons of the roads flung out across the Flats towards the northern hills and mountains – towards our own lovely valley.

"Claude," said Rima. "How does your change of plan affect Loire? Will you come back and manage the place for Uncle Etienne as you originally intended?"

"There's the problem, Rima. I just don't know what this'll lead to. I've no idea when I'll come back. If ever. So what do I say to Dad?"

"Surely you can leave the future flexible for the time being," suggested Simon. "A man's life can't be planned in advance from birth to death."

Claude removed his spectacles and let the soft night air play on his undefended eyes.

"Research chemistry is the thing I really want to do. It's always fascinated me. To be honest, I don't give a damn for agriculture. Flocks and herds and crops leave me stone cold. Now, how do I put that to Dad, who expects me to dedicate my life to Loire?"

"Loire's a religion with your father – like A. & B. is with mine," said Rima. "Aunt Clare too. She's suffered for it. Mum says it was colossal the way she kept it going during the war. Loire isn't just a farm to them. It's a sort of immortality – the past and future of the Lamottes."

"And I'm the one who'll let the side down." My brother brushed his hand across his eyes. "You see, it just hasn't got the same meaning for me. A strip of wilderness that was made to flower by our ancestors has a nice sentimental flavour about it, but – to me – it doesn't constitute a shrine."

"Don't you *love* Loire?" It seemed impossible to me that Loire could fail to move my brother's heart.

He smiled. "In a way I do, Maxie. But not like Jamie loves Bergplaas. I don't want to feel that one of these days I *must* farm Loire. I may quite likely prefer to sell it."

In the silence that followed this heresy we could hear the crickets scraping and a night-bird call mournfully. The diffused murmur of the city carried up the kloof. I felt as if my brother had hit out at something loved and living. It was my first warning that one day he might not hesitate to break with a family tradition. I stared at his slight silhouette, at the gleam of his glasses still lightly held between his fingers. His attitude was remote and detached.

"I only ask to live my own life in my own way. Surely that's a freedom any man has a reasonable right to expect. I don't want family fetters to tie me down."

"Will you say these things to Daddy – as frankly as you've said them to us?" I asked. But it was Rima who cut in before he could answer for himself.

"Of course not, Maxie! He mustn't! There's no need to – yet. The time may come when Claude'll *want* to farm Loire. Or he may have a son who'll love the place as a true Lamotte loves his land. Let the whole question ride for the time being."

"Rima's right," said Simon. "Why upset your parents now? Go your own way for the present. Wait and see what gives, and make no decisions until you have to. Uncle Etienne doesn't want to hand over the reins yet, in any case. Loire is your heritage, but that's far in the future."

My brother put on his glasses. "Who knows?"

Rima jumped to her feet. "It's hot. Let's swim."

We could see the silver gleam of the pool through the trees as we strolled across the garden to the little creeper-covered pavilion. Rima and Simon went ahead of us. In the dark she was as nimble and sure-footed as a cat. Simon always said of her that she was a nocturnal animal. Claude linked his arm through mine.

"I know what you're thinking, Maxie."

"Do you?"

"Yes. You're fighting the thought, but it's there."

"What thought am I fighting?"

I slipped my arm out of his grasp, needing to be separate from him. The others were at the water's edge already, and Simon called: "Hurry up, you two!" I didn't want Claude to say what was in both our minds. Too much had been put into words already.

"You think I'm a traitor. Perhaps, in a way, I am. But sometimes one has to choose between being a traitor to a tradition or a traitor to oneself."

I said: "You'll go your own way. None of us has the power to stop you. Not even Loire."

"You have so many ties, Maxie. So many things and people you care about. You think with your heart. People like you get hurt."

"I'm luckier than you. I get hurt and heal, and stick my neck out for more punishment. But you follow such lonely ways. Who wants to be without ties? So terribly alone."

"Dear Maxie, loneliness doesn't mean the same to me as it does to you. We're brother and sister, but temperamentally we're two quite different animals." His voice was warm, with a smile in it. "You move, like a young lioness, in a pride. I prefer to hunt alone."

"You always have done," I said. "But I'm sorry for you, just the same."

He laughed. "Don't waste your sympathy. Let's go and join the rest of your pride."

8

CONTRASTS

IN THE FOLLOWING AUTUMN Corinne, the granddaughter of the Wise Woman of Bergplaas, came to Rosevale to help old Annie, who had decided to postpone the finality of retirement.

"If I retires, Miss Maxie, I mus' go an' live with my married niece, an' I don't want to leave Miss Kate yus' yet. But I can do with a girl to give me a han'. My bones isn't as young as my heart."

Aunt Kate, always easy-going and indulgent, agreed. And Uncle Gideon said, "It's all in accordance with Parkinson's law. The more people you employ the more you need. Big fleas and little fleas."

Corinne was a very small flea in the household, and soon found herself taking on all sorts of odd jobs. Rima's studio became one of her chores, and doing the flowers was another. Aunt Kate discovered that Corinne had a natural gift for arranging flowers and we all offered her advice and encouragement with an eye to shelving a job that often came our way. I had quite got over my ridiculous apprehension about Corinne coming to Rosevale. The haunt of the night of the fire was no longer revived by her neat figure and the diffident smile that betrayed a gap of four missing front teeth. This gap under the full lip had the childish charm of the moment between lost milk teeth and the big frilly boulders that so quickly take their place.

"Annie'll bully her," I said to Rima. "Poor thing!"

"She's used to her *ouma*," smiled Rima. "At least Annie hasn't got a reputation for putting the evil eye on her enemies!"

In fact, after the stern discipline of Lizzie, Annie held few terrors for the new young housemaid. Corinne was as gay as a bird by disposition, and her manner to Rocky and Goodwin gave them no cause to complain that she treated them like "black donkeys", as Annie was sometimes inclined to do. In fact, Rocky, who had a roving eye, was once caught by Annie pinching Corinne's behind as she went upstairs.

Corinne's squeal of protest was half a giggle, but Annie's wrath was tremendous.

"He says it was only fun – to make her feel at home!" Annie muttered to me, with a face like a thunder cloud. "I know where dose black donkeys gits wit' deir fun! What would Lizzie say if she knew a *Native* had touched her gran'child?"

I shuddered to think. Natives – even parsons – were still regarded as fairly wild animals by the old-fashioned Cape Coloureds, who identified themselves firmly with the White way of life. Rocky, wounded in his pride, sulked for a week, but after that everybody settled down.

When Corinne went into the garden with her basket and her secateurs, Leslie amiably allowed her the freedom of the picking-garden behind the house. But the roses he always cut himself.

About this time Leslie was preparing for his biennial visit to his distant country, and he brought his nephew, Lenno, to take his place during his absence. Of course Uncle Gideon paid Leslie's train fare both ways, but, while he was at his *kraal*, he received no wages. This was the custom, and it was up to Leslie whether he stayed away for weeks or months. It generally took him about half a year to deal with his family affairs, such as hut-building, cattle-coping, starting a new piccaninny, and so on; and, in the meanwhile, Uncle Gideon knew that Leslie would send impassioned pleas for money, penned in flowery but urgent terms by the Indian scribe at his nearest general store. This too was a matter of custom, because it is acknowledged that every good master is also his servant's banker and the only money-lender who will not demand interest. But, like most borrowers, Leslie always appealed for more than he hoped to receive, and Uncle Gideon's postal orders were made out on this assumption.

For a month before his departure Leslie worked with Lenno, teaching him about the garden. The roses had been pruned and the new shrubs planted, most of the vegetables were in, and, by the time the summer pests became a menace, Leslie would be back at Rosevale. In any case, Aunt Kate could be relied upon to instruct Lenno with spraying and fertilising when necessary. He was a splendidly built young Bantu with the springy step of the tribesman who can cover endless miles of bush country at a steady lope. He kept his round bullet-head near shaven, and his teeth were huge and white in his merry coal-black face. When he laughed, which was often, he ducked his head shyly. Rima and I thought he was full of charm.

"He only talk littie-bittie English," his uncle informed us. "He have work in a mine on the Rand. On top, not under. He can speak Afrikaans. Now he want to learn English." We promised to help, and, after that, whenever we saw Lenno, we taught him a few new words of English, and he remembered them well.

We often heard them signalling to one another across the garden with curious bird whistles. They talked in the deep-throated Shangaan language and seemed to have a lot of jokes. Lenno sang to himself a great deal, monotonous calypsos in a minor key. He came of the Bavenda tribe, which is very musical and famed for the beauty of its women.

"In my country there are only two nations," Leslie explained. "Shangaan and Bavenda. Once they kill each other. Now they marry." I never got used to Leslie's casual use of the word "kill". But then knifings among the Bantu are commonplace, and even the most gruesome ritual is, to them, an understandable necessity. "Lenno, his auntie have marry my father's cousin," added Leslie, to prove his case.

We nodded gravely. Bantu relationships were too complex for us. We were more interested to know of Lenno's romance. He was betrothed to a beautiful maiden of his own tribe who had attended the same Swiss Mission school, and who was, in his uncle's eyes, an admirable match.

"Her father is a doctor," he told us. "Very *very* clever."

The doctor had not, however, graduated at Wits or U.C.T. He had inherited his wisdom from a long line of distinguished and terrifying witch-doctors, who could, at will, turn themselves, or other people, into reptiles, for the Mamba was their totem. Lenno's father was the grandson of a chief. So socially everything was in order. But, in the true biblical fashion, he had to work long and hard to win his bride. It was understood that in two years' time he would be in a position to pay the *lobola* of thirty head of cattle for this treasure.

Both Leslie and Lenno knew all about wild creatures, and they both loved Rima's budgies. We'd see them standing near the sunporch, gazing into the aviary where the blue, yellow and green love-birds twittered in the branches of their dwarf tree or swung on their toy ladders, or laid their careless eggs in tiny pigeon-holes without making the smallest pretence at nest-building. Rima's tame birds attracted wild ones, and sugar-birds with slender curved beaks and long tails hovered round the big cage. Then Leslie and Lenno would help us to identify them from our bird-book, which gave us all great pleasure and satisfaction.

In June, when the rains of winter were falling, Leslie caught his slow train to the north. He travelled across the jagged mountains of the Cape, the wide semi-desert of the sheep-breeding Karoo, the sun-drenched high-veld with its grain and its gold, and the lowveld with its lions, and on into the land of forests and peaks and great rivers where his people dwell in their reed huts, where a man measures his prestige by the number of his cattle and his wives, and where the mysterious powers of the witch-doctor are supreme and no magic is impossible.

Simon, too, left us at this time. Uncle Gideon sent him to the Durban and Johannesburg branches of A. & B., after which he was to go to the Federation; and then on an extensive African tour to examine the possi-bilities of trade in the new Negro states emerging so rapidly to the north of the Union. He would be away about a year in all. He missed Claude by a few days.

My brother returned from Wits in June, and, after a fortnight at Loire, he made his headquarters at Rosevale as he had a good deal to attend to in Cape Town before sailing for England.

That was when the contretemps over Fara September blew up. You couldn't exactly call it a row. Anyway, it left a bitter taste in our mouths.

Fara, a highly educated Coloured girl, was a fellow student of Rima's at the University. She was studying music, dramatic art and elocution, and she had already made a name for herself in the famous Coloured Operatic Group which can sell out the City Hall with a wildly enthusiastic mixed audience any time it puts on a show. She was the daughter of Mr August September, who worked in the upholstery department of A. & B., as his father and grandfather had done before him. The Septembers were com-paratively prosperous and highly respected Coloured people who lived in a nice little house at Sea Point.

One day Rima came home very elated.

"Fara September has promised to sit for me. She has a wonderful head and I just can't wait to begin work!"

"She has a lovely voice," said Aunt Kate warmly. "Her performance in Tosca was superb. Mr September nearly burst with pride when I con-gratulated him on his daughter's success – and rightly too."

No one offered the slightest objection to Fara posing for Rima, and Claude and I often went up to the studio during the sittings.

Rima, who had been so secretive about her Mother and Child sculpture, didn't mind in the least when we stayed and watched her at work.

"This is quite different," she said. "The other was creative, this is a portrait. In a way, having other people here helps Fara relax."

She modelled in plaster with the intention of casting the bust in bronze if it turned out good enough. And, because my cousin was a perfectionist, there were many sittings.

Like most Coloured people Fara was temperamental, up one moment and down the next. Sometimes she was wildly over-animated, and then again she might be unaccountably dejected. She was surprisingly free of the Cape Coloured accent, which has a lilt all its own, and she determinedly tried not to mix English and Afrikaans in every sentence she uttered.

"She takes her elocution very seriously," Rima told us in confidence. "She likes coming here because she thinks Maxie and I speak well, and she learns from us. She's terrifically observant."

"She's a born mimic and actress," agreed Claude. "She plays the part of Rima Antrobus."

Fara was small and slight, with smooth night-black hair, like an Indian woman's, and a brown skin the colour of winter bracken. She had a softly sensual mouth, a graceful neck, and glistening almond eyes that looked ready to brim over with laughter or tears any moment. She was one of a large family, and she worried a good deal because she felt that her father was spending too much on her education.

"Why worry?" said Claude. "When you're rich and famous you can help the other children. Your father's investing his money in your talent."

"How can I get rich and famous?" she pouted. "That sort of thing doesn't happen to Coloured people here."

"It doesn't *happen* to anybody anywhere. You have to *make* it happen." He frowned as he added, "All the same it's bloody that it should be harder for your people to get rich and famous, but it is."

She was sitting with her slender hands folded in her lap, her head proudly poised, tilted up a little. She didn't disturb the pose, but she looked at my brother with a searching downward glance through lashes thick and black over the moist shine of her eyes.

"You're famous here already," remarked Rima. "The Group's going on tour next year – all over Africa. Why don't you go with them? You'll be through Varsity by then."

"I ought to start work. I'll be qualified to teach – to earn money. And you know the Group isn't paid."

"To hell with teaching," said Claude. "Get away from here! Chance your arm and go for bigger game. You could bring it off."

I think that was when the dream was conceived – Fara's big brave dream. I added my quota.

"If you want something badly enough – if you set your whole heart and mind on it and really know what it is you want – it'll come to pass."

Rima wiped her hands on her smock and pushed back her copper hair. "Would that apply to tea, Maxie?"

I laughed. "I'll put the kettle on right now."

One of us always drove Fara home to Sea Point, usually Claude, because Rima knew how he loved to drive her little open red sports car. Any excuse was good enough for Claude to get his hands on the wheel of Red Devil, as we called it.

That evening we were all exhilarated. Rima had nearly completed the portrait and we could see that she had caught a special quality in Fara, the spirit that was to enable her to follow my brother's advice and chance her arm on a very long shot.

"Look," I said. "You're brave, Fara! That head is full of courage."

She gazed at the small tilted head as if she found it strange and foreign, yet exciting. Her laugh was nervous and high-pitched. It was the one thing she'd not studied and tried to improve. All her unsureness about herself was in that laugh.

"I don't know myself so beautifully white!"

"Clown white," said Rima. "Mask white, deader than a corpse. I hate plaster. Wait till you see it in bronze."

Rima disappeared into the little washroom, and Fara moved slowly towards the sunlit aviary. She watched the budgies, so lively behind their bars. She's not just seeing the birds, I thought. She's seeing something else.

"They're like little children," she said at last. "Unfitted for freedom."

"Rima'd never cage a wild bird."

She glanced at me quickly. "No. It'd dash itself against the bars. They'd cripple it. Or kill it. This is a nice pleasant cage. The world's full of cages, some not so pleasant, some very crippling."

Claude began to say something and stopped. I felt him waiting. She went on.

"My skin is my cage. A pretty, brown cage. I'm told that's nonsense – that I'm free to develop along my own lines. There's a word for that sort of freedom – *apartheid*. Or is it more polite to call it parallel development? One layer underneath, the other – the White one – on top."

I felt her intensity and frustration, and I wanted to put my arms round her and say, "That isn't so. You're free." But it *was* so, and Fara wasn't free. Separate development, separate cages. No roaming here, there or anywhere for the brown beasts. Fences on all sides. Ceilings, too. No freedom of the upper air for the brown birds. My brother took a step towards her, and suddenly I knew that the feelings inside me were not my own, but his. It was *he* who wanted to comfort Fara.

Rima came back into the room. She was still in her smock, but her hands were scrubbed and she was drying them. She flung down the towel.

"Can you spare me the time for one more sitting, Fara? Just one more."

"Of course."

Fara turned to the little wall-mirror and applied her bright geranium lipstick and a generous touch of rouge. She was more beautiful without make-up – "With it she looks like a *houri*," Claude had said to me once – but she'd have felt undressed without it. She swung round with one of her theatrical gestures.

"I'll be sorry when it's finished. It's been wonderful, coming here. You've been . . . very nice to me . . . you three . . ."

Rima smiled, as she cut in. "Tomorrow then, Fara?"

"The day after. I can't manage tomorrow. I'll be here as usual the day after."

She folded her rainbow-coloured kerchief and tied it lightly round her inky hair. The hood of Red Devil was down. She got into the passenger seat beside Claude and drew the collar of her lavender wool coat high about her throat. She looked young and attractive and rather tarty. It was the *houri* look.

As they turned out of Rosevale drive they were heading straight into the setting sun. I don't think either of them saw Uncle Gideon and Aunt Kate come through the little wicket from the Kloof Nek woods. We did though. Rima shaded her eyes with her hand as she watched her parents stand quite still and stare after the little red car as it roared off in the direction of the Glen.

C

9

STORM OVER FARA

THE NORTH-WESTER ROSE and piled the rain clouds over the mountain and, by the time we had finished dinner, the cold bright winter's day had turned into a stormy night with hail pelting against the window-panes.

We sat round a cosy fire in Uncle Gideon's study, my uncle and aunt in their usual easy chairs, Claude in a corner of the big couch with Trout, the tabby cat, and Pim, the poodle, curled up next to him. Sambo, the labrador, sprawled on the hearthrug, twitching and snoring. Aunt Kate was working on a tapestry firescreen to match the cushions on which my cousin and I were sitting on the hobs jutting out from the big open fireplace. There were fir-cones among the burning logs and they gave off a vivid blue and gold blaze and a resinous scent to counteract the wet dog smell of Sambo.

Uncle Gideon, who wore his old velvet smoking jacket and fleece-lined slippers, leaned forward and flicked the stub of his after-dinner cigar expertly into the flames. He folded his evening paper and put it on the stinkwood stool at his side.

"Maxie," he asked, "when do you finish your course at the Technical College?"

"In a few weeks' time."

"Your father's planning a trip to Europe next year, I believe?"

"Yes. We've had two fat years, Daddy says, and he reckons we can afford it at last."

"You'll want to fill in time before sailing. We could take you on as a mannequin at A. & B. in the spring."

"A mannequin? Not me, Uncle Gideon. I'm not the type. Not tall enough, for one thing."

"You could do the teenage stuff very well. I've mentioned it to Miss Pratt. She agrees."

"I'm eighteen – a bit old for that, surely!"

Aunt Kate smiled. "You have the fresh juvenile look, dear. And you're a graceful creature."

Claude glanced up from his book and grinned. "Juvenile! Do you want to aggravate her, Aunt Kate?"

"The late teenage stuff was what I meant, of course," said Uncle Gideon. "I'm not suggesting Maxie models school uniforms."

"I'll gladly work in the show-room – or in the office. But I don't want to be a mannequin. You've got to have a feel of the theatre to model clothes. It's not my line."

"As you like," Uncle Gideon turned to Claude. "Talking of the theatre, was that Fara September in Rima's car with you this evening?" He switched off the reading lamp at his elbow. His craggy features and grey thinning hair were in shadow, except for the firelight. Claude's voice went cool as he answered.

"I took Fara home this evening. She'd been sitting for Rima. I've driven her home several times."

"So I've noticed. Her father works in our upholstering department. The Septembers are well known to us at A. & B."

Rima stiffened. "Claude takes Fara back at my request."

Aunt Kate was threading her needle, holding it up to the light. "A bus passes our gate," she remarked.

"In the peak hour, between five and six – and with bus *apartheid* – Fara could wait a long time by our gate!"

Uncle Gideon said calmly: "No need to get heated, Rima. But if you feel that Fara must be taken home in your little open car, I suggest that in future you drive her yourself. Or let Maxie."

My brother's face had turned to stone, but Rima was leaning forward, her brow puckered, her mouth obstinate. She never hesitated to stand up to her father.

"What are you getting at, Daddy?"

"Take a guess."

"You mean because Fara's Coloured?"

"Anything else?"

"I suppose you don't like the daughter of one of your Coloured employees being seen around with your nephew."

"You've assessed the situation very accurately."

She made an impatient gesture. "Listen, Daddy. At Varsity the students thumb lifts into Cape Town all the time. They stand in queues at the bottom of the steps, girls, boys, Europeans and non-Europeans – thank God U.C.T. is not *yet* forced to close its doors to non-Whites – and motorists give them lifts. Every day of the week. It makes no difference what race the student may be. In fact, a lot of drivers say, 'I'll take you and you and *you*' and *pick* on the non-Europeans. That's one of the ways the public conscience works. You do it yourself, Mom."

"I daresay," said Uncle Gideon. "But a young White man, alone with an extremely striking heavily made up Coloured girl, in a very aggressive little open sports car is quite a different cup of tea to someone like your mother giving a lift to a mixed bag of student passengers on the road from U.C.T. into Cape Town. I don't really have to explain that to you, Rima. Nor to Claude."

Rima's eyes flashed a silent rebellious "So what?", and I saw a tiny muscle twitching in my brother's cheek. I knew that sign. Uncle Gideon changed the direction of the conversation.

"Under what terms is Fara posing for you, Rima?"

"Terms?"

"What do you pay her?"

"Pay! I wouldn't insult her. She's at Varsity like I am. She sits for me out of friendship."

"*Friendship?*" My uncle's heavy black eyebrows arched up. "Quite what do you mean by friendship?"

Aunt Kate let her work fall into her lap. Her features were sharp and bony like all the Beefords, but they were softened by the habitual gentleness of her expression. She said quietly.

"I know what Rima means. She means good will, Gideon. There's no harm in that. We could do with plenty more of it in our country. In any case, Fara's sittings are over – or very nearly – and I think you've made your point."

But Uncle Gideon frowned at his wife, and gave his attention to my brother.

"What has the procedure been? Do you appear – *after* Rima's sessions with Fara – to act as chauffeur? Or are you present during the sittings?"

Claude kept his temper.

"Maxie and I often go to the studio while Rima's working. Maxie makes tea for us – and serves it."

"And you . . . four . . . enjoy a nice sociable chat?"

My cheeks were burning and I couldn't keep back the words that jumped to my lips. "Yes, we do, Uncle Gideon! Fara's highly educated and gifted, and as nice as she can be. Why shouldn't we behave in a civilised way and talk to each other like civilised people?"

He didn't appear to resent my interruption.

"I'll tell you why, Maxie. Because, rightly or wrongly – and, I admit, many people think wrongly – it's not our way of life."

"But we're changing our way of life. We've got to go with the times."

"We're passing through an industrial revolution," he said. "The sort of thing England went through over a century ago. I quite agree that we're living in a period of readjustment and change. But it doesn't affect our private lives."

"It very soon will," said my brother. "The one follows the other. England's industrial revolution led into her social revolution. The time is coming – and soon – when education and civilised behaviour will be the only criterions of social status. And money, of course. Pigmentation will be a matter of taste. No more."

"What do you mean by soon?"

"In your lifetime."

"The *herrenvolk* are doomed," said Rima. "And they know it. But they want to hang on to their privileges and power as long as they can and leave the blood-bath to our generation and the next."

"There's only one real answer," I said. "Intermarriage. When we're all mud-coloured we'll be able to live together without patronage or pretence – without fear and humiliation."

Aunt Kate said, "You young people talk to show off."

"No," said Claude. "Any scientist would agree with Maxie. I study science and mathematics and world trends, and it doesn't take a great brain to realise that the world trend towards the freedom and dignity of the individual – which abolished slavery and emancipated women – is on the wing again. In a very big way. Add to that the overwhelming numerical superiority of the African, and his uninhibited fertility, and you get a fair picture of the future in Africa. The White man's best chance of survival on this Continent is gradual absorption. Miscegenation."

Aunt Kate folded her tapestry and put it into her deep work-bag as if she no longer had the heart to work on it.

"If that day is to come, Claude, I pray I never see it."

"In the meantime," said Uncle Gideon, "there's a law against that sort of thing. Let me remind you that sexual association between any European and non-European – inside or outside the bonds of matrimony – is a criminal offence, punished with increasing severity."

"And what a cruel idiotic law it is!" Rima cried. "One's upbringing should be enough to look after something so personal."

"Not everybody has a good upbringing, darling," said Aunt Kate. "These laws are intended to maintain racial purity."

"To enforce it," I put in. "As if you could! Human beings aren't robots. They love and hate. They *feel*."

"So it seems," Uncle Gideon gave me a caustic smile.

My brother has two voices – one warm and personal, one cool and objective. It was the second that chimed in now.

"It's strange to me – all this trivial thinking and acting. Here we are, challenging the stars, rocketing into the space age, and we make tremendous issues of inconsequent social and ethnological differences. Surely to goodness we should forget about the importance of being White or Black, or members of one nation or another, and think only of being sensible and united earthmen."

Aunt Kate made a rather helpless gesture and Uncle Gideon reached down to select a log from the iron basket. He placed it carefully on the fire, added a few fir cones, and stared into the rainbow coloured blaze as if he sought there the mythical salamander. After a while he said, "You go too fast and far, Claude. You're soaring into the realms of science fiction. I'm a contemporary fellow. I look ahead – I need to, because I'm the head of a big business concern – but I keep my earthman feet on the earth under them. I'd advise you to do the same. While you're in this country – or when you come back to it – observe its traditional customs."

A glance passed between Claude, Rima and me, and we rose on the same impulse, like sea-birds on a rock when the tide is coming in and a wave breaks nearer than the wave before it. We went to the old schoolroom and turned on the electric fire and, very softly, the wireless. A rotating gadget in the radiator produced an unconvincing illusion of flickering flames, but its heat was dry and concentrated. Rima put a bowl of water in front of it. Trout, the cat, who'd followed Claude as usual, investigated the bowl, and, finding no milk, turned away in disgust and began to wash its nether quarters with the clinical concentration of its kind. Rain spattered gustily against the windows behind the heavily lined chintz curtains.

Rima stood in front of the fireplace, her hands clenched.

"They're like the rest of their generation – blind with preconceived prejudice, steeped in it. What'll open their eyes?"

"You can't open their eyes," I said. "They've been blind too long. They're too old. Uncle Gideon looks ahead, like he said he does. He sees how things are likely to develop. He can even apply new ideas to his business – and I mean the big ideas now, the basic ones – but he can't bring them into his private life."

"He doesn't want to. He's frightened to," said Rima.

"That's about it. He was giving me a warning tonight." Claude took off his glasses and wiped them with the little polishing chamois he kept in his spectacle case. "Your father knows damn well that these days every single bridge between the races is charged with dynamite, especially where a man and a woman are concerned. He was handing me a clear tip to watch my step."

"It was insulting. There was an implication behind it – that you . . . physically . . . were interested in Fara—"

He shrugged his shoulders. "I took a long time seeing her home. If Uncle Gideon saw me leave Rosevale with her, he may have heard me come back. Then he'd know what a long time it took." Without his glasses my brother's eyes had their young defenceless look.

I caught my breath. "Why, Claude? Why did you take so long to see Fara home?"

Rima was curled up on the huge old sofa with the broken springs. She looked up curiously.

"Yes, why?"

"You know the September house?" Claude asked.

"I do," she said. "Maxie doesn't. It's a pleasant, solidly-built cottage in a lane at the end of Sea Point. A little garden, where the kids keep their pets. They have a couple of good-tempered tortoises. And there're fig trees and a big old loquat tree. A nice view of the sea and Lion's Head. A few chickens."

"That's right. The September family have owned that property for over a hundred years – nothing grand, but they love it."

"Of course. I've had tea with Fara there," Rima said. "They've some very good furniture. Mr September understands about things like that. It's his job. And Mrs September keeps the place like a new pin. She has a couple of my budgies in a cage on the stoep."

Claude put on his spectacles. "When I got there with Fara one of the kids ran out to say Ma was crying and Pa couldn't comfort her. I went in with Fara. I thought there might have been an accident. Mrs September was weeping fit to break her heart, and the old man wasn't much better. They'd received their notice to quit."

Rima sprang to her feet. "But that's impossible! It's their property – their home!"

"That lane has been proclaimed a White area. They'll be given time to . . . make other arrangements. Then they must go. All the Coloured families in that lane will have to go. The authorities are sympathetic, but you can't have a Coloured pocket in a White group area—"

"It's horrible . . ." I knew of these instances – who didn't? – but this was personal, not just another distressing case of individual hardship necessitated by the master plan for social segregation.

Rima's face was sharp with fury. The skin had shrunk back on to the bones, leaving her nose prominent and her eyes blazing.

"Disenfranchise! Disinherit! What power gives one group the right to persecute another? To throw a decent man out of his very own home and hand it to some other person whose skin is lighter?"

She looked Jewish now, ready to storm and wail and tear her hair and decry persecution in all its forms.

"What did Fara do?" I asked.

"There was a jar of artificial floewrs and dried bulrushes on the mantelpiece. Fara seized the flowers and rushes, threw them on the floor and stamped on them. Then she hurled the jar against the wall and screamed, 'Take that!' It smashed to smithereens. It was rather an ugly jar. Fara couldn't have liked it much."

Rima was amazed into a quiet pallor. "What next?"

"She spat on the mess, and swore, and yelled to one of the kids to come and clean it up and *maa' gou!*"

"What good did all that do?"

My brother grinned.

"It cleared the air no end. It got the kids busy tidying up. It infuriated Mrs September out of her tears. Mr September threatened to fine Fara for the breakage. And some invisible and unidentified official's thick skull was smashed to atoms when Fara took her pot shot at authority in general."

We tried to laugh, but we weren't really amused. We were angry. We were so often in a rage, so sore at the injuries inflicted on those with no redress.

I said, "That's how it snowballs – the hate."

My brother looked at me. The tiny muscle in his cheek was jumping again.

"Fara threw an empty jar at a blank wall. No harm in that. But multiply that impulse by several million and see what answer you get. It adds up to a savage sum."

"Yes," said Rima. "But why were you so late getting back to Rose-vale?"

"I took Fara for a drive to cool her off and calm her down. G'night girls, I'm going to bed."

He went out, leaving the door open behind him. After a few moments the cat plopped off the sofa and snaked round the door on its way upstairs to Claude's bedroom.

"Two of a kind," said Rima. "They do as they like, and be damned."

Part 2

NEW HORIZONS

IO

EAST COAST

I SAILED FOR ITALY with my parents in the following January. A. & B. had packed the most wonderful hampers of tinned food, and bales of blankets for the peasants who had helped Daddy while he was hiding in the Italian mountains during the last winter of the war.

"It's a debt long overdue," he said, "and one that can never be repaid, but at least the stuff'll be useful to them and I know what they need."

It was all packed and stowed in our station-wagon, which was shipped with us in the Italian liner.

Rima was sad to see us go. She sat on the bunk in my tiny single berth cabin looking skinny and miserable. The cabin was air-conditioned, almost cold in contrast to the heat of the summer's day.

"I envy you, you lucky dog! I long to go to Italy. Italy and Greece."

"Your turn'll come. When you've finished your Fine Arts Course."

"Two more years. An eternity."

"You can cut it shorter than that."

For her sake I tried to subdue my own intense excitement, but I knew that it bubbled through my voice and danced in my eyes. It was making its own music and colour inside me. I had never been away from the Union, and now new oceans and seas, new coasts and countries lay ahead. Adventure. And Mombasa. Simon was to meet us there for the twenty-four hours our ship would be in port. He was going to fly down to the coast from Nairobi, specially to see us.

Rima looked round and made a gesture that embraced the whole ship, Africa, Europe, and a great deal else as well.

"All this – and Simon too!"

"If he can make it."

"He'll make it, Maxie. He's already invented a business excuse for going to Mombasa."

She looked so peaky and disgruntled that I tried to cheer her up.

"Never mind, Rima. I'll get a glimpse of him, but after that he'll be on his way back home to Rosevale and you."

"Not Rosevale," she said.

I stared at her.

"Not Rosevale? What on earth do you mean?"

"He wants to find a bachelor flat somewhere."

"But why?"

"Can't you understand how it'd be for him at Rosevale once he's working regularly at A. & B.? Dad pushing him around in the office and the departments all day, and Simon coming home in the evening still harnessed to the job – like somebody who's baled out and can't get rid of his parachute!"

"But Rima, what'll Uncle Gideon say?"

"He'll agree. If I play my cards right, he'll think the idea was his."

"Whose is it?"

"Mine."

We were wary and mistrustful. Suddenly she tossed her head back.

"Can't you see that we *have* to get clear of each other? All four of us! That night, when Dad let Claude have it about Fara, you and I got hurt too. We've been like four puppies in one basket all our lives. Crack the whip at one and you scare the lot."

"But, Rima, we're out of the puppy basket now. We're scattered."

The shiver that passed through her chilled me too.

"It's going to be cold for me – alone in the puppy basket."

"You could have kept Simon with you. He belongs in your family. He's one of you."

"No!"

I recognised the echo of an old cry. He mustn't be allowed to belong too closely. He mustn't share her parents and think of her as a sister. She must shift the ground and manoeuvre him on to some neutral territory where he could be separate and free. She must risk losing him in order to gain him. The cold tremor, born of Rima's loneliness and fostered on me, crept through the pores of my skin and into my bone-marrow. Did she love Simon so much? Could she be plotting so deep? Or was I reading too much into an entirely natural situation?

"This cabin's icy," she said. "A fridge. I don't think I go much on this air-conditioning – though you may need it later on in the tropics."

There was a hammering on the door and laughing voices as our gang of friends surged in with books and chocolates and flowers for me. No room to put anything or anybody. Everything was fun and warm again. We swarmed all over the ship, and I heard a young wolf say in Italian to his friend, "Not to hope! The pretty blondes always go down the gangway at the third bell." I smiled to myself and wondered if he'd be my *flirt* for the trip. Why should he imagine I didn't speak Italian? He'd soon learn better, and then he'd feel a fool!

Later, when we were leaning over the rail to wave goodbye to friends and relatives, his friend looked sadly after Rima's small figure. "There she goes, the little red one! I love them red, like little flames." And, in the evening light, Rima's copper head burned as she looked up and waved her yellow scarf.

By sunset the wind was singing a cold song in the rigging, the Twelve Apostles were fading in the distance, the noisy pursuing gulls were fewer and the ship was meeting the Indian Ocean swell with a resigned long-suffering groan. Mummie decided to go to bed and trust to "getting her sea-legs" during the night, and Daddy and I ate a magnificent dinner, and cautiously assessed those of our fellow passengers who appeared for the meal.

"Don't make your new friends too quickly," he warned me. "There's always a reshuffle a few days out."

We toasted his "pilgrimage" in chianti, and he said, with his eyes twinkling, "To my past and your future, young Maxie!"

When I went to bed I thought of Rosevale, pink against the purple shoulder of Table Mountain, and of my cousin, Rima, cold and alone in that big "puppy basket". And then I thought of Simon, who'd meet us in Mombasa, and of the unknown world waiting to be discovered and explored. That night I heard it, for the first time, the thin tuning-fork note that seems to girdle a ship at sea with a high secret song. And I wondered if the other passengers could hear it too, or if it was just my imagination, or the song of my own blood.

This was my father's *bonanza* year. I shall remember it always for very many reasons, certain turning-points in my own life, but also for the special radiant quality of my father's pleasure during this holiday that was so much more than a holiday to him. His usual effervescent charm was shot through with deeper vibrations, and I found myself with a phrase running through my heard. This must surely be *the summer of his deep content!* Mummie was aware of it too. I believe she and Daddy rediscovered one another that year. They had both shed their responsibilities for the time being. Loire, which had done them proud with bumper harvests, rested in the care of the foreman, promoted manager; and his wife, under an arrangement profitable to herself, had taken charge of Mummie's precious poultry. My parents were more carefree than I had ever known them.

I was soon absorbed into the little world apart of shipboard life, chasing around with a pack of young folk, including the two Italians who had noticed Rima and me before sailing time in Cape Town. Our happy hunting-grounds were the sports-deck under the awnings, the boat-deck under the stars, and the open air swimming-bath. We played games, went ashore together, danced and flirted, and I gained self-confidence. Somehow, without Rima there, I was more completely myself. Perhaps she was right. We had been too close for too long.

We left the thriving ports of the Cape and the Eastern Province behind, and in Durban the first humid colourful breath of the Tropics touched us. Another girl and I went up into the Thousand Hills with the two young Italians, and into the dreaming valleys of Zululand, where the tribesmen herd their cattle, and the naked chocolate breasts of the women bounce under collars of beads. This excited our companions, who were easily inflamed, and we had trouble keeping them in order on the way back to the ship through the emerald cane-fields where the Zulus worked in the hot sun. A century ago the Zulus had been proud warriors and coolies had come from India as labour for the sugar belt, but now the Zulus wielded the machete and the Indians, by and large, were artisans, store-keepers, money-lenders, professional men and owners of land and property.

That evening we watched the green Bluff of Durban recede in the dusk, and bade the Union goodbye.

The steamy heat, increasing daily as we sailed up the East Coast and "bumped" over the Equator into the Northern Hemisphere, was as relaxing as a Turkish-bath – or so everybody said – and we were glad of our air-conditioned cabins. The tourists' cameras whirred and clicked as they sauntered through picturesque streets and markets, where the voice of the *muezzin* called to the faithful from minarets etched against a fierce blue sky, for this was the fringe of Moslem Africa. But the biggest thrill of all was when we passed an Arab *dhow* close enough to take a picture. The cameras were out in full force for that!

Daddy grinned as he watched the delighted amateurs. "I don't mind all these people taking photographs," he said. "It's the poor buzzards who'll have to look at them I pity."

Mummie laughed. "I'm sure Maxie's diary would be more interesting."

"Do you really want to see it?" I asked. "My impressions and secret thoughts—"

"I'll buy it."

But, when I gave her my scribble book, she opened it and burst out laughing.

"You win, Maxie. This is like Rima at her most abstract."

"I've got to try and keep up my shorthand some way. Might as well be this. All that stuff I learned at the Tech was wasted at A. & B. A dead loss."

Daddy passed his hand over my head, as if I were one of his beloved springer-spaniels and the fall of my hair a long silky ear to be fondled.

"Nothing you learn is ever wasted. Be it good or bad, learned in or out of school. No experience is a dead loss. None."

Mummie said, "All the same, she's wise to practise her shorthand."

He smiled. "Her private cypher. It's no effort to you, is it, Maxie? You love writing. Like Rima loves drawing. And maybe, when you practise your typing, we'll be able to read what you've written."

"The abridged version," I said. "Pity Rima can't illustrate it."

"She'd catch the feel of life better than our ship's busy photographers," said Daddy. "She has a gift for that."

He was right. Rima's pencil could evoke a whole mood with a few strokes. I could picture her curled up in a chair in some corner of the deck, her sketch-book in her lap, as she studied the jabbering rabble swarming on board to work cargo or falling asleep between shifts, lying like dogs on the hard deck. Yes, Rima would capture the White languor and the Black turbulence, the urgent African bodies of the men under their white robes, the fecund curves of the black-veiled women, the quick life in the huge moist eyes of Negro children and the sharp precocity of little Arab boys bent on some form of exploitation.

In a way I missed Rima quite intensely, yet I was glad that I would have Simon to myself at Mombasa. This thought was so thrilling that every time it came to me it took my breath clean away. It was my last-thing-at-night thought, the one I saved up till my head was on the pillow and the lights were out. Then I'd whistle it up, softly, and secretly, the way I used to smuggle the dog into my bed when I was a child at Loire, knowing it to be naughty and forbidden, but feeling happy and warm and luxurious because I also knew that it was a harmless thing to do, not really wicked. I nursed the dream of Mombasa night after night – a formless, green, moon-lit dream, with Simon moving through it in situations that would have astounded him and appalled my parents.

When we arrived at the lovely spice island of Zanzibar, there was a cable from him to say that he would meet us as arranged and that he had booked provisional accommodation at the Nyali Beach Hotel. We asked the Chief Steward about Nyali Beach and he told us that it was some distance from the port, "very beautiful for a small holiday, beautiful beach, nice hotel, but food not so beautiful as on board our ship."

"It'll do us good to get out of the ship for twenty-four hours," said Daddy. "Make a nice break."

But the day before we docked Mummie was running a temperature and the ship's doctor gave his verdict. "Influenza . . . and the *signora* must remain in bed."

"Daddy," I pleaded that night. "I'm terribly sorry about Mummie, but it won't stop my going to Nyali Beach with Simon, will it?"

"For the day? Of course not."

"I don't mean just for the day. I mean for the time we're going to be in port."

"I don't know, Maxie. I'll have to think about that."

I bit my lip, choking on my disappointment, working up a red-hot resentment.

"If there were someone else from the ship—" he added, "a chaperone—"

"Not that ridiculous word! Who ever heard of a chaperone in this day and age? Why, everybody goes off with everybody else – all over the place. Heaps of the girls I know take their holidays with their boy-friends and nobody thinks a thing about it. And Simon . . . Why, Simon . . ."

"Simon's like a brother to you – is that it?"

I nodded. Suddenly I couldn't meet his eyes, and, to my dismay, my own had filled with tears.

"We'll decide tomorrow, Maxie. Your mother must give the decision. You may think we're old-fashioned, but we've been young too, you know."

"Everything's changed since then – but *everything*!"

He laughed good naturedly. "Manners and customs may have changed. But I don't suppose human nature has. Fathers know the male animal. That's why they cherish their daughters."

"But Simon—"

"Come off the boil, Maxie. Simon's different, you want to tell me. How long is it since you've seen him?"

"Going on for a year."

"A year at your age – eighteen – makes a big difference. Go and take a good long look at yourself in the glass – when you've finished fuming – and perhaps it'll surprise you to see how you've grown up. I'm sure it'll surprise Simon."

To surprise Simon was exactly my intention. But I said indignantly. "Daddy, how can you do this? How can you try to change things between Simon and me? It's horrible!" Did he guess how much I wanted to change things? I felt found out and furious – and pleased – because my father had noticed that I had become attractive to men, because he thought that Simon might find me desirable. As I glanced up I met his eyes, reflective and penetrating, and knew that I had spoken too passionately and impulsively. He looked away from me as if he felt that he too might have said more than was wise.

"All right then, Maxie. As you were. When we've seen Simon tomorrow, we'll make a plan."

But what plan? A tiny slice of life – a day and a night in Mombasa, sandwiched between long months apart – and they had the power to spoil it! It was intolerable that I couldn't make my own plan without asking anybody's permission. The sooner I was independent the better – financially, of course. That was most important. The rest would follow automatically.

That night I hated my parents.

11

DAY IN MOMBASA

W<small>E DOCKED IN THE MIDDLE</small> of the hot steamy morning, and there was Simon waiting for the gangway to go down. He was wearing a Palm Beach suit and waving a panama hat I had never seen before. Three very small boys scrambled on board at his heels.

"Meet the Johnsons," he said, when he had greeted Daddy and given me one of his bear-hugs. "Mathew, Mark and Luke."

Three soft green-lined hats were snatched off three flaxen heads, and small limp paws were pressed politely into ours, but the bright eyes of Simon's little friends were darting in all directions. I was speechless with excitement. It was whirling round inside me, sparking and bright as Catherine wheels.

"How and where did you acquire this ready-made family?" Daddy laughed.

"I've been staying in their home in Nairobi. Sandy Johnson's mixed up with A. & B. one way and another. He and his wife have been marvellous to me. I promised to bring these chaps to see the ship. They've been in a ferment since dawn!"

"We flew to Mombasa yesterday," volunteered Mathew, and instantly the other two chimed in, their voices drowning any further information we might have received from their elder brother.

"You'll get used to that," laughed Simon. "Mark and Luke always open fire when Mat utters, so Johnson junior conversation is pretty chaotic."

Mathew, aged eight, was bright as a button, Mark didn't allow a slight stutter to interfere with his determination to express himself, and Luke had learned that the only way to assert himself was to shout his brothers down.

"Where's Aunt Clare?" Simon asked.

"She's got herself a dose of flu, so I'm afraid we aren't starters, as far as the Nyali Beach Hotel is concerned," said Daddy.

I threw Simon an agonised glance, and he said quickly. "But Maxie? You'll spare us Maxie? We've made so many plans for the next twenty-four hours—"

"Are your friends staying at the hotel? Will you be in a party?"

"Very much so – and June Johnson'll be delighted to chaperone Maxie, if that's what you're thinking about." (*Chaperone* – that obsolete word again!) But Daddy's face cleared, and suddenly I realised that he'd hated the idea of spoiling my fun. He heaved a sigh of relief.

"Then Clare won't worry. That's fine. You look after Maxie's expenses, and I'll settle with you when you bring her back tomorrow."

So I loved my father again. Mummie, who wouldn't allow us any nearer than the cabin doorway, said, "Enjoy yourselves, my dears, and, Simon, be sure and have this girl back on board in time to sail at noon."

I'll remember Mombasa all my life – the looking forward and the looking back and every single second of that short precious time that changed so much for Simon and me. The happiness all mixed up with the beginning of guilt.

It was quite a way from the harbour to the hotel in the ramshackle taxi, and there was so much to say and to hear that we both kept talking at once. Simon had really missed Rima and me. I knew by his voice and his eyes. Laughter and pleasure were brimming over when he said, "Oh, Chick, it's good to see you! We keep interrupting each other, like our three Apostles here. Eh, Mat?"

"Everything's bliss! I didn't think Mummie'd let me stay at Nyali Beach without her and Daddy. Bless the Apostles and their parents."

We passed an enormous old baobab tree, and Mathew, Mark and Luke explained that it was haunted. "*Full* of ghosts! And down there's the boat-house. We can use Mr Bird's boat—"

"He's lent it to us while we're here. He's g-gone on s-safari—"

"So he doesn't need it himself."

The words all tumbled out together, but already I had learnt to find my way through the three-point barrage.

"There's the hotel – *there!*"

"We c-can see the beach from our room."

It was rather a rambling hotel but it looked wonderful to me. The Johnsons were waiting for us in the entrance lounge. I liked them at once.

After all, they'd tipped the scales in favour of my being there. They both had chubby, cheerful moon faces and light hair. They might have been brother and sister. June Johnson read my mind, and smiled.

"Don't tell me we look alike. We're cousins, and they say cousins shouldn't marry because of their offspring. But there's not much wrong with ours, touching wood."

"Go and wash your hands and brush your hair, boys," commanded their father. "See they do it properly, Mat."

They scampered off as Simon came over from the reception desk.

"Here's your key, Maxie. I'll show you your room, and then we'll join Sandy and June for a drink."

I took the heavy key from him. I can feel its weight now, its coldness in my palm, its teeth; and I can feel Sandy Johnson's eyes on my back as I went with Simon. Men did that nowadays. They looked at me, and looked again, and I liked it.

A Swahili porter carried my light suit-case, and we followed him up a flight of stairs and along a narrow corridor to the last door on the left but one.

"This is you," said Simon. "I'm next door – end of the road."

The Swahili porter put down my bag, was rewarded, and disappeared.

The room was cool and pleasant, with a private bath, and French doors leading onto a balcony that ran the length of the corridor. We looked down onto a shady garden meandering away to the sea-shore. The sea was quiet, glittering and aquamarine, with a white line of surf far out to mark a coral reef. A huge flame-tree, alive with honey-birds stood in a pool of blood-red petals and cast its elaborate shadow on Simon's end of the balcony. Brilliant butterflies hovered over the exquisite intricate scarlet flowers.

"Chick, look at me!"

I raised my face to Simon's. His hair was curly in the damp heat, his eyes narrow and gleaming, the same colour as the sea.

"I believe you're grown up at last. Quite grown up."

I gave him a long very special look. It's a look women learn quite suddenly. It shoots a line for a man to catch and draw tight if he wants to. Simon caught it and his breath, both at the same time. His nostrils flared and his eyes flashed, but he threw my line back at me.

"Hey, Maxie, who's been teaching you Lorelei tricks?"

I laughed as I leaned against the balustrade in the fragile shade of the flame-tree. All its host of little birds was singing inside me, it's scarlet blossoms were opening in my blood.

"Go, powder your pretty nose," Simon was brusque. "Hurry up! And, when you're ready, sing out for me. It's time we joined the Johnsons."

"Time we joined the Johnsons – sounds like a song-hit."

The world was full of song today. I went into my room. I wanted to dance.

"I don't mean to be unsociable," said June Johnson, when we'd ordered our short drinks in the bar. "But eating with the Apostles is an ordeal. A menu card excites them. You two must have a lot to talk about so you'd better have a table to yourselves for lunch. We can meet on the beach round four this afternoon."

We could hear the little boys sucking their raspberry-ades on the verandah outside. Mat was telling his brothers not to blow bubbles through the straws. "It's bad manners in a hotel." A gurgling chorus answered him as Mark and Luke went on blowing bubbles and argued at the same time.

"They're not very relaxing company," said Sandy. "But on the beach or in a boat the effect is diffused."

After lunch Simon and I wandered down to the beach in our bathing things, and lay in the shade of a grove of trees. How drowsy it was! The silky lap of the sea, the high whine of cicadas, the cheeping of birds. Our towels were folded under our heads. When I looked up through the leaves, the cloudless sky was blanched, not brilliant blue like ours at home.

"Everything's pale here," I said. "Except you. You're grilled to a turn. Crisp and brown."

"Trouble with the equatorial sun is it boils instead of frying. Makes people look like steamed fish. I got my brown in Rhodesia."

"You're the colour of the maroela wood you sent Rima. She was utterly thrilled with it."

"What did she make of it?"

"An African rain goddess – rather weird."

"She gets that African feel in everything. Simple, primitive, and sometimes a bit sinister."

"It's her inspiration. Tribal customs, rituals, dances, the lot."

"She studies them."

"It's more than that, Simon. Rima is *of* Africa – in rather a mystic way."

He opened his eyes wide. He was interested. He liked talking about Rima.

"D'you really think that, Maxie?"

"I'm sure of it. Leslie knows it. Leslie'll talk to me about lots of strange things that happen in his country. Magical things. He'll even mention the witch-doctor. But he'll tell Rima more, because he knows she understands. She could very easily *believe* in sorcery. That's why Corinne is so attached to her. Old Lizzie is a bit of a witch and Corinne's full of superstition."

"Corinne? You mean Lizzie's grandchild – the little Coloured girl from Bergplaas. How's she doing at Rosevale? I'll bet old Rocky tries a trick or two."

"Annie keeps her eye on him. She needs to. He's a proper old sultan. But Corinne doesn't worry. She looks after Rima's studio, and she's got Lenno tame in the garden."

"Rima made me a delightful sketch of Lenno in one of her letters. He really is a magnificent looking young warrior. She drew him leaning against his garden rake as if it were an assegai."

"He's a true warrior type, but he's more modern than Leslie at heart. A step further away from the old Africa."

"Never a very long step. They throw the bones in the city locations just as they do in their tribal kraals. Funny that Corinne and Lenno should get on all right. Usually the Coloureds and Bantu despise each other."

"Not the young ones any more. At least not nearly so much. I think the whole attitude's changing."

He rolled over and looked at me. I wanted to move into his arms, and I closed my eyes, so that he shouldn't see the way I felt. We were quite alone in our grove between the garden and the sea. Simon said:

"Everything's changing. I've seen it all over Africa – the new attitude. The realisation that there *is* the possibility of equality between different races. Not in a broad sense, mind you, because that simply isn't so – yet. But individually. It's a beginning."

"It's a beginning Uncle Gideon doesn't care about."

He was tracing patterns on the sand with his long narrow finger. He stopped doodling, and grinned. "You mean that row about Fara September. Rima wrote me that Dad was pretty curt with Claude for treating her as an equal."

"With all of us."

"Rima doesn't take very kindly to the hand of authority these days."

"None of us do."

"You're right. When I go home – and I fly south the day after to-morrow – I'm going to find a flat of my own."

I began to ask him about it, but the high eager voices of children cut through our solitude.

"Goodbye sweet peace," said Simon. "The Apostles are upon us."

They raced across the soft sand, pebbles rattling in their tin pails. They wore miniature red bathing trunks, and their soft sun-hats, and they carried little striped towels over their shoulders. They flung themselves down beside us, all talking at once.

"Can you swim?" I asked Mat.

"Yes, yes, yes," they cried. "Let's swim *now!*"

"They can't. Not a stroke," said Simon. "But who cares?"

He swung Luke up onto his shoulder and loped down towards the sea with the child clutching at his hair. I followed, Mat and Mark clinging to my hands. The water was tepid and rather sticky, very different from the fresh turbulent waves that washed our own far away peninsula. But the little boys revelled in it, and held onto us, shrieking with delight. I thought how wonderful it must be to be married and have children and all be young together. Afterwards we got cold drinks and lollipops from a kiosk near by, and Simon said, "I take it all back about you being grown up, Chick. You aren't. It was just a momentary hallucination."

Presently Sandy and June came down for a bathe, and Sandy said, "We've been lent a boat with an outboard motor. What about taking a turn round the island in the cool of the evening?"

"Heaven," I said.

An old grey man came down to the shore to dig for bait. He was dressed in a fetching Swahili pill-box cap and short tunic. His spindly legs and splay feet were bare. He had a knife and a stick. He'd stare at some place in the wet sand, waiting for a sign which only he could discover, then he'd plunge in the knife, burrow like a terrier, stab the stick into the hole and accurately impale a long pink worm as big as a small snake. I shuddered. "Ugh, what a horrid operation!" But the Apostles were enthralled. They stood, awed into rare silence, watching spellbound as he went about his curious business.

Their shadows sprawled on the beach grotesquely long and thin for three such little boys, and I knew that my lovely day with Simon was slipping away into evening almost before it had begun. The familiar "sunset sadness" crept over me, and then Simon picked up my towel and put it round my neck and said, "Time to get ready for the next thing. It'll be nice on the water."

I knew that he understood my mood and wanted to change it, and wondered if he guessed that the way I loved him was a new way, or that the touch of him and the look of him was as dangerous to me as a lighted match thrown into summer grass.

12

NIGHT IN MOMBASA

S ANDY JOHNSON TOOK us round the island in a boat borrowed
from friends away on *safari*.

Maybe the Apostles were sleepy after the activities of their busy
day: at all events, they were peaceful at last, sitting amidships with their
mother, their fair heads uncovered, their curls a nimbus in the golden glow
of the sunset. Mat leaned over the side to trail a small hand in the water,
Mark seemed welded to one side of June, and Luke was cuddled against her
on the other. She looked tranquil, as if she found it good to have all her
family contained in this small space, safely under her wing. Simon and I
were part of that all-embracing maternal tranquillity. It held us in a
charmed circle, and our composite heart was the throb of the outboard
motor.

The damp blanket of heat had been lifted by a cool breeze, filling the
sails of little yachts and dinghies, ruffling the dense foliage on shore,
feathering the smooth surface of the sea. A fleet of Muscat *dhows* lay at
anchor under the forbidding windowless walls of Fort Jesus, the grim
prison fortress with a long bloody history. Their woodwork was all picked
out in blue, so that it appeared more like a mosaic of tiles. Seamen with the
tough dark faces of pirates peered down at us as we cruised round their
wooden vessels. Little model aeroplanes flew at the high prows instead of
figureheads, and intrigued the little boys. They understood the aeroplanes
but the *dhows* belonged to the far past. June wrinkled up her nose as their
musky aromatic smell was carried to us on the breeze.

"All the perfumes of Arabia – good and bad!"

Music was echoing in my ears, the subtle strains that sing in certain
phrases . . . *gold and silver; and ivory; and apes and peacocks* . . . I asked Sandy
what cargoes were carried by the *dhows*.

"Persian carpets outward bound. And things like elephants' tusks,
rhino horn, Indian tiles, cloves and copra—"

"What's c-copra, Daddy?"

"Dried coconut, Mark. The basis of margarine and soap and things like that."

"What's marga—"

"A sort of butter, Luke." June smiled at me. "The world's very full of questions when one's four."

"I must have a look at those Persian rugs tomorrow." Sandy's gaze was on the *dhows*. "We're here on holiday, but I really include business. Not like Simon, who only pretends to."

"Were these slave-ships once?" I wanted to know.

"Maybe they still are," said Simon. "Just littie-bittie slave-ship one way and another."

When I protested he laughed and glanced at June.

"My cousin doesn't know the facts of African life. I've been in West Africa – the old Slave Coast – quite recently, Maxie. You hear the African bellow that he can rule his own country the democratic way in this democratic age, and, all in the same breath, he beats his political opponents and slings them into prisons like Fort Jesus here, to rot."

"If he sold his brother down the river it wouldn't be the first time," said Sandy. "The White slave-trader never did catch his own Black meat. He bought it from the chiefs, who sent it to the coast by boat and on the hoof. Sounds cynical, but that's life in Africa. Cynical. We're all guilty of her sins and crimes – the whole blinking lot of us, White and Black."

The *dhows* receded into the distance as we chugged out of the creek. Sea-birds swooped over the pearly water or rested on its surface. The haloes faded round the heads of the Apostles, who were just sleepy little boys once more. June looked down at them with the secret anxiety of mothers the world over, wondering what lies in store for their sons.

"What does the future hold for them?" she asked. "The future in Kenya?"

Sandy shrugged the question away. It was too big, too difficult to answer.

"What does the future hold for anyone, anywhere? The whole world's a flash-point, with over-population on one side and nuclear annihilation on the other. But so much fun and adventure in between! Life's worth while. Life's wonderful. Just live it! You modern women cling to a dull word that's all the fashion. Security. Your grandmothers asked for adventure."

She touched the silky hair of the youngest. "We want security for our children. Not just for ourselves."

"Pooh, children worth their salt soon learn that life's second name is danger. Find yours a safe funk-hole – if such a thing exists – and they'll burst out of it at the first opportunity! The men of my family have been trader-adventurers for generations. We break new ground, we chase up a new opportunity. And that's what we'll still find right here. In Africa."

"I'm with you," said Simon. "Dad's forbears – and Maxie's too – believed in trying their luck in a new land. And a damn good thing they made of it."

"And a damn good thing they'll go on making of it, so long as there's a good strong Navy to keep their trade routes open. The trader'll always be wanted all over the world. And Africa certainly won't throw him out. So relax, wife of my bosom."

June smiled. "Thanks for the words of cheer. As a matter of fact, I'd hate to leave Africa. I love it."

"So do I," said Simon. "I wouldn't want to be anywhere else in this day and age. What's happening here is dangerous, but it's a constructive sort of danger. Something here – all over this continent – is struggling to be born. And there's no birth without blood and risk."

Freedom, I thought. Freedom wants to be born. But it was a nebulous thought. It had no face. What is freedom? A pattern of light and shade, like one of Rima's abstracts. You'd ask her what it meant, and she'd say, "You tell me." If you pressed her and said, "It must mean something to *you*," she'd only smile and say, "That's not the point. It's what *you* see in it that matters." Freedom has a different meaning for each of us.

"Maxie's not with us any more," said Simon, with a glance at me. "She does that. Goes off on her own."

They smiled and went on talking, threading their way through threats of change and danger in the world about us. But nothing they said disturbed me, any more than it did the children. It skated over my mood of Sleeping Beauty happiness, still in its hour of enchantment.

When we got back to the hotel Simon called me out onto our balcony. "Maxie! There go the *dhows*!"

They flew before the prevailing wind like a flock of white graceful birds, their great *lateen* sails billowing as they set course for the open sea, for home and Muscat and the far ports of Arabia. Simon's arm was linked in mine.

"They've made that voyage for thousands of years – even before the days of Solomon and Sheba. Who watched them from this shore? You and I, perhaps, in some other incarnation. In the days of Scheherazade and The Thousand and One Nights."

The idea was part of the magic of being with him here in the scented purple dusk. The swallows in the eaves were twittering as they settled for the night. They too, like the *dhows*, had set out on their long seasonal migrations since time immemorial. They made a kissing noise that reminded me of Rima's budgies. The *dhows* were no longer vast white birds, they were butterflies upon the horizon, and then they were nothing. They had ceased to exist.

"Maybe we did," I said. "It's a nice thought. A phoenix thought."

"A phoenix thought? The fabulous bird that rises from the ashes of destruction. Tell me more."

I hesitated. The phoenix thought was something special between Rima and me. It was one of the fancies we'd always shared and loved as children, like our love for the warrior horse of the Book of Job. Whenever we'd heard a particularly bell-like bird-call we'd stopped dead in our tracks, believing it to be the phoenix. Perhaps it was our personal version of Leslie's sort of magic.

"But you know the legend," I said. "Everybody does."

"Never mind. You tell me – and its special thought."

"It's just one of the things that caught our imagination when we were small. Rima and I used to read anything we could get hold of about the phoenix. We read that it was a bird of Africa, sacred to the sun ..."

"Go on."

"Well, it was the most beautiful bird in the world, with gorgeous brilliant plumage and a strangely sweet voice. It lived for about a thousand years, or longer, and, when its time came to die, it built itself a nest with the twigs of spice-trees and set the nest on fire to burn itself alive. The new phoenix was born of the flames, and, as soon as it was strong enough, it flew away to Egypt with the ashes of the nest and offered them up on the altar of the Sun at Heliopolis."

"It's a lovely myth. The glorious rebirth. So that's your phoenix thought."

"And a bird – such a free creature! Rima and I used to make believe we could hear it in the woods. We'd act the legend. Sometimes she was the Priestess of the Sun, other times she was the bird. We took it in turns."

"Quaint little pair you were – with your overworked imaginations!"

"I didn't like being the phoenix. I always jibbed."

"No fancy for the flames? You've always been scared of fire."

"Not just that."

"What then?"

It was nearly dark now and the first stars were glimmering. His chin was resting on my hair. He bent his head and I wondered if he knew that I could feel his lips moving against my hair. I said:

"It was a very lonely bird. Lonely in life and lonely in death, the bird without a mate."

"Independent and indestructible. Have you ever seen a phoenix?"

"Rima and I saw one the year Daddy and Mummie took us to the Game Reserve. A real one."

"When Claude and I were left at Rosevale to work for our exams. I remember. Where did you see your real phoenix – and what was it?"

"It was just after sunrise, near the river. A beautiful fire-coloured bird with a crest and a long tail and a blue cap."

We'd both seen it at the same moment, Rima and I. We'd caught hold of each other and gasped. "It's *him* – the phoenix!" We'd had no doubt about it.

Simon laughed softly. "You still believe in it, don't you?"

"Nearly," I admitted.

It was quite dark now. Lights were springing up all over the hotel, shining across the balcony from bedrooms further along. Not the one next door to mine, which should have been occupied by my parents. My parents and the ship were of another planet tonight. There were voices, people coming upstairs to get dressed for dinner, or popping out onto the balcony to take in bathing things that had been drying on the rail. In the garden the night watchman had come on duty with his mangy old dog. The dog barked at a cat, and we could hear the watchman talking his own language to one of the room-boys squatting outside. Jabber, jabber.

I thought of my new evening dress hanging in the cupboard, and wondered if Simon would be proud of me when I wore it. It was the lightest frothiest cotton, printed with tropical flowers. Not much top, but a short full skirt like a Spanish dancer's. My blue sandals had heels as slender and elegant as the beak of our fabulous phoenix. My perfume was called Blue Hour – the hour of dusk and midnight. Suddenly I could bear to say good-bye to my lovely day because the dress and the sandals and the perfume were waiting for me. And there'd be music and dancing in the palm court open to the sky.

Simon said the dress was breath-taking, and when Sandy Johnson saw me, he went "Whee-ew!" and raised one expressive eyebrow.

"Take heed," he warned Simon. "Cousins are dangerous animals. I should know."

The evening went as fast as equatorial twilight. It came and it was gone. One moment we were dining, the next we were dancing, and, almost before Sandy could complete one of his wolf-whistles, the band had packed up and disappeared, the palm-court was empty, and June was yawning, "Bedtime for me. The boys wake with the birds."

"I've half a mind to take a dip in the sea," suggested Sandy. "All that healthy exercise has heated my blood."

But June tugged at his arm. "Oh, come on, darling! Settle for a shower. It's long after midnight, and you'll wake me if you come in at all hours."

Sandy laughed. "Marriage is a dog's life, Simon. Before you know what's hit you, you find you're one of the children."

So Simon and I went alone to the sea – a kind maternal sea quite unrelated to our own boisterous oceans.

"It's warm and breathing," I said, as we floated on the swell. "It breathes deeply and peacefully in its sleep."

Phosphorus was iridescent round us in the water.

"You're silver," he said. "A shining silver girl."

"Sea-magic . . . little sequin scales to turn us into a mermaid and a merman."

He swam to my side and caught me in his arms. For once he didn't duck me. No horseplay now. He held me against him. We were out of our depth, treading water with our strange flowing limbs, our gleaming bodies together, rocking with the sea, as if we danced, weightless, no floor, no music, only the rhythm of this great gentle element, only its beat and its soft breathing.

"You," he said. "You and your magic!"

Why must it ever end, this night of stars and warm sea? I would willingly have drowned there in Simon's arms. But the tide had pushed us towards the shore. He was standing now, steady, his feet on sand. We were cloaked in the shimmering light of our sea-magic.

"Get along with you! Go!" He launched me from him, as if I were one of the little boys, and I swam away, trailing my opalescent fire.

The tide was low and we had quite a way to walk across the pale open beach into the shadow of our grove. Here and there a lighted window still glowed in the hotel high on the green flowering rise. Up there someone else was sleepless. Maybe the night-watchman was making his rounds with his scruffy old dog at his bare heels, or more likely he dozed against the corner of the white wall.

We were wrapped in our towel gowns. It was hard to make an end of being together. I was wide awake, terribly awake in every pore of my skin, every particle of my body. But Simon had picked up our wet bathing things and wrung them out. He shook the sand from them, and then he held out his hand to me.

"The night's nearly done, Chick. It's beginning to fade."

Up in the hotel we saw the last lights go out. Now all was darkness and silence save for the sea. We wandered up the winding shingle path through the dreaming garden, his arm holding mine lightly, for I am not like Rima who can see in the dark. I'm lost in the dark, quite lost and frightened. A bat flew low and almost touched us. I stopped with a stifled cry, my hands to my hair, and buried my face in the hollow of Simon's shoulder. We stood in the deep shelter of a mango-tree, and, as he held me, I felt him trembling. But I knew that he was not afraid.

"Don't let me make love to you," he whispered. "Don't let me!"

But the wakening of my body had set a thousand pulses beating under the thin surface of my flesh. A thousand little throbbing hearts told me that I belonged to Simon. For me that garden in Mombasa was Eden before the serpent and the knowledge of good and evil, before sin and guilt and banishment. We were alone in the garden, the first man and woman. But it wasn't so for Simon. If he'd wanted me he could have had me. Instead he unlocked my hands from round his neck and put me from him. Gently. It was, for a moment, as if he'd severed me from part of myself. Yet I knew that this act of severance was not an act of cruelty but one of love.

"Come," he said.

And I walked with him, hand in hand, through the fading night.

He left me outside my room. The doors onto the connecting balcony were open and I saw the gold patch fall across the boards as Simon switched on his light. Then his silhouette darkened it as he stood in the doorway. I heard him go out onto the balcony to hang our damp bathing things on the rail.

D

I undressed and lay down under the mosquito-net draped over my bed. The gold oblong vanished from the floorboards outside. It was the hour before dawn when the tropic night is flimsy as gauze. I lay naked, without the sheet over me, yielding my burning skin to the light touch of a breeze cooled by the fragrant hours of darkness. I'd have to put on my shortie-pyjamas presently, or I might fall asleep and not wake before the boy brought my early tea. The breeze was a phantom hand, tender and cool, drawing the fever out of my body, which had become unfamiliar to me, aching, as it did, with frustrations more insistent than pain. Was Simon asleep? Did he care that he had wakened me in this new way that would surely never let me rest again?

I pushed the net aside and drew on my pyjamas. I stood in the open doorway and watched the gossamer dawn slashed by the silver swords of daybreak. The swallows were silent under the eaves; the colony of little birds in the flame-tree were quiet and invisible. Perhaps they were not there at all. Perhaps it was only their playground of the day. Even the cicadas had ceased their scraping. Only the sea purred softly.

I moved out onto the balcony and touched Simon's bathing-trunks, hanging on the rail. Already they were nearly dry. I wondered if he could be asleep. There was no sound from his room. I had to hold onto the rail to stop myself from going to him. Was this what they called temptation?

Then he was there, his arms encircling my body as he lifted me over the threshold into my own room and set me down on my bed with the dis-ordered folds of the white mosquito-net about me like a wedding veil gone awry. A striped towel was a loin-cloth round his waist; his chest was bare. In the cobweb half-light I saw the swift power of his neck and shoulders, the tapering shape of him, the long muscular legs. He looked down at me.

"Listen, Chick – dear Maxie. Sir Galahad's the man who never was – nor ever will be. You're going to be on your own an awful lot soon. For Christ's sake, watch out! The others won't kill themselves to take care of you. You're only eighteen. The answer isn't this sort of thing . . . not yet."

The others . . . this sort of thing . . . what did he think of me? I wanted to say. "It's only you I want – only you!" Instead my throat tightened and the sharp stinging tears welled up. They ached in my neck, streamed down my cheeks. The grey light was seeping into the room.

"Oh, God, I've made you cry."

His own eyes were desperate. He sat beside me and rocked me in his arms, and I wept against his broad bare chest.

"You tear me apart. What in hell d'you think I am? One of Rima's wooden figures?"

He was soaked with my tears. I tried to wipe them from his chest. "You'll catch cold, Simon."

"I'm drenched – a red-hot shower."

Although his lips smiled, his face was strained in the grey dawn. It was the way he had looked as a boy when he was upset. Uncle Gideon could make him look that way. Rima could too. I never had.

"It's all right, Simon. Forget it . . . and don't worry about me . . . There'll be no others . . . and, with you, it's as we were."

"Is it ever?"

"This time it is."

He had no sooner gone than I fell into a deep dreamless sleep. I didn't even wake when the boy brought my tea. Not till they started polishing the floors by skating up and down the corridors with pads strapped to their feet, and yammering. Heavens, how Africans can yammer! I opened my eyes reluctantly. The sun was high and the heat of the new day was gaining strength. I lay, bathed in lassitude, waiting for my spirit to return to my body from some far place. I don't wake quickly, like Rima – all in one piece. My soul goes wandering while I sleep and comes back at its own pace, cat-like, pausing to wash its face on the way, refusing to be hustled. By breakfast time it is with me.

Simon and I had breakfast together. I was ravenously hungry. We didn't speak of the night before. The morning was glorious, but too short. A few hours, a last swim. Oh, to hold back the clock!

I had packed my things. Simon looked in.

"I'll go and settle the bill, and organise our taxi."

"Daddy insists on squaring my share with you."

"We'll fix that on board."

"Shall I come now?"

"I'll send the porter along. You give him our stuff. I'll be waiting in the hall."

I stood alone on the balcony, staring at the flame-tree with its little flitting yellow birds, joined now by a swarm of black hornets sharing the honey from the blood-red blossoms.

The sea was molten metal and the palm trees swayed against a steely sky.

There, nodding over the winding garden path, was the big mango tree. In its dense night shadow Simon had held me and said, "Don't let me make love to you!" But he had wanted to.

Remember that he wanted to, I told myself. And know that one day he will want to again.

13

PILGRIMAGE

AFTER MOMBASA IT SEEMED to me that everything became sharper and more significant. The impressions in my scribble-book, jotted down in the shorthand Daddy described as "Maxie's Arabic script", were concerned more with thoughts and feelings – my own and other peoples' – than with scenes and activities.

Lush tropical Africa and the damp heat were left behind as we sailed along the barren Red Sea coast, its golden wastes creased through the centuries by dry winds blowing interminably from the far amethyst hills. The vampire sun sucked the moisture from our bodies as it sucked the water off the salt-pans, but the nights were brisk and cold.

We steamed through the narrow Suez Canal in slow convoy. There were modern towns on the Egyptian Bank, and the camel and the ass ploughed in double harness in the green strips between the sun-baked mud villages. On the other side the empty sands of the Sinaii Desert spread to infinity, broken only by the shimmer of mirage.

"The thirst," said Daddy, as he drained his tankard of beer. "That was the terrible thing in the desert. When we were in the bag – thousands of us – Rommel said, 'Your own people have beggared up the wells. My fighting men'll get their water ration, and you'll have what's left.' There wasn't much left."

The deserts drew my father with an awful fascination. They seemed to call him back into the past, back into his war. "Our torture was mirage," he said. "The false promise of water. You have to be burned and parched before you can really appreciate the shade of an oasis and the tinkle of a fountain." He threw me one of his laughing sidelong glances. "One goes through life discovering the obvious as if it were a great revelation. Eh, Maxie?"

I understood his preoccupation with the past. I too had a separate inner existence. At night in my cabin, when the strange life-rhythm of the ship encircled me with its mysterious heterodyne note, I relived Mombasa. It was not just an East Coast Port to me. It was Simon and a garden by the sea.

One of these times – it was in the Mediterranean – the obvious became clear to me with all the wonder of a revelation. Moonlight came and went with the sway of the ship. It poured through the porthole in a milky stream. I lay and watched it come and go, luxuriating in my brief day and night of memory, disturbed only by one troubling question. I'd thrown myself at Simon's head and he'd turned me down. Was that really love, as I'd thought – a sacrifice to him? I ached for it to be sacrifice, but I was no longer sure. Suddenly the shaft of bland benevolent moonlight flowed right over me, drowning me in its radiance, and, all in the same moment, I knew that what Simon felt for me was only great affection and the natural hunger of any young man for any attractive girl. And, of course, he'd judged my feelings by his own. To him I was still Maxie, but an adult Maxie susceptible to romantic circumstances and a man's magnetism. Any man's. That was all.

This revelation freed me from the humiliation of loving with greater intensity than I was loved. *Simon didn't know.* I was bathed in a sensation of cool fresh freedom. I no longer felt bad because I'd tried to take him from Rima. My body and spirit were gloriously light, no longer divided by the splinter of guilt. That night they stayed together, dreamless and at peace. When I woke next morning, it was still that way.

We disembarked our station-wagon and ourselves at Brindisi on the toe of Italy, and drove up into the snow-capped mountains of the Abruzzi. This was the true beginning of my father's pilgrimage. Here he had lived as a fugitive, dependent upon the peasants for his life. It was hard for Mummie and me to visualise his hunted existence.

"War is a man-thing," she said. "Like having babies is a woman-thing. Marriage may make you one flesh from time to time – as the prayer-book says – but you stay two people. Especially in a war."

The air was strong and pure and touched with spring as we drove through the passes. My father's prison camp had been in the north, but our destination was the village where he had been given refuge throughout the dangerous winter while making his way south towards the front line of the Allied advance. He had lived with the wood-cutters and the shepherds, he had shared rough shelters with the autumn lambs; he had been housed in barns and cellars, and clothed, fed, guided and protected by the mountain people. Most of the winter his hiding place had been a stable with a pair of snow-white oxen, gentle, strong, and beautiful as sacred cattle. They'd belonged to old Mario, his host.

At last, late in the afternoon, Daddy said, "There! Across that valley you can see my village."

It clung to the slope of the mountain, small and straggling, a few humble houses little more than hovels, a tiny church, a scattering of primitive farms. We could not speak. We rounded a bend in the winding ascent. Daddy turned the station-wagon into a farm track and drew up in a cobbled courtyard near some outhouses and a white-washed dwelling. Children played under a fig tree, there were goats and fowls and a fat pig. An old man with a face like wrinkled leather rose from a stool outside the door and shaded his eyes with his hand. The children stopped playing to stare. Mummie and I didn't move. Daddy got out. He was hatless, and the wind with its breath of snow lifted his shock of thick grey hair. Oh, God, let them recognise him! I thought. They don't know he's coming.

He moved away from the car, a gaunt figure in the golden evening light, a silhouette to the old man and the children who watched silently.

"Mario!" cried my father. "Mario!"

The old man uttered a great shout of welcome and held out his arms. "*Sei ritornato!*" My son, you have returned! They went towards each other like that, arms outstretched, and both were weeping as they embraced.

The excitement of the villagers; their chatter in a harsh dialect my father spoke, rustily at first, then freely; their exclamations of joy over the useful presents Daddy had chosen with such care and thought; the church bells pealing, and the sense of being part of a large family and a small miracle, are things I shall never forget as long as I live. Someone killed chickens for a feast, someone else produced flagons of country wine; even mattresses were found to put on the floor of the warm living-kitchen so that we might sleep there, wrapped in the new blankets we had brought as gifts.

That night, with the family of Mario moving softly in the loft overhead, I understood why Daddy had felt that he must return. It was an act of faith.

We left soon after dawn, and, as we waved goodbye, we all knew that this time it was really farewell, but there was no bitterness in the thought.

We stopped for a picnic lunch in a narrow valley. My father stood a little apart from us, listening. We heard the sound of a shepherd's pipe, very sweet and clear in that rarefied air, and the tinkle of the sheep-bells.

"That was the music of freedom," said Daddy. "You can never believe how intoxicating it was after the years behind the wire. Freedom! It tasted like this mountain air – sharp and pure, and it was full of danger. It came in bursts of sheer exhilaration, and then one was a fugitive again, a hunted creature."

He came and sat down near us, and took the coarse black bread and cheese my mother offered him. He looked shy, as if he had spoken out of turn.

Mummie said, more gently than was her way: "Claude would tell us that freedom is relative, a matter of degree, an interval, perhaps, between one slavery and another."

I too tried to give him time to recover himself. "I wonder how the slaves felt, Daddy, the day they were freed – when your great-grandfather told them to leave Loire because now they were free people."

Daddy filled a mug with red wine and tossed it back. "My great-grandfather, like many others, freed his slaves long before the day of emancipation. For generations on Lamotte land every child born to slaves was freed. You need to be conditioned to freedom, Maxie."

"But there must have been other farms where that didn't happen."

"There were. And their freed slaves did what anybody else would have done. They went out into the fields and got drunk on wine and the thought of liberty. But, when the wine and the wonder wore off, many were afraid, and they went back to their masters as paid servants. Others wandered round in thieving vagrant bands. Farmers were ruined, and the Great Trek began, with the Boers moving north to seek a new country – at just about the same time as the powerful Bantu warriors were moving south, destroying lesser tribes as they came. So, up in the mountains of Natal and the Transvaal, you got the first great clash of Boer and Bantu – a clash that'll come again."

"Only next time we'll all be in it," said Mummie. "Up to the ears. The whole shooting match, everywhere in South Africa."

"And why, Clare?" My father's eyes flashed. "Because men will die for the mirage of freedom!"

Mummie began to pack up the picnic basket. The sound of the sheep-bells was nearer now. The shepherd with his flock came in sight. He was a shaggy fellow, grim-faced, but he smiled when Daddy addressed him in his own dialect, and he accepted food from us with a dignity that blessed our offering.

As we went on our way, Daddy said, "Men like that shepherd back there risked their lives for *our* freedom, even though the enemy was offering a reward for every prisoner recaptured."

So we left the mountains and returned to the ports and cities where nobility was measured by titles and coronets, and riches by money and possessions.

We spent a few days at Naples. Vesuvius flaunted her pennant of smoke like a battle ensign, and we visited the ruins of Pompeii, a city gassed and buried in the midst of life. Later, along the road to Rome, my father could hardly believe in the astonishing revival of this lovely country that had been one of the bloodiest battlefields of the war.

"It's more than reconstruction. It's a rebirth. A phoenix risen from the ashes."

His words evoked Simon and the "phoenix thought". I saw again the Muscat *dhows* flying before the wind, and heard the swallows twittering in the eaves at Mombasa. I had given Simon our itinerary. Would there be a letter from him in Rome? But there was nothing.

Next morning we stood on the dome of St. Peter's and looked down upon Rome, with the Vatican City at her heart, secluded and sublime. The Seven Hills were soft undulations, the Tiber a shining ribbon through the Campagna, the Colosseum ruins a reminder of the cruelty and magnificence of man. Art and history basked in the sun, layer upon layer of civilisation. The callow youth of my own land was a distant reproach. Daddy snorted when I said so.

"Our country is young and vigorous, and that's no crime. Its history is being made and its culture is growing. We're part of it. Let's do the best we can."

No letter when we got back to the hotel. Nor when we arrived in Florence.

Our rooms were on the riverside. From my window I could see the jade green Arno spanned by its graceful bridges – phoenix bridges, reborn in exact imitation of their past beauty, but I looked at them listlessly. We spent the next day on a dutiful sight-seeing tour and Daddy pointed out that Italian art and architecture had been greatly blessed by powerful patronage and the inspiration of a living religion. The palaces and churches of Italy were her art galleries.

D*

Tourists gaping round the Duomo offended my sense of reverence, but I liked the quiet alcoves and altars dedicated to special Saints. And I looked with longing at the carved confessionals where your sins could be confided to an unseen confessor and washed away with absolution and a penance.

"You and Daddy leave me here," I whispered to Mummie. "I'll walk back to the hotel. I'd like to."

So they left me alone in the black and white cathedral with its shrines and treasures. I knelt in a quiet pew, where the light was filtered by a stained glass window of unimaginable beauty. Presently I found myself silently telling my problem to a plaster figure in a blue robe spangled with golden stars.

"I love the man destined for my cousin, who is also my greatest friend. She too has always loved him. When she was only a child she told me so. It is still so. Yet I want to steal him from her. I am possessed of love. Help me!"

I waited for the answer. I could hear a priest intoning, and the fluted voices of boys singing a psalm in Latin. My answer came soundlessly, like the shaft of moonlight that had danced across the sea, through my porthole and into my cabin and my heart.

"You have belonged to this family as if it were your own. Would you find happiness in stealing her lover from your greatest friend?"

I knelt for what seemed to me a long time, hoping for resignation. But, when I rose and went out into the sunshine, I was not at peace. A little boy selling flowers on the steps of the Duomo held out a bunch of daffodils, narcissi and violets more fragrant than any we have at home. He thrust them into my hands, crying "Beautiful flowers! *Bellissimo*. Like the *signorina!*" I laughed and buried my face in their cool sweetness. No! I thought rebelliously. I'm young and in love and I won't give in. I'll make Simon love me!

When I looked up he was there, with the sun in his laughing eyes. The flowers fell from my fingers, and the boy bent to gather them from the pavement.

"It can't be you! How can it be?"

"Your parents said I'd probably find you here. *Ragazzo*, I'll buy that bouquet for the *signorina*."

He paid the boy, and, as I took the flowers, he said, "Come, and I'll tell you all about it."

We walked down the narrow street. Above us, on a tiny Romeo and
Juliet balcony jutting over a carved portico, a young woman was singing
for the sheer joy of spring. Her voice was rich and sweet, and the word
"amore" floated down to us through air as scintillating as the stars on the
Madonna's robe.

14

ITALIAN PLAN

S IMON EXPLAINED EVERYTHING to us at dinner that evening. From Mombasa he had flown home and Uncle Gideon had almost immediately decided to send him to Europe with the buyers to learn that side of the business and establish the necessary contacts.

"I found that our schedule overlapped with yours," he said. "Here, and in Milan, so I thought it would be a good plan for Maxie to horn in and learn some of the ropes. Quite unofficially, of course."

Mummie thought it an excellent idea. "If she's really going to work in A. & B. eventually, she should certainly know what goes on at the buying end. How long are you here for, Simon? And where are your colleagues?"

Simon had booked in at our hotel, but Miss Pratt and Mr Williams, the buyers, were at a hotel in the centre of the city. They were all to be two days in Florence and a week in and around Milan.

"After that we split up," said Simon. "I'm to open up certain new markets in Scandinavia, Miss Pratt goes to London and New York, and Bill Williams to Vienna, Switzerland and London, and we all meet up in Paris homeward bound."

Glorious vistas unreeled in my imagination. I longed to be a buyer, and was more than ever determined to concentrate on languages and on learning as much as possible from A. & B. buyers and agents in the meantime. Miss Pratt, who was soigné and middle-aged with blue hair and eyes, was keenly aware of my Beeford blood and Antrobus backing and at once decided to be helpful. I couldn't have had a better guide and adviser.

"Your Uncle Gideon Antrobus sets great store by enterprise," she said. "He always welcomes new ideas, even if he throws them out, and you have plenty. You have good taste too, and an excellent sense of colour combinations. You'll make the grade one of these days."

So I went around the wholesalers and shops with Miss Pratt and helped choose sportswear and lovely Florentine leatherwork for our gift department. But, when the day ended, we parted and Simon took over the lighter side of my education. The evening before we were to go to Milan, he said, "I'm going to dodge my colleagues and drive up with you and your parents tomorrow."

"I hoped you would."

We had fallen back into the old comradeship of holidays at Loire. On the surface it was as if Mombasa had never been. I wondered if he had organised this trip so as to see me and be with me again, and came to the conclusion that it was pure coincidence.

We were walking along the Lungarno in the evening sunshine. It was chilly and I drew my warm travelling coat more closely round me.

"It was just about here that Dante is supposed to have seen Beatrice and her girl friends for the first time. Remember that picture by Rossetti?"

I nodded. "So strange that he never really knew Beatrice. Yet she was his grand passion and his inspiration."

Simon smiled. "Unrequited love. Maybe it's the best sort for a poet, but we ordinary chaps like something more substantial."

We sat on a wooden bench and watched some children playing on a sandy spit at the water's edge in the shadow of the rebuilt Ponte Trinità. The river, full and swift with the melting snows, raced between tall historic houses and mediaeval palaces. The soft green hills and distant mountains were gilded by the slanting rays of the sun. Mimosa and lilac nodded over the high walls of hidden gardens.

As if he continued his thought, Simon said, "Rima'll adore this city. For her it'll have everything."

"When will she come here?"

"Year after next when she's completed her course and got her degree."

"That's centuries away."

His hands were lying easily in his lap, half linked. Good hands on the reins, feeling a horse's mouth, giving whenever possible, gentling, yet never losing control.

"What's your plan, Maxie – after Milan?"

"It's not changed. I'm going with Daddy and Mummie to England via the Riviera and the Château Country."

"And the big idea about taking a job in Italy and carrying on with your French and German. How about that?"

"I'll come back."

"I wonder if you will."

He didn't take me seriously. Maybe he was right. I hadn't made the least attempt to inquire about a job. I was just drifting lazily and contentedly from day to day. I looked at him and smiled.

"You came out of the blue. In the same way something else'll turn up. I've a hunch about it. I'm not fighting fate. I'm floating with it – like that stick the boys have thrown into the river. There are times to plan and fuss, and times to let nature take its course."

"A nice philosophy for those who can afford it. You've no responsibilities."

"Nor have you. Not really. Not yet."

The long hands moved outwards, and he rose and drew me to my feet. It was odd how he could look down at me and still keep his head so high. I wanted, quite dreadfully, to touch his face, to trace the curve of his mouth with my finger – that indentation in the shape of a heart between his nose and the bow of his upper lip. His shoulders were back. He never had to brace them. He carried them naturally with pride. The cold breeze blew his hair forward so that a brown lock fell across the breadth of his forehead. His ears were rather pointed, sign of a satyr, or a very young dashing centaur perhaps. I was aware of all these things, and afraid to look at him. We began to walk back to the hotel in a roundabout way, through shadowy colonnades and narrow streets curving like scimitars, lost to the sun already.

"I may not have many responsibilities, but Dad takes a dim view of drifters. You're not in his orbit for the present; I am. Tomorrow Milan, and that's one of our most important centres. No drifting for this lad once we're there!"

Milan had none of the leisurely slightly decadent atmosphere of Florence. The thrusting Milanese lived at an entirely different pace from the cultivated Florentines. This city, the heart of the industrial north, existed intensely in the present.

"Not far from here Mussolini and his mistress were shot by the Partisans," said Daddy, "and hung by their heels outside a filling station."

"A shameful end for a great man," said my mother. "Because nobody can deny that he did a lot of good for his country in the early days of Fascism."

"Milan is a cruel city," said Simon. "Cruel and vital, according to our friend Roberto Angeli. He says that everything worth while is initiated here. Movements are born and are killed in Milan."

During our week in the city we became very friendly with Roberto Angeli and his German wife, Bertha. Roberto was the representative of a powerful industrial concern with connections all over the world, including South Africa, and he had, on occasions, spent a couple of days at Rosevale during his flying visits to the Cape. One night we went with them to the famous Scala Opera House to hear La Tosca. We met beforehand at their penthouse apartment for a snack. Roberto led me out onto the roof-garden.

"There's something you must see, Maxie. Our evening miracle."

From where we stood we looked across at the magnificent cathedral with its frescoes of saints and the golden Madonna on the spire. As the last rays of the setting sun touched her she seemed to step right forward in a blaze of glittering glory before yielding to the shadows of the night.

"It's a heavenly illusion," I said. "I wonder if it happened by accident."

His bony well-bred features had the sardonic princely look of a Renaissance portrait. He shrugged his shoulders. "What does it matter? It is enough that it happens. Our little daughter Lucia loves to watch it. You'll meet her when you spend the day with us at our villa on Lake Como next Sunday. She's only four and she spends most of her time at the villa with her grandmother."

My parents had decided to spend that Sunday pottering round Milan, so Simon and I took the station-wagon and drove out to Lake Como. The Angelis' villa was perched on a terraced wooded cliff, and we had to leave the car and follow a winding footpath between the trees and flowering shrubs. Across the water rose the snow-crested Alps, and I said to Simon, "Wait a moment! I have to smell and feel this beautiful place." We paused in the warmth of noonday, and, for the first time in my life, I was aware of the peculiar quality of a mountain lake – the fresh fragrance of water rising up to cool the sun-drenched air. It was both scent and sensation.

We heard voices as Roberto and Bertha came to greet us. Lucia, the little girl, was clinging to her father's hand, skipping and dancing. I saw a pert tip-tilted nose, wide-set blue eyes, a pony-tail of flaxen curls, and sturdy limbs full of grace. Instinctively I went down on one knee and held out my arms.

"Lucia!"

Roberto let go of her hand and she ran to me. The child and I looked at each other. We laughed with delight. We were friends.

"Love at first sight," said Simon.

The villa was large, airy and modern, but it contained some pieces of old Italian furniture and marble-topped tables with graceful carved gilt legs and ornamentation that even I recognised as being genuine and valuable. They belonged to Roberto's mother, *Signora* Angeli, who spent the greater part of the year with her son and his wife in their lakeside villa, though from time to time she went to stay with her daughter in Venice. The old lady had her son's high bridged nose and air of breeding, and, like many northern Italians, she was fair-skinned with grey eyes. I had the impression that she was the true mistress of the house, but perhaps that was only because of her natural authority and poise.

"Mama seldom comes to Milano," explained Bertha, as she introduced us. "She prefers the quiet of the countryside."

Out of deference to the *signora*, who spoke no English, I did my best in Italian which Bertha spoke correctly but with a marked German accent. Roberto talked to Simon in English, and little Lucia was equally at home in the language of either of her parents.

"But she must learn English," said *Signora* Angeli. "You can see how handicapped I am by my ignorance of it, and even Bertha cannot sustain an intelligent conversation in English."

She was speaking to us but at the child who stood by her knee and who quickly grasped her grandmother's strategy. Lucia was obviously the pivot of the household and precocious in the way of only children. She glanced up at me with mischievous eyes.

"I will learn English from Maxie."

Bertha smiled. "You've made a conquest, Maxie."

We spent most of the afternoon on the lake in Roberto's speedboat, and had tea in a *ristorante* on the waterfront under a pergola of roses and honeysuckle. It was there that Roberto broached his plan. He suggested that I should spend a year with them. I could teach Lucia English and help Bertha with hers, which was very elementary. It would be nice for Bertha to have a young companion in the house when he was away on business. When he was home he always had a great deal of English correspondence to deal with and he would need my help as a part-time secretary. On my side, I would be able to improve my Italian by regular conversation periods with his mother, and all the normal opportunities of life in an

Italian home. Bertha would be only too glad to give me German conversation. Would I consider the idea? If so, we could discuss further plans later.

He had spoken in English, so Lucia had not understood what was said, but, like an animal, she sensed what was in the air and snuggled closer to my side.

I wanted to say "Yes" at once, but I hesitated.

"When do you want me to start?"

His aquiline face assumed the sharp executive expression I had come to expect whenever he discussed business matters with Simon or the buyers. He was always absolutely clear cut and precise on such occasions. No loose ends.

"As soon as possible. Right away, in fact. There would be a salary, naturally."

I would willingly have taken the job on an exchange basis alone. Feeling slightly dazed, I said as much. He laughed.

"No, Maxie. I'm a business man, and, when one is seeking for a unique commodity, one mustn't underrate its value. If you come to us, we'll be very lucky."

"But you hardly know me—"

"I met you at Rosevale, when you were a young girl. One remembers certain people. I know your background, and now you know ours. There will be some travel too. Venice in the fall where we stay with my sister in a beautiful little palazzo; and the Dolomites for a month's skiing in the winter."

Bertha put out her hand and touched mine gently. "And perhaps a visit to the Rhineland – to my old home – when Roberto is away on one of his trips. But what matters most is that you are *simpatico*. We like you very much, Maxie, and Lucia has lost her heart to you."

"I'm overwhelmed, Bertha. I don't know what to say. But I have to talk to my parents. I can only tell you now that I want very much to accept your offer – this very instant!"

"We'll leave it till you've had a chance to discuss it with your father and mother," said Roberto. "Not another word on the subject till then."

Moonlight was blue on the Alpine snows as Simon drove me back to Milan. I was tremendously stimulated by the prospects opened up by the Angelis' plan.

"It means missing out France and England," I said. "I'd have to take it on at once. Roberto made that perfectly clear."

Simon agreed. "But what does that matter? England won't run away, whereas the job might, unique as you are, my Chick."

"I did promise to go to Eights Week at Oxford with Jamie Vermeulen. It's years since I've seen Jamie—"

"To hell with Jamie! Be an opportunist. Get out of your rut. Forget your valley. You've never been afraid to take your own line."

"You were the one who really hatched this plot, weren't you? Come clean. You wanted to keep me safe in a respectable family, complete with Grandma."

He laughed. "Smart girl, aren't you?"

"Yes."

I laid my head back and closed my eyes.

"Poor Chick. You're tired. It's been a long day, and it's brought its own problems. Go to sleep. I'll wake you when we're home."

I nodded.

When my father and mother left Milan they went without me. Both were delighted at the turn of events. They were relieved to know that I would be safe and happy with the Angeli family.

On the following day Simon took off on his Scandinavian tour. Roberto, Bertha and I saw him off at Milan airport.

The plane was a speck in the sky, smaller than the birds round the head of the golden Madonna. Suddenly I felt very much alone.

Bertha slipped her arm through mine as we walked to their car.

"I understand," she said in German. "You see, Maxie, I too am a foreigner here."

15

RHINELAND INTERLUDE

HOW EASY IT IS to lose one's heart to a child!
Lucia was a darling – quite frantically naughty some times and we had a few imperial tussles – but spontaneous and responsive in everything, like her mother. When she was pleased she'd launch herself into my arms, a human rocket, her own clasped round my neck in an affectionate stranglehold.

"Hey, you'll throttle me!"

"T'ottle, t'ottle!" She shrieked with laughter. She tried new words out, learned them quickly and often found them hilarious. For instance, Bertha was a forceful tennis player, and, after one of our games, I said, "Compared with you I play bumble-puppy."

The expression caught Lucia's fancy. She rolled on the grass in helpless mirth, repeating, "Bumble-puppy, bumble-puppy . . ."

When she was given a cuddly toy dog for her fifth birthday she instantly named him Bumble-puppy. He was her favourite animal and was seldom far from her.

I shared her room, and, when she lay asleep, fair curls tossed on the pillow beside Bumble-puppy's brown head, something inside me turned over. Love, perhaps, simple and uncomplicated, bland as milk. Her little silver rosary lay on her bedside table, the Madonna and Holy Child were framed over her head, and St Francis and his wild creatures looked at her tenderly from the opposite wall. There was a little faun at the Saint's side, with a daisy chain round its dappled neck.

Bertha was always equable with the child, but Roberto could be capricious. She sensed his moods, as her mother did, and skirted warily round the bad ones. Her intuition was as quick as her intelligence. She was, in everything, intensely feminine. She was devoted to her grandmother, though *Signora* Angeli never spoilt her. The *signora* had her son's haughty air and caustic wit, but softened by graciousness, and from her the little girl learned manners as exact and precise as arabesques or religious responses. I shall see Lucia always, curtseying to one of her grandmother's friends as if the elder lady were a queen; shaking hands gravely with a small visitor of her own age; being lifted by her father so that she might cross herself devoutly with holy water at the entrance of the little country church; genuflecting in a deep obeisance outside the Angeli pew, or stealing inquisitive glances at the swaggering apple-cheeked altar-boys, swinging their incense-burners. These were her attitudes. Her laughter and tears and tantrums, her deep innocent sleep and her arms round my neck were the essence of herself, and now they are part of me too, like so much else that is good, bad, happy and sad.

I used to look forward to my Italian conversation periods with *Signora* Angeli. We discussed so much, from spaghetti and the human soul to South Africa and sorcery.

"You love your homeland very much," she remarked once. "When you speak of it – and, in particular of Loire or Rosevale – you forget to hunt for words. They fly to you on the wings of your enthusiasm."

Her perception sent a stab of homesickness through me. She patted my hand.

"There, Maxine. It comes and goes. Bertha, poor girl, is always wrestling with nostalgia. She and my son married for love. I doubt if that is really the best way."

"Surely it is the *only* way!"

She raised amused eyebrows. "An alliance of suitability, based on practical considerations and interests and on the same faith and background, has just as good a chance of survival, if not better."

"I can't believe that."

"But it is so. Bertha's countrymen, only a few years ago, were first the allies and then the enemies of Italy. My son was a Partisan. At fifteen years old he was an experienced saboteur who had killed Germans. That is hardly an ideal introduction for marriage with a German girl – even if she is a Catholic."

I said passionately: "But it's wonderful, *signora!* It's love rising above all outside difficulties and enmities – like Romeo and Juliet."

She laughed outright. "Poor Romeo and Juliet! How would their love have stood up to the daily wear and tear of matrimony and the hostility of their in-laws."

"But theirs was a great love."

"It was never truly tested. They were very young and they wanted the one thing they couldn't have. That's the way of youth – and of love. Forbidden fruit . . ."

As I was silent she threw me one of the shrewd piercing glances that reminded me of Roberto when he was conducting a difficult business deal or dictating an important letter. At those times he always made me think of Uncle Gideon. They both saw far beneath the surface of their transactions. In her own way *Signora* Angeli too had a stiletto mind.

"You've already discovered that, Maxine?"

I felt the colour flood my cheeks as I murmured something about inexperience of the world – of love. Her eyes sparkled with life and gaiety.

"Now listen to me. Human existence is as full of love as a garden is full of flowers. Each season brings its own blooms, and, when one withers, it would be stupid to think there will be no more."

But I didn't think of love in flowery metaphors. Love was Simon – his voice, his face, the way his eyes narrowed and shone when he laughed, the surprising softness of his lips, the feel of his skin, close-knit and cold in the sea and tasting of brine, his body against mine. These thoughts made me dizzy, and I was sure that *Signora* Angeli was much too old to guess at them, which was just as well. To her, no doubt, all the fire and anguish of love had long since been sublimated.

That summer Roberto flew to America on a month's business, and I went with Bertha and Lucia to the Rhineland. It was there, in the home of Bertha's childhood, that I met Jamie again. It was there that the disrupted pattern of my own young life began to re-form. It seemed as if destiny looked round and said, "Hey, these threads have been scattered! I must pick them up and weave them together once more."

Bertha's father was a retired country doctor. He and *Frau* Hahn lived in a small house above a loop of the Rhine. The green hill opposite was crowned by a mediaeval *Schloss* with a crenellated watch-tower. Here, in the olden days, the robber barons had controlled this strategic point of road and river. Behind the house was a little orchard where the doctor kept his beloved bees. Lucia was terrified of the hives and gave them a wide berth, but Bertha used to help her father take out the combs. She'd puff the smoke-gun to soothe the agitated bees while the old gentleman, in netted hat and gauntlets, collected the apple-blossom honey that had in its flavour an intoxicating touch of the flower of the vine. All round us glowed vineyards that had ripened in the sun for over a thousand summers.

Herr Doktor and *Frau* Hahn lived very simply. Anna, their cook-general, attended to their few wants, and, during our visit, Anna's married daughter came in daily to help, bringing her six year old daughter, Gretchen, so that Lucia should have a playmate. The two little girls were as happy as larks together. Both were intensely maternal, and we'd see the flaxen heads bent over dolls' cradles or prams.

"Our dolls are alive," explained Lucia. "We make them come alive."

"*Ach, so?*" chuckled her grandfather. "The world is full of make believe. We physicians must never forget the human will to believe what it pleases."

He was over seventy, but his face was smooth and cherubic, for he loved nothing more than a laugh and a joke. He had a way of laughing right down inside himself so that his shoulders shook and his blue eyes disappeared, and then *Frau* Hahn smiled too, although she was hard of hearing and often missed the cause of his merriment. Nothing gave her greater pleasure than to see us over-eat ourselves.

"Eat up, my child!" she'd say to me. "Eat up, and come again!"

The appetising smells from the big airy kitchen always made us hungry before we reached the table, so her orders were not hard to obey. Except for the smoked raw ham or fish. I never liked those. But *Frau* Hahn's *Apfel Strudel* and *Sandtorte* were out of a dream.

Bertha had two sisters behind the iron curtain in Eastern Germany and a brother in South West Africa, but, remote as they were, I came to know them and their families quite well, for the house was full of photographs and snapshots, especially of the grandchildren, and *Frau* Hahn loved to talk about them. Everything in that house was homely, from the cuckoo-clock in the dining room to the pipe-rack on the wall by the doctor's big leather arm-chair with its fancy studs. Such a collection of pipes I have never seen before or since, but our host's favourite was his *meerschaum* with its curved stem and deep bowl, elaborately carved and embellished with the figure of a young mermaid. His fine gnarled fingers held her gently cupped in his hand as he puffed contentedly at this cherished pipe.

I'd given Jamie Vermeulen our Rhineland address because I knew that he hoped to visit his mother's German relations in the summer vacation and there seemed a slight possibility of seeing him. Yet, in the end, he took me by surprise.

We had had our supper – high tea really – and Lucia was tucked up in bed. Her grandmother had kissed her goodnight and said, as usual, "*Hast schön gebetet?*" and the child had answered, yes, she had prayed for everybody including the dolls and Bumble-puppy. The cuckoo had pounced out of his little door to announce that it was eight o'clock, and Bertha and her parents had gone to sit in the rose-covered arbour at the corner of the low stone wall above the river. Every evening we sat there and watched the river traffic – paddle-steamers crammed with tourists, boats of every sort, strings of barges in tow of a jaunty tug, or great flat rafts floating timber down from the Black Forest. I was never tired of watching this scene in the peace of the lingering summer twilight so different from the swift nightfall of my own homeland. But, on this particular evening, I had wanted to write to my parents. They would be on their way home now, westabout this time with only one stop at Las Palmas, and I meant to have a letter waiting to greet them at Loire and assure them that I was well and enjoying the job I had taken so impulsively.

I came out of the front door, my letter in my hand, intending to stroll along to the village post office with it, so as to catch the early morning mail. Then I saw him striding across the grass, the last of the amber light on his wheat-fair hair. He was in shorts and a blue sweater and he looked like an overgrown boy.

"Maxie – you!" He repeated the word in German with its added intimacy. "*Du!*"

So long since I had seen him. I lifted my face and looked at him as he took my hands, and saw him staring down at me with wonder in his eyes.

"Jamie . . . Why didn't you warn me?"

Bertha was running towards us across the garden. She was laughing as she came up with us.

"Papa says I must bring out a tray with beer and biscuits. Come and help me, you two!"

"You've introduced yourselves—"

"Of course! You've spoken of him, don't forget. We know Jamie Vermeulen and Bergplaas, and *Mutti* and *Oom* Gert, and the moment I saw him standing at the gate – a bit lost and uncertain – I said, 'That's Maxie's Afrikaner friend! It can be no one else.' And, just imagine, he's brought a tin of South African tobacco for Papa. Such thoughtfulness!"

Suddenly I was tremendously excited. Happiness was lighting candles inside me. I could feel myself glowing. Bertha was still chattering away in

German and Jamie was answering in the same tongue. He belonged here. He was one of us. They had accepted him for himself. His being here completed everything.

While we helped Bertha prepare the tray he explained that he was staying at the village inn with two fellow students. They were on a walking tour.

"We've come from the Main, where we've been staying with *Mutti's* relations. They gave us a wonderful time. I seem to have met dozens of new cousins and friends in the past fortnight. But I couldn't go back to England without a glimpse of Maxie."

"A glimpse?" I said. "How long are you staying?"

"Till the day after tomorrow."

"We'll see about that," smiled Bertha. "I don't think we'll let him go so soon, Maxie."

Nor did they. As Jamie carried the heavy tray to the arbour, Dr Hahn's wise old eyes were summing him up.

"You are an athlete?" he asked.

I cut in with quick pride. "He plays football for Oxford, and he has played for South Africa. He has his Springbok colours."

"*So?* Then he is a powerful player, this Jamie! But he is limping. The knee – it is giving you trouble?"

"A bit," Jamie admitted. "It does from time to time."

From long habit the old doctor saw everybody through the eyes of his profession, and Jamie was no exception. Before he returned to the inn his knee had been properly examined and Dr Hahn had convinced him that it would be very foolish to continue with his walking tour.

"For the first time in my life I'll take medical advice without kicking," grinned Jamie, as he bade me goodnight at the little gate above the river. "The other two can go on, and I'll get a river boat to the coast."

We stood in the growing darkness. The huge red face of the harvest moon rose above the eastern vineyards. A steamer, pricked out with lights, hooted as she rounded the horseshoe bend. The intermittent beam of headlights swept the river-road and passed on. We hesitated, unwilling to part. Once he would have shouted "*Totsiens!*" waved, and gone whistling on his way. Now he leaned on the gate as if he could not bear to leave me.

"There's so much to talk about, Maxie. Can't you come out to lunch with me tomorrow – just the two of us?"

Lucia took her siesta after the midday meal. I could be back before she woke.

"I don't see why not."

"Where shall we go? I'm the stranger in these parts."

"There's a little *Gasthaus* about half a mile down river from here. We could eat there – out in the garden."

"I'll call for you at a quarter to twelve. If you aren't ready I'll wait."

"Jamie," I said. "I'm so glad you came."

"Not so glad as I am. Did anyone tell you how lovely you've grown?"

"Don't be silly . . . *auf wiedersehen*, dear Jamie."

He took my hands and held them against his cheek for a moment.

"*Auf wiedersehen*, Maxie."

I watched his broad figure out of sight, shadowy in the darkness, limping slightly. He was whistling through the side of his mouth the way he'd always done as a boy. Long ago, when we were children.

Lunching with Jamie became a habit. Every day during that week we went off together. Not far. But from noon to three o'clock was our time. Sometimes the people at the inn put up a picnic hamper for us with delicious crisp *Brötchen* and *Wurst*, cheese and fruit and a thermos of fragrant coffee. Or we ate out of doors in one of the little beer-gardens on the water front. That year was Europe's wonder summer. It was mine too. The lull before the storms.

Bertha and *Frau* Hahn encouraged my holiday feeling, and Jamie was touched at their hospitality. He had a standing invitation to supper in their home.

"I love my women-folk," chuckled the old doctor. "But I can do with a man's conversation from time to time."

He and Jamie would hold long discussions in the little arbour above the river. Dr Hahn, one hand lovingly clasped about the decorative bowl of his *meerschaum*, would mull over the African problem in the light of history and philosophy, geography and anthropology, and Jamie went along with his views, glad to talk without the heat and immediacy which distorts the picture when we see it at home.

"Even with education, you can't civilise a continent like Africa overnight," Jamie pointed out. "Wherever you look, from Cape to Cairo, you'll see tribes and individuals in various stages of education and evolution."

"Some being advanced too rapidly, and others being held back." The old gentleman plugged his professorial pipe with a deft finger, and puffed at it comfortably. "Races grow up, you know. Like people."

I smiled to myself as I saw the mask come down over Jamie's open face. I thought, You've hit your head against the wall, *Herr Doktor!* Every right thinking Afrikaner knows that the White man is God's appointed trustee for the Black man, and will be from now unto all eternity. Yet, the more I listened to their conversations, the more I realised that Jamie's years at Oxford had opened many doors in his mind. He clung tenaciously to his own ideas, but he didn't refuse to consider any others.

Those summer nights I felt closer to him than ever before. With him I was content – almost bovine. It was not a bit like being with Simon, who could make me feel like one of Dr Hahn's beehives, full of honey, but full of bees as well, full of dangerous stinging sweetness. All the same I knew that Jamie was changing towards me, discovering the new grown-up Maxie. There was a time limit to contentment.

Lucia and Gretchen followed him round like puppies, and he'd tell them exciting tales of Bergplaas and our valley with its birds and beasts. Most of all they loved to hear about the baboons, who were clowns and made them laugh.

"When do you go home to begin life as a farmer?" Bertha asked.

"About this time next year."

"Why don't you join us for a skiing holiday in the Dolomites next January? There's a little place we go every year. Good snow and a good *pension*. Cheap, but not fashionable."

"Sounds wonderful. I'm no skier but mad keen to try."

His eyes sought mine, questioning. Would I be there? Did I want him? Bertha intercepted the glance.

"Maxie'll still be with us then," she smiled. "And four's a good number for a party. We'll be four grown-ups – and Lucia."

So we planned it that evening in the long twilight between the Rhine and the vineyards. We'd meet again in the New Year, in the snows of the Dolomites. We'd be a party of four.

But, when the time came, we were a party of six.

16

DAZZLE OF SNOW

WE WENT TO Venice in the late autumn to stay with Roberto's sister, who was married to an elderly Venetian nobleman whose family tree and small but beautiful *palazzo* dated back into the mists of the Middle Ages. It was like living in a museum.

I detested everything about it. I disliked the cold patronising *contessa* who made me feel exactly what I was – a cross between her niece's nursery-governess and her brother's part-time secretary, a gauche uncultivated intruder in a distinguished family circle. I couldn't bear her lascivious old husband or their sleek slippery son. The *palazzo*, with its painted ceilings, gothic windows, marble staircase and floors, chilled me to the marrow of my bones, and I was perfectly convinced that the room I shared with little Lucia was haunted by the groaning ghosts of bygone guests poisoned or stabbed by our host's illustrious ancestors. He wore an elaborate "poison-ring" on the fifth finger of his right hand, and sometimes, when he looked at his elegant wife or his mother-in-law, I suspected that he was tempted to find new uses for it.

The labyrinth of canals, spanned by pretty humped bridges, hemmed me in and gave me a sort of aquaphobia, and I pitied the narrow houses compelled to wade forever in those stagnant waterways. I loathed the Lido beach, where I took Lucia when the sun shone. I was bored with the chiming church-bells; with serenades and graceful gondoliers; with avaricious guides and merchants battening on camera-festooned tourists; with pigeons in the Piazza San Marco and gulls squawking round the pink Palace of the Doges. I was sick of the past. Always the past.

Really, of course, the trouble was chicken-pox.

Even Lucia, usually so volatile and adorable, had been listless and irritable, and one morning, Bertha, with her palm on the child's forehead, said to her sister-in-law: "*Senta*, Gabriella, I think Lucia's sickening for something."

The *contessa* wasted no time. She called in her doctor, who suspected chicken-pox. She was outraged. The threat of quarantine loomed over her parties. But Roberto took a firm line fast.

"We will leave Mama with you, Gabriella, and the rest of us will return instantly to Milano."

The *contessa* did not protest.

When we arrived at the apartment in Milan Bertha's doctor confirmed his colleague's opinion. There was no further doubt about it. Lucia had chicken-pox. So, it seemed, had I.

By the time we were "clean" again, as Lucia put it, winter had set in. Outside it was bitterly cold, but the apartment was centrally heated and too warm for my liking. I longed for a log fire, for the crackle and hiss of dry wood, for the blue flame and resinous fragrance of fir cones. We had had tea and I was alone with Lucia. We sat in the window alcove, and a book of English fairy tales lay open on the table beside us. But Lucia was not in the mood for fairies.

"Tell about birds and baboons, Maxie."

She leaned against me, Bumble-puppy in her arms. The sky was low and leaden, and we could see the frosty breath of people walking in the Piazza. The swallows and swifts had long since deserted the Cathedral saints for summer lands and only the pigeons remained to keep them company.

"Birds and baboons? Let me see. In our mountains at home it is early summer now, with the oaks all green and the vines coming into leaf – vines like those in the Rhineland. The squirrels are stealing the eggs of the doves, and scolding – *ch-ch-ch-grr!*"

She laughed. I loved it when Lucia laughed. It was such a merry gurgle. "Dove noise too," she begged. "Doves and squi'lls."

I obliged. "– and the weaver-birds'll be teaching their little ones to fly. Their nests cling to branches above the pools where buck and baboons and ostriches come to drink in the evening. The wild ponies come too with their foals—"

"Foals, Maxie?"

"Young horses, with gay little pony-tails, like you." I touched the fair curls tied with a blue bow. "And lambs skip beside their mothers in the grazing lands all day, but, when night comes, the shepherds take them to their kraals, so they can be safe from the leopard behind their stone walls."

She knew it all by heart. Lucia could have told about every bird and beast at Loire, but she never tired of hearing about our wild creatures. "Tell, tell!"

"Well, then the baboons go to their sleeping-place up in the kloof, and the old grandpa – the sentinel – sits on his rock to keep watch against the hunting leopard . . . the moon rises, the bush is silver, the pools and the river are looking-glasses for the moon to see her face . . ."

Lucia put up her little hand and touched my cheek. "Is sad – this story, Maxie?"

I shook my head and buried my face against her hair, inhaling the sweet familiar warmth. Silky skin, little fragile neck, scent of innocence, the touch of those small fingers on my wet cheek, the taste of homesickness in my throat. One should never be ill away from home. Silly to talk of the summer in my valley . . .

"Look, Maxie! Look! Snow!"

She had run to glue her pert little nose against the window-pane, misting the glass. Outside, something so beautiful, so new and strange to me, was happening that I caught my breath in wonder.

Snow-flakes were falling softly through air grown luminous with pale wintry radiance. They swirled and spiralled with unbelievable delicacy, landing lightly as white petals on the ground, on the rooftops, on the shoulders of people hurrying homewards. They drifted into the niches of the saints and haloed the head of the lonely golden Madonna. They covered the sacred spires and the common chimney-pots alike, and mantled the city in white muted magic.

Roberto found us standing there, silently gazing out of the window. Entranced. The air was so quiet that no snow blew onto the panes protected by their overhanging eaves.

"Our first snow this winter. Pretty, isn't it?"

"It's my first ever – to see it actually falling – changing a whole busy city into a white dream while you watch!"

He came and stood beside us, his thin, almost feminine hands on the little shoulders of the child.

"Which of you is younger now? You have the eyes of a child, Maxie."

"It's so beautiful, Roberto. I never imagined anything so beautiful."

He looked at me, half smiling. "To hear great music for the first time.

To see your first fall of snow. Only once in your life can it come – the first time of anything. The sight of stars, the taste of wine, the kiss of love."

"Or chicken-pox," I said. But I was thinking of Mombasa, of the sea, and Simon. Roberto laughed.

"We could make a long list between us. But listen, Maxie. I have a letter here. From Simon."

He took a flimsy air-letter-card from his pocket. "He writes that he wants to come with us to the Dolomites in January—"

"Simon – to the Dolomites!"

"Then later, in February, he suggests that he takes you with him to England – to fix you up with a suitable job in London."

I gasped. "When did this letter come, Roberto?"

"By this afternoon's mail. It sounds a good idea. He seems to be his cousin's keeper." He was watching me with his sharp interested expression. "I can arrange his accommodation easily enough, and it would suit me well to give him lire and recover from him in sterling later."

Don't dance and sing with glee, I thought. Talk calmly, like a grown-up person. Practical. To see Simon again. In a few weeks! I said, in my most secretarial voice, "Bertha made that arrangement – about currency – for Jamie."

Jamie? Now that Simon was coming with us, I didn't really want Jamie.

Roberto said, "But must you leave us in February? Do we have to lose you so soon?"

Lucia, who hadn't seemed to be listening, turned now and grasped my hand.

"Not go, Maxie! Not go!"

I smiled down at her, but I did not answer. I only knew that the time had come for me to begin leading my own independent life. The flakes were falling thicker and faster now. Happiness was shining through me like snow-radiance.

"There's a postscript." Roberto turned to the end of the letter. "Simon says here, 'I hope to bring Rima with me. Will confirm this later.'" He glanced up quickly. "That'll be fun for you, Maxie. Your South African group – Simon, Rima, you, and your friend, Jamie."

"Great fun . . ." But my voice had gone far away. It was muted in my ears, like the sounds of the city were blanketed by snow. My blood was draining out of my veins, a weird invisible process, leaving me cold and white. The world was darkening. The short winter's day was nearly done.

Street lamps were opening their eyes and lights were jumping up in windows across the Piazza. The Madonna on her spire was a slender ghost fading into the night. "It'll be lovely . . . the greatest fun."

"Pity your brother, Claude, can't come too."

"He's taking up his new appointment in January."

"Yes, of course. A research chemist. Well, never mind. Six is an even number. And we've many friends who go every year. So there'll be another new experience for you. Winter sports."

The *pension*, high in the Dolomites, was old-fashioned and comfortable, with big bedrooms and double windows and central heating. Huge stoves warmed the reception rooms, where we ate enormously, danced and sang and lived a cheerful communal life after sunset. Most of our fellow guests were young and easy-going and not a bit grand or fashionable. We lived in our ski clothes by day and in the evenings we changed into shirts and slacks. We were looked after by fresh-faced Austrian maids and waiters whose greeting *"Grüss Gott"* made us feel that the day had started right.

Rima and I had Lucia in our room with us. She never woke when we went to bed, even if we giggled like a couple of schoolgirls or whispered till our eyes wouldn't stay open another minute. After all, it *was* the greatest fun being with Rima again.

"Basically the old pattern," she said, as she snuggled under the feather "cloud" buttoned into its washing cover. "You, me, Simon and Jamie, and everybody else added unto us. Claude subtracted. But one might expect that." She glanced at Lucia, asleep with one arm flung across Bumble-puppy. "Does nothing disturb her? Not even your nightmares?"

"She sleeps like an angel."

"Does she always sleep with you? A little *duenna*."

"Always. Bless her heart. She can be very naughty, but she's so affectionate, such a honey-child. I adore her."

"You hurl yourself at love, don't you, Maxie? Your dog, your horse, your father . . . this little girl. When it's a man – one of these days – you're going to hurt yourself. Badly, if you aren't careful."

I was sitting at the dressing-table, rubbing cold cream into my face. I could see Rima in the mirror, her fluffy hair flaming on the pillow, her face bronzed like Simon's by the South African sun they had both so recently left. Even at rest she was vivid and alive, watching me, looking deep into me with that extra intuition of hers that saw through the soft exterior down to the elemental truth. A year had passed since last we had seen each

other, but we didn't have to get to know each other again. We belonged
to the same "pride", as Claude had once put it. Back with Rima I realised
that, fond as I had grown of Bertha, there could never be this absolute
unity between us. With Rima anything could be said and everything was
understood, even when we clashed. There were no barriers – save one.
When we spoke of Simon we had become cautious. She no longer
appeared to assume with childish assurance, that she would marry him or
expected me to take it for granted that she would. Being in love with
Simon was our only barrier, and that was made of glass because we could
see through it into each other's hearts just as we could see through the
mirror now into each other's eyes. Even then, I believe, we knew that the
day was coming when we'd be forced to shatter that barrier and get to
grips, and that one of us would bleed to death in the process. The greater
the love, the greater the injury.

Much of this came to me while I sat massaging cream into my skin as a
matter of habit, with Rima's reflection behind me, her hair so red against
the white pillow. I began to shake with dreadful cold in the warm room,
and she said, "Hurry and get to bed, silly-billy. I can see you shivering."

I turned to her and broke the spell. If only we could be children again.
Everything simple. Yet Rima had flawed the simplicity long ago at the
age of thirteen in another shared bedroom on a hot February day at Loire.
Or perhaps it was I who made this one thing complex by refusing to bow
to her will – by fighting my secret battle against the inevitable.

"Rima," I said. "I've missed you this year in Italy. It's only now I know
how much I've missed you."

"Same here," she said. "We've all missed you at home."

"The empty puppy-basket. Remember? The day you came to see us
off you said that."

"It was like that at Rosevale after you left. Big, empty. Till Simon
came back."

"He was going to take a flat. You said so – that day in my cabin."

"He didn't, though. He still talks about it. But he flits around too much.
It's pointless at present. Dad's always sending him here, there and everywhere. He comes and goes. In a way my studio has become *my* real
home – the heart of it."

Now her face was different. Talking of her studio, thinking of her
art.

"When do you take your degree?"

"End of this year. Then Mom's going to do a sort of grand tour with me. Including Greece. And Italy, of course. I may stay and study for a few months in Florence after Mom goes home."

"The Angelis could help you there. They know scores of Florentines. Roberto loves Florence. He often goes there."

"I know. I think that's partly why Simon was so keen on us coming here – even apart from the winter sports and all that. He wanted them to meet me – to be friends."

"He's thoughtful for us. I suspect that he really engineered this job for me."

I cuddled down under the huge cosy "cloud". Rima said:

"Not engineered, Maxie. Just put you in the way of it, for you to take it or leave it, if they made the offer."

"It's been a wonderful year. I've learnt a lot—"

"I'll bet. Italians being what they are!"

We giggled. "Roberto's rather stern," I said. "When his friends make passes at me he bites them. If he guesses."

"He knows his countrymen. Matter of fact, it wouldn't surprise me if he had a thing about you, himself."

"You're crazy! He adores Bertha. And she's my friend."

"Would that count so much? If you really loved a man would you let friendship stand in your way?"

The laughter had gone out of her voice, and she wasn't thinking of Roberto. Lucia stirred in her sleep and muttered. I said "*Shh* . . ." and turned off the light.

" 'night, Maxie."

"G'night, Rima."

We were so close, so strangely close, drawn even closer by the very thing that most separated us.

Roberto and Bertha were expert skiers and took the ski-lift daily up to the high peaks. We'd see them coming home for tea, zigzagging down the slopes among trees hung with glittering icicles, carving their indigo *spoor* in the crisp snow. Simon, who was a good water-skier, was the quickest and boldest of our South African four on snow skis and was soon able to join in long excursions. Jamie, who'd done ice-skating in England, excelled at ice-hockey, which he played with forceful intensity while Rima and I shot hilariously down the toboggan-runs or sprawled, helpless with mirth, on the nursery slopes with the other beginners and the children.

Lucia skied under supervision with parties of children, and Rima made sketches of her in action that I shall treasure always.

We laughed so much that holiday. Everything was gay and glorious and funny, and all our enjoyment was shared – part of a whole. It was as if we'd made a pact. No pairing off. And the Angelis' acquaintances joined up with us too, so that we seemed padded out in a brief sociable existence with no time or room for personal considerations.

One morning, when we were tidying ourselves before lunch, Rima stopped brushing her hair to look out of the open window. She waved her hair-brush at the noonday snow-scene.

"You know something, Maxie. Happiness is like that. Slopes of wonderful white dazzle, with dark sharp shadows for contrast. Sorrow, to point it up."

"Maybe to some people it's the other way round. Mostly shadow, with a few gleams of sunshine."

"Maybe. We can't tell. We're too young – and too lucky. We've never really suffered."

"We've cried."

"So has Lucia. When you leave her it'll be the feel of sorrow for both of you. But it'll pass. When we were kids and my dog, Rover, was run over, Daddy told me that happiness lasts longer and means more than sorrow. He said, 'Your dog made you happy while it lived and sad when it died. The happiness will swallow up the sadness.' "

It was a good thought, full of comfort. But, when the time came for me to part with Lucia, when her little face crumpled and her arms locked round my neck till Roberto gently forced them apart, I could not believe that Uncle Gideon was right. I thought that I would hear an echo of her sobs for ever.

One must never love anybody too much. Never.

17

LONDON WITH CLAUDE
AND SIMON

C LAUDE MET SIMON and me at London Air Terminal on a bitter
night at the end of February. There was sleet on the rain blowing
into our faces as we got out of his old second-hand car in a quiet
backwater off Kensington High Street. My brother's coat was shabby, and
it struck me that he looked unkempt, in need of a woman to take care of
him, but he was cheerful and obviously delighted to see us.

The solid Georgian house in which he lived had been converted into
three flats, and, carrying our bits and pieces of baggage, we followed him
up the steep staircase to what had once been the attic.

"How about the car?" asked Simon.

"Matilda lives the hard way," grinned Claude. "Sits outside in all
weathers with her little radiator-muff to keep her warm when it's
freezing."

As he opened the door of Flat Three and switched on the light much of
my tiredness and sadness at parting with the Angeli family fell away. The
place had a threadbare but lived-in look, like the favourite worn out
jackets men refuse to throw away.

"Three rooms, bath and kitchen – spacious for a bachelor," said Claude.
"Simon can sleep on the living-room divan and keep his clothes in the
linen cupboard. You're here, Maxie."

He turned on an electric radiator in a simply furnished single bedroom
with a deeply sloping roof. The curtains and bedspread were a gay floral
design, faded by many washes.

"I'm next door," he said. "Twin room to yours. Bathroom and kitchen
across the passage. Living-room at the end of it. Come and have some
sandwiches and coffee when you're ready."

I unpacked my few things and joined Claude and Simon in the large living-room.

"It's nice," I said. "It's homely – like our old playroom at Rosevale."

Claude smiled. "I was lucky. I got it from a doctor friend. He and his wife have gone to the States for a year. This lease is just a friendly arrangement."

"So it doesn't show on their income tax return?" grinned Simon.

"That's just about it. Relax while I heat some coffee."

"Who does for you?" Simon asked Claude. "This place is clean as a whistle."

"I get my own breakfast, and sometimes my supper. Mrs Ash is my daily lady – and darn good. She came with the flat. She even washes and mends my socks." He lit a cigarette and I noticed that his fingers were stained with nicotine as well as the chemicals he worked with in the laboratory. "Cigarettes cost the earth in England, but they're still my major vice. What are your plans, you two?"

Simon stood with his back to the radiator, hands linked behind his back.

"I fly to New York a week from today, then home direct from there. I hope to fix Maxie up with a job in Stokes & Staines before I leave. Dad's keen on it. You know how he is about members of the Antrobus and Beeford clan. They must prove themselves somewhere else before he takes them into A. & B. – preferably somewhere abroad."

"Well, if that job comes off, you can share this flat with me if you want to, Maxie. How long will you be here?"

"Six months. I'd love to go shares in the flat."

"There's just one thing . . . one thing I must make clear before you commit yourself . . ."

He hesitated, frowning a little. His deepset dark eyes, so like our mother's, were sunk in their hollow sockets. I kicked off my shoes and curled up on the divan, my feet tucked under me. Hail pattered on the thickly curtained windows. The wail of the wind merged with the roar and mutter of traffic from the High Street. I was to know that sound well, the voice of London, less full-throated but always more articulate in the small hours between midnight and dawn. It was past midnight now.

"People change," said Claude. "Or, rather they develop, become, perhaps, more essentially themselves. I've made my life here in my own way – though I doubt if our parents realised that when they were over in the summer. I tried to conform then, to fit into their picture, but this is my own set up." He glanced round the rather bare room with affection. "If you come in with me, Maxie, you'll have to take the rough with the smooth . . . and that's fairly inclusive."

"Doing for ourselves, you mean?"

"Everybody does that, one way or another. No, I'm trying to tell you that some of my friends – most of them – are pretty leftist in their politics and outlook. Liberal we'd call them at home. Rima'd understand and fit in better than you will—"

"Why should you say that?" I fired up, and saw Simon raise one eyebrow and smile.

He said mildly:

"Science and art know no barriers. You've heard that before. Claude and Rima stand for science and art respectively. We are duller birds."

"For instance," Claude went on, "I have a friend who is an Indian doctor. In fact, I got this flat indirectly through him. He and his wife come here often. They're always welcome – as I am in their home. Then there's a Nigerian law student—"

"Look," I cut in. "If you want to tell me that you don't apply the Colour bar in London, I'm with you – all the way."

Claude smiled. He has a truly beautiful smile. "All the way is a mighty long way. The main thing is that we should understand each other. And, just in case you're wondering, I don't ask Coloured people here to prove my broad-mindedness or register my objection to an outmoded principle. I do it because I respect those particular people and find their company – and behaviour – congenial. Intellectually and socially we must speak the same language to a great extent, or I'd see no point in cultivating them."

How exact he always was – as if everything in life could boil down to a mathematical problem! I thought suddenly of the folk at Rosevale. Old Rocky in the house. Leslie and Lenno in the garden. Corinne, and her Coloured relations at Loire and Bergplaas. Rima and I knew them as Claude could never do. We cared about them, personally. To Claude they were dependents to whom he owed a certain responsibility, but there his interest in them ceased. Fara September had been different. She had been a university student of charm and talent, striving to get on, hitting her pretty head against an *apartheid* ceiling. He had seen in her the seed of equality – given a chance. So she had interested him as a human being – too much, perhaps.

Claude had begun to put the coffee things on a tray and I jumped up to help him.

"Got a hot-water bottle?" he asked.

"Yes."

"Fetch it. I'll put the kettle on."

When I went into the kitchen he took the rubber bag from me.

"I'll put this in your bed. Just for tonight you're my guest. After tomorrow you'll be my partner. Now you take first rub at the bathroom. Simon and I are perfect little gentlemen."

I flung my arms round his neck and hugged him.

"Careful! If I spill boiling water over you, we'll all be sorry."

We settled in – the three of us. Simon and I took turns to get breakfast during the next week while he was still with us.

"Maxie does it in her sleep," he laughed, when it was my turn to be cook. "She's never awake till she's eaten."

Claude agreed. "She's like one of those fancy cameras where two images have to fuse before it's in focus. Maxie's body and soul part for the night and are only fused by the sight of eggs and bacon."

Simon, hair on end, raincoat over his pyjamas, fetching in the milk and morning paper; Claude, always in a tearing hurry to catch the Underground to the Laboratory in Western Avenue; me, dreamy and lazy in my warm dressing-gown and fleecy slippers; the B.B.C. news coming over the radio; the slow grey light beginning to brighten; the roar from Kensington High Street increasing and speeding up with the urgency of a great city on its way to work; and the morning when the pale sun showed its face for the first time and Simon pointed out young buds swelling on the chestnut tree outside our living-room window. All these things marked the beginning of my new life.

Mrs Ash mothered Claude and me. She came in of a morning, her string bag bulging with household odds and ends, her pleasant face blotchy with the cold. She'd hang her worn grey coat and woollen muffler behind the kitchen door and stuff her knitted cap and gloves into the pocket. Her brown hair was glossy and well cared for because her daughter, Janice, worked in a hairdressing establishment and practised on "Mum".

"I'll put the kettle on," Mrs Ash would say, "and we'll get cracking."

Between us we'd have the flat "shipshape in no time", and then we'd take our ten minutes' break and a "cuppa" at the kitchen table. The

English are just as bad as South Africans about tea. Anytime – morning, noon, or night – is teatime.

"I like mine strong and sweet as a good woman," she smiled. "That's what my old man always says."

I came to know her "old man" and all the rest of the family quite well before I was in a full time job myself, and she was interested in South Africa "now we've so many Coloured people in this country. London's stiff with 'em."

"I'm glad you're here," she said. "Your brother needs somebody to look after him. I don't see him but once in a blue moon, but it's my belief he doesn't eat enough. I can tell by the washing up. He scratches a bit of supper here, often as not, but a tin of soup and a lump of cheese won't keep a man on his feet in this weather."

"He probably has a huge midday meal in the canteen. All the same, he *is* much too skinny."

"You've got to build 'em up, I always say. Now, what about your cousin's socks? I take your brother's home for washin' an' darnin'. I could throw in Mr Simon's without killing myself."

"It'd be very kind of you."

Her charming smile lit her face. "I can see you're like my Janice. Washing men's socks gives her the heaves. 'When you're married,' I tells her, 'you'll be washin' nappies as well as socks.' 'That'll be the day!' she says. 'I'll dump the lot on you!' "

There was a school across the road. It was the mid-morning break and Mrs Ash went to the window as if under compulsion.

"My Danny's down there. He's my youngest – the one who's mad on animals."

The noise of playtime came up through the window, a bird-squealing that made me think of Rima's aviary in the spring, amplified a thousand times. She dragged herself away from it, wrapped the soiled socks in a piece of newspaper and stuffed them into the accommodating string bag.

"I must be on my way, Miss Lamotte. The old lady downstairs'll be getting scratchy. I do for her too, and she likes things on the dot."

I smiled. Mrs Ash was seldom "on the dot", as I'd learned already. At the door she turned.

"Oh, tell your brother our Danny's hamster's clawed its way out of the cage my old man made for it. That beast could claw its way out of anything."

I gave Claude her message. He grinned. "That hamster is the one-that-got-away. It clawed itself out of a fate worse than death when I saved it for Danny Ash."

I shuddered. The hamster and guinea-pig aspect of Claude's work was more than I could take.

"It's medicine murder. Torture and vivisection for the so-called good of the tribe."

"Oh, come now. Our ritual is strictly scientific and painless."

"Like solitary confinement and brain-washing."

"Why can't you women be rational and take a long view? You're ruled by your emotions."

"Aren't you – once in a while?"

He shrugged his shoulders. The misshapen black cat, who followed him upstairs regularly for its saucer of milk and taste of human company, jumped onto his lap. His thin stained fingers stroked the creature idly, and I knew that my brother had retreated into his own peculiar isolation where he was beyond hurt or criticism.

"He's inhuman," I confided in Simon. "I doubt if he's ever really felt pity or passion. Affection, yes, but not love."

"I envy his detachment."

"It's bleak. How can a person go through life without falling in love?"

"Give him time. When the explosion comes it may surprise you."

Before he went to America Simon introduced me to Mr Stokes, the Managing Director of Stokes & Staines. It was in this great department store that Uncle Gideon had long ago served his apprenticeship, and so, in his turn, had Simon. There was considerable reciprocity between Stokes & Staines of Knightsbridge and Antrobus & Beeford of Cape Town. Many features of our organisation were modelled on this old established but up-to-the-minute firm.

It was decided that I should work through the various departments over a period of six months, acting as Italian and German interpreter when required. My shorthand and typing might be useful to me in the Export Department, for Stokes & Staines had a large foreign clientèle. The salary was good.

"That means Daddy can discontinue my allowance altogether," I told Simon proudly. "He had to reduce it drastically while I was in Italy, but now I'm really self supporting."

I was to begin work on the Monday after Simon's departure for New York.

How fast it went – that week before he left! He had a number of business engagements for A. & B., and, whenever possible, he took me along with him and introduced me as "Maxie Lamotte, who's training to be one of our buyers." We ate expense account luncheons at fashionable restaurants, and explored dear sprawling London with its grandeur and squalor, its scars of battle, its "villages" tucked away in quiet corners, and its river. I could never get used to London River. This city with such a gift for pageantry wore its long brave history as my grandmother Beeford had worn her triple pearl necklace, casually, without pretension and as a matter of course. So different from the tourist-conscious cities of Italy! When London put on a royal parade it was for the benefit of her own people. I could hardly believe my eyes the first time we saw the Household Cavalry trotting down the Mall from Buckingham Palace to Whitehall. The glitter of the plumed helmets and cuirasses in the pale March sunshine, and the tracery of domes and spires and splendid trees against a smoky sky had the enchantment of a fairy tale. It was still with me when we went back to tea in the flat.

There was something dreamlike about that too. Coming home with Simon, hearing the door close and knowing that now we were alone, that Claude wouldn't be back till six-thirty; turning on the radiator, drawing the curtains, making a late tea with hot buttered crumpets, sometimes preparing supper with Simon's help so that it would be ready later whenever we might want it. Such domesticity, such fun! Maybe he'd sprawl on the couch and watch me arranging sprays of almond blossom or pussy-willow in a tall vase near the window, or a few daffodils and tulips, and I'd wonder if he wanted me as I wanted him, if he ever for one second wished that this was really *our* flat – his and mine.

That afternoon when the gorgeous black chargers clattered down the Mall was a Friday: his last day. Tomorrow he'd be gone. Every moment had become precious and important. We'd had our tea and I took the tray into the kitchen.

"Don't wash up!" he called. "It's so warm and cosy here."

I went back and he pulled me down beside him on the couch.

"You're a honey when you play house-house. But lay off it now. We're going out to dinner somewhere tonight. Nothing to fuss about."

E*

I leaned against him, relaxed, his arm about me, his chin nuzzling my hair.

"I like playing house-house."

"Next week it'll be shop-shop."

"And you'll be gone. Six months before we meet again."

"A lot can happen in six months."

"A lot can happen in six days. In six hours. In six minutes."

He grinned. "Six seconds can change the course of a lifetime. Let's play that record from 'Island Love.' "

I found it and put it on Claude's beloved new radiogram. "Island Love" was the most popular musical in the West End, but we'd failed to get tickets for it. It was fully booked till the end of July.

"That man's voice . . ." I said. "Black velvet. He sends me."

"And the Brazilian sex-kitten sings like an angel."

"She leaves the cast next month. You've missed your chance of seeing her."

I sang the words of the theme song softly under my breath.

"I've never heard you sing – except in church, piping the hymns and missing out all the high notes."

He tilted my face, and, as I fell silent, he kissed my lips. We were in a tower, in a lighthouse, islanded against the world outside, against the tide of week-end traffic flowing strongly from the city, against the cold spring wind and the gathering dark. Nothing, nobody could intrude. He drew me into his arms and held me tight. His heart beat against mine, as if clamouring for admission, and neither of us could speak. It wasn't horse-play as it had so often been between us; but I knew that it wasn't love either. It was danger and a deep need in both of us. We were caught in a whirlwind of desire that would, if we let it, suck us into the quiet core of absolute peace.

Away in the Kensington High Street we heard an ambulance wail and clang its urgent way through the traffic and the robots, a matter of life or death; and here, in the warm living-room, on the table by the couch, right beside me, the telephone shrilled, strident, insistent, refusing to let go, the one voice a woman can never bring herself to ignore.

"Oh, God, let it ring . . . for pity's sake let it ring!"

But I moved out of his arms. Dazed. If I picked it up it would stop ringing. I lifted the receiver and put it down on the table, but my brother's voice was saying "Hullo – hullo!" I had to answer. My mouth was dry.

"Maxie . . . is that you?"

"Yes – it's me."

"What's wrong?"

"Nothing. I've just got back—" Back from where? From what? From the heart of the whirlwind.

"Well, listen, I've been given three stalls for 'Island Love'. For tonight."

"Island Love! How wonderful!" I must get back to reality, into the world again. Be grateful to my brother for that cruel, intrusive, well-meant call.

"Can you let Simon know? Tell him not to dress. I won't have time to come home and change. I'll clean up here, and we'll meet at the theatre at seven forty-five. All right?"

"All right. But who—"

"I'll tell you all about it later. We'll go to supper afterwards at the Ivy."

I put the receiver back on its hook and turned slowly to Simon. He was sitting with his head in his hands.

"Simon . . . did you hear what Claude was saying?"

"Vaguely."

I tugged at his hands. "Look at me!" He raised his face. His eyes were narrow and shiny, bloodshot as if he'd been in the sun and the wind.

"Chick," he said slowly. "I have to tell you some—"

"No! You don't have to tell me anything. A man and a girl in the mood. The time, the place, the opportunity – and the telephone rang. That's all there is to it."

He shook his head. "It's a good job I'm going tomorrow."

"Forget about tomorrow. Tonight we're going to 'Island Love'. Claude's got the tickets. We're to meet him at the theatre at a quarter to eight. I must bath and change. Then we'll go to the theatre and have a drink and a sandwich."

His face was changing and clearing. It was all right because now I'd made him think I didn't care. He wasn't afraid that perhaps I loved him. What had he meant to tell me? I didn't want to know. I didn't want to think about that. Sometime it would catch up with me. Sometime I'd have to face it. But not yet.

18

FARA SPRING

C LAUDE WAS WAITING for us in the foyer.
"Just in time! I've got our programmes."
He seized my arm and we were swept down the short flight of
stairs into the stalls. I could feel his excitement. So unlike my reserved
restrained brother. It was the more electric for being pent up.

The orchestra was already tuning up as we took our places in the third
row. Almost at once the lights went down. There was no time to study
our programmes, but Claude leaned across me to tell us that he'd been
given the seats because Carmen Brazilia, the star, had been taken suddenly
ill. "So it'll be the understudy," he added.

"So long as da Silva's singing I can bear anything," I whispered. "That
black velvet voice!"

It had been da Silva's black velvet voice that had changed the mood for
Simon and me only a few hours earlier. I was very much aware of Simon
beside me now, his arm resting against mine in the darkness. Though he
did not touch my hand his nearness and physical magnetism vibrated
through me. There had been many times when I had told myself that it
was only "animal attraction" I felt for him, but the memory of our childhood and my young hero-worship had denied the wishful thought and I
had to admit to my inmost self that it was the other way about. I attracted
Simon, but he had never in our lives suggested that there was more to it
than that. In fact, if I'd let him finish what he'd been trying to tell me this
afternoon, I would probably have known, finally and for sure, that he
was not for me.

The curtain rose on a primitive pearl-fishing island in the Pacific, a palm
beach on the shores of a blue lagoon, with the masts of a pleasure yacht in
the offing. The effect was tropical, drenched in sunshine. Beautiful Poly-
nesian girls and their fishermen sweethearts were celebrating some local
festival. Nobody wore much more than a loin-cloth and a knife, or a grass

skirt and a *lei* of flowers. A sigh of pleasure went up from the audience. This was sheer escapism. No question of being made to think, only of being allowed to enjoy.

I knew the story, of course. The paradise island, almost un-touched by modern civilisation, invaded by the pleasure cruise party of a playboy millionaire. His goggle-fishing friends, with all their underwater cameras and fancy equipment, coming into conflict with the simple local pearl-fishers; and, needless to say, the brief romance between the Chief's beautiful daughter and the dashing playboy. It had everything, love, mystery, vengeance, violence and a happy ending when the yacht sails away and the girl returns to her island lover. The songs were haunt-ingly familiar already and I was looking forward to seeing the interludes of superb dancing that are such a feature of any lavish modern musical.

I yielded myself to the enchantment of the music and the scene and was soon lost in the world of make-believe. Suddenly I was wrenched back to reality by my brother's fingers biting into the flesh of my wrist. His touch was dry and feverish, his gaze was concentrated on the stage.

The limelight was on the Chief's daughter as she made her first entry, dreamily alone, one single scarlet flower in her lustrous night-black hair, her dark skin glowing with a deeper richer gold than that of her short grass skirt. The garland of flowers that completed her costume emphasised the firmly rounded seduction of her breasts. The understudy, I thought. Wonderful to look at, and probably can't sing a note.

In the tranced moment when she sees the stranger – the playboy owner of the yacht – for the first time, and bewitches him with her beauty, my brother's grip tightened on my wrist. It is the man who recovers himself and finds his voice, and the girl who answers with a sweet faltering note; then the romantic duet that is the theme-song of "Island Love" gathers strength. Carmen Brazilia's understudy sang with a pure sweet voice, warm and true, gaining confidence with every note. Claude's fingers relaxed and I felt him heave a sigh of relief as she held her audience spellbound.

"It can't be . . ." I whispered. He looked at me, speechless, and smiled. I leaned towards Simon.

"It's Fara September . . . *Fara*."

She took curtain after curtain at the end of the first act. It was a triumph. As the lights went up at last, Claude rose at once.

"I'm going back-stage, Maxie. See you later."

"Coming out for a cigarette?" Simon asked me.

"I need one."

We found a quiet corner in the bar and he brought us each a drink. While he waited his turn in the crowd milling round the bar I collected my wits. Simon had never seen Fara September, either on or off the stage. She had made her name in the Coloured Operatic Group while he was in America. But he knew of her. I opened my programme and saw the slip attached to it. '*Owing to the sudden illness of Carmen Brazilia her part will be played by Fara Spring.*' So she'd taken a stage-name? In South Africa the months of the year are usually the names of Coloured families, yet she had kept the essence of her name, for September is the spring at home. I saw her again as she had stood looking at Rima's aviary, and heard the echo of her voice. "My skin is my cage – my pretty brown cage—" Well, she'd flown clear of her cage tonight, she'd crashed the Colour-ceiling and it would be fair to say at last, "The sky's the limit!"

Simon was edging through the chattering surge of an audience which had expected disappointment and found itself present at the birth of a new star. There was elation and interest in the air. He put the long glasses in front of us. "Lemon squash for you – with a dash—"

"Simon, do you realise *who* she was?"

"The little bronze in Rima's studio come to life. And how!"

"I can't get over it."

"Are you pleased?"

"Of course . . . for her."

"Pretty mixed feelings, eh, Chick?"

I bit my lip. I couldn't put my misgivings into words.

"Did you know she was in this show?" he asked.

"Not an idea. But Claude clearly knew. That's why he brought us – how he got the tickets. He must have been in touch with her, yet he never mentioned it before—"

"There's been a lot to talk about these last few days, and we don't see so much of him. Only in the evenings."

"Listen, Claude stipulated that if I shared the flat I'd have to forget the Colour-bar."

"Fair enough. I took it to mean people like his friends, Dr and Mrs Devi Chand, or that Nigerian – Vincent What's-his-name—"

"And Fara. But we've met the others. He had them in. He never said a word about Fara."

"An actress isn't free to go out to drinks or dinner when she's lucky enough to be employed. I shouldn't attach too much importance to Claude's not saying anything about her. It probably just slipped his mind."

But I remembered the burning touch of his fingers on my wrist, the mounting fever in his blood communicating itself to me.

The bell was ringing and people had begun to move towards the different stairways. Claude was in his place when we took our seats. When we were settled he said:

"Fara's coming to supper with us after the show. We're to meet her back-stage. All right?"

I was conscious of Simon's raised eyebrow, of the half-amused question in his glance. But Claude was not looking at Simon, he was looking at me, waiting for my answer. On it depended the fate of our friendship and our partnership in the six months ahead. This was a challenge. "No Colour-bar – I'm with you all the way," I'd said only a few days ago, and now I was hesitating, feeling that this was "something different". I drew a long breath and met his eyes squarely, accepting the challenge.

"All right by me."

"And you Simon?"

"I'm with you."

Fara wasn't just a success. She and da Silva received an ovation. His experience had tided her over the difficult moments and everybody realised that he had helped the new star to make the most of her opportunity. It was also common gossip that off stage he and Brazilia were bitter enemies.

When we went round to Fara's dressing-room – the star's – she was the centre of a great deal of attention. The cast, who had no love for arrogant spoilt Carmen Brazilia, were buzzing round this dangerous rival who would give her plenty to worry about. The press had got wind of a good story and were there with cameras and notebooks. We heard some of the inevitable questions.

"You're from Cape Town, Miss Spring. How does *apartheid* affect a stage career in the Union?"

"No, no, no," she laughed. "Not all that stuff! Not now. This is a happy night for me. I'm from Cape Town. I learned to sing and act there—"

"Would you like to go back?"

"One day, of course. It's the most beautiful city in the world."

"In spite of—"

She put her hands over her ears. "Another time I'll talk to you, if you want it that way. Not now – *please!*"

She had all the emotionalism of her people, the laughter and tears so close together that her great liquid eyes were constantly abrim with one or the other. At last she was free and we were in a taxi on our way to the Ivy. But Fara wasn't in a stuffy little box smelling of stale cigarettes and the heavy scent of the last passenger, she was riding, high, wide and handsome, on the glittering wave that was carrying her into the headlines, into the ultimate dream of her name in lights over a West End theatre.

We had a corner table and we gave our order. We were all as hungry as wolves. The wine-waiter brought champagne in an ice bucket to be opened later. We drank dry South African sherry with our smoked salmon. Simon offered Fara a cigarette, but she shook her head.

"I don't. I keep in strict training."

"It's worth it. When I get home I'll have great news to tell your father at first hand."

I had forgotten that her father was in upholstery at A. & B. How proud he'd be! She looked at Simon with suddenly swimming eyes. Tonight was the justification of all the sacrifices imposed upon her family. She'd always felt guilty about that.

"It's like a fairy tale," she said. "Poor Carmen! Last night, after the show, she collapsed. Acute appendicitis. She was rushed off to hospital, and this morning I knew my chance had come. Do or die."

"We're proud of you," I said. "I wish Rima could be here."

"Rima gave me the courage in the first place. Quite a while ago. Rima and Claude. You too, Maxie. D'you remember that afternoon in the studio when you all advised me to go on tour with the Group? I felt it my duty to start work as a teacher, but you put big ideas into my head . . . dreams and ambitions that seemed crazy . . ."

"I remember very well." That was the night Uncle Gideon had seen her drive off with Claude in Rima's little red car, the night there'd been a row about it.

"That was the beginning. That was how I came to be spotted by a London agent in Johannesburg. He reckoned he could get me a small part in this show. I jumped at it."

As she talked we began to realise something of the loneliness, the hard work and determination that had gone into her struggle towards the great chance that had come her way. Living in sordid lodgings, sending money home to her family, spending what remained on lessons. Speech training, voice production, dancing. The dancing had been important. Without that she would never have been selected to understudy Brazilia.

"Claude knows how terribly thrilled I was when that happened."

She threw him a dazzling smile. How long had they been on these easy intimate terms? She had come a long way since that afternoon in Rima's studio. There was still a hint of the Cape lilt in her voice, and her laugh, when she was unguarded, came a little too frequently, and was high-pitched and nervous, but the flamboyance of her race had been disciplined. She was simply dressed, except for the bizarre ropes of many-coloured beads about her throat; they suited her, accentuating the length and grace of her neck. Her make-up was more restrained too, reduced to iridescent eye-shadow, the mascara on her thick lashes, the petunia lipstick she had always fancied, and nail varnish to match. She used her hands a good deal in conversation and I noticed their expressive delicacy, a characteristic of her people.

We toasted her in champagne. She drank very little herself. "I mustn't. I have to watch that. You know how it is with my folk. My Pa's always warning us." When we had finished our coffee she said that she must go home.

"You've been my true friends tonight. I'm happy and grateful. But tomorrow there'll be two performances, and the audiences won't be so kind. They'll expect more of me."

"I'll drive you back in Matilda," said Claude. "I parked the old jalopy round the corner from here on my way to the theatre. What about you two?"

Simon looked at me. "Want to go dancing, Maxie? After all, it's my last night in London."

So we danced that last night away in the hazy half-light of a Chelsea night club. When we went into the cold street in the raw early morning my eyes were smarting from the thick smoky atmosphere.

"That's the smell and the tang of London," I grumbled. "Murky. Theatres, night clubs, taxis, even here in the open air. Murk. It makes one yawny."

"That's not murk, it's lack of honest sleep."

We had to walk some way before we picked up a prowling taxi, and by then I was awake again. But I put my head on Simon's shoulder and closed my eyes in the shelter of his arm with his cheek against my hair.

He always did that, nuzzled through it, so that I could feel his breath warm on my scalp, a tingling delicious sensation. When we were near our cul-de-sac and the old Georgian house he tilted up my face and kissed me as he had never done before. It was all part of a day that had been quick with undercurrents of danger, like power humming along invisible wires, carrying warmth and light, but a threat too. Keep clear!

The milk and the cat were on the doorstep when we let ourselves in. Simon took the milk bottles and the cat surged past us up the steep stair and waited to be let into our attic flat.

"It's been such fun, this week."

"Hush, Simon! We must be quiet as mice and not disturb Claude."

The cat slipped into the dark little hall and I switched on the light. The door of Claude's bedroom stood open. The bed was as neat as when we had left to meet him at the theatre. No one had slept in it that night. I swung round and stared at Simon.

"He hasn't come back!"

He shrugged his shoulders. "Are you your brother's keeper?"

My teeth were chattering. The flat was icy cold.

"Let's heat some milk," I said. "I'm frozen. Puss would like it too."

We went into the kitchen followed by the cat. Simon put a small saucepan on the electric plate and poured some milk into it.

"Stop shivering, Chick! It's not as cold as all that."

"I'm scared."

"Why?"

"I don't know. I feel like a hamster."

"Well!"

"A hamster when it catches a glimpse of the needle."

The cat was purring and rubbing itself against Simon's legs. The milk in the saucepan smelt different as it warmed, thinner, more innocuous. But if you turned your back on it, even for an instant, it would bubble up and boil over. Milk in a saucepan was never to be trusted.

"How does a hamster feel when it sees the needle?"

He set two glasses and a saucer on the kitchen table. If Simon deigned to drink milk at all it had to be out of a glass.

"Shivery – like I am. Because it senses what's going to happen."

He switched off the electric plate, lifted the saucepan from the stove and poured the milk into our glasses and the saucer.

"There you are, Puss-cat," he said as he put it down.

I took the saucepan from him, filled it with water and left it in the sink.

"About the hamster?" he prompted. "What does it sense?"

"That something sinister is about to begin."

He flung his arm about my shoulder and gave it an affectionate squeeze.

"The only hamster I've ever known personally is the One-that-got-away. Danny Ash's pal who can claw himself out of any situation. You've got a milky moustache. You look very young and sleepy."

I wiped my mouth with the back of my hand. I was sleepy. I couldn't keep awake another minute. The cat stalked into Claude's room and jumped onto his too tidy bed. It began to wash its face.

In Kensington High Street the roar of the city was swelling. It was nearly morning.

19

ENGLISH SUMMER

FARA HIT THE HEADLINES in the Sunday papers the day after Simon flew to New York.

She was every sort of news. Show business news, success story news, and, of course, anti-racial segregation news. She fired the British imagination. "In her own country she can't stand in a White queue to post a letter, but she's something to write home about, this Fara Spring!" commented one paper, and many others took much the same line.

Mrs Ash didn't come in on Sunday mornings, and I was still asleep when Claude came into my room with the bundle of papers under his arm. He brought me a cup of tea too.

"Wake up, lazy-bones, and read this lot! I managed to get most of them."

He left me to make my lingering return to the daytime world.

Interviews, rave notices, rumours of film offers, pictures of Fara, formal and informal. One paper with a circulation of millions promised readers that next week they could begin "the life story of this beautiful gifted girl, cursed in her own homeland by her dark skin. Read how she escaped the cage of South African *apartheid* and soared into stardom overnight!"

Claude found me dazed by the impact of the sensational Sunday press. In drowsy old Cape Town we don't have so much as one Sunday paper.

"Well," he said, sitting on my bed. "Danny Ash's hamster isn't the only one to claw its way out of a cage." His eyes gleamed behind his glasses. I had seldom seen my brother look more pleased.

When we had eaten our breakfast I stacked the papers on the table, folded back at the Fara notices.

"I must send these to Rima. She'll be thrilled."

Jamie arrived from Oxford just before noon. I winced at his kiss of greeting.

"I'd as soon kiss the Abominable Snowman! Your face is frozen stiff."

"Don't grouse! Just to see you I've driven seventy miles in an open car with a wind keen enough to bite your ears off."

I looked out of the window at his vintage sports model with a long bonnet strapped in place. He came up behind me and stood with his arm about my shoulders, peering down at the joy of his life.

"Lovely, isn't she? Goes like a bomb. But the hood's being repaired."

"What's under that bonnet?"

"A paddock full of horses."

"I can't wait to try them out."

"Fine!" He turned to Claude. "Where are we going to lunch? There's quite a good pub on the river near Kingston."

"Sorry, but I've my own fish to fry today. You take Maxie."

Jamie knew Claude better than to ask questions.

"Put on strong shoes and a warm coat," he said to me. "We can go for a country walk after lunch."

While I was out of the room he leafed through the papers, and I heard him say, "Hey, man Claude, this rings a bell! When we were in Switzerland Rima told me about a Coloured singer she'd sculpted – Fara September. Sounds like this is the one!" But I missed my brother's reply.

That afternoon Jamie and I went for a ramble in Richmond Park. Suddenly he seized my hand and we ran helter-skelter down a gentle grass slope with the wind in our faces. We stopped, breathless, laughing and glowing, in the shelter of a huge plane tree. There was bracken on the bank, and deer grazed quietly not far from us. We sank down on the lee side of the tree, leaning our backs against the trunk.

"How long will you be in England?" he asked.

"About six months. I want to be home in September – for the spring."

"Me too. Talking of September and Spring, what about that Cape Coloured girl? Oughtn't we to make a plan to go and see her in 'Island Love'?"

I took a long breath. "I've seen her – the night she made such a hit. Didn't Claude tell you?"

"Not a word, except that she was the one Rima'd sculpted."

"He had tickets for that particular night. He took Simon and me."

"Is she so wonderful? Or do they love her because she's Coloured . . . oppressed by the brutal—"

"Don't be so touchy, Jamie! It stinks of guilt."

He glanced at me, offended. He looked naïve, like a child. I wondered why I felt quarrelsome.

"Fara *is* wonderful. She can act, and she has a glorious voice."

"She must feel right on top of the world. Being a star in the West End is a very different matter from making your name in Cape Town."

"Even now she doesn't feel safe. How can she? When the whole way of your life has trained you to feel inferior you don't lap up success as your due. You stare at it and wonder if it's real. And you know you can only hang onto it if you go on working for it day and night without ever letting up."

"Did you read all that in the papers?"

"No. She told me herself."

"*So* . . ." The way he said it, with the s hard, was reminiscent of Germany and of his mother. It was *Mutti* Vermeulen's expression of amazement, that "*So* . . ." with the lips very round and the little word long drawn out.

"We took her to supper after the show. We went to the Ivy. Claude, Simon, Fara and I. It was a celebration. Claude's party."

In the silence that followed I could hear the voices of children playing hide-and-seek and the thud of hooves as a party of riders cantered by. What would Jamie think? His prejudices went deeper than mine. He had played no part in our Rosevale lives and those endless insoluble discussions in Rima's studio. He was of our valley. He belonged not to the city but to the *platteland* – the country where feudal notions continue to flourish and are taken as a matter of course by both the land-owner and his labour. I stole a peep at his face. His chin was in his hand and there were two vertical furrows between his strong fair eyebrows. He could be this way, slow to answer because his thought was taking shape. At last he said, mildly enough:

"You'll find your brother very liberal these days. We all become more so over here, but let's put it this way; some of us are passively liberal, and others are actively so. Claude goes a long way towards liberty, equality and fraternity."

"You don't approve?" I was up in arms, unreasonably on the defensive.

"Within limits," he said. "At Oxford we meet all sorts; and that's good. I like exchanging views with foreigners, and I don't give a darn what colour they are. Claude meets the scientists and their friends, and he doesn't care about their skins either, so long as he finds them interesting as human beings. But he goes further than I do in getting to know them because he happens to have a flat and he invites them there. That puts it on a different footing—"

"Which you think is a mistake?"

"Stop cutting in! I like Dr and Mrs Devi Chand, though I don't go so much on the Nigerian, but there's a difference between treating *them* as friends and palling up with Fara September."

"I don't see it."

"Whether you see it or not, it's there." He had his stubborn look now. "This girl comes from Cape Town, and making friends with somebody from your home town involves continuity, which you know perfectly well isn't on."

I sprang furiously to my feet. "It ought to be on! That's what makes me so mad. People who've never achieved a thing in their lives consider themselves superior to Fara simply because they happen to have been born pink instead of brown. That's what's wrong with our country – this obsession with White *baasskap*."

Jamie had risen too.

"I hate that term. Call it leadership—"

"And call *apartheid* 'the principle of separate development with each ethnic group developing along its own lines'. That's more palatable, isn't it?"

He was stung by my tone.

"It's a perfectly reasonable theory."

"So you say. And what about the Coloureds with their ballet and opera companies turning us inside out with their productions? They've gone further in European culture than the Europeans. But dare we share a theatre – much less a stage – with them? No! As for the Bantu, they're growing up too. You can't lure the city Natives back to their kraals to squat by the reed fence making grass mats and bead skirts and little wooden animals. White education and industry have seen to that."

"More's the pity."

"It's too late to howl about that. In any case, culture and education are world wide, and every individual with the ability and desire should be able to choose what he wants from them – if he has the means and the brains. That's why Claude and I fight for open universities in South Africa – and it's why we welcome Fara into our home here. We're proud to!"

"Claude hasn't taken long to convert you. He's made a thorough job of it."

"Corrupt me. Isn't that what you really want to say?"

That was when Jamie lost his temper. He grabbed my shoulders. His face was suddenly very close to mine, his eyes blazing.

"This isn't a matter of principle. It's personal. Or you wouldn't be back to the wall, snarling like a *rooikat*. What are you fighting? What are you frightened of? Or *who*?"

I stared at him, my chin beginning to quiver. The next moment his mouth was on mine, hard and demanding, and I was in his arms. The cold wind blew about us, but our faces burned. There was nothing gentle or insinuating about his fierce embrace. I struggled in his grasp, and when at length I was free of him we stood, hostile and apart, discovering each in the other, a new person, aware for the first time of the explosive element between us. We seemed to be alone in Richmond Park in the gusty English spring. But Jamie was right. I was afraid of something – someone – but as yet my fear was formless.

"Maxie, don't look like that! I didn't mean to scare you."

"You didn't scare me. Not you."

He drew me towards him once more. His hands locked themselves across the small of my back; my bowed head rested in the curve of his powerful neck; we were at peace once more. An old memory stirred in me. Rima, with her clever fingers working a lump of putty. Later the wood had "dictated", and she had delivered it of "Oneness", the design conceived the day she had come upon Jamie and me together as we were now. The skin on my back flinched where once it had been burned and blistered. It is strange how my skin refuses to slough off its experience. I look at it sometimes – my young woman's skin, smooth, firm and un-blemished, except for a few small scars and freckles – and I know that it bears a thousand secret imprints, the invisible *spoor* of love and suffering known only to me. I heard Jamie's low voice.

"I love you."

I shook my head. But he went on.

"*Ja*, I must tell you. I loved you in Switzerland, I loved you in the Rhineland, and I loved you long ago at Loire when you nearly got your-self burned to death. I love you now, and one day I want to marry you."

He let me go, and we began to walk slowly across the Park towards his crazy old car.

"I can't think about marriage, Jamie. It's too big for me still. I want to travel and see the world and meet people. I want a job that'll give me those things."

"Marriage is a long way off for me too. I only know that, as far as I'm concerned, you're my girl."

But I wasn't his girl. I wasn't anybody's girl, which is a lonely thought in a strange land. Claude had his private life, and I knew by now that I could not expect to share it very fully. Nor did I wish to.

"I couldn't go steady with anybody. I have to be free."

There was a nervous edge to my voice, but he only said "*Moenie bekommer nie* – don't get in a fuss. It's nice knowing you're in the same country. One way and another, we'll have fun."

We did too.

It was hot that summer. Everybody called it the hottest summer in years. Scores of our South African friends turned up in London and grumbled about the heat. "It's worse than Cape Town. All the air disappears. Too many people breathe it." I used to slip out of Stokes & Staines in my lunch hour and take a few sandwiches into Kensington Gardens right near the store. The Londoners made a picnic of their long hot summer. They lay about the parks and gardens in cotton dresses and sandals. No hats or gloves, often no stockings, and they were friendly and talked to strangers. Stokes & Staines had an active social and welfare organisation and I soon made friends among my fellow workers.

Although Claude and I went our own way a great deal, the little flat was a real home to both of us. Some of our simplest and happiest evenings were spent there. He liked to have small dinners there, for four or six. "So much more fun than going to a pub. We can be at our ease and talk more freely, thanks to you, Maxie. You manage marvellously."

With Mrs Ash's help I had evolved a simple method of entertaining. "Casserole Lamotte" was our main dish – a savoury stew that only needed popping into the oven to heat up – supplemented with a cold course from Stokes & Staines' food hall, or fresh fruit-salad and ice-cream. Mrs Ash made most of the preparations in the morning, so my task was easy.

The Indians, Dr Devi Chand and his wife, Lala, came often. So did several of Claude's scientific colleagues, men and girls. Vincent, the Nigerian, was another regular guest, but he always arrived in mortal terror of the black cat.

"I'm allergic to cats," he'd explain, when the animal snaked round his legs or sharpened its claws suddenly on the back of his chair so that he jumped sky-high, his frizzy hair rising in horror.

Danny Ash usually showed up after he'd finished his homework, to "lend a hand with the wash-up" and earn half a crown and a portion of ice-cream. The hamster was always in his pocket, but it scrambled out to play with the cat. Of course neither Dr Devi Chand nor Vincent would have dreamed of helping in the kitchen.

"They don't get around to it," said Lala, as she helped me tidy things away while the men smoked and talked round the table. "They've been raised in a man's world."

"They'd be a nuisance under our feet, but it wouldn't kill them to offer."

She giggled, her black eyes moist. "It would if you took them up on the offer!"

Fara never came to these parties. Carmen Brazilia had returned to South America, and Fara Spring had become as big a draw as "Island Love" itself. So her free time and Claude's seldom coincided, except on Sundays. Maybe that's why I got into the habit of spending my Sundays with Jamie. I didn't want to know if Claude was seeing Fara or not. I wanted to be clear of it if he was. But often, when I came home, I could tell she'd been there. Her scent, heavy and cloying, lingered in the flat.

As the summer advanced I often took the train to Oxford after work on a Saturday morning. Jamie'd meet me there and I'd stay the night at "Ma Walmer's". "Ma Walmer" was a war widow who'd been left a large house in the Banbury Road where she let accommodation on bed and breakfast terms. Her rooms were quiet and comfortable and she was, as she put it, "particular" about her guests, who were, for the most part, friends and relatives of undergraduates or dons.

We explored Oxford and its surroundings in Jamie's old car, and sometimes he met me in London and we rayed out from there into the green enchanting countryside with its picture-postcard villages and ancient towns steeped in history. We never ceased to marvel at the infinite variety of scene and climate, speech and temperament to be found in this one small island. We decided to return to South Africa by the same ship.

A fortnight before we sailed for South Africa at the beginning of September I gave up my job at Stokes & Staines and Jamie and I visited my mother's Beeford relations in Scotland and Cumberland. It seemed natural to me that here, as at home, he should share the country part of my life. Claude joined us for a week in Wales and we climbed the mountains and fished the rivers and were saturated in bucolic enjoyment.

We left Jamie in Oxford. He stood beside Claude's car, the faithful "Matilda", his face burned copper by long days of sun and fresh air.

"*Totsiens*. See you at Southampton, Maxie. I'll take good care of her, Claude. I'll cherish her like Ferdinand, my Jersey bull."

We had booked our passages in the mail boat, tourist class. Jamie had been determined to go by sea because he was responsible for the transport of a new pedigree bull for Bergplaas. He had chosen and bought that bull and it was very dear to his heart.

It was my last night in London. Claude came into my room. I was packing my dressing-case. Everything else was ready. The window was open. It was still light and a flock of pigeons wheeled across the sky. We could hear the sparrows chirping on the fire-escape, a close, cheeky, intimate sound against the murmur of the city. My brother sat on my bed, I felt sorry to be leaving him. He needed someone to take care of him. He wouldn't eat enough when he was on his own. I must tell Mrs Ash to keep an eye on him. He lit a cigarette and I put an ash-tray near him. He examined his stained fingers thoughtfully as he said:

"I suppose you'll marry Jamie one of these days."

I closed the dressing-case, and went to the window.

"I don't know who I'll marry. I'm going home to a job in A. & B."

He ignored my answer, following his own line of thought.

"Bergplaas and Loire. Those farms could be run together—"

"I don't know what you're talking about. Loire will be yours."

"Loire will never be mine."

"You'll inherit it. If you don't want it you'll sell it. We've been through all that."

"Things have changed since then . . . since we went through all that."

"I know you'll get a big rise in the New Year – that you'll never give up your research job now. You'll go on up in the scientific world. But I don't see why that alters anything. You'll marry some time, and eventually you'll retire. You might have a son who'll want Loire."

"I might indeed. But I don't think my father would wish any son of mine to own Loire. In any case, a great deal would have to change before such ownership would be possible."

Outside the window the golden leaves of a plane tree were fluttering to the ground in the autumn breeze. I leaned against the sill, quivering like an animal in terror, cold, my mouth full of saliva, as if I might be sick. Claude was pale, his cheek twitching and suddenly I saw him at Rosevale, driving Rima's little red sports car into the sunset, Fara at his side, my uncle and aunt staring after them.

"Claude . . .?" The name came heavily, questioning, past the lump in my throat. He was still looking down at his hands.

"Yes," he said. "It's Fara. It has been for longer than you know. When the run of 'Island Love' is finished we mean to marry. I can't say when that'll be."

No, not this! Not my own brother! He had spoken quietly, with the deadly, unalterable decision I knew so well. But I cried out.

"No! No, Claude! You can't. You haven't thought about this properly – all that it would mean to both of you."

"I've thought of little else."

"It's infatuation. You'll get over it."

"I don't want to."

"If you marry Fara you can never go home and live together as man and wife. You'd be social and legal outlaws. Exiles. You'd be cut off from your own people – both of you."

"Because of a cruel sinful law that'll have to go. The day'll come when we'll be able to go home openly and honestly – if we want to."

"And if you do . . ." Tears choked me. Hot and salt, they poured down the back of my throat. "If you do go back . . . with your Coloured family . . . you'll break our father's heart."

He took off his glasses and wiped them. Through a mist I saw the sadness on his face. I ran to him and caught his hands, and his glasses fell to the floor. I knelt beside him to pick them up and felt the frame crack beneath my knee.

"Don't do it, Claude! Don't take this step! Fara can have anybody. She doesn't need you now she's a star." I pleaded desperately, as if for my life, but he shook me off and began to grope for his glasses. If there were children there'd be a line of the Lamottes tainted for all time. Dared I say that? He had found the damaged frame.

"They're broken. You knelt on them. You broke them."

"You've others. You're not listening to me."

"What's the good? I'd hoped you – of all people – might understand. Rima would. You're tolerant in theory, but, given the fact, you can't take it, Maxie. So now I have to lose my sister. Altogether."

His myopic eyes were wounded and his mouth was grim.

"Must I tell our parents?"

He shook his head. "Tell nobody. I'll do my own dirty work when the time comes."

The pain and bitterness in his voice hurt me.

"Whatever happens I'll stay your friend."

"Will you?" he asked. "I wonder. Hers too?"

"Hers too."

But surely it wouldn't happen. Not to my brother. There'd be somebody else for Fara Spring, the star of "Island Love". She could do a great deal better than Claude Lamotte. In six months' time she'd be through with all that. This sort of thing didn't happen to people like us.

"It's getting dark," I said, "and cold."

I turned on the light and drew the curtains. The room looked bare with all my things packed. I heard Claude go to the desk in the living-room. He'd be hunting for his spare glasses, cursing me for my clumsiness.

20

RETURN TO ROSEVALE

THE MAIL SHIP arrives in Cape Town early on a Thursday morning to connect with the fast up-country trains.

I was awakened before daybreak by the strange cessation of the liner's life. I pulled slacks and a coat over my pyjamas and ran up onto the deserted deck. We were rocking gently on the Cape swell, waiting for the pilot's tug.

Table Mountain, Lion's Head and Devil's Peak towered against the paling sky. Dark rags of cloud scudded in from the north-west. A loom of lights blinked between the foothills and the sea. The wind was fresh against my face still warm from sleep.

The voyage had been fun. I liked my Rhodesian cabin-mate, and Jamie had found himself sharing with her brother and another young tobacco planter. We'd formed a lively gang with a few others, competing keenly in the deck sports and dancing most nights.

I'd stopped worrying about Claude and Fara. It's odd how when you are away from a trouble you stop thinking about it, or even believing in it. Everything would be all right. All I felt as I stood on deck that morning was anticipation and excitement. I was home again, and now my real life would begin. The past two years away had been a sort of apprenticeship. The future was here in my own country, for better or worse.

The neutral light was growing. The white wings of gulls swooped above the swaying masts and the white horses of the bay tossed their manes. The ship heaved and groaned. I wondered if it had looked as forbidding as this to the first Etienne Lamotte to settle at the Cape in 1688 with his wife and family. That had been no pleasure cruise! It had been a voyage of many months and many hazards. A Lamotte child had been born at sea and another consigned to the deep. Danger and tragedy lay behind those early Huguenot refugees and danger and endeavour ahead of them. But, for all that, the Cape had been their threshold to a new freedom.

There, in the Western kloof of Table Mountain, was Rosevale. Much further afield lay the lovely Paarl Valley and, in its most remote corner, the grant named Loire in memory of a lost homeland.

"Wonderful sight – finest in the world, eh Maxie?"

Jamie was beside me. He had come from the well-deck where the beloved Jersey bull had his stall.

"How's Ferdinand?"

"Flourishing. The bull of all time!"

Jamie slipped his arm through mine, and I felt it coursing through him, that deep Afrikaner love of his land that is his strongest purest emotion. I looked at his rapt face. There was worship in his expression, and exaltation. It's all mixed up with religion, I thought. God and South Africa. Whoever marries this man will be marrying the land itself.

The pilot tug was breasting the swell towards us and I said, "I must go and get ready. See you later."

My parents and *Oom* Gert and *Mutti* Vermeulen came on board to meet us. I don't know which *Oom* Gert was more delighted to see, his son or the new bull. Rima came too. She was wearing stove-pipe slacks and a yellow sweater, and she'd cut her hair very short so that it licked round her small head like flame. My mother looked drawn, and it seemed to me that my father was greatly changed, subdued, unlike himself, all the old exuberance gone. Even his affectionate smile of greeting could not hide the anxiety in his eyes.

"We're hoping you'll stay at Rosevale tonight and tomorrow," said Rima. "Daddy's keen to get your new job taped before you go home, and tomorrow's my birthday. So we thought Jamie could come in for it and we'd have a party. Simon can put him up – yes, Simon has his own flat at last – and then Jamie could take you back to Loire on Saturday morning."

Mummie smiled. "After two years we don't grudge you two more days, Maxie. I think it's a good idea to talk to Uncle Gideon about your work at A. & B. Daddy and I have to go back immediately after lunch today."

So it was arranged as Rima suggested.

"Simon's in Johannesburg, and only gets back tonight," she said. "You won't see him till tomorrow."

We made our plan with Jamie and then went straight from the ship to Rosevale.

The day had turned gusty with sun and rain fighting each other. Rosevale had never looked lovelier, freshly painted, candy-pink against the violet buttress of the mountain, the kloof behind it sweet-scented with mimosa and the tips of the silver trees spear-bright where the light caught them. Aunt Kate kissed me warmly.

"Now my second daughter is home again – just when I need her most!"

I wondered exactly what she meant, but there was no time to ask because Daddy wanted to know which suit-case I needed, and Rocky was waiting to get it out of our old station-wagon. His broad black face was wreathed in smiles, he was portlier than ever, and it was good to hear his rumbling voice as he welcomed me.

"Miss Maxie must stay at Rosevale now. With Mr Simon gone to his own place, and Miss Rima going to Europe in December, my Madam will have no children left to keep our house young."

Corinne came quietly into my room to unpack my suit-case. Two years of Aunt Kate's training had taught her the arts of a lady's maid. But I was surprised to see her. I had thought that by now she would have found her way into a factory or a restaurant, something more independent than domestic service.

"I'll take this dress for pressing," she suggested, shaking out the "little black number" that had served me so well in London. She spoke in English, and that too was new, for Corinne was a girl from the *platteland* where English was seldom heard among the Coloured people.

I buried my face in the bowl of roses on the dressing-table.

"How lovely these are!"

"Lenno cut them for Miss Maxie," she said.

"Did Lenno think of it?" I asked. "Or you?"

She smiled. "*Albei*. The two of us."

"Isn't it time he went to his country to build a hut, and marry his girl and start a family?"

She was putting things into the chest-of-drawers and her face was hidden.

"He isn't going. He doesn't want to go. Leslie went last month."

"But surely, when Leslie comes back—"

"*Nee;* Miss Maxie. Lenno *wil nie terug gaan nie.*"

She had broken into her own language to emphasise that he refused absolutely to go back. I changed the subject and asked after her grandmother, old Lizzie, the Wise Woman of Bergplaas.

"I haven't seen my *ouma* lately, but I hear she is well."

My mother came in and Corinne slipped unobtrusively out of the room.

Mummie sat on the bed. She looked worried and drawn, her resemblance to Claude striking. I wondered if she had heard anything about him to trouble her, and then I realised that her concern was for my father.

"How did you find Daddy?" she asked.

"I've hardly had time—"

"A first impression. Speak your mind."

"Not himself. The sparkle's gone . . . he used to have so much."

Mummy nodded and frowned.

"Is it his health?"

"No, it's not physical," she said. "He's bothered about money. We overspent on that trip of ours, and the fat years are over. We're in a lean period. The farmers are suffering, and it's not easy to raise a loan these days."

"When Daddy wrote to me in Italy . . . when he asked if I could manage with a very much reduced allowance, I guessed things were bad."

"He hated having to do that. You were very good about it."

"I can earn my own way, Mummie. I don't need subsidising."

"So you've proved, darling. Uncle Gideon is anxious to get you established in the firm as soon as possible. Now tell me about Claude. How is he? Does he mean to come back?"

"He's doing very well in his job. He's getting a big raise next year. You mustn't count on his coming back. Not for a while, anyway."

She ran her hand through her short grey hair. "Daddy needs help. You know, Maxie, I've often wondered how much Claude really cares about Loire. You were the one who always loved the place."

"I still do – more than anywhere in the world."

"Yes," said my mother. "I believe that. The sad thing is that your father never really understood Claude. They simply aren't on the same wavelength. Such a pity."

She had never talked to me like this before, as if I were an adult and an equal, as if I might be able to help and advise her. As she sat there on my bed, twisting her thin hands together, her features sharp and drawn, I was conscious of a subtle change in the balance of our relationship, a shift of dependence from one to the other. I had no desire to tell her about Claude and Fara and add to her anxieties, whatever they might be. I only wanted to ease them. But she rose briskly, all her nervous energy and determination in her bearing and her taut smile.

F

"*Alles sal reg kom*. Just having you home again is good enough for a start."

Everything'll come right. The old South African optimism.

My parents went home after lunch and later in the afternoon Rima and I strolled across to her studio. The wind had changed and blown the rain clouds away. The rockeries behind the studio blazed with pink and purple *vygies*, orange and blue Namaqualand daisies, and many-coloured everlastings. Long tailed sugar-birds hovered over the proteas, their scimitar beaks robbing the flowers of their nectar, and little sun-birds darted among the shrubs with flashing wings and trills of song. It was all so beautiful and familiar. I might never have been away. The dogs, even Trout, the cat, took my return for granted. Lenno was singing one of his monotonous Shangaan songs as he weeded the lawn. Nothing was changed. And, under the pleasure of homecoming, was a current of warmth and looking forward. Tomorrow I would see Simon.

"You've got new birds in your aviary," I said, "The *rooibekkies* and two pairs of weaver-birds."

The golden weaver-birds, bigger than the budgies, had hung their neat kidney-shaped nests from the top of the big cage.

"They insisted on being taken in," smiled Rima. "They stuck around till I gave in to them. They get on terribly well with my budgies. Corinne'll have to take care of them when I'm away."

"Are you sticking to your plan of going to Florence?"

"Yes. Mom and Dad are taking me to London first. We'll have Christmas with our English Antrobus relatives, and then Mom'll take me to Greece. After that she'll leave me in Florence."

"How long will you be away?"

"Maybe a year. Maybe a few months. I don't know." For a moment I had the feeling that she wanted to tell me something intimate and important, but it passed. She said instead: "Mom's counting on you to stay here while you're working at A. & B. She seems to think she'll miss me a lot, and having you around will help."

I knew that my mother would expect it too, for reasons of economy as well as the old established custom of our childhood when Rosevale had been as much our home as Loire. But I wanted to be independent. Rima was watching me as if she guessed my thoughts.

"Even Simon is gone," she added. "It's a very empty puppy-basket these days."

"Puppies grow up. Peter Pan's the boy who never was." I touched the flanks of a carved horse that was like no blood horse and like every blood horse. At home, at Loire, was her picture of Snow, the white charger, with a knight and a small fair maiden on his back. "Sir Galahad's another myth, the man that never was."

I wandered round, examining her work, recalling Simon at Mombasa, and how we had talked about Rima's awareness of the *mystique* of Africa. It was more than ever apparent – a basic simplicity, a haunting rhythm. Some of the sculptures were familiar, a few were new, and two or three I remembered were absent.

"Where's Mother and Child and Oneness?"

"They're on exhibition in Johannesburg. They were selected for the Artists of Fame and Promise show."

"Rima! What a triumph! But you're doing great work. It's poetry in sculpture. It's frightening, too."

Bronze casts, *ciment fondu*, and, above all, the carved wood interpreted the dark rituals of Africa, fertility rites, harvest dances, and the propitiation of the Old Gods. She had tapped a symbolism outside her personal experience.

"That's why I have to get away . . . now . . . just when I least want to. I need new influences before it's too late. I'm too deep in the primitive. It's getting a fantastic hold on me. I can't seem to escape it."

She turned from the massive brooding pieces to the portraits, among them Fara, Claude, Corinne and Lenno. Only Lenno was full length, a young warrior with his shield and long throwing assegai. Fara's head seemed civilised and conventional by contrast. I touched the contours of cheek and lips.

"Their faces are soft and fleshy; sort of swollen, like sleeping children or birds at nightfall."

Rima smiled. "That's why it doesn't matter when they have their teeth out. Their mouths don't fall in and give them the witch look. I enjoyed our sessions with Fara. Remember the fuss Dad kicked up with Claude?"

"He was right."

"Why do you say that?"

"Claude and Fara want to marry."

"No!"

"Claude said I was to tell you. *Nobody else.* He said you'd understand. Personally, I hope to heaven it'll never happen."

Rima said slowly. "She's made the grade in a big way. Her own people are awfully proud of her."

"And ours are just embarrassed. Another Coloured girl flying high." I glanced at the carved face of Corinne. "People here don't seem able to distinguish between a famous Coloured actress and a Coloured farm girl. Both are brown. So both are inferior."

"Snap out of it, Maxie! Look ten years ahead. The world doesn't stand still. This country is bound to become multi-racial. It's inevitable. If it doesn't happen peacefully it'll happen the other way."

"Do you think that'll console my father?"

"I s'pose not. Why can't Fara be content to be Claude's mistress? They'd be gaoled here for that, but nowhere else in the world. Let them get it out of their systems. In any case, if you want to marry a woman, you must sleep with her first to be sure that part of it's right."

When I didn't answer she threw me a sly glance. "So they're lovers already? Well, I guess it works two ways. If it's not a cure it's habit-forming."

"Look," I said. "Claude doesn't want to come back to South Africa. He doesn't mind being an outlaw. You should know that."

"It's damnable that he should be any such thing – that either of them should suffer. There's no difference between Fara's culture and ours – and she's not much darker than some of the proudest in the land! Now *this*" – she indicated the warrior – "this *is* different. This is undiluted Africa. The Bantu is Pagan and polygamist. If he turns Christian he interprets the Crucifixion in his own way. Human sacrifice for the good of the tribe. Slow death and a share in the body and blood of the victim. You can't blame him. It's the old old African way to strength and still goes on. Neither the law nor the missionaries have been able to stop it."

A cloud covered the sun, and, in the shadow, the primitive sculptures seemed to crowd in upon us. With Rima I so often felt perilously near the elemental mysteries. She went on.

"The Coloured people stand between the two worlds. They can come our way, or they can go back to the tribe. But that's dangerous. It's a long step back. They are moving forward. They belong with us."

Outside the window we heard a warbling call, very clear and sweet, birdlike, yet human. And then it was answered from away down the garden.

"Surely that's the signal Leslie and Lenno always used?"

Rima nodded. "But Leslie's home at his kraal now. You're hearing Corinne and Lenno calling to each other."

"Corinne!"

"Yes. Lenno's taught her the bird-call."

Rima placed her portraits as if they were opposing pieces on a chess board – Fara moving towards a plaster cast of Claude, and Corinne facing Lenno, the noble savage.

"A pattern of revolt, Maxie."

"So that's why Lenno doesn't want to go home and marry the witch-doctor's daughter?"

"Your guess is as good as mine."

"But betrothal among his people—"

"If you jilt a girl – leave her on the shelf – her father avenges her honour by killing you."

"And this girl's father knows a trick or two!"

"With Lizzie at this end and the witch-doctor at the other I shouldn't say the outlook was rosy."

"Like jilting one of the Borgias!" I said. "Asking for trouble."

We began to giggle. We knew the witch-doctor very well by reputation. Leslie had often told us of his powers and exploits and we had felt all along that Lenno was about to marry into a sinister family. For instance, there had been the case of the missing man who had turned into a crocodile. It was famous throughout the Shangaan country. This man had annoyed the witch-doctor and had then disappeared. His wife, going to the river to draw water, had seen a large crocodile basking on a flat rock. She had instantly recognised her husband, and rushed back to the village to call her friends and relatives. Everybody had flocked to the water's edge, and all had agreed that from the neck up the croc was the missing man. The spell had evidently not yet taken full effect. The unfortunate monster had plunged into the water with an agonised roar and had never been seen again in any shape or form, human or saurian.

Rima said: "Every morning I look out of the window and wonder if I'll see a crocodile mowing the lawn."

We laughed helplessly. What fun it was being home, being back with Rima!

"Tell about you," I said at last. "You haven't told me a thing about yourself."

The western windows blazed in the sunset. It was time for us to go to the house and change for dinner. Rima's back was to the light. She stood, slim and straight. Our childhood was very near – the "phoenix game". She looked like the Priestess of the Sun, the heart of the phoenix legend. Dedicated.

"Rima! There's something special. You have something special to tell me."

She was motionless at the Altar of the Sun, and I must play the part I had always dreaded. I was the bird without a mate, the bird with the sweet voice, collecting the twigs of the spice tree, preparing the nest for my own immolation.

"Tell me, Rima!"

"Later," she said softly. "Later, Maxie."

21

CELEBRATION

I N MOST LONDON STORES the escalators are tucked away outside the showrooms, but in Antrobus & Beeford of Cape Town they move in a leisurely way through six floors and the heart of the store.

As I ascended, on the morning after my return, it occurred to me that never before had this moving-stair been put to better use as an "observation car". Showrooms, springlike with glamorous displays, cunningly led the "traveller's" eye on into the distance where he or she could glimpse vistas well worth exploring later. I recognised ideas that Simon had discussed with me in London. Good for him! He'd got away with it!

The Chairman's office on the top floor was more like a luxurious study-library, with its prints of Cape Town in the early days, and its valuable first editions in the glass-enclosed book-cases that also contained the archives of the firm.

As children, Rima and I had often giggled over the faded catalogues of the past century when hour-glass ladies in flowered hats and feather boas were dressed from London by A. & .B and gentlemen bought their mole-skin trousers and fancy cravats from dashing young Charlie Beeford, himself the very soul of English – and colonial – elegance. We were amused too by faded press photographs of dignitaries of the new Boer Republics, and of Presidents and Generals in splendid but restrained uniforms, and their ladies in tasteful Victorian regalia all evidently supplied by the already well established Cape Town firm of Antrobus & Beeford.

"Study the history of your family business," Uncle Gideon used to tell us, "and you'll learn a great deal about the history of your country over the past hundred and fifty years."

He was standing at the tall window when I went in. As I joined him he indicated the new matchbox buildings shooting up all along the foreshore. Ugly angular skyscrapers.

"We're well placed here, at the foot of Adderley Street," he remarked. "With all that foreshore reclamation going on we'll soon find ourselves in the new city centre."

"Since I've been away – only two years – everything has changed. I hate these office blocks."

"They're graceless and impersonal, but they're twentieth century. Wouldn't you love to turn back the clock for twenty-four hours? Back to three centuries ago when there was nothing down there except the sea-shore and the beginnings of the old Castle-fortress. And higher up the mountain – where Rosevale is today – Governor Van Riebeeck was planting out his market-gardens to supply the Dutch East Indiamen with fresh fruit and vegetables."

"It must have been paradise to the sailors to come ashore in this lovely place after months at sea. How brave they were – those early mariners!"

"They lived in adventurous times. Trade opened up the world, Maxie. Trading bases came first, and colonies followed. When there are no more colonies there'll still be empires of commerce. That's the picture of the future." He smiled and put his bony hand on my shoulder. "Let's not get onto my pet subject. We'll let the past and future take care of themselves for the moment and stick to the present. What we want to find out is where you fit into the scheme of things at A. & B. Simon wants you trained as a buyer."

"That's what I want too – why I took such trouble learning Italian and German, and a bit of French too. And Simon made a point of introducing me to our agents and contacts in Italy and London."

"I know he did. You're very young though."

"Twenty. That's not so young."

He raised his thick grey eyebrows and laughed.

"And Rima's twenty today. No longer teenagers. Maybe you're right. If a girl's old enough to marry she's old enough for almost any responsibility. Now, to business."

Half an hour later he spoke to his secretary down the voice-pipe.

"Miss Boshof, I'm sending Miss Lamotte along to Mr Trevor-Antrobus. And I want to see Miss Pratt right away. Ring the showroom and get her for me."

Simon's room had none of the imposing grandeur of the Chairman's. As he rose to greet me my heart warmed and lifted. It was more than six months since I had seen him, and even here, in this dull office, his vigorous maleness was stimulating. He took my outstretched hands, but he did not kiss me.

"Welcome back, Chick! You look wonderful – right on the crest. Sorry I couldn't meet you at the ship."

An obliging typist brought us cups of strong sweet tea, and blushed when Simon glanced up at her with his quick smile and said, "Thanks, Sally." When she had gone he turned back to me.

"What did you fix with the Chairman?"

In A. & B. he never referred to his step-father except as "the Chairman". His manner was pleasant but brisk, very much Simon on duty. I took my cue.

"I'm to work in the showroom under Miss Pratt. She'll teach me the ropes about local buying. Later I'm to get the hang of the various departments a woman can buy for abroad – find out what lines go well, and why, and so on."

"Good show. When do you begin?"

"Monday week. I thought I ought to have a little time at home first – at Loire." I wanted to explain that I was worried about Daddy, to ask if Simon had noticed any change in him, but the moment was not right for personal confidences.

"After so long away it's only reasonable you should spend a little time at home before getting into harness."

"I'm to get to grips with old Prattle this morning. Uncle Gideon's talking to her now. This afternoon I'll be free till I start in seriously."

"Salary all right?"

I told him, and he gave a low whistle.

"Well done, Maxie! I'd never have dared suggest as much for a start. But if the Chairman offers it he reckons you're worth it. He doesn't mix charity with business."

"It seems Stokes & Staines gave me rather a special write-up to Uncle Gideon. I didn't know about that."

"I'm proud of you. That's yet another thing to celebrate. What are you doing for lunch today?"

"Nothing special."

F*

"We'll go to that little Chinese joint on the foreshore. Suit you?"

The Chinese restaurant looked across the bay. As usual on a Friday, the mail steamer was in, due to sail for England in the afternoon. Only yesterday Jamie and I had been on board her sister ship, saying our goodbyes, exchanging addresses with fellow-passengers and promising to meet again; but already that world in a vacuum meant less to me than Mars or Saturn. The lavender hull and scarlet funnel had no more significance than any of the other normal sights of Table Bay, the tankers and cargo-boats, the fast little catchers of a whaling fleet, and the visiting warship berthed along side her host cruiser of the South African Navy.

We had eaten our chicken curry with flaky rice and all the other garnishings of the Orient; Ah Ling had taken away the tiny china cups that had held our hot rice wine and brought clear fragrant jasmine tea and set it before us. The spring sunshine streamed through the sliding glass windows that in summer were screened by light bamboo blinds.

"The sun on your hair, Chick. I suppose that's what the Edwardian novelists described as 'spun gold'. I'll bet a voyage in your company shook old Jamie to the marrow of his solid bones."

I laughed. "Why drag Jamie into this?"

"You'd shake anybody."

"That's more like it. Wait till you see my new dress tonight. It's a honey. I bought it for my twentieth a few weeks ago. A present from me to me. We're getting long in the tooth – Rima and I."

"You both wear well." He grinned. "There'll be only the four of us tonight. You and Jamie, Rima and me. We're dining and dancing at a new place in Sea Point—"

"There's always a new place in Sea Point."

"This one is fun. We'll meet at my flat for drinks first."

"I can't wait to see your flat."

"You'll like it. I'm mad about it. Rima was the interior decorator."

He lit a cigarette for me and one for himself.

"By the way, it's not just Rima's birthday we'll be celebrating. It's rather more than that. It's a secret still, and will be till Rima comes back from her travels and her studies in Europe. But we wanted you to know about it – you and Jamie, and your family, of course. No one else."

I put my cigarette carefully on the side of the soapstone ashtray, so that Simon should not notice that my fingers had begun to shake. In spite of the chicken curry and the jasmine tea I felt empty in the pit of my stomach.

"What did you want us to know?"

"Rima wants to tell you herself – as a surprise."

"No!"

"Chick . . ." His eyes were troubled, but I wasn't going to make it easy for him.

"*You* tell me! You tell me . . . now."

Under the table-cloth my hands met and clasped. They didn't feel like my own hands at all. They were strangers to one another, cold and clammy. I hated them for their dampness and their fear. Go on, Simon, club me, and get it over! It was as if he had said it already. Maybe I heard his thought before his voice made truth and fact of it.

"When Rima comes back from Florence next year we're going to be married."

It was curious that I should still be sitting there with the sun on my hair, on my naked undefended face, that I should be saying quietly: "She's always wanted you. Not as a brother. She's always known that one day she would marry you."

He said slowly, "Even as a child she was grown up. She took short cuts to all the fundamental facts of life. She knew instinctively so much that I had to learn bit by bit."

"She was sure of this – about wanting you, about intending to have you – even when we were kids. She told me so – one day at Loire – when we were thirteen."

His eyes had grown cold and indignant, as if I had insulted her. In a way that helped. But I knew that I must keep it short and get away. Words were dangerous. You started to say something and it was too much for you. It broke you down. Just now my voice had trembled. Keep the words few and short. Then get away. Simon must never know how much this hurt. Nor Rima.

"Does Aunt Kate approve? Uncle Gideon?"

"Yes."

"They've wanted it too. For a long time."

I dared not look at him. I dragged my right hand from the icy grasp of my left and picked up my half-smoked cigarette. Steady now!

"It's out," said Simon. "You can't smoke that. It's dead. Don't try to relight it."

I sniffed at it. Yes, it was stale and dead, like the brief flame that had once flared between him and me. I crushed it into the ashtray and stood up.

"I've some shopping to do. I must go."

He paid the bill and followed me out into the sunny breeze. We got into his little car.

"Where shall I drop you?"

"Medical Centre. It's on your way."

Medical Centre was nearer than A. & B. I must get away. But there was something I must say first. Only a few seconds to go. He braked by the kerb outside the fountain between the docks and the city. Behind some hoardings the noise of the pneumatic drills screamed and throbbed into my nerves.

"Here you are, then. And, when Rima tells you and Jamie our news tonight, let it come as a surprise."

"Oh, I will."

He leaned across me to open the door nearest the pavement. Traffic swirled past us on his side of the circle with a swish of tyres. I felt his warmth, his arm over the front of my body, his shoulder against me as he found the handle and released it. The breaking point was very near. I must force myself to say it now. If I failed he'd know how it was with me.

"You'll be happy with Rima. Bless you both."

He smiled. "I know it. Thank you, Maxie."

I got out quickly and walked up Adderley Street, straight-backed, head up. I heard his little car accelerate and pass me as he swung right handed towards the car-park. Now a bus to Kloof Nek, to the mountain. There can be an interval between injury and pain. It was like that with me.

The pain was there, waiting for us to be alone so that it could strike with fangs of hate and jealousy. It was with me in the bus winding up to the Nek; it stepped out with me, shadow-close in the hot sun of early afternoon; it paused with me as I decided which way to go. Up the kloof or down into the glen? I turned into the shelter of the woods, and it went with me. All my life I would have to fight the pain and humiliation of Rima's victory.

I stayed a long time among the oaks, till the sun sank into the sea in fiery splendour, and at last I climbed the steep woodland path and crossed the kloof to Rosevale. I slipped up to my room without being seen. Thank God Rima and I had never shared a room here!

When I looked into the mirror I was frightened at what I saw. Surely that sick spent face was never mine? Could youth and charm die at a single blow? It wasn't a pretty reflection that stared back at me.

"You can take it!" I told the pale image. "Be proud! If you're proud you're brave and you can take anything! Wash your face and pull yourself together!"

Simon's flat was at Clifton, less than ten minutes from Rosevale, right above the sea. Rima's touch was there. Not in the colours. Those were Simon's. So was the modern plainness and comfort. But there were panels of birds she had painted, sunbirds among proteas, effective as Japanese scrolls in their bare simplicity. And her Rain Goddess brooded in a corner of the room. It had been carved from the first wood Simon had ever given her – maroela wood from the north. It glowed with its own smooth brown life, the product of a tree bound up with strange fertility rites. Over the open fireplace was a picture I had never seen. It was austerely framed and it bore Rima's signature, but, in any case, I'd have recognised it as hers. It had her unmistakable "feel" of Africa. A buck, dappled by the shade of leaves, stood in a glade. It seemed frozen in an attitude of watchful suspicion. Yet it was helpless too, for along the branch above it crouched a leopard about to spring.

Jamie stared at it, fascinated.

"The buck. It's a haunting picture, Rima. A bit scary. The buck – that's what the Native witch-doctor calls his victim, the person picked out for a medicine murder – for human sacrifice."

She moved to his side.

"I didn't think of it like that. It was just a design of light and shadow, nature's camouflage. Funny, Maxie and I were talking about ritual murder only yesterday. Bantu sorcery seems to find its way into all my work, whether I want it or not. That's why I must go to Italy and change the whole metabolism of my art. I desperately need a classical period." She laughed, but she meant what she said.

We had drinks on the covered glass-enclosed balcony that was like an extra room. Simon had mixed champagne cocktails.

"To celebrate Rima's birthday and Maxie's homecoming?" smiled Jamie.

"All that and heaven too," laughed Rima. "We have a secret. We wanted you two to be the first to know. The only ones to know – till I come back from Europe."

She put out her hand to Simon. She had never been more vibrant or more seductive. Her hair, her skin, her eyes glowed. I felt that if the night were dark she would still shine through the gloom with this strange inner radiance. But I wanted to call out, "Keep your secret! Don't tell us!" I sensed, as I had done long ago at Loire, that the knowledge of her secret was a trap, the "No Trespassers" warning. But Jamie gasped, as if her new luminous quality had winded him. She put her hand in Simon's.

"We're engaged. When I come home from abroad we'll announce it, and very soon after that we'll be married."

We raised our glasses to them.

"It's a surprise," said Jamie. "Yet it's not. It's somehow right. *Veels geluk*, Simon and Rima. Good luck to you both and happiness always."

"That goes for me too. Every word of it."

I said it gaily. The devil was in me. This was the second time Rima had tied my hands and tossed me over to Jamie.

Jamie put down his glass and took her in his arms and hugged her. Her bright hair was splashed against his dinner jacket, and her muffled laughter was young and full of excitement. I looked from them to Simon.

"Do I kiss you good luck?"

Was he piqued by Rima in Jamie's arms, or did he find my mood infectious?

"Indeed you do!"

But he kissed me as if I were a child he loved. His lips were soft. I let my mouth rest against them, let it give a certain small quirk he knew as I pressed myself closer to him so that he should feel the shape of me, the sharpness and the softness. I heard him whisper, "Chick!" under his breath. He never called me that in front of anyone. He clasped me very tightly for a second, no longer as if I were a child. The fresh scent of his shaving lotion was on his skin and I longed to raise my hand and run it up from the back of his neck through his crisp hair. But Rima was saying "Hey! Break it up!" And she had stopped laughing. I looked up at him as he let me go.

"Good luck. Be happy!"

Jamie brought the champagne bottle and refilled my glass.

"We just need Claude," he said. "What a pity Claude isn't here with a girl of his own to complete our party."

"Yes," said Rima. "We miss Claude."

Her eyes met mine with a guarded look. Another secret. There were too many secrets between Rima and me.

22

RETURN TO LOIRE

I WOKE EARLY on Saturday morning. The birds were singing and the growing light streamed through the open window. I never sleep with my curtains drawn except when it's stormy.

My room looked east, and the bones of the mountain glowed pink in the sunrise, deceptively near and exactly chiselled, every rock and tree separate. This was what Rima and I called its "stereoscopic mood". The strengthening sunshine caught the roses on my dressing-table, and my delight in all these things cascaded over the dark heavy despondency that lay like a boulder in my chest.

Corinne brought my tea at seven, and I got up and dressed for breakfast. Jamie was coming for me soon after ten when he'd completed some business in Cape Town.

Aunt Kate was the only one in the dining-room when I went down. "Uncle Gideon's left already," she said. "And Rima's still asleep. Corinne'll take up her coffee and toast later."

After breakfast we went into the sunporch and she sank into the garden-swing and patted the cushion beside her invitingly. She wanted to talk.

Aunt Kate loved what she called "a nice little chat". I rather dreaded this one. Showing enthusiasm about Rima and Simon's private engagement wasn't going to be easy, but it was one of the things I must learn to do. I'd reached that conclusion yesterday afternoon in the glen.

"Were you surprised when they told you?" she asked.

"Not really. But, yes, perhaps in a way I was."

"How do you mean?"

"If they want to be engaged why not do it properly and tell the world? Or leave it alone altogether for the time being?"

She hesitated before answering.

"It's Rima's art. If it weren't for that, they could get married right away. We'd raise no objections. But Rima takes her art very seriously, as you know—"

"So she should. It's not merely good. Even I can see that she has something quite special."

"Her teachers have great faith in her talent. In fact, they seem to think it may be more than talent. She's set her heart on studying in Florence for several months at least. Perhaps longer. And her father didn't want the engagement announced till after her return. He didn't want her tied. He regards absence from Simon as a sort of test. After all, Rima's very young and she might change her mind."

"She won't."

"You sound very sure."

"I am."

"Frankly, I am too. But Gideon wants her to feel perfectly free while she's away."

"How about Simon?"

Aunt Kate glanced at me with a quick shrewd look that reminded me of my mother.

"He'll be free too, of course."

"Not quite so free – with Jamie and me in the know." The joking words were barbed, but Aunt Kate didn't seem to notice.

"Rima insisted on telling you."

"We've always confided in each other. She was thirteen when she told me she meant to marry Simon."

"She's a strange girl. Even as a child she had a purpose in life. Your friendship has been important to Rima. She's never had masses of friends of her own age and sex, like other girls."

"We've been brought up as sisters."

"One needs an intimate woman friend. Your mother and I were like you and Rima. We still are – when we get the chance. Nothing makes any difference. We can always pick up where we left off. Perhaps because the same things make us laugh."

She looked so happy that I hated myself for my resentment against her daughter. I might feel that Rima had been too clever for me, that she'd cheated, but I knew very well that plain jealousy lay at the root of the feeling.

"Rima and I laugh at the same things, too. And we also pick up where we left off. Are you pleased about Rima and Simon, Aunt Kate?"

"Delighted. So is your uncle. He's prepared to trust his business and his daughter to Simon. I can't say more."

We smiled. My aunt had few illusions about her husband.

"And, of course," she added, "it's marvellous for him to think that any son of theirs would be Antrobus in blood as well as name."

I'd always known that would mean a lot to Uncle Gideon, but I didn't want to think about it. As I made a move to rise Aunt Kate put out a restraining hand.

"Just a moment, dear. There's something I'd like to get set."

She's going to nail me down, I thought. She's like Mummie in wanting things cut and dried. I knew the signs.

"This is your second home, Maxie. You must feel that so long as you're working at A. & B. you're more than welcome to live here. In fact, I think Rocky's already invited you!"

I tried to answer her affectionate smile, but I was seized with panic, and words tumbled out.

"It's wonderful of you, but I must stand on my own feet . . . be quite independent. I must stop being a parasite, Aunt Kate—"

"But if you know you're wanted, surely you wouldn't—"

"It's something I can't explain. Don't think I'm ungrateful. I couldn't bear to hurt you . . ."

I broke off, my face turned away from her, conscious that I was in what my mother called one of my "emotional states". But, if Aunt Kate was hurt or disappointed in me, she didn't give it away. She said in a practical voice.

"Don't upset yourself, Maxie. Of course I understand your need to spread your wings. That's why we let Simon go – willingly. He felt that way too. Anyway, my dear, if you want to make Rosevale your headquarters while you're hunting for a flatlet – or whatever it is you have in mind – remember there's always a big welcome for you here."

She rose from the swing lightly, like a young woman.

"I have to remember not to grunt when I get out of that swing. I'm getting fat."

"You're just right."

"And you could do with a few extra pounds, my girl. That's what happens when you young people are on your own. You starve because you're too lazy or too occupied to cook."

When I went up to my room I found Rima sitting in my bed with a breakfast tray on her lap and Pim, the poodle, curled up at her feet. He gave me a sulky look. Rima was the only person who allowed him onto her bed.

"I came in to find you, and decided to wait for you in the most comfortable place. I told Corinne to bring two cups. You'll have some more coffee?"

She poured it, strong and not too sweet, the way I like it.

"Thanks," I said. "Your mother's been talking to me."

Her eyes were clear and questioning, wide-set under the fluffy hair. Her beautiful mouth was amused.

"I suppose she's tackled you about staying at Rosevale?"

"Yes."

"You're kicking at the idea."

She knows, I thought. She knows why I'm kicking. She knows we love the same man, but neither of us will ever admit it. It's the one barrier between us – strong but invisible.

"She was sweet. She says I'm to do as I like. Stay here while I find somewhere of my own. She's terribly generous—"

"She's very fond of you."

"They're thrilled about you and Simon."

"I know. Daddy's keen to have us live in Kloof Cottage up on the Nek. It's Rosevale property, so he controls the tenancy. It's near my studio. It would do rather well."

There was a tap on the door and Corinne came to tell us that Mr Jamie was downstairs.

"Shall I take your suitcase, Miss Maxie?"

"Please. And say I'll be down in a minute."

Rima looked after the girl's trim figure.

"Mom could spare her," she said. "Old Annie always threatens to retire and then does a prima donna act and stays on. If Corinne marries Lenno the two of them could work for Simon and me. He could do the garden and outside work, and Corinne could be cook-general."

"She couldn't marry Lenno! Old Lizzie'd throw a fit."

"Old Lizzie's at Bergplaas. That's a long way from Cape Town. Her fit would lose its effect. So would her threats. Corinne talks to me and I talk to her. Nobody gives much away, but ideas go out on the air. Don't underrate the power of ideas!"

"It's not fair, Rima. You said yourself it would be a backward step for a Coloured to marry a Bantu."

"This is the exception that proves the rule. The Coloureds can go either way. They are the people of no-man's-land. The neutrals. And Lenno's not just any Bantu. He's a magnificent specimen of humanity, bursting with charm and virility. No wonder Corinne's got him under her skin."

"You're selfish. You're not thinking of them. They're just two servants you'd find it convenient to have."

She fidgeted. "Do take this darn tray. It's giving me claustrophobia."

As I took it from her and put it outside on the landing table, Aunt Kate called up the stairs.

"Maxie! Jamie says you should be on your way."

"Coming in a second."

I went back into the bedroom. The dog still lay on the bed, but Rima was standing by the window in her yellow silk kimono. Heavy clusters of wistaria flowers trembled behind her, their scent the very essence of spring. I returned to the attack.

"Rima, you'd do anything for your own convenience – your own entertainment. You've no more conscience than a cat. But, I beg you, don't encourage this thing between Corinne and Lenno! Send her back to the farm—"

"Do you think for one instant that she'd go? She's a city person now. So is Lenno. You can't rusticate them all over again. It's much too late. You know that perfectly well."

I had to admit that she was right, but, as I stared at my own bare arms, I saw the goose-pimples rising, although the day was warm and the sun was on us. Her gaze followed mine, and she ran her strong finger-tips over my skin.

"How curious! I believe you still associate Corinne with fear and danger and pain. I remember now. You hated her coming here in the first place. I thought you'd got over that years ago."

"I had. This is different."

"Your burnt back, Jamie's burnt hands, the dark little house and old Lizzie . . ."

"No, that's finished and forgotten. It's them I'm thinking about – Corinne and Lenno."

"Marrying against the will of his tribe – against the social sanctions of her people. Like Claude and Fara. You know something, I daresay you unconsciously link these two affairs in your own mind. You instinctively feel that both are dangerous."

"If that's so I could be right."

"Pooh, why worry? It may never get that far with either couple. Especially this pair here. Brown folk are more sensible than White. The man generally prefers to marry the girl after he's put her in the family way. Then he's sure she's not barren. That makes a lot of sense to me."

My arms were smooth again. Under the window Aunt Kate was showing Jamie the roses. She looked up and waved to us, and Jamie did likewise.

"I can't come down," Rima sang out. "I'm not dressed."

I left her calling gaily through the window, her voice sweet and clear as a bird's. By the time I was downstairs my moment of foreboding had passed. Lenno was weeding the lawn. He was in no part a crocodile. He was very much a fine supple young man, ebony in the sun, crooning to himself as he worked.

Jamie drove fast. Past the shanty settlement towards the far amethyst mountains. The fruit trees were all in blossom; the blue, white and yellow lupins spread their vivid carpets across the landscape; and the many-coloured wild flowers bloomed in the bush and the fields. The vineyards had just begun to show leaf; the olive groves changed from smoke-grey to shining pewter with every breath of wind; and the guava orchards were already in fruit. Poplar and cypress windbreaks cut the valley into cultivated patterns and the Berg River threaded it with green-fringed silver. Once we had crossed it we ran into more open country, into the sheep, cattle and grainlands of the long arm reaching up towards the furthest foothills of the first mountain range dividing the coastal belt from the uplands and the Karoo. Here farms were bigger, orchards and vineyards fewer, and trees sparser, except for the oaks and gums sheltering scattered homesteads, the cool charm of great willows mirrored in gleaming dams, and my father's young plantations.

Children hung on the farm gates, and opened them for us, skipping with joy, and shouting greetings to "baas Jamie and Miss Maxie" as I threw them sweets and pennies. Seeing them again was tremendously thrilling.

"Jamie," I said. "Now I'm really home!"

"You're very pretty when you're happy."

He didn't fling flattery around. This golden mountain at my side had to be considerably impressed in order to produce so much as a small grey mouse of a compliment. Jamie, like most Afrikaners, could burst into an oration, if he were sufficiently moved, but small talk wasn't in his line. When he thought I looked good it was there in his eyes. I'd teased him about it that summer in England. Once I'd said, "You're looking at me as if I were a stand of ripe wheat."

He'd grinned. "Ready for the harvester." And he'd kissed me with the enthusiastic vigour he brought to his love-making.

He'd become necessary to me that hot green summer. In a way, I suppose, for those few months I'd been "his girl". On the ship too. When he saw that it worried me he had stopped talking about marriage. I'd found his company a relief from my brother's. Although my mind agreed with Claude's multi-racial attitude and way of life, my instinct went with Jamie, who quite frankly preferred to stick to his own kind.

"To me," he'd said, "those exotic friendships of your brother's would be artificial. I am as I am."

"And as your father and your grandfather were before you. Amen."

Claude and Jamie were often more tolerant of one another than I was of either of them. Perhaps they were too different in outlook to clash, whereas I stood somewhere between the two. Neither expected the other to conform, yet each hoped for full understanding from me.

"Jamie's a *boer* to his bone-marrow," Claude said of him. "And I mean that literally. He's a natural born farmer. He'll never make a hash of it as I should if I tried. He's mighty sure of himself when his feet are on the mealie-lands. No split mind. No sense of guilt. His labour, in his view, belongs on Bergplaas as much as he does himself. He'll call the *volkies babiaans* and *pampoens* and *skelms* and worse, he'll lash out their tot of wine and crack a joke with them and take it for granted that they know damn well that Bergplaas is the universal provider – for their families as well as his own – and in the long run they'll be content because they'll know who's *baas*, and they know when they're well off."

Claude sincerely envied the natural way in which Jamie fitted into the pastoral frame predestined for him.

Sometimes, when I was chilled by my brother's objective approach to life, I'd grumble to Jamie.

"Claude could live in the wastes of Antarctica or a desert. He doesn't need scenery or a climate. He hasn't even a sense of beauty."

"He'll develop that – when he meets the right girl. For the rest, he feeds off his intellect. He's a man of the mind. You need a different diet."

"What do I . . . feed off?"

"*Og*, you, my Maxie! You feed off your feelings and your love of life."

And of Loire, I might add. Now, after two years, the sight of the old house in the morning shade of its oaks poured contentment into every bit of me. With Loire to come back to nothing would ever be unbearable.

As we turned out of the blue-gum avenue into the white gates of the homestead, we met my mother's turkeys meandering round the garden at their own sweet will, as they had always been allowed to do, and Daddy's springer spaniels pounded round the house to bark at the car, and then, as we got out, to leap all over me with whines of eager recognition after the first few moments of uncertainty.

I flung myself into Daddy's arms. "I can't wait to ride all over the farm!"

My mother's eyes shone. "I wonder what she'll think of Snow-White, Etienne?"

"Ssh . . . that's a surprise. We'll take the horses out after tea – this very afternoon."

I turned to Jamie. "Will you be coming?"

He shook his head. "*Nee*, Maxie. You go alone with your pa today. Tomorrow you can come with me and see Ferdinand. This afternoon he's got to start meeting the right people."

So Daddy and I rode out alone together in the cool of the evening, my favourite time of day. I was mounted on Snow-White, his gift to me, the elegant spirited little mare sired by Snow and born and bred on Loire. The big roan had died, and Daddy rode Snow, the stallion so dear to my heart.

"Which round do you want to make, Maxie?" he asked.

"The vineyards and the lower camps and paddocks first, and then up into the berg and home by the dam. I'm longing to see the foals and ostriches, and the buck coming to the water at sunset. How good it is to be home!"

He was hatless and his thatch of hair was as white as Snow's flowing mane. The gold filling in his tooth glinted merrily, but the buoyant quality of his smile had gone. It no longer had the effect of swinging one's spirit high into the air with the laughing elation of a child lifted, tossed and caught again by powerful loving hands.

"It's fine to have you back. We need you."

He questioned me a lot about Claude, but I trod cautiously over ground I knew to be dangerous. One thing I could say with perfect truth. My brother was working hard and doing well in his firm. Both his pay and his prestige were high.

"And you, my child? Do you really fancy yourself as a career girl?"

"Yes," I said with more firmness than I felt. "Uncle Gideon's taking the idea of training me for a buyer quite seriously. When that happens it'll be the world at my feet."

"*Couleur de rose.*"

But, though his eyes mocked me gently, he was delighted when I told him of my new job at A. & B.

"You've worked for it," he said, "and you've shown forethought – all along the line. But you owe a good deal to Simon."

"I know."

"Will you live at Rosevale? That's what your mother hopes."

"Only till I find somewhere of my own – a tiny bachelor-girl flat."

"No more supervision?"

"I want to be on my own."

"You've had a taste of freedom. In England. You ran around quite a bit with Jamie, didn't you? Your mother's relatives took trouble to write and say that they approved of 'Maxie's young man'."

"Six thousand miles of ocean between us – but gossip gets here before me!" I felt the colour rise in my cheeks. "Jamie had a car and seeing the countryside with him was more fun than trekking round by myself. That's all there was to it."

"Of course. In any case, we're very fond of Jamie."

The All Clear. Thanks very much, dear Daddy. But I'll do my own picking when the time comes. At the moment my heart's quite empty. Dreadfully empty.

We were up in the foothills now, skirting the marshes. Westwards we could see right across the valley to the blue glimmer of the sea seventy miles away. Table Mountain and its Peaks were dwarfed by distance and gilded by the setting sun. Already some of the grainlands were beginning to turn amber. All round us furtive wild life was quickening. A skein of geese flew down towards the dam. South of us, a large flock of sheep, led by a huge hamel with a bell round his neck, moved down from the hill. We reined in our horses as the shepherds drove the jostling animals past us.

"Those aren't our shepherds."

"Nor our sheep," said my father. "The North-West Cape has had a murderous drought – years of it. These past months there's been the biggest sheep and cattle lift ever known. Our valley's too densely culti-vated to spare much grazing, but out here it's possible to help a few flocks."

I'd heard about the long drought and the nation-wide effort to save the drought-stricken farmers from ruin, but, even so, after the long rainless years of struggle, hope and prayer, hundreds of them were in a desperate plight.

"We're so lucky here," I said. "Always a reasonable rainfall. I'm so glad you can graze those poor sheep on Loire land."

"Maxie," said Daddy, after a long pause. "Those sheep are not on Loire land."

If he had leaned out of the saddle and struck at me with his *sjambok* I could not have been more shocked.

The mare stood quietly, but Snow fumed and fretted while the red dust rose from the scrub as the sheep milled in the direction of the old Bergplaas border a mile to the south of us. It was extremely still, except for the cries of the young shepherds, the bell of the big hamel, and the pawing and snorting of Snow. At last I looked straight at my father and met his unwilling eyes.

"I don't understand, Daddy. If it's not our land, whose is it?"

"Gert Vermeulen's," said my father.

23

ON MY OWN

"**B**UT HOW IS IT that Gert Vermeulen is in a position to buy when Daddy has to sell?" I asked my mother. "Loire and Bergplaas . . . side by side . . . if one can do well, surely the other—"

"Look, Maxie, the answer's terribly simple, but I hate giving it."

Mummie ran her fingers through her short hair in the harassed gesture I knew so well. We were sitting out on the loggia after supper, and the scent of jasmine was overpowering.

Daddy had gone to his office, sayinghe had some business that needed attention.

"I suppose you mean *Oom* Gert's a better farmer than Daddy."

"In a nutshell, yes. But life isn't contained in nutshells. There's so much – so much! Experience, disposition, even, perhaps, incentive. Daddy and *Oom* Gert are farming the same sort of land under the same conditions, and there's no real excuse for failure here, like those poor devils in the drought areas. But your father makes mistakes. He's over-optimistic and too trusting. He delegates authority to the wrong people. And he's fundamentally idle. There, now I've said it!"

She heaved a sigh of relief, and I was aware once more of her need to confide in me, of her loneliness and her loyalty. She'd never speak like this of Daddy to anyone but me. Not even to Aunt Kate – certainly not to Aunt Kate whose own husband made a success of everything he touched. I knew that Mummie was right. Daddy had the faults of his virtues. He was generous and happy-go-lucky and he had always detested the commercial side of farming, probably because he feared his own limitations. I think my father regarded his land in much the same way as a Bantu Chief regards his cattle – as an asset to enhance his personal prestige, to be gazed at, tended, loved and admired for itself alone. No self-respecting Bantu ever thinks of his herd as so much beef or hide worth such and such a sum when slaughtered, it is to him a thing of living beauty to be cherished and increased, the reflection of his standing in his community. Loire, to Daddy was a family glory, a proud heritage in his keeping. He felt that he was letting it down.

"Perhaps he lost touch during the war," I suggested.

My mother gave her sharp little laugh.

"If Gert Vermeulen had been a prisoner of war he'd have spent his time mugging up agriculture, diseases of stock and crops, the latest methods of soil conservation and so on and so on. But your father studied the mythology of Ancient Greece. He said it relaxed him."

"*Oom* Gert got a long start on Daddy during those five years," I said resentfully.

"Without his help we'd have been sunk. It was he who made it possible for a city-bred nitwit – me – to keep this place on its feet."

Her eyes flashed in their deeply hollowed sockets, and suddenly I saw her as she must have been then. Young, attractive, determined, and very dependent on her middle-aged neighbour for help. He'd have been about forty then – tanned, tough, with Jamie's wheat fair hair and deep furry voice. *Mutti*, a few years older than her husband, would have been plump and maternal already, the mother of a large family of which Jamie was the youngest. Had she possibly been plagued by jealousy? Had my mother been tormented by a pent up physical need for a man? Curious how one took one's elders for granted. They too had been young.

"When your father came back from the war he took the reins into his hands with more energy than wisdom. I got on with raising poultry. Up to a point we did all right. But, when we came back from Italy, after that jaunt of ours, we found there'd been neglect and mismanagement. Daddy had placed too much faith in the foreman. Gert Vermeulen doesn't go gadding about and leaving *his* farm to underlings to run for him. That's the long and the short of it."

"So now what?"

"So now we're selling off land. And what we still own is bonded. Meanwhile Daddy plays the horses in hopes of easy money."

"Your poultry pays?"

"Oh, yes. *My* efforts show a profit."

"And there's your income from A. & B. – your investments in the firm."

"My investments in the firm have gone into Loire long ago. Down the drain – except for a small block of shares Uncle Gideon just about forced me to keep. I get the dividends on those and I'll hang onto them, come hell or high water. I love Loire and I love your father, but between them they're making an old woman of me before my time."

The grandfather clock struck ten and Mummie rose to go indoors.

"We mustn't judge your father too harshly," she added. "When Claude turned his back on Loire, something died in Etienne."

She stood waiting for me to reassure her, hoping to hear that Claude intended to return. I had no consoling answer for her. Poor darling, she didn't know the half of it!

The weeks before Christmas flew.

A. & B. always made a big thing of the Christmas season, as much for its employees and their families as for its customers. Uncle Gideon called me into his office and explained that, as one of the family, it was my duty to be closely connected with all the firm's welfare and entertainments.

"Especially the non-European children's Christmas party and sports. They look forward to it all the year, and it has to be the tops. The sports part of the show is always run by Mr September. He's splendid. You know who I mean? In Upholstery."

"I know, Uncle Gideon. I've been meaning to hunt him out anyway – to give him news of his daughter."

"The papers do plenty of that," he said drily.

I found Mr September alone in the workroom. The Malay polisher had gone to lunch and the tall Coloured man was preparing to follow him when I entered. The place smelt of horsehair, plush and polish, a shabby Victorian emanation of old crocks awaiting repair and re-covering. I held out my hand.

"Mr September? I'm Miss Lamotte. I saw your daughter in England and promised to give you all sorts of messages from her."

He wiped his fingers carefully on a chintz remnant before shaking hands with me. He was light-complexioned with hawk features and wavy blue-black hair. His eyes filled with pride and joy at mention of Fara. I wondered how much he knew about her affair with my brother.

"Glad to meet you, Miss Lamotte. We've been hearing a lot about you from Fara."

"She's worked terribly hard and deserves every bit of her great success. Shall we sit down for a few minutes?"

We sat on two threadbare arm-chairs waiting their turn to be re-upholstered. I felt stiff and ill at ease. If anyone were to come in now and see us Mr September would be frowned upon as "too big for his boots".

Yet, if he had not been Coloured, I would simply have said, "I'm Fara's friend, Maxie," and we'd have gone from there. It was all right to talk to him about jobs to be done, about the Children's Christmas Party, or anything else to do with his work, but the "equal footing" attitude here in Cape Town, in the family stronghold of A. & B., didn't quite come off. He offered me a cigarette, and, although I smoked very little at that time, I took one from the packet.

"They're not what you're used to. Not the best brand."

"I wouldn't know the difference."

He gave me a light.

"Fara's a good daughter, Miss Lamotte. She wants us to go overseas – the wife and me. She says the holiday will do us good, and she can afford to treat us. What do you think of the idea?"

"That's what she said I must tell you – that she really means it."

He looked at me with the sad eyes of a people never quite sure of themselves.

"We'd hinder her. How could we keep up with her – with her friends?"

What could I say? He was sensitive. Everything in his whole existence had hammered the Colour bar like a brand into his soul. I spoke the truth.

"Mr September, the Colour bar's on its way out – everywhere. Fara lives in an atmosphere where talent is the test."

He smiled. "Fara has the talent, sure. But what have we? *Niks.*"

"If you want to go and share her success, *go!* That's her message to you and her mother. Now I've given it and I can't do more."

Yet, even as I said it, I wondered if I was being fair to Fara. Or even to Claude. One member of such a family might reach the top, but it could be dizzy going for the others.

"Are you still in your house in Sea Point?" I asked.

"Yes. They haven't thrown us out yet. Our poor old neighbour, *Oupa* Hendricks, hanged himself from the fig-tree in his garden. That sort of thing makes the authorities take a deep breath before they get on with moving people around *sommer soos* sheep – here the black ones, there the white ones. The Hendricks family lived in that little *huisie* for over a hundred years – since the days of the first Hendricks to get his freedom . . . a slave no longer . . ."

His voice lifted and broke on a note of cynical doubt. Then he threw me a sudden penetrating glance.

"How would *your* father feel, Miss Maxie, if he was told to clear out of *his* home – out of that fine farm in the Paarl Valley?"

It had been "Miss Lamotte", and the change to "Miss Maxie" was a significant step towards informality. So was the trend of the conversation. It seemed he knew all about us, who I was and where I came from. Did he know the rest – the Claude and Fara part of it?

"It would be very hard for my folk to part with Loire," I said. "My ancestors found freedom there – like *Oupa* Hendricks' ancestors found it in your lane. Only for my people it meant freedom to worship God in their own way. I'm young and stupid, Mr September, but I've learnt that freedom is a word with many meanings."

"If you've learnt that you aren't stupid, my young lady. Your parents must be very happy to have you home. All the same, I suppose they wish their son would come back too. A father needs his son as he gets older, specially on a farm."

His sad, dog's eyes were full of wisdom; and questioning too. He knows, I thought. He didn't say that out of the blue. He knows that love of Fara may cost my brother the right to Loire.

I made a move to go, and he sprang to his feet with wiry agility. I remembered that Mr September had been a noted athlete in his day.

"It was nice of you to seek me out," he said. "I 'preciate it."

"We'll be meeting soon again – at the Christmas party."

"The party for the non-European children. Yes, Miss Maxie."

The slight, perhaps unintentional, snub flicked me as we walked down the stairs together to the Staff Canteens. Over one door was printed "NON-EUROPEANS" and over the other "EUROPEANS". Antrobus & Beeford, like any other firm, had to comply with the regulations.

"You go your way," he said. "I go mine. Bye-bye."

I had forgotten the Cape "bye-bye", the end of every meeting and telephone conversation. As I left him standing there outside the non-European Canteen I felt sorry and ashamed. It seemed strange that one of the many rules expressly intended to safeguard White dignity should leave me with this second rate feeling, as if I, not he, were the one whose value as a human being had been diminished.

I had eaten my sandwiches and was sipping a cup of piping hot coffee when Simon joined me.

"Where are you, Maxie? Not in this canteen; that's sure. Your spirit's gone wool-gathering."

I shook off my mood of abstraction as he sat opposite me.

"How's the flat hunt?" he asked.

"I've found somewhere."

"Tell me more."

"It's a dog-kennel by your standards, but it's just what I want. At Mouille Point. One big all purpose room – living and sleeping combined – a kitchenette and bath. Unfurnished and inexpensive. I can furnish it from Loire. It'll need one or two new things, like curtains and a bed-cover, but those odds and ends won't break me."

"Is it on the sea side?"

"Yes. And it's a powerful strong seaweed-scented sea – much more ozone than your Clifton sea – and the freshness of it comes pouring in through the windows. Most of one wall is window. It's no distance from town, and I'm working out my finances to see if I can run to a motor-scooter. Then I'll be independent of buses."

"When d'you plan to move in?"

"Next week."

"Our van lift could bring your stuff from Loire. There's always transport coming from the north. Let me know the details and we'll make a plan."

Before long I was settled in. The things I brought from Loire fitted happily into the modern flatlet. The "all purposes" room was big enough to absorb them. There was an old stinkwood and yellowwood chest of drawers and a useful and decorative camphor-lined bride-chest to match. My folding dining-table was antique too – a trek-table that had made many journeys under the tented hood of an ox-wagon. Daddy had given me one of his Chinese blue and white carpets and some priceless Delft plates for a wall alcove above a bookcase. There were built in cupboards for my few clothes and possessions, and I was delighted with the gay effect of my new chintz curtains and divan cover.

Rima approved everything.

"It's full of character. It really is you. And that hyacinth chintz is just right with the view of sea and sky outside."

We were sitting on the cushioned window-seat. It was past six o'clock anb Simon was coming to fetch us to dinner at Rosevale. Rima had a glass of bitter lemon beside her. She seldom touched hard alcohol. Only wine.

"That picture – how well I remember dashing that off! It was a peace offering."

"I love it. At first I couldn't make up my mind whether to leave it in my bedroom at home or bring it here. Then I found I must have it with me. You were a kid when you did it, but it has something quite special."

She studied it, her eyes narrowed. The western light fell full on the white charger so haughtily carrying his burden of a knight and a small fair maiden. The storm-tossed flurry of leaves in the fitful sunshine breathed the same wayward life as the horse and his rider.

"It's a long time since I've seen it," she said thoughtfully. "I doubt if I've ever really looked at it since I did it. But I see what you mean – the something special—"

She broke off, and I said eagerly. "What is it? Can you analyse its quality?"

"The warrior horse and the knight have a terrific look of Simon – that spirited look he shares with your father's stallion, Snow. And the slip of a girl – the sickle moon of a girl . . ."

"Yes?"

She shrugged her shoulders and smiled. "Let that pass. It's signed with the dove of peace."

"Perhaps it signifies our childhood."

"Adolescence. Holidays at Loire. Quarrelling and making up."

And Simon between us, I thought, then as now.

"Is Simon invited to Loire for Christmas and New Year?" asked Rima.

"If he wants to come, of course." I said it carelessly, as if it didn't matter. Stupid. Rima's eyes widened. I had so much to learn.

However, Simon didn't come to Loire.

After Rima and her parents sailed for Europe in December he went to Durban to stay with Charlie and Linda Beeford. Charlie, one of my many Beeford cousins, was the manager of our Durban branch.

So our Christmas at Loire was a quiet one. There was the usual tree for the children, of course, with toys and a box of goodies for each child and a *braaivleis* for everybody afterwards. It had always been so, and, although the shadow of debt lay over Loire, outwardly nothing was changed. On Christmas morning there was a wonderful present for me. Mummie had bought me the much coveted motor-scooter which, after all, I hadn't been able to afford.

"But Mummie, you can't afford it either!" I gasped.

Her face was alight with pleasure. "It's out of my poultry savings, and it's money well spent. I'm glad you're pleased—"

"Pleased! It'll make all the difference."

"Jamie's going to teach you its tricks. He chose it."

So the lovely mare, Snow-White, my father's homecoming gift, had a noisy rival in my affections.

On New Year's Eve Jamie and I were invited to a dance given by the owners of a beautiful farm near Somerset West, where so many historic homes of the Cape stand on the vine-clothed slopes between the mountains and the sea.

The lovely old homestead was floodlit, silver white in its grove of magnificent trees. It had been the delight and extravagance of one of the earliest Dutch Governors of the Cape.

We danced in the lofty raftered *agterkamer* and out onto a wide paved terrace leading down to lawns and flower gardens. Fairy lights hung like clusters of many-coloured grapes from shadowy boughs and rose-covered arbours; magnolias glimmered among their dark glossy leaves, and pale moonflowers distilled their sweetness into the night.

After the supper-dance we strolled down to the long white wall that had once been a line of defence against the marauding Brown cattle thieves. Now it was just a boundary parapet.

Jamie spread a clean handkerchief for me to sit on, and put his hands on either side of my waist to lift me up.

"How light you are! Like a dancer."

He stood beside me, his head on a level with my heart. From up at the house we could hear the throb of the three-piece band.

"Could there be anywhere more glamorous?" I said.

"It's fine. But it's not my idea of a home. Or a farm."

"Whyever not? It's both, in a big way."

"No. It's too much of a show place. A place like this eats huge fortunes. It's only kept alive by money made in some other concern – or inherited money. It doesn't support itself."

I thought of my mother's private fortune poured into Loire – down the drain – and of Bergplaas, a simple rambling house serving a flourishing farm. Bergplaas was unhampered by traditional obligations, unexploited by a continual flow of friends and visitors expecting to find the highest standards of "gracious living". Bergplaas hospitality was generous but homely. Loire was more pretentious, and seldom without weekend guests.

"Places like this live too much in the past," Jamie went on. "Their history throttles them. I want to build something good for the future – a dairy herd maybe that'll produce the best butter and cheese in the whole of the Cape. The best fruit, the best wheat, high grade wool – and to hell with it if the house hasn't got hand-wrought silver fittings on the doors and a gable by Thibault! Do I make you mad?"

"No, you don't make me mad. You're talking good sense."

Suddenly his arms were round me.

"I love you, Maxie. Help me build for the future!"

I made no answer and he buried his face in my breast. I looked down at his hair, pale in the starlight, and let my fingers stroke it silently. I felt the ardent heat of his face against my bare flesh and his lips covering my throat with kisses.

"I love you – I love you . . ." He said it in English and in his own home language, so rich in little words of love. He was very dear to me. I knew that we could build together for the future. But not yet. Not yet.

He drew me down and crushed me to him, and when at last he let me go I was weak and breathless with the force of his passion. The old panic rose in me, the horror of being driven into something for which I wasn't ready. Marriage, babies, the responsibility of a home and family. I'd lived on a farm, I knew how hard a farmer's wife had to work. I'd seen my mother at the end of the day, dog-tired from the endless chores that were never done. And I wasn't in love with Jamie.

"I'm not ready for marriage—"

"You will be one day. Soon you will be."

"No! I've a job that'll give me travel and the chance to live my own life before I settle down. I'm not willing to belong to you . . . or anyone else . . ." My voice trailed away on the lie.

"You don't love me?"

"Not enough to give up my freedom."

"All right," he said slowly. "We'll leave it alone."

Oh, God, I thought. I've lost him.

Up at the house the music had stopped and the ancient slave bell in its high white tower was clanging its message into the hot summer night. The Old Year was dying and the New Year was waiting to be born.

I seized Jamie's hand and we raced across the lawn, between the dreaming flower-beds, up to the lighted house. On the terrace the band had broken into Auld Lang Syne and we joined the widening circle, arms crossed, hands linked. I thought of Simon, wherever he might be this night; of Rima and my uncle and aunt somewhere in England, of my brother and his dark love in grey old London; and my eyes filled with the tears I could not wipe away because my hands were held and swinging to the rhythm of the sentimental song that old and young were singing together so lustily ". . . we'll tak' a cup o' kindness yet for the sake of Auld Lang Syne . . ."

Louder and louder the heavy slave bell pealed across the vineyards, ringing in the new year – the year of fate for my country. And for me.

Part 3

YEAR OF FATE

24

SOUTH-EASTER

IT WAS ONE of our nastiest February days, when pedestrians battle against the south-easter with their heads down, and motorists on the mountain road, or by the sea, feel their cars veer and shudder under the gusty impact of the wind, while the whole city – usually so clean and pleasant – is prey to a plague of demented scraps of paper whirling about in the gutters and the air as if every wastepaper-basket in Cape Town had just been emptied out of the window.

The summer was nearing its end and the grass of the Devil's Peak nature reserve, where the buck, zebra and wildebeeste graze, was dry and tawny. The dead oak leaves flew before the wind; ships groaned at their moorings or tossed out at sea among the white caps, and the fishing-boats stayed safe in harbour. But in the showrooms of A. & B. all was peace and customers came in out of the blast, sighed with relief, did their shopping and had to nerve themselves to go out again and face the elemental fury of the summer gale in Adderley Street.

Just after my lunch hour I saw Simon stride over to Miss Pratt's desk and exchange a few words with her. She called me at once.

"You're free for the rest of the day, Maxie. Mr Trevor-Antrobus wants you to help him check that everything at Rosevale is in apple-pie order for Mr and Mrs Antrobus's return tomorrow."

My scooter was in the garage for servicing, and, in any case, I hated riding it in rain or wind, so Simon ran me up to Rosevale in his car. I adored my scooter but it was a fair weather friend.

Strangely enough, although the Niagara of cloud poured unceasingly down the face of the mountain till it seemed that Rosevale must be engulfed in the snowy torrent, it always dispersed before it reached the garden. The big house rested so closely in the lee of nature's mighty rampart of rock and forest that the gale passed harmlessly over its head.

Rocky beamed as he let us into "Mizz Antbus' Rezzidence". He led us through the spacious rooms with pride. The windows had been cleaned, the silver shone, the floors and furniture had been polished, Corinne had arranged flowers as Aunt Kate loved to see them, and Goodwin had planned a welcome-home dinner that made our mouths water. Rocky chortled when I said so, and Goodwin's black face was gratified. They explained that we had been included in their catering as a matter of course.

"My master and madam will be sad to come home tomorrow without Miss Rima," said Rocky. "Master Simon an' Miss Maxie mus' keep us young now."

We laughed and accepted the invitation and the responsibility of producing youth about the house. Rocky always did the honours of "Antbus Rezz" with tact and in style. He was also an accomplished *major domo* with an eye to detail. He had arranged for Fatima, the Malay laundress, to be at Rosevale next day to meet Aunt Kate and help Corinne with unpacking, washing and pressing. Old Annie had retired at last and was living with a married niece in Kensington.

"With Miss Rima away, we can do without Annie," said Rocky smugly. "Annie ate and slept and Corinne did the work." Yet I felt that he would miss his old enemy. They had sharpened their tongues on one another for a quarter of a century.

"Leslie came back from our country yesterday," he added.

"Now it's Lenno's turn to go home," I suggested. But Rocky was too wise to take the bait. Lenno's private life had become something of a problem, and none of his countrymen were keen to be mixed up in it.

"Where shall I bring tea, Miss Maxie? The study or the drawing-room. It's too windy for the stoep."

"The old schoolroom."

His fat chuckle was knowing. "Miss Maxie always likes the old school-room because the animals is welcome there."

So we had tea in the bright shabby room that was full of memories of our childhood and of the joint young life we four had shared, Antrobus and Lamotte. Pim, the poodle, curled up on the shabby leather sofa, and Sam, the labrador, spread himself where we could hardly help falling over him. Trout jumped onto the tea-table and began washing. Simon smiled.

"This dear undisciplined room! Trout reminds me of Claude and that absurd cat in London – the one he adopted."

"They adopted each other. Rima used to say of Claude that he was a cat man. Goes his own way and cares for nobody."

"That's Claude all right. Where's it going to get him?"

"Heaven knows. I remember so well coming in here the night Uncle Gideon let fly at us when Claude drove Fara home in Rima's little Red Devil. We came by instinct. It was always our refuge – this room."

"Our ghosts'll wander here one day."

"More tea?"

He shook his head. "I think we ought to hunt out Leslie, and then we'll see if Lenno's looking after Rima's birds properly."

We found Leslie in the vegetable garden. He greeted us with the diffident grin that revealed an extravagant number of strong well-kept teeth. He twirled a blue cap in his narrow hands. His bright blue pullover was decorated with a striking red and yellow geometrical design, and his socks were the candy pink so much in favour with the city Bantu. But we knew at once by a certain sheepish look in his eye that he was going to borrow "littie-bittie money" from Simon.

"My heart is sore," said Leslie, after the usual polite preamble. "While I sleep, the train he stop at station and a man get off and take my bundle. All my things."

We did not doubt it. Everything happened to Leslie.

"He's accident prone," said Simon, with an amused glance at me as he took a pound from his wallet. "He's a trusting type too, not like Lenno who's a smart lad."

"How is everything at home?" I asked. "Your wife and family."

"They are well, Miss Maxie. But we must move to another place and my wife, she like too much her mother. She don't want to move."

Were they being pushed around by the Government "for their own good", perhaps because the pastures in their district were grazed to the quick? To our relief we gathered that the decision was personal. Leslie was moving his family onto the land of a friendly Chief because in his present neighbourhood there were people who wanted "to make trouble" for him.

"How far is the new place from your wife's mother?" I asked.

"Only littie-bittie far – like Langa to Salt River."

"That's nothing," I said. But Simon threw me a reproachful grin.

G*

"Not everybody has a scooter, and I should doubt if there's a bus. You try walking from Langa to Salt River every time you want to visit your favourite relative."

Leslie merely rolled his protruding orbs so that the saffron whites turned to heaven with resignation. Women were unreasonable – particularly his wife in the far away Shangaan country.

Rocky came out to say that Master Simon was wanted on the phone, and I was left alone with Leslie. I asked the indiscreet question.

"That girl Lenno left behind. Has she found another boy?"

The gardener's face clouded.

"That girl is now too old. The others – her sisters – have their own huts and children."

This was a serious matter. A Bantu girl expects to keep pace with her age-group. Her tribal "sisters" had left Lenno's betrothed behind. They were wives and mothers. To the jilted girl this must be "a shame" in every sense of the term. Her value had depreciated literally and figuratively. She wouldn't be worth many cattle now.

"What does her father say?"

But the blinds were down. It was like trying to peer into a night-black room filled with formless, menacing shapes.

"Her father ask me where Lenno is. I say I really don't know. I say I don't know where Lenno lives, or where he works."

I recognised the impenetrable Bantu "ignorance", the dead-pan "don't know" of a black iron cooking-pot giving back not so much as one gleam or reflection of inconvenient knowledge.

"What would happen to Lenno if he went home? Would the doctor try to kill him?"

"I really don't know, Miss Maxie."

I attempted to press him one point further – to determine the extent of his fear. I suspected that his own move might have been influenced by the witch doctor's interest in Leslie's nephew, Lenno.

"And if Lenno stops here – can the doctor harm him?"

I was wasting my time. "I really don't know," said Leslie.

Simon rejoined us.

"Are you fixed up all right at Langa, Leslie?"

"Yes, Mister Simon. I have my same room in the bachelor quarters."

"Sharing with Lenno."

"With Lenno, and another man from our country."

"That's all right then."

We left him and sauntered over to the studio to see Rima's birds. Lenno and Corinne were there. They had just finished cleaning out the aviary, putting fresh water in the little bird-baths and new sea-sand on the floor. Corinne had washed the miniature mirrors and toy swings and ladders; and the nesting-boxes had been taken out and put away. The dwarf tree was already in its autumn foliage, early this year. The weaver-birds had grown restless and been freed.

I half expected Rima to come out of the little wash-room in her painting smock and jeans. The studio had no appearance of having been deserted by its owner. And then suddenly, seeing Lenno and Corinne together, I had one of my moments of prescience. This studio was as much their sanctuary as the birds'. They too made love here, and they too were in the habit of calling to one another with the fluted whistle of the wilds. I fancied that Corinne's skin had darkened, that her hair was frizzier and her body heavier. Her movements seemed to me more leisurely, as if her quick lively Coloured rhythm had been slowed down to the unhurried tempo of the tribal woman. In some subtle mysterious way she was becoming more African, the thin White blood in her veins thickening like her body. She was careful not to look at Lenno, and, after a few words with me, she went back across the garden to the big house, her buttocks rolling as she walked.

When Lenno too had gone, Simon and I stood alone in the studio. In Rima's stronghold. Nothing was covered or changed, except that the usual open sketchbook and unfinished sculpture on the big work-table were missing. The bronzes had recently been dusted and the wooden carvings had been oiled. A gnarled log stood in its corner.

"Waiting to give birth," said Simon. "Waiting for its midwife to come back. This – all this – is the side of Rima that's beyond me."

He touched the slatted canvas roll in which she kept her chisels – the instruments of delivery. A rough pastel design was still set up on the easel. "Recognise it, Maxie? The original idea for the big picture over the fireplace in my flat."

Cunning, fear and violent death were brilliantly portrayed in the rough impression of the leopard crouched along the bough and the fawn beneath it, frozen, aware of danger, leaf-like ears alert. For contrast, I remembered the picture of St Francis of Assisi in Lucia's nursery, and the dappled Bambi, a garland of flowers round its neck, safe under the gentle hand of the Saint, surrounded by wild animals and birds rendered tame and trusting by the innocence of love.

"There's something cruel in Rima's work. Something pitiless – as if the dark soul of Africa takes possession of her here."

Simon raised his head at my words, nostrils quivering. So the warrior horse might have looked at the first distant challenging note of the trumpet.

"Here Rima is never mine. Here she belongs entirely to her art. Once it was a meeting place for all of us. Now it has become her lair. Sometimes I hate this obsession of hers."

"You're jealous of her work?"

He ran his hand through his hair. "Jealous? No, not that. More a notion that I must fight against it. It's growing too powerful. Even dangerous. It possesses her. How can I explain? It *uses* her. Surely it should be the other way about?"

"She's very close to genius."

He loved her, but he didn't understand her essence. She was the wise one. She had lived a score of lives before ever he was born for the first time. This was the noisy hour of her birds – before sunset. How pretty they were! But I knew that Simon only put up with them for her sake. He disliked a cage, any cage, even when it served as a protection to creatures that could never exist in the world outside. These were Rima's birds, but others flew into my mind, swallows in Mombasa, making their soft kissing sounds under the eaves of the hotel above the sea. Sunset and the *dhows* flying before the trade wind. Two years ago – two centuries ago!

Those – before we scattered – were the days when we had all been at home in Rima's studio. It had been hers, and yet, in a way, it had been one of the many places shared by all of us. Not now. The dark primitive sculptures had begun to crowd us out. Even Simon had been driven to say that here she was never his. Where then was she his, if not here? In his flat above the sea? In some mountain glade? A knife was sliding under my skin – my thin sensitive skin that burned and bled so easily. There'd be somewhere that belonged to both of them. She'd always sworn that she'd never marry any man who had not been her lover in the fullest sense. "How otherwise could I be sure he was really the one for me – in every way?" Was she sure with Simon? He'd see her soon.

Next week he'd be in Florence for A. & B. – for Rima. The knife turned in the small new wound.

He was standing behind me. If his body had been touching mine from heel to crown I could not have been more intensely conscious of him.

"I must get home," I said faintly. "I'm going to the flicks with Alma Jansen and we're eating early at her place. I must get home and clean up and change."

I didn't turn and look at him. The light was reflected in the tiny mirrors of the love-birds, flashing nonsense signals into my eyes. I heard him draw a deep breath and knew that his nostrils were flaring, that he wanted me, wanted to put his arms about me and cup my breasts in his hands. My breasts ached for his hands. I put my own arms across them, hugging myself as if I were icy cold. The wind roared over the long flat summit of the mountain down into the Bay. The blood drummed in my ears. Simon's voice was a long way off.

"All right then, Maxie. Let's go!"

The next time I saw him alone was at my flat the night after his return from Europe. He'd met Rima in Italy and Claude in London. It was half past nine when he rang me from Rosevale where he'd been dining.

"Can I come round, now, Maxie? It's important."

"Of course."

I did things to my face and hastily pulled on my blue velvet slacks, a rather dashing tunic, and flat gold slippers. The south-easter season was nearly over, but once again the wind howled at my windows and whistled under the doors, threatening and exhausting. It was as if we were destined to meet in tumult and confusion. As I opened the door to him the sudden blast snatched the handle from my grasp and the door slammed to behind us. One look at Simon's face told me that what he had come to see me about was neither easy nor pleasant. He took my hands and kissed my cheek.

"Hullo, Chick."

"Hullo, Simon. What'll it be? A beer? Brandy and ginger ale . . .?"

"Horse's neck for me. And you?"

"Bitter lemon."

We got our drinks and he lit our cigaretttes. I perched on the window-seat, but he was restless, pacing about. Though the windows were closed against the wind the curtains were not drawn and we could see the angry waves silvered by the waxing moon. The beam of Mouille Point lighthouse swept the sea, faded, blacked out, and swept again.

"What is it, Simon?"

His face was hard as stone.

"Claude. He's coming home. He arrives on Monday – March the twenty-first. The evening flight. Now get a grip on yourself, Chick, because you won't like this. Claude has married Fara September. Secretly. A fortnight ago. Her old folk were there. That's why she was so anxious to get them over to England. It was a church service. All in order. I was one of the witnesses."

"You! How could you?"

I buried my face in my hands. But he seized them from my eyes. He was as angry as the weather outside.

"Don't treat me as if I were an accessory after the fact in a criminal offence! Nobody knows your brother better than you do. He'd made up his mind and he told me he'd given you fair warning of his intention before you ever left London. The least I could do was sign the register and help keep the thing in the family for the present."

"I thought he'd get over it. I put it from my mind . . . wrote it off as infatuation."

"Then you misjudged Claude and Fara. I hate the whole damn business, but what the hell! He wanted you told, and now I've told you."

"What about Daddy and Mummie?"

"He's coming here expressly to break the news himself. So that's none of your responsibility. And don't forget it!"

"Why didn't he write to me and tell me he meant to go through with it?"

"There'd have been no point in it. He didn't want to stick his neck out for more arguments and pleas. He was absolutely adamant. I may tell you that Fara's father tried to dissuade them."

I was stung. "Why should *he* care?"

"He doesn't want a scandal any more than you do. He knows damn well that here in this crazy country his daughter'll be held to blame for *ruining* the only son of Etienne Lamotte – the heir to Loire. Gifted and successful as Fara is, there are plenty of people here who'd use the word *dirty* about this marriage, who'd be ready to spit in her face for making an outcast of your brother. Gert Vermeulen for one—"

"And Daddy for another! This'll kill my father."

He sat down wearily.

"Let's cut the dramatics. Do you want to know the situation as far as I'm able to give it to you?"

"Please, Simon."

" 'Island Love' ended its run last month. Fara's film tests were disappointing, so there's nothing doing in that line at the moment. But she has an excellent contract with T.V. She's a rich young woman now, with a future."

"On the stage, you mean?"

"I doubt it. She hasn't the stamina for an operatic star. 'Island Love' nearly did her in. She's an odd girl in that she learns her limitations fast and uses her brains to get by in some other way. She's had offers for Christmas pantomimes and variety, and then she has this T.V. contract that'll keep her in the public eye and ear as a singing star. It's profitable and won't interfere too much with her married life."

"Where will they live?"

"They've already taken an attractive cottage in Middlesex – not far from London and quite near the Factory. It's ready for them any time. At this minute they're still on honeymoon in Cornwall."

"How long does Claude propose to stay here?"

"Not more than a week. He wants to go straight to Loire and get that part of it over. The news story will break from this end. Claude absolutely refuses to cringe about it. He's proud of Fara and he loves her with all his heart, and that's the beginning and the end of it, as far as he's concerned. When he goes back they'll move straight into their cottage."

"Does Daddy know about Claude coming home to see us?"

"He should get a cable tomorrow."

"I must go to Loire this weekend. I must! Come with me, Simon! Please."

He strode over to me as I sat staring out at the storm-tossed sea. He put his hands on my shoulders, strong and firm. It was curious that I, who cry so easily, felt little now except profound pity for my parents. Somewhere in the back of my mind I wondered how Jamie would take it – whether it would finish whatever there was between us. But it was my father who would suffer most. For him it would be goodbye to his son, goodbye to his hopes for a Lamotte to inherit his beloved Loire. It would be the ultimate humiliation. He would see it as an irrevocable dark shadow on the name and blood of his descendants: and none of us would ever be able to persuade him otherwise.

"Look at me, Chick!"

I looked up. Simon's eyes were kind, smiling down at me.

"Of course I'll come with you to Loire if it'll be any comfort to you. But don't look so despairing, darling! Once you get used to the idea of this marriage, it's really no tragedy. We only make it so with our hide-bound prejudice. A brilliant scientist has married a highly successful singing star. Let it go at that. I'll pick you up here on Saturday after work and bring you back early Monday morning."

"You're very sensible."

"Why not? Nobody's sick, dying, or in desperate need. Let's have a sense of proportion. Now go to bed and sleep well, and, when Claude arrives on Monday, we'll both do our best to help him over a difficult hurdle. All right?"

He touched my hair with his lips.

"Till Saturday, Chick."

The wind surged in as he opened the door. I was alone again. Saturday – the day after tomorrow – we'd be on our way to Loire.

25

IDES OF MARCH

T**HE WIND HAD** dropped at last.

The unforgettable beauty of that weekend moved me deeply then; and haunts me still. Our valley was steeped in the peculiar peace that follows the harvest. The grain had been cut, the grapes gathered and crushed, the last of the fruit stripped from the trees and sent to market. Orchards and vineyards were turning colour, their leaves thinning now that their sheltering duty was done. The wide wheat-fields were pale and spent under the hot sun. The lands had given birth and were resting.

The guest sheep from the thirstland were still fattening on Bergplaas grazing, but my father saw in them a constant mute reminder of a great agricultural tragedy. The drought in the Karoo and the North West Cape remained unbroken.

"How long can they hold out – those poor buzzards of farmers – before they have to give up and admit that the drought has beaten them? Four waterless years! In some places more than that." He shook his head.

Oom Gert Vermeulen and *Mutti* and Jamie had shared our Sunday supper and we were sitting in the patio. The moon stencilled indigo leaf shadows on white walls. The fountain tinkled in the quiet night, and Daddy's Springers slept at our feet, some still hunting, no doubt, as they twitched and uttered the little grunts and whines that break through a dream. *Oom* Gert's Boer tobacco was pleasantly aromatic in the open air. Mother's turkeys roosted in the lower branches of the trees. A halo of tiny insects and moths fluttered round the wall lantern.

Oom Gert blew a careful smoke ring, and so still was the night that the wavering hoop hung unbroken while he puffed a second ring through it with the accuracy that had always fascinated Rima and me.

"The whole country will suffer," he said, "One can only hope that the Government will learn from that suffering. Irrigation schemes for the thirstland are more important than fine tarmac roads for tourists."

"They've cried out for irrigation schemes for years!" growled Jamie. "And now it's too late."

"Too late for some," said his father. "But those that come after will profit."

"That's not going to be much comfort to the families who face ruin now! Fathers of young children who've staked everything they possess in trying to carry on."

Daddy looked thoughtfully at Simon who had spoken brusquely. How much my father had changed of late! His expression, once so infectiously vital and optimistic, had settled into a stony resignation that tugged at my heartstrings. Perhaps the financial burden of Loire was too heavy for him; perhaps he, like the men of the drought area, had seen the Gorgon face of failure.

"You're right, my boy. Ruin staring at you – when you have young children to support – must be the cruellest thing of all. Especially when the fault is not your own. Those wretched farmers might well cry out, 'My God, my God, why hast thou forsaken me!' "

His words were hurled into a silence we found it hard to break. *Mutti* let her knitting fall into her lap as she tried to picture those abandoned homes, the parched land and dying stock beyond the watershed of our mountains.

"We're so lucky here. Such good water, such a fertile valley!"

"No excuse for failure here," agreed my father quietly.

Mummie jumped up abruptly. "You'll have a nightcap, Gert. A *brandywyn* – and you, *Mutti*, a mug of beer? Jamie, yours is beer, of course."

Simon was on his feet. "Let me see about it, Aunt Clara. I know my way about this house pretty well. Here, at least, there's no thirstland!"

She nodded, her taut smile answering his grin. She sat down once more, but she had been upset. Daddy glanced across at her with sudden tenderness, and it seemed to me that *Oom* Gert looked away deliberately as he said: "A *brandywyn* would be just the thing, Clare." I was oppressed by the hidden troubles in each of us, betrayed in a word or a gesture as impossible to interpret as the moans of Daddy's favourite dog breaking the sound barrier of sleep.

The conversation was desultory now, the overtones and deeper significance lost. *Mutti* had discovered a delicious new way of making Russian salad and was explaining it to my mother, and Daddy and *Oom* Gert were thinking along Russian lines too. Communist. They were talking about this business of the Natives threatening to make a bonfire of their passbooks next day.

"These bloody Communist agitators!" grumbled *Oom* Gert with no particular animosity. The "bloody agitators" were part of his political faith – the blame-takers for all our country's troubles. "They get at the city Natives. Now why must those poor niggers be incited into burning their passes?"

"Passes are symbols," said Daddy patiently. "Passes represent restrictions on a man's liberty – his right to go here or there, or change his job at will. We know they are safeguards – that without them foreign Natives would flock in and take the work from our own Bantu – but, let's face it, the pass and the policeman are too closely related."

"And do you wonder?" put in my mother acidly. "When a policeman has the right to knock up a Native at any hour of the day or night to demand to see his pass; and, if he can't produce it there and then, the poor devil is picked up, gaoled and fined. To any decent law-abiding Native that sort of treatment is the end – just what the agitators want!"

"It's not the system that's at fault," put in Jamie, "it's the application. It creates a genuine grievance. And a genuine grievance is a good fertiliser for bad seed."

There was nothing new in the conversation. It slid over my head. My secret knowledge of my brother's reason for coming home weighed on me much more than the many and various trials of the Black man. Would we ever again sit here in the patio – the Vermeulens and ourselves – amicably discussing the knotty problems of our lovely land? Tomorrow night – maybe when the foolish Natives were making ash-heaps of their passes – my brother would be here at Loire, dropping his bombshell into our family life. The Press would get wind of the story and splash it in heavy type. After that the talk and the scandal, the looks of shock or pity. Would Gert Vermeulen bring *Mutti* here again? Would he put our home out of bounds? Would he take a charitable view for the sake of an old friendship? Or would he feel that my brother's marriage – illegal here – had outraged and morally disgraced an entire social group? Examples were set at a high level, and what Claude had done was, by all *Oom* Gert's standards, unforgivable.

The Vermeulens had expressed great pleasure when my mother, glowing with joy, had greeted them with the news that Claude was paying us a flying visit, but Simon and I had been silent, and Daddy's smile had been touched with its new sadness.

Oom Gert knocked out his pipe and put it in his pocket. He rose to go, and Daddy stood up too, tall and spare beside the stocky, powerfully built Afrikaner. They paused for a moment under the lantern, two trusted friends and neighbours who had shared so many of the hazards and tribulations of a farmer's life and the same profound passion for the land. A breeze rustled the dry leaves of the pergola and lifted my father's shock of white hair. Memory stirred in me, and I saw again the snow-capped mountains of the Abruzzi, and Daddy standing beside the station-wagon, head up, the chill spring breeze in his hair as he waited for recognition from the old peasant who had been his father and his saviour in a time of great danger and hardship. And Mario's cry. "My son, you have returned!" Why did I think now of Daddy's "pilgrimage" to those who had helped him back to freedom? His act of faith. That humble mountain village had been his private Mecca. Perhaps because my heart was aching with a premonition that these two old friends might be saying *totsiens* for the last time.

Simon whispered, "You've been off on your own long enough, Maxie. Join in!"

Mutti was saying that the evening had been "*sehr gemütlich*"; and she added, "When Claude is home – after tomorrow – you must bring him over to Bergplaas to see us. We'll kill the fatted calf!"

Jamie grinned, "What's more, we'll take him to see Ferdinand, the father of all our fatted calves on Bergplaas."

"After tomorrow" *Mutti* had said. But after tomorrow nothing would be the same again. The *gemütlichkeid* we had known tonight would be gone for ever.

Simon drove me back to Cape Town through a pastoral landscape Rima would have loved; colourless under the moon, the tumbled peaks and ranges mystic.

"You're very quiet, Chick."

"Everything seems to be for the last time."

"Oh, come now! This thing with Claude . . . it's not a foretaste of death, after all."

The words, intended to reassure, only served to alarm me. I pressed against him for comfort. The city lights were in sight, spangled and sprawling. The shanty settlement on the Flats was mercifully shrouded in the secrecy of night. Who could tell what trouble might not be fermenting there together with the "witblitz" brewed in illicit stills by the "shebeen queens" and sold in the black spots and the brothels?

We sped along the foreshore, through dockland to the Atlantic coast and my little flat above the sea. Simon came in with me. It was very late. He drew me to him.

"You're so forlorn. I hate to see you sad. Ah, your scent! The Blue Hour . . . one doesn't forget a scent . . ."

"Blue Hour matches my mood tonight."

I twined my arms round his neck and drew his head down, lifting my face to his. I didn't care if he was Rima's. Tonight I couldn't bear to let him go. I needed him desperately – his arms, his kisses. This was my place – not Rima's studio, not Claude's flat, not Simon's – it was my very own. We hadn't turned on the light. The room was bathed in moonlight. Everything, inside and out, was strangely still and waiting. Simon was pale as marble, but his face against mine was burning and his lips were fierce as I clung to him.

"Chick, for God's sake! You're all temptation!"

I knew so little of love! Only that I wanted him – that I was faint with this inner yielding – that if he left me now I would die. But he did leave me; and, though his going was agony for both of us, it was not death. Some day he'd be mine – all mine. Some day Rima's spell would be broken.

I woke late next morning. Heavy and tired. The sun was up. It was already seven-thirty. Funny that the newsboy's loud ring and rat-tat as he left the morning paper outside my door had failed to wake me. I was so used to that double "call" that I seldom bothered to set my alarm clock. But, when I opened the door, neither the paper nor the milk were on the mat.

I got myself a hasty breakfast and fetched my scooter from its corner in the garage next door to the flats. The cheerful clownish Bantu attendant wasn't at the pumps, and I thought uneasily that I hadn't noticed the cleaners sweeping and chattering as usual in the foyer.

"It's a stay-away strike," said Miss Pratt in the show-room. "None of the Native delivery boys have shown up. Of course, it's to do with this nonsense of burning their passes. A gesture – and a strike to ram it home."

Aunt Kate came in during the morning for a fitting and a hairdo. She called me into her cubicle after the fitter had gone.

"Leslie and Lenno haven't turned up," she said. "And Rocky's in a flap. He says there's trouble brewing at Langa – that there are men from other countries – that's how he puts it – in the township, talking to the people."

"Rocky hasn't stayed away—"

"No, but he's far from happy. He's ordered his family to stay indoors today, whatever happens. As for Goodwin, he doesn't want to put his nose outside Rosevale."

"I wonder what Rocky means by 'men from other countries'?"

"Oh, Xhosas, I expect, from the Transkei – or northerners from the Transvaal tribes. Zulus possibly. Who knows. Trouble-makers, you may be sure. And do you know what? Corinne's fussing too. She came to me this morning and says she and Lenno want to marry as soon as possible. There's a nice kettle of fish!"

"Rima would like her to marry Lenno."

"Rima's selfish," said Aunt Kate frankly. "She wants a couple to work for her when she's married, and she'd like Lenno and Corinne. They're good models too. That means a lot to Rima. And she doesn't seem to appreciate that mixed marriages of any sort are a bad thing."

"Maybe mixed marriages are the best answer to our country's troubles."

"Nonsense, darling! Though I must admit I've no real objection in this particular case, especially as Lenno calls himself a Christian. But Lizzie, the highly respected Wise Woman of Bergplaas, won't be too delighted at her granddaughter picking a Native for a husband! I'll have to persuade Uncle Gideon to build quarters onto Rima's studio for them."

"But what about you, Aunt Kate? You'll miss Corinne."

"I can find someone else. Rocky'll get me a Native girl. Really having a mixed crew isn't a good plan. It was forced on me in the first instance when Grannie Beeford died and we felt we ought to keep old Annie in a job."

She stubbed out the cigarette she had been smoking, and touched up her lips.

"What time are your parents coming in to meet Claude this evening? We're expecting them to an early supper."

"It'll only be Daddy. Mummy wants to wait for Claude at home. She says he and Daddy'll have a lot to talk about on the way out to Loire."

I had encouraged that idea, thinking that Claude might be glad of the opportunity to break the news to Daddy first.

"Daddy'll be at Rosevale about five-thirty," I added.

"Well then, we'll all meet there. Pity you can't go back home with your father and brother. Still, you're a working girl now, and no extra privileges."

"I'm going to meet Claude at the airport. Just for a glimpse."

She frowned. "Not alone, I hope. Not on that awful scooter."

I laughed. "Not on that awful scooter. Simon's going to take me and bring me back. He wants to see Claude too."

Miss Pratt popped her head through the screen. "Your customer, Maxie. Mrs Howe's just come in for her fitting."

"Sorry, Aunt Kate, I must fly!"

"See you later," she said.

Daddy was by himself in the rose garden when I arrived at Rosevale just before seven. The summer blooms were at the height of their beauty. The towering wall and flying buttresses of Table Mountain were still bathed in the afterglow of a spectacular sunset. The evening was mild and tranquil. It matched the calm of my father's mood. Never – except in Italy, in that "summer of his deep content" – had I seen Daddy look so serene, almost as if some great sorrow had passed from him. A wave of relief swept over me. Whatever he might have to tell or hear from his son, he was prepared. As I watched him gently touch a creamy bud on the point of opening, stooping to inhale the fragrance of a red rose in the fullness of its glory, and silently marvelling at the pearly perfection of Peace, the thought came to me that my father, who so seldom went to church, was listening to "the voice of the Lord God walking in the garden in the cool of the day."

He raised his head. "Hullo, Maxie. Could there be a better evening for your brother's home-coming?"

Aunt Kate was calling to us.

"If you want a glass of sherry before supper, Etienne, it's now or never."

After supper Daddy said, "I'm going to get along. I know it's early, but I'll take my time."

"Shall I come with you?" I asked.

He looked down at me, smiling and ruffling my hair with the flat of his hand the way he'd done in my childhood.

"No, darling. You come along later with Simon."

He tilted up my chin and kissed me. "Sweet as any rose." His old merry grin lit his face for an instant – a flash out of the past. As he was about to leave he turned to Simon.

"Which way do you recommend? I don't usually approach the airport from the city side."

"I always go by Gunner's Circle, Vanguard Drive and the Klipfontein Road. That way you cut out all that dreary congested stretch through Athlone."

"Good. See you at eight forty-five. These planes have a habit of coming in early."

"We'll be there."

"Have some coffee," Aunt Kate said to us. "You two have plenty of time. It's certainly not more than twenty minutes the way Simon drives!"

We were out on the stoep and we heard the grandfather clock in the dining-room strike eight with its melodious Westminster chimes. The luminous dusk held the garden in Madonna-blue enchantment. Lights were blinking in the city. We saw them here and there between the trees. The stars brightened as night fell. So did a weird red glow down on the Flats.

Uncle Gideon looked at it, frowning.

"Doesn't seem like a bush-fire."

We knew the low, spreading blaze of a bush-fire well. This was different. Nearer, with high leaping flames making a lurid beacon of the huge power-station condenser bordering the Coloured area of Athlone and the Bantu location of Langa.

"It's Langa!" exclaimed Simon. "And Vanguard Drive skirts it. Uncle Etienne will probably be headed off some other way. We'd better get going, Maxie."

I heard the undercurrent of anxiety in his voice. The fire was clearly between the city and the Klipfontein Road to the airport. If it was really Langa then Rocky's family and Lenno and Leslie would be there in the midst of whatever might be happening.

We heard Aunt Kate say, "If it's the Natives making a bonfire of their passes—" But we didn't wait for anything. Within seconds we were in Simon's fast little convertible, racing down the Kloof Nek Road.

26

NIGHT OF GRIEF

L ANGA IS NOT a shanty town. It is a well-planned Bantu township which has grown up in over a quarter of a century on the industrial fringe of Cape Town. With its neighbouring Nyanga it houses some forty thousand Bantu from the tribal territories.

There are many families in Langa like Rocky's, and also a great number of misleadingly named "migrant bachelors", like Leslie, who go back to their homes at regular intervals but always with the intention of returning to the city. These "bachelors" are housed in the long brick barracks and hostels known as the Bachelors' or Single Quarters – the stew-pot of every sort of trouble, from that brewed by political agitators, to the simple human problem of harlots and *dagga* and *shebeen* liquor smuggled in for the furtive pleasure of men forced by circumstances to lead unnatural lives. The Single Quarters are the constant scenes of fights, knifings and police raids, and very often the innocent are sucked into the mire with the guilty.

Simon and I knew Langa well enough long before that night of March 21st. Only last Christmas we had taken in Christmas trees and gifts organised for the Bantu children by A. & B. and by various charitable organisations employing our firm.

The sandy wastes of the township are traversed by broad shady avenues. There is a shopping and civic centre, recreation grounds, free schools, clinics and crêches, and a number of churches of different denominations. Rocky's home was typical of the best type of dwelling in the old established part of the location. It was solidly built, gaily painted and well furnished. He had a small well-kept front garden, a mealie patch, a few hens, a dog, a cat and a car. In the city a man's importance is judged by the quality of his radio and his furniture; and a reasonably good car is the equivalent of a herd of cattle in the territories.

It was odd, though, how when you looked westwards from Langa –

which means Sun, as Nyanga means Moon – all you could really see was the majesty of Devil's Peak, and I found in this a strange diabolic symbolism, especially in the evening when the Peak, lit by the strawberry globe of the sinking sun, seems to soar straight out of Satan's inferno and the fires of hell.

"Have you ever seen Devil's Peak so dominant?" I'd said to Simon. "It blots out everything else, even Table Mountain and smug old Cape Town, and one feels that the Devil is master here, riding high, wide and handsome against a blood-red sky."

He'd laughed. "Maybe he's master a good deal of the time. Where isn't he?"

Yet here I had felt that he might be very much at home – the ace agitator in this Black hive, where the languages and customs of innumerable tribes created their own Babel, and where the superstition and sorcery of the Old Gods of Africa waged their perpetual warfare with city civilisation.

The Christmas spirit had been abroad that evening and the Devil's shares had been low. But tonight – less than three months later – all hell had broken loose.

Till that night of March 21st I don't believe that I had ever in my life feared any human being. And then – in that short space of time between Rosevale and D. F. Malan Airport – everything changed.

The hood of Simon's convertible was down and my hair streamed back from my face as he stepped on the accelerator and let her go, regardless of speed limits. Ahead of us a fire-engine clanged its furious way towards the burning location. A police cordon at the fork into Vanguard Drive made way for it and Simon charged through in its wake.

"I'm not stopping for anyone," he said. "Your father will have come this way unless he was headed off."

"Even then he'd have to skirt Langa on the other side," I said.

We rounded the sharp bend by the bridge. A thick wattle screen divided the location from the road, but behind this hedge was a holocaust. A deafening and terrifying noise beat on our ears. The roar and crackle of flames consuming schools, churches, the town hall and the administrative buildings was mingled with the howling of a maddened mob, intermittent shots, wailing ambulance sirens and the fierce clanging of fire-bells.

Suddenly we saw a hail of broken bottles fly out of the concealing wattle at the fire-engine ahead of us, and as it turned, undaunted, into the location entrance, a fireman clutched at his face and slumped sideways.

Simon prepared to rush the ambush, but a half brick splintered our windscreen and another just caught him on the side of the head and opened up a jagged wound. The little car swerved and almost crashed into a burnt out vehicle on the side of the road. Then approaching headlights blazed along the tarmac and we saw the menacing shape of a police Saracen coming towards us, followed by a patrol van. Our tyres screamed as we skidded to a halt a few yards past the wrecked station-wagon.

"Simon! Could it be—"

"Yes, it could. Stay where you are!"

But I followed him as he leapt out of the car and ran to a dark form sprawled on the verge. As he knelt beside it I came up with him, and, at the same moment, the lights of the patrol van were turned full onto what lay there.

"Maxie!" Simon shouted hoarsely. "For God's sake don't look!"

But it was too late.

They must have stoned Daddy's station-wagon and dragged him from it before they fired it. His unknown murderers had killed him because his skin was white and thus he was "the enemy". They had hacked him with knives, they had burnt and mutilated his body. Death is not enough when a mob goes mad. I didn't feel hate then. Only horror. There was no room in me for anything but this awful horror.

Ice cold sweat burst out on my forehead and poured down my face, my palms tingled and red mists swirled before my eyes. My legs were giving way and I felt Simon lift me as if I were a child. Then everything was black and I knew no more.

Voices filtered through oblivion. Someone was holding smelling salts under my nose. I could not bear to open my eyes. My face was wet with the dews of death. There could be no cold like this. Yet a jacket covered me. I raised a feeble hand to push the salts away. As it fell back onto the jacket, I knew the weave of the material.

"Simon . . ."

"Feeling better, Chick?"

I made a sound from the dark sea in which I drowned. When I opened my eyes I saw at once that the charred tragic thing that had been my father was gone from the roadside where it had been lying. The police van had gone too. A small ambulance was stationary near us. The noise from the location had died down. It was strangely quiet now. Showers of sparks from the burning township floated down through the windless air. Devil's Peak was black against the starry sky, girdled by the moving lights of cars along the scenic drive, jewelled by the great façade of the University blinking down upon the Flats from scores of lighted windows.

"Drink this," said the ambulance attendant. "It's sal volatile."

I shook my head. "I'd be sick."

The gash on Simon's head, above his left ear, had been patched with sticking plaster, but his shirt was blood-stained and his face was grim as he smoothed my soaking hair back from my brow. Everything was fitful and lurid, pockets of darkness and light under the fine dangerous fall of fiery rain and snowy ash.

"Where have they taken . . . him? To hospital?"

"It was too late for that."

"Then where—"

"Darling, don't worry about that part of it. Please."

"Claude!" I tried to sit up. "We've got to do something about Claude!"

"Can you take care of her?" The ambulance man sounded worried. "There's the patrol van coming to give me a lead through to Athlone. What about you two?"

"We'll go along under the same escort. Then we'll carry on to the airport."

"Is the young lady up to it? You could take her to the hospital."

"No!"

I was already on my feet, shaky but determined. We must fetch Claude. And Mummie . . . what about Mummie? Someone must tell her.

The police escort turned back at the T intersection of Vanguard Drive and the Klipfontein Road, where the ambulance forked right towards Cape Town and we headed left to the airport.

Simon was always a fast driver, but now he had good reason to give the little car her head. It was long past nine and the Johannesburg plane would have landed more than half an hour ago.

The wind of our passage revived me with its life-giving breath. But confused nightmarish thoughts wandered into my mind and hovered over the appalling image of what I had seen. I touched Simon's hand on the wheel with cold clammy fingers.

"Stop . . . I'm going to be sick . . ."

Within moments he was holding my head as I retched my heart out by the sandy side of the road. Panic caught me again. Impressions of wattle and drifting dunes hiding nameless horrors on the lonely badlands of the Flats; a group of ragged Coloured children staring at me silently as waves of faintness washed over me. Icy sweats and legs of jelly; Simon kicking out at a mongrel dog; the strength of his arms supporting me. "That's better, Chick!" The blessed breeze when we set off again. The stars above us in a clean cloudless sky. What about Rocky's wife and family there in the devil's cauldron behind us? Leslie and Lenno in those sinister Single Quarters? I must have muttered my fears, because Simon answered.

"Rocky told his family to stay at home tonight. Their house is nowhere near the area of the fires. Langa's a big place – very big and straggling. Leslie and Lenno? I wouldn't know about them, but I guess they can take care of themselves. We're nearly there now. Claude'll be in a state."

"I must clean myself before I see him. I must wash." But would my jelly-legs hold me up?

Claude was waiting outside the main hall. I saw the slight figure and the gleam of his glasses under the light, and the blackness of his untidy hair. He never wore a hat. He had a suitcase beside him.

"Simon! Maxie! What in God's name . . .?"

"We've been caught up in riots – the Langa road."

"We saw the location burning from the air – a shocking sight. I couldn't get near a phone, or I'd have tried to ring Rosevale."

As he spoke he helped me out of the car. I swayed giddily. A big young woman – a perfect stranger – said "'skuus", and took my arm. "She better come to the wash-kamer with me." Before we could say "yes" or "no" she had swept me off and was dealing with me in a sensible and practical way. She had a strong Afrikaans accent, a pair of kind eyes and the manner of one accustomed to being obeyed.

Simon brought a tot of brandy, and she made me sip it, raising my head and shoulders firmly from the couch on which she had told me to rest.

"Now you stay here a while, my dear – just till your people are ready for you. I'll be around. I'm a trained hospital nurse, so you can feel safe with me."

"I've had a very great shock . . . my father . . ."

"So your friend told me, the one who brought the brandy. Don't try to talk. Just take it easy."

She saw me through that desperate half-hour while Claude and Simon got through to Rosevale and Bergplaas. Then she led me to a quiet corner of the hall where they were waiting for me.

"I'm so grateful—"

"*Nie te danke nie.*"

She smiled at me, patted my hand and turned to wave at someone who was evidently expecting her. The next minute she was gone – the guardian angel whose name I shall never know.

Claude lit a cigarette and put it between my lips. Simon pushed a cup of strong sweet tea towards me.

"Drink it, Maxie. It'll help pull you together."

"I am together." But I drank the tea and felt the better for it. He told me what had been arranged.

"The Vermeulens are going over to Loire right away. Jamie'll drive your mother in to Cape Town and *Mutti*'ll probably come with them. They'll leave Aunt Clare at Rosevale and get straight back. *Oom* Gert must stay at Bergplaas in case of trouble, though all's quiet there at present. Claude's talked to Dad and he says we're to bring you to Rosevale without delay – unless you want to pick up some night things at your place first."

"I'll do that. Simon, will *Oom* Gert tell Mummie what's—"

"He'll tell her there's been an accident."

"But she'll know . . . she'll know . . ."

The floodgates opened and I began to weep. With the tears some of the dreadful sickness was washed away.

We drove to my flat first so that I could pack a suitcase. When we arrived at Rosevale all the lights were on. Aunt Kate took me upstairs at once to the double spare room Corinne had prepared for Mummie and me. She made me get straight into a hot bath, and lent me a warm dressing-gown to put over my pyjamas.

"You'll want to wait up for your mother," she said. "And, however warm the night may be, you must be cold. Claude'll sleep in your old room."

She was pale as death but calm and masterful like the unknown nurse who had looked after me at the airport. She didn't leave me, and from downstairs we could hear the radio announcer giving news of the riots interspersed with music. A news flash, music, then another news flash, blurred and indistinguishable to us. Suddenly it was blotted out.

Rocky, green with grief and apprehension, had put coffee and sandwiches on the hot-plate in the dining-room. It was nearly midnight. Aunt Kate had told me to talk to her if I wanted to.

"Tell me about it if it helps, my poor child. Tell me anything."

But I had shaken my head, unable to talk. I could never say what I had seen. I must begin to bury what I had seen, dig its grave deep inside me. Only Simon would ever know – ever understand – Simon, who had shared the horror.

When we went down Uncle Gideon said: "It's all quiet now. The army have reinforced the police and the riot seems to be quelled. The location is cordoned off, and the roads round it are being patrolled."

Later I knew that the announcer had told about cars having been stoned and burned, about the murder and mutilation of the Coloured driver of the car which had taken a newspaper reporter and photographer into Langa; and about Daddy – though not by name. That was when Uncle Gideon had switched off the wireless, afraid that the message might be repeated and that I would hear it.

Soon after midnight Mummie arrived with Jamie. She'd refused to allow *Mutti* to leave *Oom* Gert and possibly run into danger on the National Road. She came in, her face pinched and ghastly, and threw herself into Claude's arms.

"Claude! Thank God you're here!"

In that moment, as he held her close, I saw how alike they were – brave and wiry, self-reliant and self-sufficient, yet torn to shreds by the force of their strong repressed emotions.

We turned away as she sobbed against her son's breast.

"He's dead . . . I must know the truth . . . he's dead?"

Claude didn't deny it. He just held her more tightly.

"Maxie," said Aunt Kate. "Give Jamie some coffee and a sandwich, and get coffee for your mother."

Jamie followed me into the dining-room. We were alone there. His voice shook as he said: "We had the wireless on in the car to get the news flashes. We heard about the station-wagon that had been stoned and burnt, about the European who'd evidently been driving. Your mother guessed."

"Oh, God . . . poor Mummie!"

Jamie went to the window and pulled the curtains aside as if he needed air. His fists were clenched when he swung round, his face tortured. Fury blazed in his eyes.

"The bloody kaffirs! The damned, bloody, murdering kaffirs!"

The words and the look pierced the numbness of fear and shock that held me in its grip. For the first time since we had come upon the wrecked station-wagon and what lay near it I knew a powerful surge of outgoing emotion. Till then everything had been incoming, one horror upon another. I'd been waiting for this, for something that had to be released. Jamie's bitter curse had set it free. It ran through my cold horrified blood – a white-hot current of rage and hate against my father's savage killers. From now to all eternity every Black man was my enemy!

Rocky came in.

"The coffee, Miss Maxie. Your Mummie needs it. Master Jamie too, with all that long drive back this terrible night."

My dazed eyes took in the helpless misery that sat so strangely on the butler's usually cheerful face. His eyes, almost lost in big puffy pouches, were red as if he had been crying, and haunted with dread and anxiety for those he loved, his wife and family there in Langa in the midst of the burning and the shooting and the fighting. All our lives he had made us welcome in this house of Antrobus, where we had been "the children" he had served, scolded, spoilt and known as well as he knew his son. The tide of hate drained out of me and left me empty. There could be no all-inclusive enemy.

"I'm sorry, Rocky. You pour it."

"This business tonight – it is a heavy thing."

"*Ja*, man, it is." Jamie's tone was quiet. "Leave that cup for me. I'll help myself."

"My youngest son is a wild boy," said Rocky in a choked voice. "He never wants to listen to his mother. Robert, he must always be in everything."

I knew the "wild boy" with the laughing eyes and the huge mischievous smile. Not one to miss excitement. We were all in it together. All of us.

"Mother likes milk and sugar," I said.

H

He set the cup on the small silver tray. He took great pride in "his" silver. As he turned to go, he said:

"My heart is very sore tonight, Miss Maxie."

"Come," said Jamie gently. "We will go to the others, and then I must be on my way."

27

STATE OF EMERGENCY

IN THIS TESTING TIME the strength of my mother's character shone
out like a beacon. For a long time she had been sharing Daddy's
burdens of which we knew nothing.

"I wanted to spare you all I could. There wasn't anything you could
have done, darling, so Daddy and I simply went ahead as we thought
best. If Claude had been here – or even if he had cared for Loire – the
struggle might have taken another turn. But, as things were, we gave in."

Ten days had passed since that terrible night, and we were sitting
on the swing on the terrace at Rosevale. My father's ashes had been
scattered over the berg overlooking his beloved Loire, and Claude
had returned to England. Mummy had taken the news of my brother's
marriage with sorrowful resignation. No storms or scenes.

"You are my son," she had said. "I will stand by you."

Uncle Gideon had neither condoned nor condemned. He tried to ease
things for Mother.

"Claude is much ahead of his era mentally. Now he has jumped the
social wall as well – into the inevitable future. Luckily the girl is gifted
and adaptable and can take her place with him anywhere in the world –
anywhere but here, of course." His smile was cynical. "However, that
won't embarrass anybody because what isn't under one's nose is easily
ignored or forgotten."

Aunt Kate said very little, but her eyes often misted when she looked
at my mother. The Vermeulens too had made no comment, but the
bonds of friendship had held. They evidently felt that our cup of grief
had already been filled to overflowing and that we needed all the support
and sympathy they could give us.

After all, the story of the mixed marriage between the son of an
old family and the famous daughter of a Coloured craftsman made
no headlines. It was swamped in the vast mass of evil tidings reported

daily in our newspapers. Individual dramas took second place now that our country was suffering at home and pilloried abroad.

After my father's funeral Mummie had explained our financial situation to Claude and me. Daddy had been selling off many morgen to try and keep Loire going, but finally he had realised that he must cut his losses and part with it altogether. So he had secretly sold the homestead and the remaining land to a wealthy English buyer who regarded it as an investment for his teenage son. The buyer, who lived in London, was content to be an "absentee landlord" for the present. So for the past few months my father had, in fact, been the salaried manager instead of the owner of Loire. He had dreaded telling Claude the truth and admitting failure. After his creditors were paid there would be very little left in my father's estate.

"When you think of it," said Mummie sadly, "each had something to confess to the other. But what Claude had to tell Daddy would have broken his heart. Your father was so proud, Maxie – too proud, perhaps."

In a way she seemed to draw comfort from the knowledge that Daddy had been saved the humiliation of feeling that his son had "ruined the racial purity" of our line. A narrow rigid point of view in my eyes, but one that he would have held.

My father's executors had telephoned the owner of Loire in London to suggest putting in a manager till further notice, and it was Jamie Vermeulen who was offered the post. Mummie was relieved when he accepted. "There couldn't be a better choice. Jamie is a good farmer, he loves Loire, and he'll have his father at hand to advise him."

Aunt Kate insisted that Mummie and I stay at Rosevale for the present, and we were thankful to do so. We continued to share a room because I often woke at night screaming and panting with terror, soaked in sweat. "Hush, Maxie, it's all right. Mummie's here." The touch of her hand would soothe me as it had done in my childhood. Yet it was I who should have been the strong one. Those were strange anxious times when no woman cared to be alone and when all the gunsmiths were sold out of small-arms.

Many things had happened in the past ten days, and it was now clear that the countryside demonstrations and strikes had been highly organised and intended to paralyse the Union's life. The leaders were the extremist Pan-Africans whose slogan was "Africa for the African". Their declared intention was to "take over the country by 1963". March 21st had been

"Launching Day" for the first stage of their campaign. Their hand was against every White man, and one stage would follow another till their aim had been accomplished. So they said.

"If our leaders are imprisoned," proclaimed their orators and their leaflets, "others will rise up, and Black men from Egypt and Ghana will come to liberate the Bantu of South Africa. *By* 1973 *all Africa will be Black. The White people will be the slaves and we will be the rulers!*" Strong inflammatory talk, and "the Old Gods of Africa" were freely invoked.

They said, "No violence". But violence explodes. It exploded most horribly at Sharpeville in Johannesburg where scores of Bantu lay dead and wounded at the end of "Launching Day".

A State of Emergency was imposed, and units of the Citizen Force, including Simon and a great many young men in our group, were called up on military defence duty. Under the Emergency many thousands of people, White and Black, suspected of incitement or Communist activities were taken from their homes for questioning, or gaoled indefinitely without redress, while all over the country individuals with reason to fear arrest fled through the "rat-run" of the British Protectorates to Ghana, where Mr Nkrumah – whose own opposition had long languished in prison – waited righteously to give the fugitives sanctuary, or pass them on to Moscow or wherever else their destination might happen to be.

"It's like a war," sighed Aunt Kate. "Everybody's sucked into it and you can't tell where it'll end."

At Rosevale, in our little circle, we were all "sucked in" one way or another, from the tragedy of my father's murder to the wounding of Rocky's youngest son, Robert, "the wild one", who always had to be in the thick of everything. He had stopped one of the bullets fired into the crowd at Langa and lay dangerously ill at Groote Schuur Hospital.

On the morning after the riots few Bantu dared to go to work and their jobs were done by Whites and Coloureds or not at all. The Coloureds, defying threats and intimidation, ranged themselves boldly with the Whites. But, to Uncle Gideon's surprise, Leslie and Lenno appeared at Rosevale and were there to meet him when he came home to lunch. Both were severely shaken. Beads of moisture stood on Leslie's grey forehead as he spoke of the shooting and the burning. "Oh, Master, it was a night of suffering!" while Lenno's young arrogant face wore its most dead-pan look, and he volunteered little except to corroborate his Uncle's statements.

"At sunrise," said Leslie, "the police cars went round Langa to call out loud, 'Who wants to go to the job let him go now and he will be safe!' "

Both he and Lenno had made a dash for it.

But we guessed that their reasons were different. Leslie, with his wife and young family far away, didn't want to be involved in trouble. Poor fellow, he was law-abiding and peaceful by nature, but things always happened to him. Lenno might easily have enjoyed the excitement of political agitation, but he was in love. Lenno wanted to get to Corinne. He wanted to marry Corinne, live at Rosevale, and clear out of Langa altogether.

"Have you burned your pass-books?" Uncle Gideon asked them.

"We pretended to, but we hid them in our hats." For the first time Leslie smiled, pleased at his cleverness. "Those men who tell us to burn ours, they do not burn theirs."

"They're not such fools," said my Uncle.

"If we go back to Langa tonight those men will kill us," said Lenno flatly.

"No violence" the Pan-Africans had promised, but they had also stated: "Who is not with us is against us"; and those who "went to the job" knew that the intimidators – or "Spoilers", as they were called – would deal with them. Uncle Gideon knew it too. He reassured his gardeners.

"You can stay here till things are quiet again."

He gave them mattresses, blankets and a primus stove and advised them to make a temporary dwelling of the big toolshed in the garden.

"The place is an armoury," he told us with his grim smile. "Axes, spades, picks, saws, the lot. They can hold the place against all comers!"

Later that day Rocky's wife came weeping to the house. She had been to the hospital and seen their son, Robert, who "does not speak."

"The Spoilers order my husband to return with me," she added through her sobs. "If he stays at the job they will burn our house and cut our throats."

Rocky groaned aloud and went like a fat ox to the slaughter. We didn't see him again for a fortnight, but we visited the boy at the hospital often, and the lively little fellow recovered and once again had plenty to say for himself.

It was at this time that I noticed the tall shadowy figure haunting our garden towards nightfall. He came with the dusk and once, under the light by the gatepost, I saw Leslie talking to him. There was something strangely threatening about that long gangling figure and heavy dark face. The stranger wore a little green knitted beret with a tassel on top.

We were on the look-out for Spoilers and next day I asked Leslie about this man.

"Is he a Spoiler?"

Leslie instantly put on his dead-pan face.

"I really don't know, Miss Maxie."

"I have seen him several times. If he's not a Spoiler, he's a Watcher."

"He is a Watcher."

"Who does he watch?"

"I really don't know."

But I persisted. "Are you afraid of him?"

"I have no need to be afraid of him."

"Who has?"

"I don't know."

"If he's a Spoiler the police will take him."

"The police will not take this man. They will never have anything against him."

When I asked Lenno about him I got the same blank stare. Lenno, it seemed, knew even less than Leslie. The gangling stranger sank into the back of my consciousness and months passed before I thought of him again.

Meanwhile, throughout the country, the Black man was destroying whatever the White man had given him.

"Such senseless baboonery," said Uncle Gideon, as we read of Bantu teachers being dragged out of schools and beaten up by the Spoilers, and children sent out of the classrooms so that the schools could be burned. Churches, welfare centres and clinics suffered the same fate, while gangs of thugs in heavy cars travelled round to ensure that no man worked. They established a reign of terror, using hostages and arson as part of their system. They stood in knots on street corners and gave the slit-throat sign to any man suspected of being at work. So there was hunger and want in the locations, and White women got permission to take food in. Many went about those errands of mercy with fear in their hearts. It was a very contradictory situation.

The police met the intimidation drive with the gloves off, and, gradually, the Spoilers disappeared and men and women filtered back to work, and White relief societies began collecting funds to rebuild what had been destroyed and to help the Bantu who had been victimised by the strike or by the imprisonment of a wage-earner under the Emergency.

Then, at 3.16 p.m. on April 9th, the final shock burst upon our country and horrified the world.

At the Union Exposition in Johannesburg a rich, highly-educated farmer, whose epileptic mind was a tormented combination of brilliance, music and madness, shot the Prime Minister in the face at point-blank range. By some miracle the attempt at assassination failed.

What made all these things even more macabre was the fact that this was the Jubilee Year marking the Union of the four provinces of South Africa into a united nation – a period of festivals during which most people felt that dreams of unity had retreated into the distant past. But the *volkspielers* danced and the celebrations went on.

Out of the chaos and confusion came questions and answers. Sharpeville and Langa, the attempt on the Prime Minister's life – all these were signposts. The South Africans stood at the cross-roads and took a long look at themselves and at those signposts, and some read them one way and some another. But from every section of the community – English-speaking and Afrikaans, industry and commerce, judges, professors, students, churchmen and members of Parliament, was heard the plea for a "new deal" for the Black man, for more bridges between the races, for better wages, for more privileges and fewer restrictions, for a greater regard for human rights and a proper respect for human dignity.

Uncle Gideon was one of those most deeply concerned in the meetings of industry and commerce. He had decided that Antrobus & Beeford must immediately give the lead by increasing its pay packets for non-European labour. And, with Simon away in the Citizen Force, he was deprived of his right hand. I asked him to allow me to go back to work. He was in his study at Rosevale and he turned his drawn face to me.

"It's too soon, Maxie. You've been through too much. Now that things are more settled you and your mother must take a fortnight's holiday. It would do Kate good to go with you."

But Aunt Kate refused to leave him. "He needs me," she said. So Mummie and I went alone to a quiet fishing village on the coast. The hotel was plain but clean, and Uncle Gideon had insisted that our bill was to be settled by him.

The autumn air was keen and bright. There were boiling rock-cauldrons where the seaweed heaved and surged as the great rollers came creaming in, and long stretches of silver sand where we walked for miles. We were more like sisters than mother and daughter, trying to help and advise each other. Roberto and Bertha had written to me urging me to come back to them in Italy and "get away from it all", and Rima had added her persuasions. Our friends from Europe were just as kind and concerned about our personal safety as they were critical of our country's "oppressive policies". Even old Dr Hahn wrote me a wise and affectionate letter from the Rhineland.

"D'you want to go to Italy to the Angelis?" Mummie asked. "Don't think of me."

"No. This is where I belong. I'm staying. What about you? Have you any ideas about your own future?"

"Oh, yes," she said. "Daddy and I had a plan. I shall stick to it . . . in a modified form. I'm going to invest what little I have in a small poultry farm . . . somewhere in Constantia, maybe. Uncle Gideon will take a bond on it and I can pay him back as I go along. It's something I understand. I can make it pay."

I left her side and ran down to the water's edge and felt the little quarrelsome wavelets of the ebb wash round my ankles. It was a good idea. She could make a go of it. But would she expect me to live with her? Suddenly I could not endure the thought of giving up my independence. When I went back to her I knew that she had read my mind.

"You might want to spend weekends in the country with me – though it won't be like Loire."

"You can't live alone."

"I'll have help – a Coloured couple from Loire probably – cook-general and a man to give a hand with the poultry and so on. I'm very self-sufficient, Maxie. I learned to be during the war."

"You're wonderful."

H*

Her face was shaded by her big sun-hat and she wore dark glasses; I could not see her expression, but her voice was not quite steady as she said:

"Freedom is the most important thing in life. Your father knew that. I wouldn't curtail yours, darling – not for anything."

The next day was Easter Sunday and we went to the little village church. It was a very simple service, but to us it was the most moving in the world. We read the Easter message in each other's eyes. There was no death.

When we returned to Rosevale Aunt Kate told us that Corinne and Lenno were married.

"We rang Rima in Florence, and she wants them to have quarters attached to the studio. A Coloured builder has the job in hand."

I too went back "to the job", and early in May Simon was demobbed, and A. & B. announced its new scale of non-European pay packets, an example quickly followed by many other big stores.

Since our holiday my nightmares had come less often and I made up my mind that I must pluck up courage to return to my flat. Mummie was already busy hunting for a suitable little farm.

Then one evening Jamie rang me up.

"I'm coming into town next Saturday. Come back with me, Maxie. *Mutti* wants you to spend the night at Bergplaas, and I'll bring you home on Sunday evening."

The old familiar arrangement, but with so great a difference!

I was half afraid to accept. But I knew now that my ghosts must be laid. I had not been back to Loire since the day we had taken my father's ashes home to the berg. The horses had been sold, yet I wore my corduroys, hoping that we would be able to ride.

Jamie drove me straight to Loire and the dogs rushed out to meet us. Daddy's Springers!

"We can't do without them. They're mine now. We'll be hunting soon. Pa's hounds are in good shape."

"And Ferdinand?"

"*Og*, wait till you see that glorious bull!"

We went through the rooms of the old homestead. The owner had bought most of the massive Dutch furniture, which suited the place so well. A few precious things had been sent to Claude, and some still waited to be fetched away by Mummie or me – rugs and china mostly.

I was touched to see that someone had arranged flowers in the great copper jugs to make the house more homely.

"*Mutti*," said Jamie. "She didn't want you to find it looking too bare. I sleep in Claude's room, and use your father's study as a sort of living-room. But I usually eat over at home."

Outside my own bedroom Jamie left me.

"Tea'll be ready in a minute," he said. "Then we'll have time for a ride."

I went over to the small-paned window and looked out at the oaks. They had shed their leaves early this dry hot year. I perched for a few minutes on the wide teak sill where once Rima and I had watched the boys come up from the dam and cross the courtyard. Simon, she had said, was the bible horse. "Canst thou make him afraid as a grasshopper? The glory of his nostrils is terrible." And Jamie, we had decided was a great antelope, magnificent in the mating season! Claude was a cat-man, aloof and alone. She had told me her secret here and tied my hands for the first time. All that was in another life.

As we strolled over to the stables we saw Mummie's turkeys roosting on a gate.

"I'm keeping the poultry for the time being," said Jamie. "The foreman's wife manages that part of it. Your mother may want it later."

A Coloured groom was saddling Snow-White.

"Not Snow-White!"

"I've bought her myself. I couldn't let her go. I have sentimental reasons for keeping her."

Dear Jamie. It was as if he had said, "I love you." He knew how little I had to give. There was neither land nor money, and my brother had brought "disgrace" upon my family. I was not of Jamie's church, and, though his parents might be kind and hospitable to me, they would no longer welcome me as a daughter-in-law.

Jamie rode his sure-footed chestnut gelding, and I was on Snow-White. When we came to the place in the hills where Claude had scattered my father's ashes to the wind, we drew rein. Jamie took off his broad-brimmed veld-hat and bowed his head.

Below us spread the fallow lands of Loire and Bergplaas, the resting orchards and leafless vineyards and the shining dams where the Jersey herd and the home sheep slaked their thirst with those from the drought-land.

As I looked down at our lost heritage all the joys and sorrows of my early life welled up in me and the taste of salt was in my mouth, for tears are the taste of childhood as laughter is the sound of it.

My father's spirit was all about us. He had failed to save Loire, and that no longer really mattered, but he had given his life and his heart to this place and in death he was part of it. I saw him on his big roan, or on the stallion, Snow, pausing here, as Jamie and I paused now, the dogs with us. Daddy's eyes, warm with love, had ranged this scene a thousand times from boyhood into manhood and middle-age. He had only lost it when, for a time, war and capture had deprived him of his freedom. Here – as at Rosevale among the last blooms of summer on the last evening of his life – he had listened to "the voice of the Lord God walking in the garden in the cool of the day".

The flat gold light lay tenderly on the tawny grass as we rode slowly home. The children opened the farm-gates for us and danced and shouted with glee when Jamie gave them a handful of *lekkers*. They were so gay, these little descendants of slaves, to whom the *baas* was still the patriarch, master of his family and his *volkies*. But their *oubaas* was gone, and the new English *baas* would not be a man born of the soil of Loire.

With sunset the air grew cold and the first sharp breath of winter whispered through the rags and tags of thinning leaves.

We dismounted and loosened our horses' girths. The wizened old groom took the reins, but I followed him into the stable. It was hard to part with Snow-White. Jamie felt in his pocket.

"Here you are. She likes her lump of sugar."

That was as it should be. A pocket full of sweets for the *kleintjies* and sugar for the horses. It was dark in the stall. Smell of hay and harness; arched neck and rippling muscles, satin-soft lips and hot breath tickling the palm of my hand as Snow-White took her sugar; Jamie watching over me; and, outside, the dreaming lands and old white homestead. What you have loved is yours for always.

Jamie said: "It's getting dark. They'll be expecting us over at Berg-plaas."

"Of course. We should be going."

We went out into the bloom of the dusk.

One day I'd come back here; ride Snow-White to *Oom* Gert's hounds; feel the yellowwood boards of Loire under my feet, and see the oaks green-gold in the spring. But I'd come back as a woman who had buried her dead and said goodbye to her girlhood. When the new wheat ripened in the sun it would not be our wheat, nor would the vineyards and orchards bear our fruit; the fleecy merino pelts would be shorn and graded for the new owner; and whatever came of good or bad would no longer matter to us. But my girlhood was part of this valley and these hills. Death and fire had turned it to dust and ashes and the winter winds would blow it away.

"You're sad, Maxie. I shouldn't have brought you back. Not yet."

His old car jolted over the rough track between Loire and Bergplaas.

"You were right to bring me back."

"Remember that fire – up on the berg over there? You were still a kid—"

"Of course."

I looked down at his hands. It was too dark to see the scars, but they were there.

"Bits of the berg are barren still, charred to the bone. Other areas are flourishing as never before. See what I mean? It works both ways."

I let my hand glide under his. Life was full of scars.

The lights of the Vermeulen home glowed at the end of the avenue of blue-gums. The night smelt of leafmould and bonfires, autumnal and aromatic, the scent of the dying season. But I knew that Jamie was right. There is always another flowering.

28

BOTTOM OF THE WELL

T HE OFFICIAL INQUIRY INTO the Langa riots of March 21st
began at the end of April. It was held in open court before the
Government-appointed Commissioner, assisted by the Deputy
Attorney-General and a team of advocates appearing *pro deo* for the
Langa Vigilance Association. A thousand miles away, in Johannesburg,
a similar Commission was examining into the March 21st riots at
Sharpeville arising out of the same country-wide Pan-Africanist
campaign against the pass-laws.

Simon and I were among the scores of witnesses, White and Black,
who testified to the events at Langa on that fateful night. But, apart
from giving our evidence, we spent many hours in court. Mummie
found it "morbid" that I should want to know any more about the
"troubles" than what I had been forced to see for myself. "It can only
stir up terrible memories," she protested. "I shan't go near the court
myself. It would be like – like going to a murder trial."

Uncle Gideon didn't share her view.

"This isn't a trial, Clara. It's an Inquiry. The Commissioner's duty
is to shine a torch into the bottom of the well in search of relevant truths.
God knows what he'll find in the process! A few human rights murdered
and mutilated; police ineptitude in mob control; restrictive laws, harshly
and unreasonably applied, acting as a perpetual irritant to people who
live in poverty in the midst of plenty; the writing on the wall, maybe,
for those who care to read it."

But my mother was a woman bereaved. "Those Natives murdered
my husband! I want to see them brought to justice and punished."

He looked at her with pity.

"My poor Clare! You won't see that – not in this court or any other.
The crime against your husband was without personal motive – a

barbaric, bestial manifestation. Etienne's killers were dark, frenzied figures in the dark of the night. Nameless, faceless."

My mother shook her head and buried her thin face in her hands. Uncle Gideon patted her shoulder.

"Simon and Maxie – especially Maxie – have been through a dreadful ordeal. If spending some time, now and again, at the Inquiry is going to help them get it into perspective I won't stand in their way."

The quiet court, cool and clinical, with soft clear artificial lighting and complete insulation from city sounds, was like an austere theatre where only the court officials parrot-played their parts. The stalls – high pews polished by much use – were more often than not half empty, but up in the gallery reserved for non-Europeans every seat was occupied. Strange that there should be so many of them with nothing to do day after day except attend "the play"!

Anyone could come and go as they pleased. Simon and I usually slipped into the pew behind the black-robed figures of the advocates. One of these representing the people of Langa we called "the old Lion" because he looked, roared, growled and purred like the King of Beasts, and every now and again he passed a blunt irritable hand over his thick white mane. But it was the slight youngish figure of the Commissioner on the carved throne, centre stage, who held our attention with his patient persistence, his quiet insinuating questions and his occasional rebukes. Above all, his humanity. To him every witness was a human being. Witnesses gave their evidence in the language of their choice, English, Afrikaans or Xhosa. If Xhosa was used there was an interpreter, a spare expressive European who interpreted not only the words but the mood of the witness with a fine sense of drama or comedy.

I often glanced round and up at the gallery, at the black intent faces listening to the Old Lion finding extenuating circumstances for the rioters and cunningly shifting the weight of blame in the scales. If a policeman was giving evidence their faces would darken still more, and, if he should happen to be a Bantu policeman, there'd be a threat in the silent accusation of their eyes, but sometimes a wave of amusement swept over them and broke the sombre façade with ripples of light, for there was often a touch of comedy in this long and varied performance.

Those were strange shut away days for me when violent human

actions and emotions came under the searching lens of the law. Gradually I realised that my own personal experience was only one small gory piece in the great mosaic of human hate, fear, and misunderstanding. And stupidity. In the end stupidity and intolerance seemed to outweigh wickedness and evil.

The facts were simple. A meeting had been called at Langa by the leaders of the extremist "Africa for the African" group. The meeting, frankly inciting people to break the pass-laws and demand a general minimum wage of £35 a month irrespective of sex, age or any other conditions, had been banned and the police arrived to disperse it. The six thousand people in the square had not obeyed the dispersal order fast enough. A baton charge had inflamed the crowd, stones and broken bottles had been hurled, shots had been fired. Death, injury and arson had followed. The whys and the wherefores were the Commissioner's headache.

"Everybody sees red at times," said Simon, as we sat in the Public Gardens during the lunch break. "And Natives see redder than most. They aren't disciplined and they're violent and volatile by nature. As you know very well, they knife each other without a thought for the consequences. Add mob hysteria and you get something very frightening indeed. Remember those nine young policemen who were literally taken apart at Cato Manor? I'll bet the police at Langa and Sharpeville remembered that slaughter!"

The Gardens are only a minute's walk from the Law Courts and we had made a habit of going there for lunch. The May days were bright and fresh, for it was the clear sparkling period between the last summer south-easters and the first north-westers of the winter. We'd sit at one of the tables under the trees near the café, and we'd feed crumbs to the greedy doves. The squirrels would ask for nuts, and scold if we had none for them, and from the other side of the Gardens we'd hear the shrilling of birds in the aviary. Yet that sound, so reminiscent of Rima's studio didn't really recall her as vividly as it might have done, for this was a time belonging entirely to Simon and me. He and I – alone – had come face to face with tragedy, and now, day after day, he was helping me find my way through disaster and shock to peace of mind.

One morning Robert Rocky was called into the witness-box. His lively face just showed above the rail. Rocky, in his sedate parson's attire, hovered anxiously in the offing. The Commissioner looked down from his throne and smiled encouragement at the boy.

"Do you go to Sunday School?" he asked in his gentle way.

Robert threw his father a smug smile, and answered vigorously, "Yes, Sir."

"Then you must tell the truth here as you have been taught to tell it at Sunday School."

Robert elected to tell "the truth and nothing but the truth" in English, and did so with self-important gusto and graphic gestures. Like every Bantu he was a born actor. He had disobeyed his mother and slipped out of the house to join the gathering crowd. Then, when he had wanted to run away, he had found himself wedged in the surge of frightened, angry, yelling people. He had heard shots. He had fallen. "I was shot!" Someone had picked him up and taken him to the hospital.

When Robert had given his testimony the Old Lion stood him up on the bench with the other exhibits and told him to pull up his shirt and show the Commissioner his scars. The boy displayed them with proud alacrity. These were things that only happened to truly adventurous lads! The Commissioner shook his head sadly, but he said he was pleased to hear that Robert had paid his last visit to the hospital, and he wished the boy good health and a full recovery.

As Rocky led his youngest and favourite son from the court he gave me one of his real old-fashioned grins, lost in folds of cheerful fat. Now that the "wild boy" was well and all was quiet in the location he was almost his old chuckling good-tempered self. If he bore any lasting grudge he did not show it. His attitude appeared to be that Robert had learned another of life's lessons the hard way.

That same afternoon Simon was called, and it was he who told our story and answered all the questions. I simply had to state that I had nothing to add. I shall always remember the kind grave face of the Commissioner and the sympathy in his eyes. I had no wish to look at those forbidding dark watchers in the gallery as I left the witness-box. I only wanted to get away. Going over it again had revived the bad memory too vividly.

Simon's car was parked in a side street near the Law Courts. The hood was up, for it was cold with a hint of rain in the evening air.

"Where shall we go?" he asked.

"Up to the Nek. For a walk."

"Your shoes?"

"They're all right."

Soon we were tramping briskly along the narrow track skirting the Twelve Apostles high above the cliffs. The sun was low, and the broad Atlantic swell prepared to receive it. The earth scents were soft and rich. After a while we stopped and looked down at the sea. I drew a long deep breath.

"It's strange," I said. "The hate seems to have gone out of me. I feel clean again."

"Hate's a cruelly destructive thing. I've felt it like you have – burning me up."

"These last weeks . . . how can I explain? . . . somehow the deed and those who did it have separated themselves in my mind. I've stopped thinking of them as people – people like Leslie and Lenno, perhaps – gone berserk. They were rage and hate materialised – mad."

"Driven mad by one set of rules for Whites and one for Blacks, by kicks and frustrations and the sheer red rabies of knowing yourself the under-dog doomed by the White *baas* to stay that way for ever and ever, *amen*."

"We've got to stop and start again – all of us. It's the only hope for our country. But, most of all, our leaders have to think along new lines."

"That's not easy," he said slowly. "This policy of *apartheid* is their chosen road. They call it the traditional way of life in South Africa—"

"It is too! But times change and traditions with them. Any fool knows that."

"Our leaders aren't fools. They know it too. Long ago they expanded *apartheid* to include a very ambitious programme of Separate Development. And their plan – as far as it has gone – has done a great deal of practical good—"

"But spiritual harm, Simon! Because it holds no hope of eventual equality. Human beings can't live without hope and freedom."

"Look," he said, "White supremacy is the cornerstone of Afrikaner Nationalism. To their way of thinking it's that or chaos. Ask Gert Vermeulen or Jamie! They're reasonable enough, but that's the view they'll hold."

"*Now* – yes! They'd be right. But surely we have to look ahead and face the future realistically. We should take a new road, make up our minds to begin to share, bit by bit, and hope that we'll keep on being able to share – on a basis of merit alone."

"A brave new road – but, according to our present Government, one that'd lead the Whites straight to the gallows. No, Maxie, make no mistake, Afrikaner Nationalism is committed to enforcing White supremacy by hook or crook from now to all eternity. Only a change of leadership can alter that."

"Or a change of heart. There's such a thing as a genuine change of heart!" I spoke passionately.

The sun had set and the sky was red as blood. His face hardened. He'd grown too thin and the fine sensitive modelling of his features stood out craggily. His eyes were curiously light against the summer tan that still bronzed his skin, and suddenly they were dreadfully unhappy.

"A change of heart. Yes, but that can come too late. *I know.* It can come so late that you daren't confess it – even to yourself. You've followed your road too blindly, too faithfully and too far. You've led too many others along it with you. There's no going back. It happens with countries and governments and dictators . . . and it happens with ordinary human beings, God knows! Suddenly something happens to bring them up with a round turn, and they experience this . . . change of heart . . . and then maybe they find they've passed the point of no return."

He wasn't talking of governments and dictators any more. He was looking straight into his own heart – at the truth he had discovered too late.

"Simon!"

"Chick, my darling . . ."

Suddenly he was holding me with his cold hard cheek pressed against mine. He was kissing me possessively, with desperation. What was he telling me? That he must go his way with Rima? I didn't dispute it then. But in his arms I was no longer proof against my need for him. I was his, giving him my lips as never before. We were lost in the mountain mist that swirled about us, chill and ghostly.

Dusk and the mist. We knew the danger. When at last we broke apart, Simon said, "Come, take my hand!"

We picked our way along the narrow contour path, at times in single file, Simon ahead, my hands on his waist. The texture of his jacket, the tweedy smell of it in the moist air, the way his hair went into crisp damp curls, the mist that made phantoms of us – all these things belong to the revelation that he loved me.

We were to have dined at Rosevale, but I couldn't face Uncle Gideon and Aunt Kate with my new knowledge threatening my loyalty to them and to Rima.

"Make my excuses," I begged Simon. "Any excuses you can think of."

"There are plenty – after appearing in court. But your mother'll want to see you. She'll want to be reassured that you could take it."

"She can come and have supper with me. I'll scramble some eggs. Take me home – please! I'll phone her from the flat."

The fog was thick when we got to Kloof Nek, and Simon had to use his fog-lights to drive me to Mouille Point. As he left me, he said:

"It's just as well I'm going away next week."

"I suppose so."

But without him life would be hollow and haunted.

On the following day Uncle Gideon sent for me in his office.

"Sit down, Maxie. I want to talk to you. Now that the Inquiry is over you must make up your mind to get on with the job and carry on as usual."

"I realise that. You've been very good to me, very patient."

"What's happened is past and done with. Nothing can change it, and it's up to you to try and put it all behind you. You appreciate that you'll have to stand on your own feet financially, so your career is more important than ever. It may even be necessary for you to help your mother for a while."

"I'll do my best."

He clipped and lit one of his small cheroots and puffed at it thoughtfully.

"I want you to see something of our other branches in the Union. Miss Pratt and I both feel that you're going to be a valuable asset to the firm, but, if you're to buy for us abroad, you must find out what sells in our other branches at home, and why, and so on. You have to develop judgment as well as flair."

"I'm keen, Uncle Gideon. What do you want me to do about it?"

"I want you to make a tour. Port Elizabeth, Durban and Johannesburg."

"Isn't Simon doing that circuit?"

"He is. So it seemed to Miss Pratt and me a good idea for you to go along with him. You'd only need two or three days in Port Elizabeth – the Bartons could put you up – and a week with the Beefords in Durban. From there you could go to Johannesburg where the Consadines will take care of you."

"Does Simon know . . . about taking me with him?"

"I've just spoken to him. He suggested – rather foolishly, I thought – that your mother might enjoy going as a passenger. But I'm against combining my firm's business and other peoples' holidays. In any case your mother needs peace for the present. She wants to look around for a suitable little farm. We're delighted at the way she's entering into the idea of this new venture. She's a brave determined woman. Competent too."

"I know. Mummie never gives in."

"Now, as to this tour. Miss Pratt will brief you. She'll give you the names of key people in the various branches and tell you what to observe and note down."

"Then it's been definitely decided that I'm to go?"

I waited, tense, as if the oracle were about to utter. He glanced at me with sudden penetration.

"We'd expected you to welcome a change – after the last weeks. The up country and east coast climate is at its best in June. And you know your cousin, Charlie Beeford, well, and the Consadines too."

"I do welcome it! Really I do. It's just that I was taken by surprise. Simon goes so soon – Monday, isn't it?"

"That's right. You haven't much time, so you'd better go to his office and find out what itinerary he has mapped out. Then you can think out your bits of packing on the weekend. Miss Pratt'll arrange your accommodation. We're going to miss her when she retires in a couple of years time."

"So soon?"

"She'll be entitled to her full pension year after next. The doctors can keep us ticking over long after our allotted span, Maxie, but they can't keep us young. However, you wouldn't know about that. At your age growing old is something that happens to everybody else."

I laughed, and his expression relaxed.

"You've been looking strained," he said. "Come back with a little more flesh on your bones."

Once I'd have been wild with delight at the programme he had offered me. Now I was scared. I've wondered since if Uncle Gideon had the least idea what he was doing when he sent me away with Simon. Surely Rima's father ought to have known better.

29

WE TWO

PORT ELIZABETH IS five hundred miles from Cape Town. We could have done it easily in a day, but Simon had a conference on the Monday morning so we decided to leave after lunch and break the journey. We were using one of the firm's new American station-wagons, a long glittering blue rocket loaded with samples for the various branches as well as our suitcases. Much of the time we cruised at about eighty, but through the mountains or along the cliffs above the sea we took it quietly. We shared the driving, Simon taking the lion's share.

The tawny winter uplands at the foot of the Langebergen were shrouded in driving rain and our windscreen-wiper flicked back and forth hypnotically. The curious rancid scent of the "stinkweed" pervaded the moist air, and then it was sharpened by the tang of the Indian Ocean. The great sweep and swell of Mossel Bay spread before us; green bush above golden scalloped beaches; flat rocks where seals basked on sunny days; and embracing this superb outlook was the softness of a new climate, milder days, warmer seas, gentler rain. We changed over and Simon took the wheel.

"We're in a different weather cycle now. It'll probably be fine by the time we get to Wilderness."

"Everything's different. I feel as if I'd left my whole life behind."

"No wonder. So much has changed for you. Loire gone. Claude gone. Your father . . . All the old associations sliced away overnight. Permanently."

"You've seen it all come about. You were with me all the way – even when it began. With Claude. If it hadn't been for Claude and Fara, none of the rest would have happened as it did."

"That's fate. What's done is done. You have to let go of the past and meet the future."

"I want to, but there's a time between – a dizzy sort of gap – and this is it."

"Sounds like the trapeze artist – that second when she's suspended in space between letting go one swing and catching another."

"Breathless, dangerous, high in the air. There ought to be a net."

"When it's the real thing there is no net."

Storm clouds hid the Outeniqua range. It was already dusk when we left George among its magnificent trees and began the winding descent through the river gorge to the coast at Wilderness. Simon reduced speed, and, as we looked down upon the meeting place of river and sea, he said, "Well, Chick, do we stop here at Wilderness or carry on to the Plet motel? We could make it by seven-thirty if we press on."

"Let's go on."

I was afraid to stop. Simon – the Simon I had known all my life – was slipping into the past too. The moment of "letting go the swing" was drawing perilously near.

The rain had ceased. The long necklace of lakes and lagoons shimmered in the twilight between the forests and the sea. This too was a moment of transition, the luminous black pearl interval between day and night. The mountains hugged the coast, and at last we came to the curve in the road with beyond it the scattered lights of the motel welcoming the traveller to a warm fireside, a good dinner and a night's rest.

There was the main house with dining-room and lounge, and, dotted about the garden were shacks of various sizes. We went into the little reception hall made bright by bowls of scarlet and orange berries and russet leaves. A Native porter called the receptionist who was young and attractive.

"Just for tonight? Let's see. Number five, that's a double—"

"Two singles," smiled Simon. "With bath."

"Sorry," she laughed. "I jumped to the inevitable conclusion! Yes, I can manage two singles with bath." She gave the porter the key. "He'll show you your way. Now, if you'll sign here."

We signed the register, and Simon said, "We'll be wanting sandwiches tomorrow."

"Ham, egg, tomato, cheese – just tell your waiter and he'll see they're ready. You can get dinner up to nine o'clock. What time would you like morning tea? Six-thirty, seven—"

"Seven would be fine."

"That way, Master. Over there."

The porter indicated the two-roomed shack across the garden and Simon ran the car under shelter alongside it. The porter unlocked the door and switched on the lights. A narrow passage connected the rooms, which were bare, only intended to accommodate motorists for a night or two, but the curtains were modern and gay with geometrical designs in red and yellow on an apple green background. The bathroom was luxurious.

The car was right beside the shack door and Simon took out our night-cases and locked it. The porter had gone and we heard him laugh and say something to the room-boy in the clicking Xhosa language.

"Funny," said Simon. "This is the suitcase you had in Mombasa. I remember it well."

We were both nervously aware of each other, of being alone together, of the forces driving us so relentlessly. In Mombasa – long ago – Simon had been put in charge of me, in trust, but even then he'd been caught off guard by the Maxie who was no longer a child and we'd found ourselves with senses spinning. It had been that way in Claude's flat too, the night the telephone rang and we went to "Island Love" and saw Fara capture the heart of a West End audience – and of my brother. And now the whole course of our lives was at stake. The thing that had been building up between us in spite of Rima – or perhaps, in a peculiar contrary way, because of her – was all about us, a sultry electrifying power heralding storm. Yet the night outside was clearing, sweet and starry.

I turned away from him to the dressing-table. Anything to break the unbearable tension. I touched the candlestick and matches.

"Evidently there's a lights-out time."

"Or the plant is temperamental. How hungry are you? It's a quarter to eight."

"I'd like a bath before dinner."

"Me too. But don't take too long. I'm famished."

When we went back to the main lounge a huge fire was blazing in the hearth. Simon ordered dry martinis, and the waiter brought us a menu card. Next to each dish were suggested appropriate South African wines.

We chose minestrone and tournedos and a Constantia burgundy "to go with a steak and a winter's night."

"Bring the bottle here to the fire," said Simon, "so we can warm it."

The wine waiter looked pained. "I can take the chill off for master."

Simon threw the man his quick smile.

"No, leave that to me. I know exactly how I like it. Bring it here and draw the cork."

I had changed from my turtle-necked pullover to one of fleecy salmon-pink that went well with my light navy corduroys; my "flatties" were the same salmon-pink and the kerchief round my neck was a deeper red and a lighter blue. I knew that I looked attractive because, as Miss Pratt put it, "Maxie's right for casuals". I was always loaned to the sports department for tea-hour mannequin parades.

Simon's long flexible hand touched the wine bottle, testing its temperature, and suddenly I was tingling all over as if the smooth thick green glass had been my skin.

"That should be just about right. I think we ought to go and eat."

There were only a few people left in the dining-room when we went in, and we were relieved to see that there was no one we knew. Afterwards we had coffee in front of the fire, and presently we found that we had the room to ourselves. It was getting late and most people were early starters.

The fire was dying down. I leaned forward to put another log on, but Simon touched my arm. "It's not worth it." The lights had begun to dim. As we went out the porter bade us a drowsy goodnight. The waxing moon was already low in the sky, obscured by rags of fleeting cloud. It was only a little way to our shack. The others were in darkness, but we had left a light burning and the window was a faintly glowing square of gold across the path between the azalea shrubberies. I shivered.

"It's cold coming from the fire."

Simon slipped his arm through mine. "It's no distance across the garden."

It was no distance. Nor was it any distance for the girl on the flying trapeze when she let go the shining bar of her swing to launch into space and grasp the hands of her partner flying towards her high above the sawdust ring.

The hum of the electric light plant died down and the golden square faded from our shack, leaving it dark and secret. In the deep silence that followed we looked back over our shoulders and saw the porter hang an old-fashioned lantern outside the main entrance of the motel.

We were drowned in this remote moonlit silence. We could not even hear the sea, but we could taste brine in the fragrance of the air.

As we strolled along the path our eyes became accustomed to the gloom and there, crouching against the wall of our shack, was the station-wagon like a big animal on guard.

As Simon closed the door behind us it was dark.

"I'm scared of the dark!" Even in my own ears the sound of my laugh was unnatural.

As he lit the candle on my dressing-table all the planes and hollows of his face, its clean-cut sensitive modelling, flaring nostrils and mobile mouth sprang into sharp relief. It was a woodcut; it shook my heart. The long fingers and prominent bones of his hands were, for an instant, transparent as he shielded the thin small flame from a sudden draught. I half closed the casement and drew the curtain across it. When I turned he was standing with the candlelight flickering upwards into the brilliance of his eyes. The look of him sharpened the pain in my heart. It was the warrior-horse look. "Hast thou given the horse his might? Hast thou clothed his neck with the quivering mane?" I covered my face as if from a blinding light.

"I love you," he said. "I love you, Maxie. Only you."

All my life I had waited for him to say those words.

His arms were round me. He was trembling as if with fever. His cheek against mine was burning hot. I pressed myself against him to still his trembling that was neither weakness nor fear, and loved him the more for it. Nervous, strong, inexpressibly dear.

"I've loved you always. There was never a time – never – when you weren't the one. There never will be," I whispered.

I heard the swift intake of his breath as if a whip had flicked him. His arms tightened about me and his mouth was on mine, but I no longer knew him. Three words had made us strangers to each other. Simon, woven so close into the texture of my whole existence, was unknown to me now – a stranger because he was my lover and there had been no other lover in my life.

The sun was up when the room-boy came in with my early tea and drew the apple-green curtains with their cubist design so that the green freshness of the morning poured in through the open window. He said "Good morning" and I returned his greeting from dazed somnolent depths, and heard his bare feet pad down the passage to Simon's room.

Voices passed by my window as early leaving parties went across to breakfast. An engine started up. Someone was evidently already on his way.

I yawned and stretched, catlike, till my limbs seemed incredibly long; I flexed my toes and felt energy tingle through my nerves. Even my nails were alive! I put my hands under my head. My tangled hair was warm and silky. Come back, my wandering spirit! Come from the far shadowy places of the night and walk in this bright garden under the winter sun! The world outside is waiting for us. So is breakfast After breakfast we'll really be together again, you and I, my spirit. I sang as I ran my hot bath, and while it filled I drank my tea. What excellent tea! I felt the flutter of water over my body when I moved in my bath, and I thought, Lovely warm water, you too are my lover, whatever touches me today is the touch of love.

I was dressed and my night-case packed when Simon came to my room.

"How beautiful you are!" he said. "Such a shining beauty!"

I laughed and glanced from him to the mirror, and, for a split second I glimpsed it – the shining look – and then my everyday face smiled back at me.

After breakfast we drove into Plettenberg Bay to fill up with petrol. The garage was on the heights and opposite it was the general store.

"Shall I pop over the way and buy a paper?" I asked.

Simon grinned. "If you want to read yesterday's news all over again."

"Of course! Yesterday hasn't caught up with us yet. It's out of this world. Everything's out of this world."

"We'll come here for our honeymoon," he promised.

When we were on the road again I said, "I suppose we'll be in P.E. in time for lunch."

"Not if I can help it. We've got our picnic lunch and we're going to dawdle. We'll make P.E. for tea."

"Won't the Burtons expect us?"

Mr Burton was the manager of the Port Elizabeth branch of A. & B., and he and his wife were going to put us up for the next forty-eight hours.

"I've fixed that. The young lady at the motel is going to ring through and say not to expect us much before five o'clock."

I relaxed, luxuriating in my new-found happiness. This wonderful day was to be all ours. The distress and sorrow of the past weeks had evaporated in the warm radiance of love.

We wound up through the wooded hairpin bends of the Blaauwkrantz Pass above the river that flowed into the sea at Nature's Valley. Waterfalls plunged down deep ravines where early arums gleamed among ferns taller than a man. Here, in the dense sub-tropical Tsitsikama forest, the soaring trees were garlanded with liana monkey-ropes and flowering parasites, and here the foresters sometimes saw the last descendants of the biggest tuskers in Africa – hardly a herd now, only a family of huge elephants, protected like every other wild creature and flower in this paradise of the Cape.

Beauty deprives me of speech. It moves me like great music; one wouldn't chatter through a splendid symphony; so I leaned close to Simon, mute and rapt; he looked down at me, half touched, half amused, wholly understanding.

At last we were up on the wooded coastal plateau, and he said, "Shall we go into the forest and see the Big Tree?"

"Let's! I've never seen it."

"Nor have I."

He slowed down and we turned off the National Road where a signpost showed the way to the famous giant of the forest.

We bumped over the rough track, veined with serpentine roots, and soon we came to a glade partially cleared by the woodman's axe. Simon didn't bother to lock the car when we got out. We were utterly alone.

"So this is it?"

We stood staring up at the Big Tree, fenced to protect it from human hands that would have carved dates and initials on its huge bole.

"*Die pluk van varings en blare en die uithaal van bolle is streng verbode*," read Simon from the notice-board printed in both official languages. "So now you have been warned. You pick ferns or leaves, or lift bulbs on pain of death. The Department of Forestry says so."

" 'Species. Yellowwood,' " I continued. " 'Height, One hundred and fifty feet. Age. Approximately two thousand years.' That makes you think! Two milleniums."

"They say it takes three hundred years for a yellowwood to reach maturity."

Moss and lichen covered the giant's base and the massive trunk was hung with stalactites of peeling bark. Our gaze followed it upwards to the spreading umbrella of delicate olive-grey foliage stroking the clear blue sky.

"Shall we go further into the forest, Chick?"

I nodded, though I was oppressed by the green gloom. We clambered over worm-eaten logs and down a winding forester's path which eventually lost itself in a carpet of thick fern under a tangled canopy of branches and creepers quivering with the wings of butterflies.

"Can you picture him?" whispered Simon. "The little yellow Bushman with his bow and poisoned arrows? Two thousand years ago, when the Big Tree was young, he'd have hunted here."

The leaves were thick and damp under our feet.

"It's eerie," I said. "Frightening."

The mighty elephant, the tiny forest-deer, the baboon, the monkey and the snake belonged here. So did the little nomad hunter of pre-history. We were the intruders. We listened to the sounds of hidden life. Bird? Animal? *"Sweee! Cheeooh! Cheecheechee . . ."* and thin insect humming. Over all, there was the unceasing murmur of the tree-top wind we couldn't feel. The humid jungle scent of streams swollen with the first winter rains lay like mist over the earth. For two milleniums the Big Tree had listened to these voices, breathed this air, harboured its wild creatures and scattered its seed.

"We're so small, Simon . . . We're nothing at all."

"We're as great as our love."

Brave words, but tremors of fear were creeping round the nape of my neck. When Simon wanted to make love to me, I said, "No, not here!"

We found our way slowly back to the glade. Once he paused to touch the smooth mottled trunk of a sapling.

"I can almost feel the sap rising under the bark."

"Rima might have said that."

His palm flung away from the tree as if it had been stung. So she was in his mind too – Rima with her strong hands worshipping the wood, divining the weird ritual figures only she could release? Even the birds flitting here and there brought her near.

"This isn't our place," I said in a sort of panic. "It's hers! It's full of things she'd understand . . . invisible wings above, and, under the ground, a whole system of growth pushing these trees up to the light. It's ancient and spooky . . . full of dark African spooks. Don't you feel them – the phantoms of the past? And Rima . . . Rima too!"

He whirled round and gripped my arms. In that weird leaf-light his skin was greenish.

"Stop it, Maxie! We've got to talk this out some time – this business of Rima. There's a hell of a mess to be sorted out, and it's got to be tackled sensibly and honestly. We're going to hurt a lot of people by taking what we want – by taking each other. We've got to face that. We've a great deal to face."

"You're not willing to face it. You can't bear to hurt those people."

"It's not easy to throw loyalties to the wind."

His jaw jutted and his face had gone thin. Did he really want to marry me or was he already regretting last night? Could any man who'd once loved Rima put her out of his heart? She was here in the forest with her narrow mocking face and her hair red as fire.

"Rima'll be between us always," I said.

"If you think that we'd better call it a day."

"She's possessed you. For years she's possessed you."

Stupid to say that, even if it were true, but my brain was reeling with jealousy and a vague comprehension of the pressures that had moulded so much of Simon's life and forced so many of his actions. Rima, spoilt and subtle, lit by the fluctuating flame of genius, determined to wake the passion of this man who might have been well content to remain her "brother". Her parents encouraging the altered relationship, pushing him gently and firmly towards the alliance that would bind him still more closely to his adopted family.

His fingers tightened on my arms and bit hard into my flesh, bruising it.

"Don't you understand anything? It's you who came between Rima and me! We could have made a go of it but for you. You were the haunting one – ever since that night in Mombasa. It's you I've fought – the thought of you always in my mind."

"Mombasa! Why didn't you tell me then?"

"I was committed. Even then I was committed. Rima and I were destined for each other. I wasn't free."

"Are you any freer now? Answer me that!"

He almost threw me from him.

"God knows! D'you think it's been easy – these last weeks? Accepting the truth with all it entails! I've been through it again and again. You haven't got around to that yet, have you, my darling – my dear love?"

I dragged him round to look at me. The bitterness and trouble in his eyes shocked me.

"*You* haven't considered this matter day after day, night after night. When I told you I loved you it wasn't because we'd had a good dinner, or because you were beautiful and we were alone, or even because every single thing about you cried out to be loved. I told you the solemn truth that had been torn out of me bit by bit – a truth that means letting down all the people who matter most in my life. Only a great love could be worth that – not a little love sick with silly doubts."

I had never seen him so pale and tight-lipped, biting off the words that made me understand that our love was no simple romance but a breach of faith.

"We daren't look back, Maxie. We have to go forward, and, if our ghosts go with us, that's part of the price we must pay."

Now he was demanding that I share his guilt in sacrificing Rima. She has her art, I thought. She'll get over this. She's dedicated to her work. But I didn't care. Simon had said he loved me, and I would never give him up. He was mine for as long as we lived, till death, and beyond.

His eyes were changing and melting as he watched my face, and, when I slid my arms up and round his neck, he bowed his head to meet my lips and we were one.

The leaves of the Big Tree whispered high above us. In time the old giant would fall or stand dead in his kingdom, but this moment of human love would never die. It would linger on in the forest, part of its mystery, of earth and sky, of the roots under the earth, and of every living thing that takes a mate.

30

SIMON

"IF IT WEREN'T for the family complications what would you want to do? About us? About getting married?"

We had taken one of the branch roads down to a secluded cove. There wasn't a soul in sight, not even a Coloured fisherman. The morning sun was surprisingly hot and we'd stripped into bathing things. We lay on a rug spread under the sheer rock face and the ledge above us formed a bar of shadow for our heads.

"I'd want us to get married soon. We'd take a flat and I'd keep on my job till we'd saved enough to buy a little cottage by the sea and have two babies. First a boy, then a girl."

"Instead of which, we'll have to give up our jobs and start again from scratch. Both of us. Somewhere else. England, perhaps. Or the Federation. It has to be a new start."

"Simon—"

"Yes?"

"When did you first feel sure it was me you wanted – only me?"

He laughed and touched the back of my neck, ruffling my hair.

"I don't know. It came on me, bit by bit, in spite of trying to turn away from it. But there was a day when you moved my heart till it hurt – the day little Robert Rocky was called at the Langa Inquiry. I was watching your face. Its tenderness, woman and child at the same time. When the Old Lion put Robert on the table and made him show the court his scars your eyes filled with tears and you bent your head. The little gold tendrils here, at the nape of your neck, were childlike, but your compassion was all woman."

He traced the curve of my neck round over my shoulder and down to the swell of my breasts. I arched my body to his hands, my eyes half shut. A little blue flower nodded on the ledge above my head, dancing against the cobalt sky. Nothing could separate us now. This love might cost him his family and his job, but we would never give it up. I couldn't see the little blue flower any more because he was covering my face with kisses, I tingled and melted under his lips.

When at last we drew apart the shadow of the ledge had broadened and the incoming tide was beating into the cove, hissing up the sand. Suddenly I wanted to plunge into that foaming ice-cold water. I sprang up.

"I'm going in for a dip."

Before he could stop me I was running down to the water and into the surf. I heard him call after me, but I only waved and laughed. The cold took my breath away, but it was glorious. A big roller, curling and breaking close inshore, caught me and knocked me off my feet. Choking and gasping, blinded by spray and my own wet tangled hair, I felt its backward suck carry me down the steeply shelving bank into deep water. One second my feet touched sand, and the next I was out of my depth, swimming frantically against the drag of the undertow that swirled in the direction of the cruel jagged rocks forming the camber of the cove. I heard the thunder and crash of the waves against the rocks and thought, This is it.

Then Simon was within reach of me, swimming strongly, washed against me, holding onto me.

"Hang onto my shoulders and swim like hell!"

I tried to do as he said. This was very different from those long ago "rescues" in the dam at Loire. This was life or death.

"The next'll take us forward," he panted. "Hang on!"

A huge roller came surging in, a wall of green glass topped with flying spray as it curled for the break. We were in it, in the pounding foam, clinging to one another, dashed and bruised as the force of the wave rolled us up the steep shelf and recoiled. Simon lifted me bodily and carried me clear of the sea. Then he set me on my feet, his arms clasped round my waist so that I drooped across them while water poured from my nose and mouth.

"You crazy little idiot! There was a warning notice further up the beach. You know our coast can be treacherous!"

He began to rub me down with a sun-warmed towel. But even when I was in my slacks and woollen sweater my teeth still chattered. I knew very well that we might both have been dashed to pulp against the rocks.

He poured hot coffee from the thermos and handed it to me, and I was glad to drink it.

"Dry your hair, you poor little drowned rat!"

He gave me the towel while he dressed. As I rubbed my hair I knew that there was a thought – something significant – floating about in the back of my mind, something that must be dredged to the surface. He was beside me again, smiling down at me.

"Could you eat?"

"Yes."

"Good."

We tucked into the motel sandwiches, and quite suddenly the thought was there.

"You saved me from drowning."

"You trained me up to it. You were always drowning in the dam at Loire."

We laughed. Safe again. Happy.

"Rima has a Chinese theory. If you rescue someone from death that person has the right to sit on your doorstep and be cherished by you for ever after."

"So you suggest that from now on you're my responsibility?"

"That's it. You've cheated destiny of its victim, so you've accepted the responsibility."

"I seem to recall that once upon a time – after a fire – Jamie had that privilege."

"You've cancelled that out."

"All right then. From now on I'm the master of your destiny."

The shadow of the rock was wider now and we knew that we must be on our way.

It was in Port Elizabeth that the pattern of our tour began to shape itself into a sort of dual existence. On one side was the job we had been sent to do for Antrobus & Beeford; on the other was our own dream world. There was the pretence that we were no more than cousins and colleagues, and there were the stolen moments of bliss when we were lovers, hungry for each other, living only for the next chance of being alone.

Port Elizabeth is a vital growing city, and, in spite of the recent disturbances, our local A & B was flourishing. Everybody we met was optimistic about the future. Our troubles would pass.

Mrs Burton, our hostess, belonged to one of the old "border families" descended from the first British Settlers of 1820.

"Eight Kaffir Wars *they* had," she said, "and look at the Eastern Province now! Port Elizabeth was no more than a camp when those early settlers stepped ashore, and today it's a thriving industrialised port, the centre of South Africa's important wool trade."

She was proud of the Eastern Province and its turbulent history, and her husband was equally proud of the record of his branch of Antrobus & Beeford.

When we thanked them for their hospitality and set out for Durban we did not go direct. We went to the Wild Coast first. Simon had fallen in love with an ingenious wooden giraffe belonging to the little Burton girl. The creature was full of character, and Mr Burton told us that it had been carved by an old Pondo craftsman down on the Wild Coast.

"I buy most of his stock for our Tourist department, and it goes like hot cakes. As a matter of fact, I've often wondered if it wouldn't be worthwhile to use the prototypes for wholesale manufacture."

"I'll visit your Pondo pal," said Simon. "What's his address?"

Mr Burton produced a map and showed us a small inlet on the Pondo coast where a river flowed into the sea.

"It's a fisherman's heaven," he said, "but very unsophisticated. You'd have to spend the night at Aunt Emily's Inn. We often go there in the summer for a week's peace and quiet. Of course, it's out of season now."

So we left Port Elizabeth behind and headed for the Wild Coast.

The city fell behind us and at once the fine tarmac road plunged into a sea of elephant bush. Travel in Africa is like that. You leave the city limits and there you are, out in the *bundu*, with dorps and filling stations hundreds of miles apart. If you give a hitch-hiker a lift you may have him with you all day, and he could hit you on the head and steal the car and no one be any the wiser. You can take your pick of a place to commit murder or make love, and be sure of solitude. Nothing but earth and sky.

Our road took us through the bleak grassy uplands of the Transkei, swept that Friday afternoon by a cold wind with a touch of sleet in it.

It was Bantu territory, the land of the Black cattle-men, grazed bare and seamed with erosion. Scattered groups of little white huts stood up boldly over the heights and rifts of this great tribal country which has gradually become the land of old men and boys, women and infants, because the young men are lured to the cities by the industrial revolution that is rapidly changing the pastoral face of South Africa. Most of the people are primitive and gay, their oiled and ocre-painted bodies wrapped in blankets fastened with huge safety-pins. The little herd-boys waved and danced as we went by, leaving them cavorting in a cloud of red dust. Here and there we came upon parties of stick-fighters and their followers, striding and leaping along the path to some distant contest. The stick-fighters were barbarically adorned, as heroic in the eyes of Bantu boys as a famous athlete would be to a European schoolboy. Every now and again we'd see the traditional African frieze of an un-hurried file of stately women, a water calabash on each turbaned head, treading the well-worn track from the spring to the *kraal*, their pic-caninnies strapped to their backs.

It was afternoon when we began to wind down through citrus and banana plantations into a lush jungle-clad canyon. The scene was more tropical and the air balmier with every mile as we followed the course of a golden-brown river to the sea. The Bantu here wore blue togas and many beads. Simon drove onto a raft at the river crossing and we were ferried to the far side by a team of chanting Pondos, glittering with brass ornaments, their legs encased in old inner tubes.

This was the Wild Coast.

A general store and a few bungalows marked the fishing village, and we drew up in front of a little inn with linoleum floors and an atmosphere of solitude and leisure. Long white rollers pounded onto the beach between the river and a rocky promontory. We looked at each other with a sense of home-coming.

My room faced onto the river mouth and the sea, and the air that came through the open window was strong and salty. When Simon tapped on my door before dinner I had changed into the same corduroys and fleecy pink pull-over I'd worn at the motel on the first night of our journey. Already that seemed long ago.

"I love it," I said, looking out at the river and the towering dark cliffs above it. "I love this Wild Coast."

"And I love you. God, how I love you! No more wondering about it – thinking this is infatuation, it will pass. It's getting dark and I can't see your face properly. Not to see your face – ever again – that would be death."

His hands cupped my upturned face and his eyes were tender in the twilight. Already it seemed to me that our happiness had entered a phase of greater safety, that the guilt and the ghosts had fled before the full flowering of this love that had grown to maturity with me. It was not a thing apart. It was me – all of me.

"Maxie," he said. "I wrote to Rima from Port Elizabeth. I told her everything. That I want to marry you. There should be an answer waiting for us when we reach Johannesburg."

Rima's answer. What would it be? For an instant a chill crept into my heart.

We went down to the homely dining-room. It was out of season and there were few guests, only a party of young men, obviously on a fishing holiday, and two other couples and a small child.

After dinner, when we were sitting in the small lounge warmed by a cheerful wood-fire, the proprietress, Mrs Travers, came to ask us if we had all we needed. I caught Simon's eye and wanted to laugh. She was our idea of what Aunt Emily should be, from the top of her grey head to the soles of her solid size sevens.

"The electricity is off at ten o'clock," she said. "We make our own. We're not late birds here. Our fishermen visitors get up with the dawn."

We asked her to sit down and Simon offered her a cigarette and lit it for her. It was obvious that she was intrigued with us.

"Antrobus," she said to Simon. "Now would you be connected with Antrobus & Beeford?"

"Very much so. The Chairman is my step-father, and my cousin here, Miss Lamotte, is a Beeford on her mother's side. We both work for the family firm. We're on our way to Durban, but we want to see the old Pondo maker of toy animals."

She smiled. "Old Noah? We all know him here. Your Mr Burton from Port Elizabeth is one of his best customers."

She was very friendly and needed no encouragement to talk. "Everybody calls me Aunt Emily," she said, "so you'd better do likewise."

We found that there was very little she didn't know about the Bantu and his habits, for her father had owned a chain of trading stores in the Transkei, and she spoke fluent Xhosa with all the appropriate clicks. She was genuinely fond of the Natives, but to her they were all still children.

"Everything has to be done for them, and is it easy to teach them soil conservation! The Government has a proper struggle there. Never ending. Of course, the trader is really their best friend and the store is their club. They come from miles around and sit all day in the sun, bartering goods and exchanging news and views. No buying and selling in a hurry for them! The store is the heart of the Bantu grapevine."

"It's always the same in Africa, the trader's the real link between primitive Black and White progress," said Simon. "Even more than the missionary."

She snorted. "I can assure you, my father knew more about the Bantu than any missionary ever did! The trader sells the Black man what he wants to buy. The missionary has to bribe him to take religion." She glanced at her watch. "Bless my soul, nine-thirty! That's my bedtime."

A little while after she had gone we went to our rooms, tip-toeing hand in hand down the linoleum-covered passage. We wanted to laugh at the expressive shoes outside the doors, the heavy walking-shoes of the young men, a woman's small brown sandals inside her husband's broad ones, the family group of man's, woman's and child's. We could imagine their owners, sound asleep and dreaming of fish – big fish on the end of a line, or minnows in a little painted pail.

"I'll come and say goodnight to you later," whispered Simon.

I nodded, butterflies fluttering in my tummy.

When he came to my room the house-lights had dimmed and died. Moonlight shimmered on the river in the shadow of the mysterious jungle-clothed cliffs and the night was silent except for the thunder of surf on the beach. Somewhere a Native woman was singing a lullaby.

I put out my arms to him.

For two days we stayed at Aunt Emily's Inn. Sometimes now I wonder if that weekend was a dream or a reality. Love. Infatuation. How can you tell them apart? For two days my world was Simon. If doubts were hidden deep in my heart I buried them deeper. There would be a letter in Johannesburg. Facts to be faced. Let them wait. I was drugged with desire, drowsy with a slumbering contentment that could at any moment wake into fiery passion.

The sun shone on our daylight hours and the night tides ran high as the full moon drew the ocean with her timeless inexorable pull. We rowed up the golden river between its high tropical banks and swam in lonely reaches with only the birds for company. Aunt Emily directed us to the hut of Noah, the Pondo craftsman who lived in the woods up on the heights above the sea. We found him squatting in the sun outside his hut, dressed in a blanket and a straw hat, his dark hands chipping and chiselling the soft raw wood into the shapes of birds and beasts.

Simon picked up a ferocious lion about a ruler's length from nose to tail. "Noah's got the Disney touch, Maxie. He puts character and comedy into his animals. They're easy to pack, unbreakable, essentially African, and great fun. I must talk to Lew Consadine in Jo'burg about exploiting this."

He bought most of the old craftsman's stock and commissioned more. But I was glad when we left our Pondo sculptor. His work, so quick with life, reminded me of Rima's. The thought of Rima was shallow in my consciousness, often rising to the surface, and I'd have to thrust it away to keep my joy in the present.

Monday came – "blue Monday, back to work!" Aunt Emily said – and the chanting Pondos ferried us back across the river on the first stage of our journey to Durban and civilisation.

Durban in June is at its best. Warm enough to bathe by day, but cold after nightfall.

We spent the inside of a glorious week there with my cousin, Charlie Beeford, who had recently been transferred from the Federation to take over the management of our Natal branch. His wife, Linda, was a dark husky-voiced American with a lazy southern drawl. Their attractive house was on the Berea high above the harbour. The day after our arrival Linda told us that she was having two friends of ours to dinner.

"You haven't seen them for quite a while. But I won't say another word about them. They want to surprise you."

We could hardly believe it when Sandy and June Johnson were shown onto the porch where we were having sundowners. Their cousinship seemed more marked than ever, and I had a vivid recollection of my first meeting with them and the "three apostles". As we greeted each other with delight, Sandy's soft wolf whistle was an echo of Mombasa that made me laugh, and pleased me too.

"What two years can do, young Maxie! You were a corker then, but now!" He grabbed me and kissed me as if he meant every moment of it. "This gorgeous South African habit of promiscuous kissing. How I adore it!"

Simon protested. "Hey, that'll do! When you come up for air for the third time you might try telling us what you're doing here – apart from devouring my favourite cousin. We thought you were settled on the Copper Belt."

June pulled her husband's ears. "He's incorrigible! You're quite right, Simon. We have our own store in Kitwe, but we've decided to educate Mat and Mark here. We've put them to boarding-school in Natal."

"So you've faith in the Union?" asked Simon.

"Most of our investments are here," said Sandy. "That should prove it. We like the Copper Belt and we're doing well, but, with the Belgian Congo getting independence at the end of this month, a good deal of trouble may spill over into the Federation."

"Central Africa's a cook-pot at the moment," said June, "with too many independent states emerging much too fast, and a scum of looters, rapers and murderers coming to the top side by side with the new Black political aristocracy."

"Where's your youngest – funny little Luke?" I asked.

"No longer their youngest," said Linda. "John arrived last year. Some people have all the luck." To her sorrow, her own marriage was childless.

"The two little ones are at home in Kitwe with my mother in charge," explained June. "But we fly back on Tuesday from Johannesburg. As a matter of fact, we're spending Monday night there with the Consadines. Charlie says you'll be with them too."

"That reminds me. We have a plan." Charlie paused in the operation of shaking gin and lime on ice to make a gimlet. "Why shouldn't we all go up to the Hluhluwe rhino reserve for the weekend and the Johnsons could go on from there to Johannesburg with you two?"

Suddenly I realised that it seemed ages since I'd been gay, sociable and carefree. I began at once to look forward to Friday as a child waits for some extra special treat.

I*

Throughout the long drive from Durban through the lush cane-fields into the blue mountains of Zululand the Johnsons and Beefords had driven together, while we carried the weekend blankets and provisions in the station-wagon.

No sooner had we passed through the gates into the Hluhluwe Reserve than the whole tapestry of bush and woodland came alive. We saw the zebra and the wildebeeste grazing together, and shy entrancing herds of buck, and the funny warthog families trotting smartly along, tails erect, with father in the lead and baby bringing up the rear. We were in the little kingdom of protected wild life where nature's only enemy is the poacher.

At dusk we drove into the grassy thorn-enclosed camp high above the tumbled hills and wide valleys. Thatched cottages and *rondavels* accommodated visitors, and the meat we had brought with us was grilled and served by camp-boys. The two couples shared a cottage and Simon and I had adjoining *rondavels*. The night was cold but so fresh and beautiful that we put on slacks and warm sweaters and ate outside in the shelter of a wild fig tree. Charlie had brought his guitar and after supper we sang the songs of the camp-fire the world over. But when Linda crooned the Negro spirituals and folk-songs of her own Deep South the rest of us fell silent and listened spellbound. At last Charlie put his guitar aside.

"Time to turn in, if we mean to go rhino-spotting at dawn."

When the others had gone to bed Simon and I lingered a while in the tranquil night. The little *rondavels* and larger cottages cast their solid shadows on the grass, and the fig tree trailed its piebald patchwork at our feet. Beyond the thorn-fence a rhino snorted and we could hear the grunting of some wild animal, perhaps a buck. Below us the ridges and knolls were clear-cut by moonlight, and, in the river-beds the silver mists lay deep.

When we called "Goodnight" to one another, loud enough for the others to hear, there was a smile in our voices.

In the early mornings and late afternoons we went out in the cars with our little Zulu guide, Zeta. Charlie had binoculars with him and we gazed into the prehistoric faces of the near-blind rhinos with their eyes and their horns incongruously placed half-way down their noses. We went to the water-hole at sundown and saw the fantastic double-jointed act of a giraffe getting himself a drink; and were enthralled when Zeta told us that the "cattle" grazing on a distant hillside were in fact buffalo. When we lazed in the camp during the heat of the day, we heard the camp-boys singing sonorously while the darting jewel-like honey-birds filled the trees with their twittering and the whirr of wings.

But once again "blue Monday" dawned and Simon came into my *rondavel* to fetch my case.

Without a word he took me in his arms and held me as if he would never let me go. We're together, I thought. We're not losing each other. Why does this feel so terribly like goodbye?

Charlie and Linda returned to their lovely but childless home; June and Sandy came with us, heading for Johannesburg and the Copper Belt, but leaving half their family behind; and Simon was no doubt wondering – as I was – what message he would find from Rima at the end of this day. No happiness could be flawless.

The great mountain ranges fell behind us and the tawny expanses of the highveld spread to the far horizon. Towards evening we drove through the pulsing dynamic city of sky-scrapers and pastel mine-dumps to Hillcrest, the Johannesburg home of Lew Consadine and his wife.

Lew and Beth Consadine did a great deal of entertaining for A. & B., and their way of life was geared to include a constant succession of house-guests. Hillcrest was always open to members of the Antrobus family, and the Consadines had often stayed at Rosevale during holidays at the Cape. They greeted us all warmly, and Lew – a big hearty man – slapped Simon on the back with cheerful good nature.

"You'll never guess who's here, my lad! Arrived at three this afternoon."

Beth was saying to June, "I think you Johnsons and Simon had better occupy the guest cottage, and the girls – Rima and Maxie – can share the old nursery."

Rima! The blood drained from my heart.

Suddenly all heads turned to the short marble staircase. There she was, smiling, swift as flame, running down the stairs straight to Simon, hands outstretched. He took them, his eyes narrow, the wings of his nostrils blanched.

"Rima! What on earth are you doing here?"

"I got your letter, darling, and I came at once. So here I am – your answer!"

She swung round to me before he could reply.

"And Maxie! I've a message for you – from Roberto Angeli. He says to tell you he'll get you a job in Italy any day you want it."

My hands clenched and my nails – my sharp claws – pierced my palms. The sudden pain shocked me back into self-possession.

"Good for you, Rima! You think of everything."

31

RIMA

Lᴇᴡ's ᴅᴇᴇᴘ ᴠᴏɪᴄᴇ rumbled comfortably into a moment of
tension.

"I'll take Sandy and June over to the guest-cottage. You can
take care of Maxie, Beth. Simon knows his way."

"Thanks," said Simon. "I'm at home."

The houseboy was taking the baggage across the lawn to the pretty
cottage which was a sort of annexe to the main house. Like the motel,
I thought, and a needle-sharp pain pierced my breast.

"Take a whiskey if you want one, Simon," called Beth, "and look
after Rima. Come along, Maxie. You must be dying for a bath and
rest. I hope you don't mind sharing with Rima, but we're full house,
and it's only for two nights. She phoned through to her father an hour
ago and he says you're to cut your time here short – pity about that –
and go straight on down to the Cape the day after tomorrow. She'll
be with you, of course. You could have knocked me down with a
feather when she rang Lew from Rome to say she was on her way here
to meet up with you two."

She opened the door into the large bedroom that had once been the
nursery for her daughters who were now married.

"We'd no idea she was coming," I said.

"No. It was evidently one of those impulsive decisions. She got
fed up with Florence. Homesick for Simon, she said." Beth laughed.
"Gideon Antrobus would like to see those two make a match of
it."

The centrally heated room was warm, and suddenly I couldn't
breathe. I went to the window, threw it open and inhaled great gulps
of frosty air. It was quite dark already and far away on the horizon
lightning forked among the stars. I could smell the veld – the dry grass
fragrance that reminded me of the wild parklands of Zululand. The city

grumbled and muttered to the east of us, a fantasy of soaring lights and winking signs, a loom of gold.

Beth showed me a little wheel on the heating tubes. "This regulates the temperature. Just turn it down a bit if you find the room stuffy."

"Everything's fine. If I'm down by half-past seven—"

"Or later. We don't dine before eight. Wear what you like. The men won't be changing."

When she had gone I tried to collect myself. Rima and Simon were downstairs. What were they saying to each other? Could she take him from me?

I was dressed and standing at the open window, trying to nerve myself to go down, when June tapped on the door.

"Child, you'll freeze! For pity's sake, shut that window! I've been sent to fetch you. Lew thought you could do with a cocktail or something."

"I could." What a horrible thing it is to smile with willpower and muscles alone.

The others were already gathered in the lounge when we went down.

"Rima, my girl," Lew was saying. "The newshounds are after you. Those sculptures of yours that were on exhibition here created quite a stir. Too primitive for my taste, but the critics like you."

Her clear laugh rang out. "You're honest, anyway."

I got through dinner somehow. As we left the table, Beth tapped her husband's shoulder in passing.

"Now don't keep Sandy and Simon talking and drinking liqueur brandy for hours! Tomorrow's a heavy day for most of us."

But it was near eleven when they rejoined us.

"Anybody want a nightcap?" asked Lew presently. "What about you, June?"

"Not for me. We should call it a day. Don't you think so, Sandy?"

"Wife of my bosom, when you say it's time for bed have you ever known me protest?"

Lew opened the French doors onto the terrace and strolled across the dewy grass to the guest-cottage with June, Sandy and Simon. Beth came upstairs with Rima and me.

"You can sleep late tomorrow, Rima. Breakfast in bed. Ring and tell Polly when you want it." She turned to me. "Eggs and bacon'll be on the hot-plate in the dining-room at eight o'clock, Maxie. You'll need to be ready to go into town with Lew and Simon at half past. Our Johannesburg branch is the brightest star in the A.&B. constellation, and Lew won't let you miss a corner of it."

"What about the Johnsons? Will we see them before we go?"

"At breakfast. I'm taking them to the airport right afterwards. Good-night, my children. Sweet dreams."

So now we were alone, Rima and I.

This wing was cut off from the Consadine's suite by the bathroom and Beth's little sewing-room. Rima stood leaning against the door, her eyes hot and dangerous, her breath coming fast.

"You always meant to take him from me, didn't you?"

"You staked your claim. I didn't fight you, Rima. I fought myself. Now it's different. Now I'm fighting you."

"His letter – the one posted from Port Elizabeth, the one trying to ditch me – got me just in time. But I had to move fast."

"He'll still ditch you."

"Oh, no, he won't!"

I faced her, my heart hammering. What new trickery was this?

"Shall we get to grips, Rima?"

"Let's!"

Her hands shot out and her fingers whipped round my wrists – those strong sculptor's fingers that could drag life out of the hardest wood. "Yes, Maxie, let's get to grips! Simon will never marry you! He'll marry me because I'm going to have his child."

I stared down at my wrists as I had done long ago at Loire when she had told me her "secret" and the invisible barrier had first begun to rise between us. If I had seen my veins slashed and life-blood gushing it would have seemed less of a mortal injury than the words she had just spoken. But Rima too was suffering. She had possessed her man, yet she had lost his love.

She began to tear off her clothes, sobbing as she did so, and when she stood naked before me, as if to offer me the final proof, tears were streaming down her face. I turned away from her tears, from her swollen delicately veined breasts and thickened waist, only slightly changed, but, to me, who knew her body like my own, eloquent enough. I wanted to escape from her, anywhere into the night. But we were fettered as we always had been. We could fight and wound each other, but we remained together.

When at last I turned off the lights there was no sleep for either of us. Cold as it was, we had left the window open and the clean frosty air poured into the room. Questions sparked in my brain.

"You haven't seen him since March – since he was in Italy. Yet it was in May . . . last month . . . that he realised he loved me! How could he have let us drift deeper and deeper into a love affair when all the time he must have known—"

"About me? He didn't. He knew for the first time tonight. I told him when we were alone before dinner."

"But if it happened in March – it must have been then – you'd have suspected weeks ago! Why didn't you tell him at once? Surely you can see that none of this need have happened if you'd told him!"

She drew a sharp painful breath and sat up in bed, a shadowy form in the dark.

"If I'd told him he'd have insisted on a quick marriage. I didn't want that – then. I had other plans."

"What plans could you have had? You'd been caught."

"My room-mate – a Swiss girl – knew of a doctor in Zurich. You pay, and no trouble. I waited till I was positive and then she made the arrangement for me. I'd have been in Zurich by now – not in Johannesburg – if it hadn't been for Simon's letter. That changed everything."

"Why should it have changed your plan?"

"I'm not handing him over to you, Maxie!" She turned fiercely towards me and I saw the pale featureless glimmer of her face. "Why should I? He's been my lover for months – all the time you were chasing round England and Scotland with Jamie Vermeulen. He wanted us to marry, but I wouldn't have it. Not then."

"Why on earth not? You've always meant to marry him. You still do. At any price."

She was hugging herself, rocking a little. She had stopped crying long ago.

"It's hard to explain. I suppose I wanted it all ways. My freedom means a tremendous lot to me. I have a sensation sometimes . . . so strange . . . of wings brushing by, wings of genius, perhaps, just touching me for an instant . . ." She tossed back her fluffy hair. "I needed Italy for my work. I reckoned marriage could wait. I hadn't counted on you sneaking in to steal him."

A torment of jealousy shook me from head to heel.

"You think you can take a man when and how you want, pick him up, use him, drop him and pick him up again?"

"So I can." Her voice was razor-sharp, out to cut me up. "Simon wasn't my first, and he knew it. But he was the only one who ever mattered a damn, or ever would. He knew that too. He took me as I was – a woman and an artist, of an age to do what I liked."

"Can you still do what you like ... with Simon?"

"Yes. Because his letter came in time. With me this way, his child – his life – in my body, he won't let me down. You know him well enough for that! It was fate that he wrote when he did. Three days later – even two – and my hold over him would have been gone. Down the drain."

I lay on my face, my head turned away from her. There was no answer to what she'd said.

"You always lie that way, don't you, Maxie? Ever since your back was burnt that night at Loire, the night Jamie saved you. How well we know each other!"

"And you could always see in the dark. Cat's eyes."

"We've shared so much all our lives. Even Simon we've shared. That's right, put your hands over your ears! Go off by yourself, if you can – very much by yourself."

"Stop it! You've got him – you've got Simon. Can't you let it go at that?"

Though my face was buried I felt her hate stretch out towards me like the neck of a hissing goose.

"No, I can't. Because you've had him – and you mean to have him again."

"It's finished. You've made sure of that. It's all quite finished between him and me."

"Nothing is finished between the three of us. Not yet."

She made it sound like a curse. But at the root of the curse lay fear.

I suppose I must have slept, because I woke when Polly, the Native maid, brought us tea and orange juice at seven o'clock. Rima sat up.

"I've decided to fly down to the Cape today. I'll go to the airport with Beth and the Johnsons and get the first plane south."

"I thought you were coming with us tomorrow."

"I can't face a thousand mile car journey all in one stretch. Not with this beastly nausea. So you'll have the long long drive alone with Simon – a chance to say your tender farewells."

"If that's how you want it, that's how it'll be."

"Anyway, I want to get home quickly and warn Dad and Mom what's in the wind."

"Will you tell them the truth?"

She frowned. "About the baby? Not if I can help it. It's not the sort of thing they'd take lightly. Let them get around to that gradually, by themselves. By the way, Maxie, have they any idea about *you* and Simon – how you feel about each other?"

"You're the only person who knows."

"That's good. It takes the sting out of the situation. Let's keep it that way and save face all round."

She dressed quickly and went out of the room. Presently I saw her small figure cross the dew-spangled lawn in the direction of the guest-cottage – and Simon.

Beth Consadine accepted Rima's change of plan as only sensible.

"Personally, the Johannesburg to Cape Town run in one jump kills me, even if I'm only a passenger," she said. "Much pleasanter to fly."

As I bade the Johnsons goodbye, June took my hands and smiled at me with intuitive sympathy. "Come and stay with us at Kitwe," she said. "It'll be a change for you. You might even get a transfer to A. & B. up there."

Sandy gave me a smacking farewell kiss. "We'll take you to the Great Lakes, Maxie – the mysterious sources of the Nile – and we'll have lots of fun. Make it soon!"

The unexpected tears brimmed as I thanked them.

I suppose that all the time, all over the world, human beings are doing their jobs fairly efficiently with one half of themselves while the other half is suffering, rejoicing or worrying about their intimate private lives. That's how it was with me that day at A. & B., when Lew Consadine took me round the store while Simon talked to various people concerned with the financial side of the business.

I listened reasonably intelligently, and made notes and observations, while all the time I was thinking, What's the use? I'm going to get out of A. & B. as soon as I possibly can. But what'll Uncle Gideon think? He's been so kind and considerate to Mummie and me ever since the horror, and Mummie's not settled yet. How can I leave her till she is? The speculations and imaginary conversations with my uncle and my mother went round and round in the depths of my mind like disturbing background music.

"You see," Lew was explaining, "we have a different clientèle here in Johannesburg. We can afford to run these expensive and exclusive glamour lines. They pay us."

"It's magnificent," I said. "I've always thought A. & B. in Cape Town was something to boast about, but this goes one better all the way."

He beamed. "The women shoppers here are less conservative and more competitive. When you buy for us you mustn't have the old aunties in Cape Town in mind, you must think of women of the world – stylish and sophisticated. That goes for household effects as well as clothes and cosmetics."

I made the conventional responses like a member of a well-trained congregation in church.

When we returned to Hillcrest at the end of the day Beth met us.

"A sundowner? You must be exhausted, Maxie. When Lew takes someone round A. & B. he gives them the works."

"Did everybody get off all right?" asked Lew.

"Rima'll be in Cape Town by now and the Johnsons should be safely home at Kitwe."

Lew gave me a gin and tonic, and poured Simon a stiff whiskey and soda.

"Why don't the four of us go to the Monkey-Puzzle tonight?" he suggested.

Beth laughed. "That's the latest night club. Lew has shares in it and he adores an excuse to go and see how his investment's doing." Then she saw my hesitation, and added kindly. "Perhaps you'd rather not. Maybe you're too tired."

"I haven't been out dancing since . . ."

"Oh, my dear, I quite understand. It's a matter of feeling. The world's grown so heartless these days and mourning of any sort seems to be a thing of the past. In any case, you'll be leaving before dawn tomorrow, so we'll settle for dinner quietly at home."

The men had business to discuss, and Simon made no attempt to see me alone. The past fortnight, where every moment together had brought its own thrills and frustrations, had become an illusion. I no longer believed in it. The motel, the Wild Coast, Hluhluwe – none of them had ever existed.

Beth gave us a picnic hamper.

"It'll do for breakfast and lunch," she said. "But you'll need a real dinner. You'll probably make Beaufort West in time for a meal. Why don't you break your journey there?"

"We're going straight through," said Simon firmly. "It's easy when you share the driving."

When we slid through the quiet empty streets of Johannesburg before dawn we were by ourselves for the first time since leaving Hluhluwe sanctuary.

We were clear of the mine-dumps, the shanty-towns and the satellite towns of the reef long before daybreak touched the frosty highveld. I huddled into my warm coat. What now? I wondered. I was too tired and numb even to hate Simon.

"Maxie, what can I say?"

"Rima's said it all. She told me everything that night at the Consadines. We shared a room for our sins."

"Everything?"

"Yes."

"Including the Zurich plan – the one she changed at the last minute?"

I was surprised that she had told him that.

"Yes, even that. It's a pity she didn't take you into her confidence sooner."

"A great pity. If I'd known, I might have saved you so much—"

He broke off, biting his lip. Fatalistically, I wondered if I would have had it otherwise.

The sun was coming up, turning the veld to a sea of rippling gold. Huge fleecy clouds, billowing above the skyline, were edged with opalescent fire. The revolving blades of tall iron windmills flashed in the bright light of the new day as did the corrugated iron roofs of isolated dorps and farmhouses among their clumps of trees. Willow-fringed dams glowed here and there.

"Poor Rima," he said.

Anger blazed up in me.

"Has it struck you that she's using her condition to force your hand – to make you give me up?"

He sprang to her defence.

"You're not being fair. Rima isn't like that. She's proud and independent. She would never try to hold me if it weren't for this baby!"

I felt my face and heart harden. Fool and dupe! Couldn't he see through something so obvious?

The miles skimmed silently by. After a time he turned the car into a lonely lay-by, one of those small acacia groves off the main road, a pleasant patch of shade in the blinding glare. There was a stone mushroom table under the trees with four little stone benches round it. A big iron litter-bin stood on one side of the farmer's fence. On the other a windmill *klonked* lazily in the morning breeze. Cattle and sheep huddled under a huge weeping willow near the overflow from the cement cistern, immobile as clay animals in a Christmas crib. A colony of yellow weaver-birds darted noisily in and out of their beautiful elaborate nests. The farmhouse, three or four miles away in the lee of a *koppie,* formed another green oasis rather larger than ours.

We got out of the car and Simon put hard-boiled eggs, buttered bread and a thermos of coffee on the mushroom table between us.

"Breakfast," he said.

"I'd choke."

"Nonsense. Drink that coffee and eat your bread and butter." He peeled two eggs and gave me one. "There's a spill of salt and pepper for each of us."

I shrugged my shoulders and bit into the egg, but the bread stuck in my throat and I went over and threw the rest of the slice into the litter-bin. I came back and drank the coffee Simon had poured. He took cigarettes from a pocket of his bush-shirt and lit one for me.

We sat facing each other across the table. I had never seen him so grim.

"You believe what you said, I suppose – that Rima's trying to force me into a marriage I don't want?"

"Of course I do. She's always wanted you on her terms – when and how she likes, as lover or husband – but I've crashed in, so she's got to put the clock forward."

"Go on. Say everything that has to be said."

"The accident of finding herself pregnant was providential. So was the fact that you posted your letter when you did – in time to stop her getting rid of your child. She's keeping it because that's the only sure way of keeping you. The timing's gone a little bit wrong for Rima – an early marriage and family – otherwise it's all according to plan."

"I didn't know you had it in you to be so cruel and venomous."

"You're learning." Venomous? Yes, I was spitting poison at him, sickened by it myself. "This past fortnight we've been living in cloud-cuckoo-land," I added.

"It seemed real enough to me."

"Seemed!" Past tense and suggestion of doubt. "Your love for me was about as real as that mirage over there – a lake shimmering in the drought. The koppies stand knee-deep in refreshing water that doesn't exist. Daddy told me once that mirage was torture to the thirsty soldiers in the desert. But of course, it's only torture if you know it's false . . . or when you find out."

The breeze grew stronger as the day advanced. By noon it would be a high wind. The *klonk-klonk* of the windmill pump, no longer lazy, was a metronome beat in my head.

Simon's eyes were hostile slits. "Perhaps I should tell you something you *don't* know."

"What don't I know . . . About Rima and you and me?"

"She offered to release me. She said it was up to me whether she went back to Europe – and Zurich – or not."

"When did she say that?"

"Yesterday morning. She came to my room before breakfast. She said she hadn't appreciated before how serious it was between you and me. She was prepared to step out of the picture if I wanted it that way."

I put my hands over my face, recalling her neat figure crossing the lawn, quick and purposeful. Clever, tricky Rima! Putting herself in the right; appearing so magnanimous; knowing he'd never call her bluff; giving us this last day together as a parting gift in which to hurt each other beyond all redemption. I stood up.

"What are we waiting for? We've a long way to go."

"Maxie! Don't look like that – so hard, so shut away! I can't bear it, knowing I'm responsible."

"Life's curious, isn't it? Less than a fortnight ago we were planning a new life together. A new beginning. In the Federation perhaps. Now, for you, it's as you were, only better, your position nicely consolidated at A. & B., while I'm out on a limb—"

"How dare you! Don't you know what it means to me to hurt you? Of all people, *you!*"

His hands were flat down on the stone mushroom table as he leaned across it, his face contorted. Suddenly I was afraid. Between us, we'd torn him apart, Rima and I.

I can see his forearms now – bare, strong and brown under the short-sleeved bush-shirt; the sinews of his hands corded and tense, the working of his throat. I can hear the *klonk* of the windmill pump and the twitter of the busy yellow weaver-birds; and smell the dry hay-sweetness of the winter grass on the wind.

"Chick!"

My face was buried against the khaki patch-pocket over his heart; my whole body wept for want of him, crying its secret need, but my will fought the fatal inner yielding. I threw my head back to defy him, and my fists pounded on his chest.

"No! Never any more . . . never again! You've made your choice."

He let me go, and went slowly to the car. The cows and sheep continued to crop the grass in the willow's shade. Death of a small human love affair today, birth of an immortal king two thousand years ago. It was all one to them.

32

NEW BEGINNINGS

S IMON AND RIMA decided to be married quietly on Friday,
July 8th.

Of all people, it was Rocky who took exception to the date.
He went so far as to beg my mother to intercede with Uncle Gideon
to exert his right as master of the household and forbid the wedding on
that particular day.

We were having tea in Aunt Kate's cosy little study when the old
butler came in, ostensibly to fetch the tea-things, but in fact to make
his extraordinary request. The rest of the family were out and Mummie
and I were alone.

"But Rocky," she said reasonably, "it's Miss Rima's wish, and it's
the bride's right to choose her wedding day. Also it's the evening the
ship sails up the coast and they're going to spend their honeymoon in
Lourenço Marques."

Rocky stuck out a thick sulky underlip.

"This special Friday is a bad day."

I wondered if the old superstition about Friday being unlucky worried
him. Did he regard it as the devil's day when evil had triumphed over
good?

"What's wrong with it?" I asked.

"In Langa there is a man who dreams strange dreams and hears voices.
He tells the people that on Friday, July 8th, the days of darkness will
come upon us. The sun will not rise, great winds will blow, and all
the prisoners will burst out of the gaols." Rather sheepishly he added:
"There are many who believe that the end of the world is coming."

"Then the sooner Miss Rima marries Mr Simon the better," said
Mummie. "So that she has her own husband to take care of her through
these awful happenings."

But Rocky only growled that such a day was not good for important undertakings like marriage. My mother laughed and told him not to be foolish, but when he had taken the tray, and the door closed on him, she shook her head.

"Ever since the March troubles there's been a recrudescence of superstition and witchcraft among the Natives. It's always that way. Upset them politically and they're wide open to the witch doctor and the phoney prophet. Even Rocky, a parson of sorts! But, of course, one has to remember that it takes several generations for a Bantu to discard the Old Gods – if he ever does."

We learned later from Leslie that the people of Langa and Nyanga were taking candles and stores into the locations in preparation for the "days of darkness". They had all been told by the seer not to stir from their houses or go to work. Throughout the whole country the same prophecy had been spread and everywhere the Black people cowered in fear.

But Rima's wedding day dawned as bright and glorious a winter's morning as you could wish to see, and throughout the land the gaols remained filled to capacity with their usual complement of criminals plus the political detainees incarcerated under the Emergency.

"There!" said my mother. "You see!"

Rocky beamed, and breathed gusty sighs of relief, and his family left Langa without a qualm to attend the religious ceremony in the little church in the Kloof Nek Road.

Jamie was Simon's best man and the Vermeulens were the only guests who were not members of the Antrobus or Beeford clans. Uncle Gideon had told me to take Saturday morning off, after we'd seen the ship sail for the coast in a flat moonlit calm, Jamie took me back to Bergplaas for the weekend.

"So much for the seers and prophets," I said. "The predestined period of darkness could hardly have been brighter, day or night."

He laughed. "They cover themselves. The seer will simply tell the people that a white hen and a black tom-cat crossed his path in the hour of cockrow and everybody will accept such a combination of circumstances as being enough to cancel out any previous portents."

"Like the oracles of Ancient Greece. They always had a get-out."

I rested my head against his shoulder, thankful to be going back to the farm with him. The night was clear and cold; the vineyards and orchards bare. This was the way Rima loved our valley, wintry and leafless, colourless under the moon, the mountains etched against the starlit sky.

"Propitious or not," said Jamie. "I'm glad that's over."

"Rima's wedding?"

"*Ja.*"

"So am I."

"Now perhaps you'll be able to settle down, my Maxie."

"I? It's Rima who'll settle down."

"Not just Rima. You," he said. "*Du.*"

A tiny intimate German word and a world of comfort in it. I didn't argue.

It was Jamie who was really responsible for finding my mother's little farm.

A farmer friend of his in the Tokai area of the Peninsula wanted to sell a cottage and a few acres of his land. Jamie came to Cape Town the week after the wedding and told Mummie and me about it. We'd been out to dinner and we came back to my flat to discuss the idea.

"It sounds just what I'm looking for," said Mummie, "and the price your friend suggests is very reasonable if the place is all you crack it up to be. What's the snag? Is the cottage dilapidated?"

"Not at all. It's in an excellent state of repair. I went over the whole property with a fine-tooth comb."

"Well then, Jamie, come clean! Forget the salesmanship and tell us the catch."

He laughed, his blue eyes dancing in his sunburnt face.

"All right, then. This pal of mine, he's Koosie Van Tonder—"

"Koosie Van Tonder, the snake man!" My mother chuckled. "No wonder you led me up the garden-path step by step. What a neighbour!"

Koosie Van Tonder had many claims to fame in the Peninsula. He was a successful nurseryman, a well-known naturalist, and a popular writer and radio personality on his favourite subjects, which were landscape gardening and South African birds and snakes. His snake-park at a seaside holiday resort was an unfailing attraction for children and tourists, and he did a lively trade in the export of reptiles and snake venom, which he "milked" from the fangs of his captives for the manufacture of anti-snakebite serum.

"Koosie's a marvellous fellow," protested Jamie. "I've known him on and off for years. He married a connection of Pa's, and has a couple

of sons at Stellenbosch University. They come to us at Bergplaas sometimes on a Sunday, and suddenly I remembered that the last time I'd
seen them they'd mentioned this cottage. So I went to have a look at it."

"You're a dear. It was kind of you to bear me in mind. But I don't
fancy living next door to a viper's nest." My mother shuddered. But
Jamie didn't give up easily.

"*Og, nee!* It's nothing to disturb yourself about. See here, Koosie
has a beautifully designed pit up at his place – quite a distance from the
cottage – and the occupants don't get out except to be milked or taken
to the snake-park. And just think of the advantage of having such a
neighbour—"

"How near?"

"A couple of miles or so. And if you see so much as the tail of a snake,
all you have to do is give him a ring and he's right there with his forked
stick and his bag to catch the creature and its relatives. If it's a harmless
useful molesnake he tells you and you keep it. Then, again, if any of
your folk get bitten any time – running about barefoot as they do – he's
handy with the treatment. Nothing to fear."

I saw my mother beginning to turn the advantages over in her mind.
Perhaps, after all, this Koosie Van Tonder might be a desirable neighbour.

"Ring him up right now, Jamie. I'll go along and see that cottage
tomorrow."

By the time Simon and Rima returned from their honeymoon the
deal had been clinched. Uncle Gideon, of course, had approved it and
helped Mummie with all the business details. He loaned the money
she needed and assured her that, from his point of view, it was a "gilt-
edged investment".

It was wonderful to watch Mummie's interest and excitement in
the new enterprise. The little farm was in a pretty corner of Tokai,
sheltered by splendid plantations and watered by a stream fringed with
ferns and arums. Behind it was a sunny protea-covered slope, and
Mummie said at once, "I shall call it Suikerbossie – Sugar-Bush." A
few avocado trees grew near the house, and my mother at once recognised
their value.

"I'll make a bit on the side by selling avocadoes, pig-lilies and proteas.
I might even start bee-keeping, or mushrooms, and I'll certainly plant
out some asparagus beds. It's not far from the main Muizenberg Road
and I can set up a farm stall for my produce."

She bubbled over with new ideas. For the first time since my father's violent death she was really living again.

I flung myself heart and soul into the whole scheme with her. All my spare time and energy went in helping her get the cottage ready, deciding where the poultry should be kept, and planning a flower and vegetable garden. The Van Tonders couldn't have been more helpful. Koosie found Coloured painters and carpenters to do Mother's odd jobs, and produced the extra outdoor labour she required; and quite soon Corinne's brother, Abel, and his wife, Louisa, moved in as handy-man and cook-general.

"All Lizzie's family are reliable," said Mummie. "I shall feel safe with Abel and Louisa."

So the thrilling weekend came when Jamie arrived at Sugar-Bush in a farm lorry packed with crates of poultry. My mother welcomed her Loire chickens and turkeys like long-lost children, and that evening Jamie and I shared her first meal in her new home.

When I went out to the lorry to see him off he lifted me into the air and swung me round as if I were a child. He was glowing with pleasure.

"She'll be all right now, Maxie. She's got an interest in life again. She's full of plans. Looking forward."

Looking forward. That was living. I put my arms round his neck and tried to thank him for his share in it.

"*Og*, love," he said. "Don't look at me like that! There's spring in the air."

I heard the old lorry trundle down the farm track with its empty crates. Mummie was waiting for me in the doorway.

"Darling," she said, her eyes shining. "This is going to work out. I think I'm actually happy again."

Meanwhile Rima too was nest-making.

Kloof Cottage was daily assuming her character. Simon had given up his flat, and, when his possessions were in their new home, I realised how much Rima's influence had once pervaded his flat. By the strength of her personality art she had made it hers as her taste now dominated Kloof Cottage.

It did not seem strange that I seldom went to Rosevale or Rima's home because it was taken for granted that, outside my working hours, Mummie had first claim on my time. Then, during August,

Uncle Gideon decided to send Simon to visit our branch in the Federation.

In spite of the intervention of the United Nations the tragedy of the premature independence of the Belgian Congo had gone its dismal way. All civilised cohesion had broken down in a welter of inter-tribal warfare. Murder, mutilation, rape, disease and starvation were the order of the day; and White refugees streamed over the border into the Federation and south to the Union with ghastly stories of atrocities. Many of these unfortunate people had experienced unforgettable horrors and agonies as well as the loss of all their possessions.

The day Simon left Uncle Gideon sent for me in his office. I found Rima with him.

"Sit down, Maxie." A cheroot hung from his lip and he spoke irritably. "Can't you persuade this daughter of mine to stay with her mother and me at Rosevale while her husband is away?"

"Couldn't Simon? Can't you?"

"We've all tried. Simon did his best. But the word *obey* was not included in her marriage vows."

"I've Corinne and Lenno within call," said Rima.

"Their quarters are attached to your studio and you'd have to shout very loud indeed to attract their attention from the cottage."

"Oh, Daddy, surely you know we've a bell wired up from the cottage to the studio, to say nothing of the telephone."

"That may be. But they take their days out together. What then?"

"I'm not nervous."

He turned to me with a despairing glance. "You see how it is. She's obstinate as a mule. These are disturbing and lawless times when it's not right for a woman to be on her own."

"Maxie is," said Rima.

"In a flat. That's entirely different."

"Well, what about Aunt Clare out at Tokai – on the edge of beyond?"

"Abel and Louisa live in." He looked at me for support. "Can't you make her see sense?"

I smiled. "Not if you can't."

"So you'd better tell her your suggestion," said Rima firmly.

I sensed a trap and kept quiet. My Uncle took the cheroot from his mouth.

"The only alternative I can suggest is that you shut up your flat, Maxie, and stay with Rima at Kloof Cottage till Simon gets back."

Perhaps dismay showed on my face because Uncle Gideon added gently, "It would be a very great relief to Kate and me if you'd do that."

"It would be fun to have you for company," put in Rima. "Like old times. I'm keen to get Corinne and Lenno grooved in their new job while Simon's away. Having you there would be a help. It wouldn't interfere with your work here. Whether you come and go from Mouille Point or Kloof Nek can't make much difference."

"Shall we take it as settled?" said Uncle Gideon.

What could I do? Mummie and I owed him so much. Rima'd put me on a spot. There was no way of refusing.

I moved in that evening.

"Why did you want it this way, Rima? I simply don't understand."

I was unpacking my few things in the pretty spare-room. Rain beat on the window-pane.

"Three reasons."

She was sitting on the bed in her working jeans and smock. She stubbed out a cigarette with one of her decisive gestures, and adjusted the shade of the bedside lamp.

"Well?"

"First of all, I really do want to train Corinne and Lenno. She's inexperienced at cooking, and he's got to learn to be a houseboy as well as outside man."

"You'll try them out on the dog."

She laughed. "Don't be acid! Then secondly, we want to bolster up the face save. Simon, you and I have all three made fools of ourselves and we've already agreed to keep that quiet. So we must carry on as usual – best of friends and so on."

"Put on the act while Simon's away."

"Exactly."

"You're a deep one, Rima. And reason number three?"

She shrugged her shoulders impatiently. "For your information, this preg thing seems to speed up after the fourth month. You can't get away with it so easily. If I were at Rosevale Mom would soon be wise to it. You know how she is, wandering in and out of our rooms and finding excuses for little chats. She doesn't miss a trick. And I'm not ready to spill the beans yet."

"Anything else?"

She rose and moved slowly over to the window. She spoke with her back to me, her hands thrust deep into the pockets of her jeans.

"Perhaps I'm being fanciful – being the way I am – but . . ." Her voice was not quite steady, and her hair quivered as she tossed her head back. She went on. "I feel a need – a great need – to be with somebody who knows everything. No pretences and deceptions."

I was hanging a dress in the wardrobe. It was very quiet in the room. Outside the rain and wind were working up to a real end-of-winter storm.

"What is it, Rima?" I said at last.

She swung round, face haggard, eyes haunted.

"If you want to know, I'm going through hell. I've never felt so utterly alone as since the day Simon married me."

"Do you want to tell me about it?"

"I must! You're the only person in the world who'd understand. But just lately I've felt like . . . like a bloody spider! Spins her web, uses her mate . . . and devours him."

"Rima!"

"It's true. It's a relief to say it. That's the thing. I can say anything to you. Anything. We're down to the bare bones of truth. We have been since Johannesburg."

"What else do you want to say?"

"He doesn't love me."

"You blame me?"

She pushed her hair back, pressing her palms against her temples so that the smallness and narrowness of her face, the prominent nose and beautiful ears, seemed naked and pathetic.

"I blame myself. I've got that far in self-knowledge these last weeks. At a critical moment in our lives I let my work weigh against Simon. So there it is. I'm left with it."

"*And* your husband."

"My dutiful husband who doesn't love me."

For the first time in my life I felt a new sentiment towards Rima, one so foreign to our relationship that at first I did not recognise it for what it was. It was only when I put out my hand to touch her and found that she was trembling that it came to me that I was sorry for her.

"Listen," I said. "When the baby's born it'll all be different. He loves children. He's good with them and he'll be proud and happy. He'll fall in love with you all over again. You can make him."

"Not while you're around."

"I shan't be. I'm going to write to Roberto – ask him to find me a job in Italy."

"You'll have to wait till your mother's properly established at Sugar-Bush."

"I'll stay till the end of the year. Then I'm through."

"My baby's due in December."

"Yes. Next year we'll make a new start. I'm looking forward, Rima. You've got to do the same."

Her eyes clouded. "I don't see the future. I've tried to, but it's shapeless – like a log of wood without a soul. For me looking forward is like looking into a black night."

"You've cat's eyes."

I wanted to speak lightly, but the goose-pimples were rising on my arms.

"Maybe Rocky was right," she said. "Maybe we were married on a day of darkness. Even though the sun shone."

33

DAYS OF DECISION

IN THE FORTNIGHT that followed Rima and I almost found our way back into the old intimacy of our girlhood – with a difference. It was still spiced with antagonism, but I was no longer under her dominion. We had fought our battle for Simon, and we had both lost. There was a truce.

My cousin threw herself into her work for solace. Her studio was her refuge and her lair. Her birds were her favourite company. But, when I came home in the evenings, she seemed glad to welcome me. We were – with Simon away – on the old footing. No pretences. Once she said:

"It's curious – to me it's astonishing – but I really believe that I might come to love this baby. It's quickened. I'm aware of it as something demanding – something I'll have to serve."

"You *will* love it."

"Especially if it brings Simon back to me. You said you thought that could happen."

"It will."

She gave me a sharp, almost laughing look.

"There's still you to compete with."

"There won't be. Mother's settling very well at Sugar-Bush. I've written to Roberto already about a job in Italy. I won't be here much longer."

We were in her studio. The sculptures that had been on loan to the Johannesburg Gallery had been returned, and, with those she had brought back from Simon's flat, the large room was populated now with weird African figures and groups.

"In a way I'll be sorry if you go before the baby's born. I'd have liked to do a portrait of you. The curve of your neck, chin to breast, has something. It's flowing – young, yet maternal. With my infant in your arms—"

"Oh, no!" It was a cry of pain, as if she'd touched an unhealed wound.

"Simon's going to bring me some wood from the Copper Belt," she went on. "There's such lovely wood in the forests of Central Africa. So soft, it's almost malleable. I want to try some new experiments in sculpture."

"African motives?"

"Yes. I stick to what I know. Nothing could be more different from the Renaissance Italian art with its religious inspiration – the stuff I've come from studying – yet, in a way, the impulse is the same. It's something that springs from inside the artist, an interpretation of legend and ritual. Mother and Child comes into that category."

"You'll have Corinne and her baby as models soon. Hers is due in November, isn't it?"

She nodded. "It'll be nice for my child to have Corinne's as a companion. I've told her she can keep hers here. We can easily add another room."

I laughed. "Your studio won't be a studio with servants' quarters attached, it'll be the other way about if you go on adding to it."

"They're my models," she said. "Corinne and Lenno. The child will be too."

She was absorbed in her work again. Whatever else went wrong, she'd always have that.

I went back to my flat the day Simon returned from the Copper Belt.

Although the seer's prophecy had not come to pass and no phenomenal winds or days of darkness had disrupted our lives, our gaols were, by less miraculous means, disgorging many of their inmates. By September the State of Emergency was lifted and political detainees, in scores, hundreds, and thousands, were trickling back to their homes.

The country was looking ahead to the October Referendum which was to decide whether or not the Union of South Africa was to become a Republic.

The White people talked and argued about little else. The Bantu appeared indifferent; they had no vote and those who were politically inclined had other plans for the future of the Union. It was the Coloured people who were once again humiliated. They knew very well that if they had not been astutely removed from the common voters' roll by a piece of political chicanery – *verneukery*, they called it – their vote would have decided the issue. As it was, it was once more impressed upon them that, as far as their country's destiny was concerned, they were children of the twilight, whose fate lay in the hands of their White masters.

This was brought home to me when I went to the upholstery workshop at A. & B. to talk to Mr September. Mr September took his lunch break in the noon hour, so I could usually find him alone and relaxed around one o'clock. I'd often go and see him then and we'd exchange news of my brother and his daughter. I perched on the arm of a tattered old easy-chair and accepted a cigarette from the packet he offered me.

"My mother had a letter from Claude yesterday," I said, "she rang me up in a state of high excitement last night. Good news, isn't it?"

"My wife is delighted," he beamed. "It'll be our first grandchild. A beautiful present for next year."

"Claude says Fara will keep on with her television programmes as long as possible. She's a very popular T.V. star. And Claude's got another promotion – with better money. They're making a good life for themselves."

"We're thinking of going over there to settle when I retire. The whole family. They'll clear us out of our home soon. The authorities have given us all the time they can, but it's to be a White area, and that's that! If we've got to dig up our roots we might as well make a job o it." A brooding melancholy had settled on his face. "We don't want to live in a Nationalist republic."

"It'll be a change in name only," I said. "It's to be a democratic republic. The Nationalists are members of a political party. We've got to build a stronger opposition more in tune with world trends. Lots of Afrikaner intellectuals and Christians feel that way, and, once they've got their republic, they'll come into the open and say so. A good many have already. This *laager* of total *apartheid* can't survive. Slavery was abolished and women were emancipated. The colour bar – enforced by law – will go too."

"If ever that happens we can come home again. Your brother and

Fara too, perhaps. It would be nice to think that there might be a place in the sun for their child in the country of its origin."

He put out his cigarette and his eyes met mine and looked away with the evasiveness peculiar to so many of his people.

"My daughter is famous. Last week she danced with a royal prince at the Savoy Hotel in London. But, if she arrives at D. F. Malan Airport in Cape Town, she must tidy herself in the non-European cloakroom and walk out into our South African sunlight by a non-European exit."

Suddenly I saw her – the Fara I knew – with all the nervous emotional temperament of a renowned singer, her pride and fire contained in the enchanting casket of her pale brown skin, degraded and humiliated. In the name of sanity, why? I flushed, more ashamed than her father because what he had said was true.

I left Mr September and went up to the European employees' canteen for a snack. Simon was sitting at a corner table and beckoned me to join him. I did so. Disciplining myself to be "ordinary" with Simon was one of my resolutions.

"Rima and I want to come and see Sugar-Bush," he said. "What about Sunday supper?"

"That'd be fine. I'll be there for the weekend."

"We'll be along about half-past five."

Mummie and I were proud to show Simon and Rima round Sugar-Bush. The little farm was at its loveliest in the spring evening with the golden western light shining through the gap in the mountains, gilding the proteas in full bloom and the creamy arums growing in profusion beside the stream. The cottage was gaily painted and charmingly furnished with many of the smaller antiques my mother had saved from Loire.

After supper the Van Tonders came in for coffee and the *naartjie* liqueur we had always made at Loire from a recipe bequeathed to my mother by Grandma Lamotte.

Rima and Koosie Van Tonder began talking about birds.

"There are some wonderfully decorative up-country birds that I'm sure could be established here," said Koosie. "There's plenty of nectar for the honey-birds in the *suikerbossies* and the other flowering shrubs. I'm going to try a couple of importations."

Rima listened fascinated to the plans of this bearded naturalist with the weather-beaten face and horny sensitive hands. I knew by her observant look that she was mentally modelling his irregular expressive features.

"How will you get hold of these birds?" she asked.

Koosie plugged his pipe and lit it.

"I've got a first class snake-handler – a chap from way up in the northern Transvaal, not far from the Game Reserve. He went home to his country shortly after the troubles, and he'll be back any day now. He's going to bring me a collection of birds and reptiles. A young cousin is coming with him – a lad who helped snare them. I'd like to give the boy a job. He wants to work here, but I really don't need another Native."

"My father's looking for a second full-time gardener," said Rima. "If this boy's from the Shangaan country he might fit in with our people at Rosevale."

"I'll bear it in mind," Koosie promised. "I'll let Mrs Lamotte know when they turn up. It should be soon."

It was just the normal course of events. You hear of somebody and maybe you engage him. It's the grapevine system. No sixth sense flashed a red light for my benefit.

"He'd be raw," put in Mrs Van Tonder. "A boy who's good with wild life may be quite ignorant of gardening."

"He can learn," said Simon. "When Lenno came to Rosevale he knew nothing about flowers. But he learnt fast. And now he's training up as a house-boy. Rima and I stole him – and his Coloured wife – from Rosevale."

Mrs Van Tonder expressed surprise. "Natives and Coloured don't usually marry."

"Much more often these days. A lot of the old prejudices are going by the board."

A little pause followed Simon's words. The conversation was getting near home. Mummie's face had saddened, and I knew that she was thinking of Claude and Fara and their coming child. But she said:

"Corinne's folk don't approve at all. They don't like her being married to a Native."

Simon laughed. "Corinne likes it very much, and that's what matters!" The awkward moment passed, and presently our guests rose to go.

"Do you want a lift to town?" Rima asked me.

"No thanks. I've my scooter. I'm staying the night."

Three days later, on Wednesday, October 5th, the White population of South Africa went to the polls in strength to decide the Republican issue.

My mother and I were still registered in the Paarl Valley, so we had to record our votes there, and I took the day off to do so. We had arranged to spend it with the Vermeulens and Jamie told me to bring riding clothes.

The day was bright and mild and the mood of the people was peaceful. The result was a foregone conclusion, but the many who voted against a republic proved that the government in power had a formidable opposition to its principles.

Our valley had never looked more beautiful with its froth of fruit blossom, the young green of the grain and the bare vineyards beginning to sprout among the blue and yellow lupins. Going to the hustings under the oaks was more like going to a country fair. All our friends from round about were helping in one way or another and everybody was laughing and chatting, and where you put your cross on the voting card was your own private business.

When Jamie took me riding in the cool of the evening, he said:

"I'll bet we put our mark for different decisions today, my Maxie. But that's no reason why we shouldn't build together tomorrow and in the future. We both love this land of ours."

"Yes," I said. "And believe in it too. But we must share it more fairly."

"*Og, ja,*" he smiled. "We will! But now this minute let's just enjoy it. You look so sweet on Snow-White – two little thoroughbreds from the same valley."

He'd brought the mare over from Loire the day before and it was wonderful to feel her tender responsive mouth and perfect rhythm as we cantered along the foothills. On our way back to Bergplaas we passed by old Lizzie's house. Jamie reined in his horse.

"Remember this huisie, Maxie?"

I would never forget it. The fire, the burns, the dark room, old Lizzie's soothing hands and balm, Jamie waiting in agony for her attention, and, in the background, Corinne's young scared face.

"I wonder if Lizzie's in. I'd like to talk to her."

As I spoke the Wise Woman of Bergplaas hobbled out onto her narrow stoep that was covered with a vine just coming into leaf.

"Miss Maxie! I heard the horses and came to see who rides by old Lizzie's house."

She spoke in Afrikaans. Her toothless mouth had fallen in and the years had reduced her to a shrivelled hag. A crowd of children quickly gathered round us, calling out and cupping their little hands for *lekkers*. Jamie laughed as he dug in his pocket for the sweets and tossed them to the children. We did not dismount and the old woman stood beside Snow-White, her gentle wizard's hands stroking the soft satin nose of my mount.

"Can I take a message to Corinne for you?" I asked. "She's very well and the baby's due next month – your first great-grandchild, isn't it, Lizzie?"

But the old woman's face had crinkled into an ugly malicious scowl and her rheumy eyes blazed with scorn.

"Dat chile of de devil will come into dis world wit' no hands an' a forked tongue – like de serpent Satan, his pa!"

"Nee, Lizzie! Moenie vloek nie! Keep your curses for your enemies. Lenno's a fine young man, even if he is a Native."

"If my family don't marry Coloured dey marries White," growled Lizzie.

"You old snob! They can't do that any more – within the law. You're our Wise Woman here on Bergplaas – our healer not our witch. Go inside and pray for your grandchild and her baby!"

The old woman muttered a few profanities; then she looked up at me and cackled with mirth.

"You hear him, Miss Maxie! A man who cheeks his ouma beats his wife. So pasop!"

We laughed as we called goodbye and rode on. When I looked back over my shoulder the old dame was hobbling back into her little white box of a home.

Two days later the result of the Referendum was known. South Africa would be a Republic. The Afrikaners went to church and gave solemn thanks for the victory that would place the responsibility of founding the new state in their hands.

"It was a matter of sentiment either way," said Jamie. "Maybe a new beginning will be a good thing all round. It might even let loose a few new ideas!"

Mummie, Jamie and I were having Sunday supper with the Van

Tonders. We'd quite got over our nervousness about meeting stray serpents in Koosie's house. His pets were kept strictly within the confines of their pit, but this evening our host was more excited about affairs of the snake-pit than affairs of state. Treasure trove had arrived from the north.

"New ideas, my boy – the breath of life!" he said. "Eh, Mammie?"

His wife looked up from pouring the coffee, her eyes alight with affectionate amusement.

"New ideas? New snakes and birds. That's all you care about, Koosie. Milk and sugar, Mrs Lamotte?"

When we had all been served she said, "Now I think of it, Koosie, we promised to let Mrs Lamotte know when Milton came back. The boy he's brought with him seems bright but doesn't speak much English."

Milton, the snake-handler, had arrived that day with Drum, his cousin, and a number of exotic reptiles and birds that they had managed to snare during the months Milton had been home in his country. Koosie was delighted with the new arrivals and could think and talk of little else.

"The boy, Drum, has only a temporary pass," he said. "I got him one so that he could come here with Milton and give him a hand with the livestock. But Mr Antrobus would have to fix up his permission to remain on. They're tightening up these regulations, as you know."

"How long can he stay?" Mummie asked.

"A month."

"Well, that would be time enough to try him out, and if he's a success I'm sure my brother-in-law will be able to fix an extension."

"Would you like to see him?"

"Very much. If I talked to him tonight I could arrange to take him in to Rosevale tomorrow evening. I'm going in then, in any case."

My mother was not one to let the grass grow under her feet. Nor, it appeared, was Drum.

Both Natives were waiting at Jamie's car when we went out. The lights from the porch cast their long shadows across the bonnet.

"Ah, here we are," said Koosie Van Tonder. "This man is Milton, my snake-handler, and this is his cousin, Drum, who wants to work in Cape Town."

The older of the two men pulled a green knitted beret off his woolly head and stood turning it between his dark fingers. He was tall and very black. The younger was hatless with a shaven head which gleamed under the light. He was well built with a dazzling white smile and alert eyes. Milton had evidently constituted himself spokesman.

"Drum is strong and clever and he will work well," Milton told my mother. "But he does not yet know English. He will learn fast. Also the garden."

Like Lenno, I thought. Rima and I helped Lenno to learn English. But in the back of my mind I was wondering where I had seen Milton before. And when? That tall gangling figure was vaguely familiar, and the green beret. Surely I had met him somewhere, like this, by night light? As Mummie interviewed them I raked my memory, but it was Corinne who came into my mind. Corinne waiting for Simon, Rima and me at the car one night at Loire, begging us to find her work at Rosevale. Rima had done so, and the result had been the marriage with Lenno that had so upset old Lizzie. Ah, here it came – a vague recollection. Lenno and Leslie in the nights following the troubles, when they had stayed at Rosevale in the garden-shed Uncle Gideon had jokingly called "an armoury". Not Rocky. The Spoilers had threatened to burn Rocky's house and kill his family if he stayed "at the job" and he'd disappeared into Langa during those anxious times. Rocky hadn't been there when the tall Bantu stranger with the green knitted beret had haunted Rosevale. Leslie had called him "the watcher".

I felt my skin shrink; the goose-pimples were cold on my arms. Ridiculous, I thought. I'm being silly because that period has terrible associations for me. All cats are grey in the dark. Who can tell one Native from another at night? Green is a smart colour among them. Plenty of them have green knitted berets.

Mummie was saying, "Now make it clear to Drum that he must come down to my house – the cottage by the stream – at five o'clock tomorrow evening. Then I will take him with me to Rosevale and he can talk to Mr Gideon Antrobus."

"He will be there," said Milton. "Thank you very much, Madam."

They melted into the night.

Jamie dropped us home. When I said goodbye to him we stood in the shadow of a moonflower tree. The scent of the long white trumpets was intoxicating. As he drew me to him and kissed me something long quiesc-

K*

ent woke in me. I clung to him. We were young and it was spring.

All the same, when I turned off the light and closed my eyes that night, it was not Jamie who disturbed my peace. It was the gangling heavy-featured "watcher" who loitered, shadow-like and sinister, at the portals of sleep.

34

THE OLD GODS

NEXT EVENING I WAS to meet Mummie at Rosevale. When I arrived on my scooter her little car was already there.

Rocky said, "Miss Maxie must go to Miss Rima's studio. The ladies is there. My Master and Mister Simon is not yet back."

"What about the new boy?"

"He waits here for Master."

I strolled up the hill through the rose-garden. Long before I got to the studio I heard Rima's love-birds twittering and kissing to beat the band. But there was something else. The big sliding-window against the aviary was wide open, and, hovering round on the outside of the wire mesh, was an exquisite scarlet and blue bird with a long tail and a bright crest.

Aunt Kate, Rima and Mummie were standing under the *keurboom* in the full glory of its cyclamen-coloured flowers. They made a sign for me to be quiet and I joined them silently and watched the spectacular newcomer darting here and there, but constantly returning to the aviary, attracted by the budgies. This was no mountain-bird of the Cape. Surely this was the "phoenix" of our childhood! Presently I saw that it was not alone. There was a less glamorous hen with the sunbird. We gazed at them, enraptured. Then, as the sun vanished behind the Nek, the two alien birds flew away and were lost among the protea bushes and mimosa trees of the kloof.

Rima turned to me, breathless, eyes shining.

"Did you recognise him, Maxie – the legend of our childhood?"

"The phoenix! But smaller—"

"A miniature phoenix, like a miniature collie or poodle. A little tiny child of the sun." She was laughing and vibrant. "That new boy, Drum, brought the pair in a cage, and we freed them here. Mr Van Tonder reckons they could live among the *suikerbossies*."

"If the hawks don't get them," said Aunt Kate.

"Koosie has another pair that he's freed near his place. It'll be fun to compare notes," added Mummie.

"It has a mate," I said. "This phoenix has a mate. I'm so glad."

Rima touched my hand impulsively, and I didn't flinch at her touch. Sometimes, lately, I had thought that perhaps I was the one most to blame for everything that had gone so wrong in our lives. Other times I hated Simon and Rima alternately.

"You always minded that part of the story, Maxie. The aloneness of its life and death. To die alone – no!" She shivered.

"Oh, come now!" said Mummie. "The phoenix has a rather special way of dying. It's the symbol of rebirth. It goes through fire and rises again more brilliant than before."

Rima smiled. "All the same I'm glad our little phoenix is less unique. I like to think it'll set about its nesting, egg-laying and hatching in the good old-fashioned way."

Aunt Kate caught her eye, and they laughed. So Rima had told her mother about the coming baby? I hadn't seen my cousin so sparkling for ages.

"Was Daddy home when you arrived at Rosevale?" she asked me.

"No. The new boy was waiting for him."

"Let's go down and meet him. I want to see Daddy before he interviews Drum. We must take that boy. Drum may not know much English but he understands the language of wild things."

What Rima wanted was, within reason, good enough for her father. In any case, he liked the look of the Shangaan boy.

"I'll take him on trial till Friday. Then we can decide whether he stays or not," said Uncle Gideon.

Rima was delighted and begged that Drum should be set to work on the rockeries near her studio.

"So that you can bird-watch together," chuckled her father. "I suppose I have to indulge you."

She was so gay that evening. Seeing her with Simon, more relaxed than she had been for weeks, I thought, It *can* work! This marriage can be all right. The sooner I clear out the better.

That night I made my decision. The very next day I took a letter from Roberto Angeli to the Chairman's office and told my uncle formally that I wanted to leave Antrobus & Beeford. I handed him Roberto's letter and he read it in silence. Then he looked at me over his spectacles.

"I see by the date that you've been thinking this over for at least a week."

"Yes. I've made up my mind."

"You really prefer the idea of working in this Tourist Agency in Rome to staying on with us – even as a buyer?"

"I'd like to try it. For a year or two, perhaps. It's an American firm. I've always wanted to go to America."

"You're more likely to go there for A. & B.," said my uncle drily. "These people are employing you in Italy. However, you seem to have set your heart on a change. According to this letter, you should leave us next month."

"They want me in November – before the Christmas rush."

"You were doing so well here. I'd hoped you'd learnt the needs of our other branches on your tour. Next year I'd intended sending you overseas with Miss Pratt and Simon."

I said desperately, "Uncle Gideon, I know I'm letting you down. I can't explain. Please don't try to make me change my mind!" The words tumbled out and the tears started to my eyes.

"I don't know what's behind this, Maxie. I can only guess that your reasons are personal – and that they are very strong indeed. I won't try to dissuade you. Write to Roberto and accept."

He passed the letter back across his desk. I have often wondered since how much he guessed. I still do.

Next morning, while I was getting breakfast, my telephone rang. It was Rima.

"What's this Dad tells us about you taking a job with a travel agency in Rome?"

"I'm going next month."

"When can you come and tell me about it?"

"I can't today—"

"Friday then. Drink-time in my studio."

"I'll have Jamie with me. He's picking me up at A. & B., and we're going to Sugar-Bush for the weekend."

"I'd love to see him. Bring him along. Simon'll be late that evening. He and Dad have a business conference, that's likely to keep them till near seven at the earliest. Mom will be out too – at Somerset West – so I'll be alone in my glory."

"All right then."

"How come Jamie can get off on a Friday afternoon – pay day?"

"His brother, Boet, is staying with him."

"So Boet'll cope while Jamie courts." She laughed. "There's something else I want to talk to you about. Leslie and Lenno are gunning for Drum. They've both told me Drum'll make trouble if he stays."

"Do they say why?"

"Not a thing. Dead-pan. But they mean to get him fired."

The sinister shadowy figure came back to my mind, the "watcher" who'd hung about Rosevale at the time of the March troubles. Rima didn't know about him. She'd been in Italy then.

"Are you there, Maxie? The line went dead or something."

"I'm here, but I must rush. See you Friday."

We'd go and see Rima before Simon could get home. I would be glad to show her Roberto's letter and let her know that I was going out of their lives. It was the only answer. I would return from Europe in a year or two cured of the infatuation that had obsessed me for so long. By then he'd be out of my system. He'd be Rima's husband, as far as I was concerned. No more. But my eyes went to the blank space on the wall above the fireplace. Rima's picture of the knight and the damsel on the white charger was gone. One day I would put it back because it was a live and lovely thing. When I could put it back and look at it dispassionately, without a sinking in my breast, I'd know that I was cured of an old sickness. I longed for that day. It would be freedom day for me.

When I got back from A. & B. on Friday evening, Jamie was already outside the flats. He had parked his car on the sea side of the road and he stood on the greensward beyond it watching the manes of flying spray stream back from the bursting lines of surf. I stopped my scooter by his car and joined him, slipping my arm through his and drawing a deep breath.

"Good drop of ozone!"

"*Ja,* wonderful. It's steaming hot in the valley today. You know something, Maxie. My brother, Boet, says there's a farm for sale Gansbaai way, only a couple of miles from the sea. Fine for cows and sheep as well as crops. It's going for a song. This is a good time to buy. Prices will go up again when folk get their nerve back and realise that South Africa is God's own country after all."

"Tell me more."

"The *huisie* is a little old farmhouse, simple but strongly built. Yellow-wood floors and rafters. No gables and mouldings. Not grand, like Loire. Just homely. I'm going out there with Boet to look at it on Sunday week. Why don't you come?"

"Why not? But what about Loire? If you buy that place it doesn't mean you can leave Loire at short notice."

"The owner's moving in next year. He can do his own farming. I'm not one to work under the boss's thumb. Only so long as he's an absentee landlord and I'm in full charge."

I laughed. "Well, that'll be something else to tell Rima."

"Rima?"

"I said we'd join her in the studio for a drink. Let's go and get it over, then we can come back here to the flat and I'll doll myself up to dine and dance with you."

"All right," he said. "But why did you say it'd be something else to tell Rima? Have you news for her too?"

"Suspicious creature! Yes, Jamie, I have. I'm leaving South Africa next month."

"No!"

In the level evening light his hair was gold as ripe wheat and his eyes were bright with sudden distress in the deep tan of his face.

"Where can you be going? And why? How will I get along without you? What *is* this thing?"

"Roberto's found me a job in an American travel agency. It's in Rome. Good money and the chance of travelling. Europe . . . America . . ."

"The Rhineland – where I fell in love with you."

"Ah, Jamie, that was centuries ago."

"Whole centuries of wanting you! Why must you go away?"

"I have to. There's something I have to work out for myself . . . away from here . . . away from you—"

"Away from one or two other people, perhaps?"

I turned abruptly from him.

"Come," I said over my shoulder. "Let's go on up to Rosevale."

We drove to Kloof Nek along the coast and up through the Glen to avoid the city. The evening was unbelievably beautiful. Below us were glimpses of dazzling blue sea and silvery sand, and above us the gaunt granite Apostles were benign in the western light.

At Rosevale we found Leslie watering the border of the rose-garden. "How is it you're still working?" I asked. "It's six o'clock."

On pay day he always left on the dot of five to do his weekend shopping.

"I wait to see Master."

I smiled. Aunt Kate would have given the boys their pay-packet at lunch time, but, when it was a question of borrowing money, it was the Master's affair. Leslie gave me a sheepish grin. We both understood perfectly.

"Master'll be late back," I said.

"I know."

I turned to Jamie. "Leslie's training a new boy in the garden – a boy from Van Tonder's."

"I remember. Your mother talked to him on Sunday night."

"Drum have go." Leslie's tone was laconic.

Jamie looked at him in surprise.

"You mean he's not going to stay here after all?"

"He have go back to his homeland. Now. There is a train at half-past five. Drum have go to catch it."

In a way I was not surprised. Rima had said that Leslie and Lenno were "gunning for Drum".

"Did Master sack him?" I asked.

"I really don't know."

The black dead-pan look warned me that there was no point in pursuing the matter. Drum's return fare to the north would have been paid by Koosie Van Tonder in the first place, and he would have received his Rosevale wages today. Perhaps he was homesick. At all events, whatever the reason for his departure, it solved a problem. Leslie and Lenno would be satisfied, even if Rima was disappointed.

We stood for a few minutes looking across the vale towards Rima's studio. The L-shaped extension for Lenno and Corinne did not show from here, and the studio itself was partially concealed by the spreading *keurboom*. The roses – the first wave of the season – formed a swathe of delicate colour and fragrance. Stirring discordant music drifted down to us. Rima's radiogram was playing Stravinsky's Firebird.

"Does Rima often work to music?" Jamie asked.

"Yes. Her little birds love it. They respond. At the moment she has a craze for the Firebird. It's too hysterical for me."

The studio seemed to melt into the kloof with the setting of the sun, though the roses were still touched with light. It is always very lovely to me the way the afternoon lingers on in certain places. From where we were we could see the city and the Flats still bathed in the liquid amber glow which we, masked by the western buttress, were losing fast.

The radiogram clicked into silence.

Jamie put his arm about my shoulders. He smiled as if to say, "This moment must never pass. It is full of peace and harmony." Or perhaps that was what I read into his smile, for a strange thing was happening to me. It was like that other time on the mountain-side when I knew that I was no longer consumed with hate for my father's killers. I felt cleansed of something virulent and destructive. There was no more hate in me for Rima.

Leslie bent to move the perforated hose sprinkling the border of stocks and forget-me-nots and early spring flowers. How delicately he touched things! I had often noticed that. From somewhere near the *keurboom*, up by the studio, a flash of jewelled colour started into the air, glittered for a second in the last rays of the sun, and vanished into the purple velvet gloom of the mountain. So the little phoenix was still around? I wanted to ask Leslie about it and to tell Jamie about the sunbird from the Shangaan country, but the strange peace held me silent, as if spellbound.

Then we heard it. Terrifying, yet familiar.

For years Leslie and Lenno had whistled to one another across the garden, and later Corinne had shared their call that was more bird-like than human. But the cry that now pierced the evening air was very human indeed. It was urgent and panic-stricken, a desperate danger signal.

Leslie dropped the hose and uttered a shrill answering whistle.

"It is Lenno – something bad!"

The next instant he was racing up the hill with long springy strides.

"Come, Maxie!"

Jamie took my hand and we too ran along the steep grass paths between the terraced rosebuds. Lenno was calling to Leslie in their own language, and then, between the *keurboom* and the rose-garden, we saw Corinne's clumsy form kneeling by a figure prone on the grass. As we came up with her she raised an ashen face.

"She is dead, Miss Maxie! Miss Rima is dead! *Die slang het haar doodgebyt!*"

Jamie fell on his knees beside Rima. She lay in a curious twisted attitude with her head buried in her arms. She wore her paint-daubed working smock and jeans, and an old paint-rag had been tied in a makeshift tourniquet above her left knee. The bare flesh between her sandal and her trouser-leg was discoloured and swollen and two angry punctures showed above her slender heel.

"Quick, Maxie! Ring up the doctor and say it's a case of snake-bite." Lenno said: "It is too late."

Jamie was applying his lips to the bite, trying to suck the poison from it. But Corinne stooped and dragged at his arm.

"Nee, baas Jamie. Don't poison yourself! There is nothing you can do."

"It is too late," repeated Lenno. "I have kill the snake. It is the bad one – the quick one."

His face was grey and beaded with sweat.

I had not moved. It was no use. Jamie turned Rima gently onto her back, but, as her hands and her red hair fell limply away from her face, he gasped in horror.

"Oh, God, poor Rima!"

The small blotched features were cast in a mould of mortal terror.

We could guess how it must have been – the shock, the cry drowned by the Firebird's furious symphony, a desperate attempt to tie a tourniquet before stumbling out in search of help. Rima – alone in so much fear!

Jamie put his hand over her heart. The baby, I thought. I stooped down and laid my ear against her body where, so short a time ago, her child had been quick with life. There was only stillness now and a deadly chill that crept icily into my own warm body and set my teeth chattering.

Jamie carried her tenderly into the studio, where her little love-birds still twittered, and laid her on the divan. Corinne moved forward and closed the staring eyes. She went heavily to her own quarters and fetched a sheet. Before she covered Rima she made the sign of the cross over the quiet heart. They know about death – birth and death. Somehow the Coloured people are closer to these things than we are.

Jamie was already on the telephone to the house doctor, who was an old friend of the Antrobus family.

"Dr Maas? . . . This is Jamie Vermeulen. I'm speaking from Rosevale – Rima's studio. Something terrible has happened . . . she was bitten by a snake . . . what sort?" He was frowning. "I don't know, but I'm afraid it's too late in any case. There's nothing anybody can do for her . . . Yes, please come. We'd be grateful."

He hung up and turned to me.

"He's coming right away. Now Simon – where can we get Simon and her father? What about her mother?"

"Simon and Uncle Gideon should be at A. & B. The meeting was in the Chairman's office. Aunt Kate was spending the afternoon at Somerset West. She won't be back till dinner time."

"Then she's probably on her way."

He was dialling A. & B. But there was no reply. The meeting must be over. They too would be on their way home.

The sun had set, the birds were almost silent now, and the long shadows of Rima's sculptures flowed across the floor, moving in upon us, dark, atavistic, the brooding spirit of Africa. The Rain Goddess and the primitive Genesis seemed to watch us. How exhausted she had been when she had completed that! As if she, the artist midwife, had herself given birth. In a corner was the poetic symmetry of Oneness, inspired by Jamie and me the day she had found us in that passionless embrace – the day he had told me about winning the Rhodes Scholarship. His burnt hands had been folded under my blistered back in the shade of the trees at Loire. Claude and Fara were here too, their portraits on the big work-table against which Jamie leaned; and there was the Blood Horse, symbolic of the brave bible-horse – "he paweth in the valley and rejoiceth in his strength" – and Corinne and Lenno. We had all been grist to Rima's mill one way or another. But it was Africa that had really possessed her – the Old Gods of Africa. My eyes fell on a rough painting lying on the table. A few bold strokes and her rare use of colour suggested the new phoenix soaring from the fiery nest to the distant altar of the sun.

Lenno and Leslie stood with bowed heads at the foot of her divan as if they guarded a catafalque. Tears streamed down Leslie's cheeks and splashed unheeded on the floor-boards. Lenno leaned lightly on the long-handled garden hoe with which he had killed the snake. Rima had sculpted him in much the same attitude, a noble warrior leaning on his long-throwing assegai.

Jamie raised his head slowly and looked at Lenno.

"The doctor asked me what snake it was. Where is the snake you killed?"

A deep silence held the room. No one answered, but beads of sweat broke out on the boy's upper lip and smooth wide forehead.

"I do not know, baas Jamie."

My skin crawled. Evil was in the air. The Old Gods were powerful still.

Suddenly Jamie sprang at Lenno's throat.

"Don't give me that! You know damn well where the snake is. You know what snake it was! The bad one, you said, the quick one. Puff adder? Cobra? Show me, or I'll strangle you!"

Corinne cried out. "Leave him, baas Jamie! I will show you the snake. Come with me."

She led us through the little pantry into her own quarters and pointed to a flat round basket of native workmanship just inside the open door.

"It is there. The mamba."

"The mamba! That is impossible!"

He removed the lid and stared down at the slim green coils and yellow under-belly of the reptile still writhing though its tiny head was crushed.

"Where did Lenno kill this thing?"

"In Miss Rima's studio – near the birds."

"How did it get here? A green mamba!"

"I don't know."

"You must think hard, Corinne." He was gentle and persuasive now. "What you don't know you must try to guess."

She stared at him as if mesmerised, her huge liquid eyes brimming, as he tried to make her speak.

"One thing you must know as well as I do. The mamba is no snake of the Cape."

She clasped her arms across her heavy pregnant body in a gesture both defensive and touching.

"Whoever brought this snake to Rosevale meant one thing only, Corinne. Murder."

Her arms tightened over her unborn child. She looked ill and near her time. She leaned against the lintel of the door as though she might faint. But Jamie persisted relentlessly.

"*Who* was meant to die? Miss Rima? Surely not Miss Rima?"

I went to Corinne and put my arms about her. I felt the spasm of pain seize her and heard her groan in the first sharp pang of birth. She forced the answer from pale lips.

"It was I who was meant to die – I and my child."

35

THE WHITE HEIFER

ORINNE'S SON WAS prematurely born that night, and, thanks to Jamie, old Lizzie – driven from Bergplaas to Cape Town by Boet Vermeulen – arrived in time to assist Dr Maas with the delivery of her first great-grandchild, a small near perfect replica of his father.

In the days that followed we pieced the facts together patiently, bit by bit. From Leslie, from Rocky, from Corinne, even from Koosie Van Tonder. Not from Lenno, who refused to speak.

Koosie was not surprised that Drum had gone. Milton too had left for the north by that same evening train.

"You never know what they're up to," he grumbled. "But at least they brought me my stuff before clearing out. Though – come to that – there's a new green mamba missing from my pit! Anyway, it seems they were offered a fat sum to work for a German naturalist who's travelling round Africa collecting specimens for European zoos. This fellow saw Milton in my snake-park and got chatting to him, and the deal was clinched. The bloody fellow's probably got my mamba!"

Jamie and I knew better than that, but we left it alone. The dead snake had disappeared mysteriously just after Dr Maas arrived and gave his attention to Corinne, whose labour was brief but severe.

It was no great mystery really. Just one of those African tragedies that happen time and again among a primitive people under the sway of the sorcerer. Only, in this case, vengeance had stretched a very long arm across time and space for its victim, and the death blow had miscarried.

The story had begun in the Shangaan country long before Leslie had introduced his nephew, Lenno, into Rosevale garden. Lenno had come to the city to earn the bride-price for his betrothed, the daughter of the powerful witch-doctor. He had changed his mind and fallen in love with Corinne, the Coloured girl. Rima and I had made a joke of it when we heard from Leslie why Lenno refused to go back to his country when his time came to do so. The witch-doctor would kill him or turn him into a crocodile. "One day we'll see a crocodile mowing the lawn!" we'd said, giggling hilariously.

Two more years had passed. The March troubles had come, with many curious repercussions. Men from the distant Bantu homelands had suddenly appeared in the Bachelors' Quarters at Langa – men with important friends among the far away tribesmen as well as in the city. A considerable number of these strangers were political intriguers and their attendant thugs, the Spoilers; they knew how to play on the superstitions of the people. Among the many messages and prophecies that filtered through the grapevine at this time was an entirely personal threat delivered to Lenno through the agency of Milton, the Shangaan snake-handler.

The young man must return to his country and pay *lobola* for the bride who still waited for him and whose value in cows was diminishing with every day that ripened her beauty past its prime.

Lenno had scoffed at the idea of paying cattle for a girl he no longer desired, and, in spite of Milton's warnings and his uncle's anxiety, he had remained in Cape Town and married Corinne. Milton, the "watcher", had taken his home-leave and reported to the witch-doctor that the girl who had supplanted his daughter was not even a Bantu but a Coloured mongrel who despised the *kraal* and mocked at tribal custom.

In the months that followed, the jilted girl's brother, Drum, had helped Milton collect reptiles for the Van Tonder Snake Park, including the deadly green mamba, whose poison sacs, after the winter hibernation, were full of lethal venom.

The chance that took my mother to Sugar-Bush may have simplified Drum's assignment, but nothing would have prevented him from carrying out his share of it. That the result was not according to plan was fate. The Old Gods had their reasons for putting a twist in the pig's tail.

It was Corinne who told me what happened after that.

Jamie drove Mummie and me up to Rosevale the day after the tragedy – the day Rima was cremated with only the family and Jamie and Rocky at the service. Afterwards, while Mummie stayed with Aunt Kate, Jamie took me up to the studio and left me alone with Corinne.

She was lying in bed with her new-born baby in the crook of her arm. Shock and fear had left their mark on her, but, when she looked at the little head covered with frizzy hair, her great eyes softened and I thought it was no wonder that Rima had wanted to sculpt her.

She answered my questions frankly, once she realised that we did not intend to call the police.

"If the police come," she said, "perhaps they make Lenno go back to his country, and I am not a woman to live in a kraal with kaffirs."

"The police won't interest themselves. They don't like witchcraft cases when there isn't so much as a piece of evidence to support them."

She smiled then. "The snake is gone."

"Only Lenno knows where," I said. "And you, perhaps."

"He tells me nothing. Drum comes here and Lenno orders me to have nothing to do with him, but he does not say why. He doesn't tell me that Drum is the brother of the girl he was supposed to marry."

"Did you obey his order?"

"Am I a Native wife to take orders from my husband? Drum shows me a friendly face and I am sorry for him because he is a stranger. He is often working up here, where Miss Rima has him busy on her rockery. When we have a cup of tea she tells me to give him one too, and he drinks it outside our quarters. He smiles and thanks me politely. Am I to look sour and say nothing – I, who can speak a little of his language?"

"It was Lenno's fault. He should have told you who Drum was."

"Natuurlik!" She spoke half in English and half in Afrikaans, but when she became excited or emotional, she fell into the language of her people. "So yesterday afternoon, when Drum comes to my door with that pretty basket and says it is a present for me, I am pleased. I am washing up Miss Rima's tea-pot and cup, and I tell him to put it down inside the door. He says goodbye and that is the last I see of him."

"Where was Lenno then?"

"He is working in the garden at Kloof Cottage. Miss Rima is busy here in the studio. She says not to disturb her till Miss Maxie and baas Jamie come. She is playing that wild music that makes the birds sing. So then I look at the basket and wonder what is in it, and think it will be nice later on for my sewing. I bend down and untie the cord round it . . ."

She shuddered violently and clasped her baby son closely to her breast.

"Miss Maxie, something moves in the basket! There is a rustling and a hiss. I scream and run over to Kloof Cottage to find Lenno. I suppose the snake slithers out of his basket to crawl into the room of the music and the birds. How do I know what happens after I run away?"

"What did Lenno do?"

"I tell him Drum has brought me something that lives and I am frightened. Lenno is wild because he too is afraid. He picks up his hoe like he wants to hit me, and he calls out, 'I told you not to speak to that man!' Then he tells me who Drum is, and I am still more scared, so I get cross and we quarrel. We stand there quarrelling, while, over in the studio, poor Miss Rima . . ."

She broke off, sobbing bitterly.

"Corinne, stop howling! Tell me calmly what happened next."

She snivelled and gulped. "It's true I must be calm. My ouma says if I cry so much my milk will turn to poison – snake poison – and this small child needs all I can give him that is good and pure. She says if I don't do what she tells me the doctor will take him away and put him in an incubator like a chicken and he'll grow up with a cock's red comb on his head."

She pulled herself together.

"Suddenly we hear that the music has stopped. It is quite still, except for the birds. Then the new bird – the bright one – is flying high up into the kloof. All day he has been playing round the big cage with the budgies, and Miss Rima is always happy when she sees him. My ouma says that bird is Miss Rima's soul. She has seen the bird. This morning he came back. Soon, she says, he will go and be seen no more."

What ancient lore made old Lizzie say such a strange thing? Who was the poet who wrote "There's wisdom in women, of more than they have known, and thoughts go blowing through them are wiser than their own"? Corinne went on talking. Excitable now.

"We run to the studio and Lenno sees the snake outside the big cage. He has the hoe and he brings it down on the thing's head. It is dead but it goes on wriggling. I rush outside to shout for Leslie in the rose-garden, and then I see Miss Rima lying near the tree."

"You're working yourself into a state again. I'm going to leave you. But remember, Corinne, nothing of all this was your fault."

I left her weeping, with old Lizzie bullying her fondly.

When I walked back across the garden to Rosevale I found Leslie in the same spot where we had heard that shrill danger signal from Lenno only twenty-four hours ago. He was picking stink-bugs off the roses, and dropping them into his little can of insecticide. He stopped when I spoke to him.

"I have been talking to Corinne, Leslie, and now I know a good deal of this affair, but there is something I cannot understand. Why must it be so complicated? Why this thing with the mamba?"

"The chief – the witch-doctor – he is of the Mamba people."

I knew about tribal totems, but still it was obscure.

"It went wrong," I said. "This wicked magic went wrong. Miss Rima was murdered!"

He said nothing. What was the use? The tortuous ways of sorcery were beyond White folk to understand. I persisted.

"If Drum wanted to avenge his sister he could have killed Lenno – or Corinne – himself. And made sure."

Leslie put down the can with its dead insect pests and stood looking sombrely down over Cape Town, sprawling among its gardens between the mountain and the sea.

"Miss Maxie knows that in the White man's city a person who kills another will be punished. He will hang. The police will not trouble to punish a snake."

"So Miss Rima dies."

Sorrow and exhaustion overwhelmed me.

Jamie was coming out of the big house. I went to meet him.

"I want to go home. Take us back to Sugar-Bush. Now."

"Yes. Your ma's waiting for you."

I wept against his shoulder while his hand gently stroked my hair.

On the following Sunday he took me to see the farm on the Gansbaai coast. In the end Boet didn't come with us. We drove out there alone.

It lay at the foot of a hill among trees and wild flowering shrubs. A sturdy white house, with wooden shutters opening flat against the wall like elephant's ears, stood in the shade of spreading acacias. When we climbed the hill we could see the sparkling blue of the ocean and fishing boats swaying beyond the surf where the gulls and duikers flew and dived. Sheep grazed in the heatherland and there were cattle in the green pasture near the dam.

In a cool stable we found a white cow with her new-born calf.

"A white cow!" Jamie exclaimed. "One seldom sees such a thing!"

"It reminds me of Italy. The pure white oxen of Italy."

I remembered my father whose long perilous journey into freedom had led him across the mountains, south to the Abruzzi, where the peasants had been his protectors and his friends and the word "freedom" had meant a bed of straw in a cow-shed with the gentle white oxen for company.

In three weeks' time I would be on my way to Rome.

I was to spend my last few days at Sugar-Bush with Mummie.

Simon fetched me at my flat to take me there. He came after work. The November afternoon was hot, with the striped canvas canopy out over my seascape window and a flimsy slatted bamboo blind lowered to cut the light. There were roses in a bowl on the table.

"It still looks like you," he said, "although you are going away. When does the new tenant move in?"

"Tomorrow. I'm leaving the key with the porter. She's a friend of old Prattle's and she's taken the flat on a year's lease, just as it is. I only had to pack my clothes."

He glanced at the two expanding suitcases, one eyebrow raised. "Everything in those?"

"No. A trunk went by sea."

His eyes wandered to the blank wall space where once the white charger had carried the knight and the little damsel through a flurry of autumn leaves.

"One day I'll put it back," I said.

His face was drawn and deeply carved. Rima, the sculptor, would have liked it this way. You could almost see the bones. But Rima, the woman, would have grieved.

"I brought you something," he said. "But perhaps, after all, you won't want it."

He was taking the brown paper wrapping from a picture which had been framed to match the one that was gone.

"This . . . it has the same impulse as the other . . . swift and strong. Immortal, in a way."

"Ah, Simon!"

I stood it on the mantelshelf, and the slatted light from the bamboo blind fell across it in slender bars as if to cage the soaring spirit. It was

Rima's impression of the phoenix, the one I had seen on her big work-table that fateful day. Touches of red, gold and blue brought the winged and crested legend to vivid life. All the fancies of our childhood and dreams of our girlhood were embodied in that enchanted bird rising from its nest of fire.

I wanted to tell Simon that I had seen it fly into the dusk in the hour of Rima's death; that old Lizzie, the Wise Woman, had said of this bird that it was Rima's soul. But my throat was working and the striped shadow of the bamboo blind blurred and misted as I gazed at the picture that was Rima.

"Her art came first . . . I resented that." He spoke humbly, which was not like him.

I unlocked the *kist* in which I had put her picture of the charger, and drew it out and set it beside the phoenix. We three, I thought. He and I, and the bright wings of genius.

"Loire and the valley," he said. "The hunts and the holidays. It all seems so long ago. It was you who understood her, Chick."

"She was my greatest friend and my worst enemy. When you love and hate someone so much you make them part of yourself."

I put both pictures into the *kist* and turned the big brass key in the lock.

"When I come back from Italy I'll hang those two pictures in a place of honour."

I slipped the key into my travelling bag, and crossed the room to draw up the sunblind and the canopy. Simon stood beside me and we looked out over the wide Atlantic. A whaling fleet was putting out to sea, bound for the ice and the midnight sun of the Antarctic.

"Do you remember a fleet of dhows sailing in the sunset? The time you told me about the phoenix thought?"

"Very well indeed."

I closed the window. The whalers were away on the horizon, vanishing over the rim of the world as once the dhows had done.

"Turn on the light, please, Simon. I'm going to draw the curtains."

He switched on the light just inside the door. The sound of the metal runners on the curtain-rod was brisk and final.

"Is that the lot? What about the other windows?" he asked.

"All done. I'm ready to go."

He stood waiting for me, there by the door.

Longing shook me like a wave of burning fever – the old familiar sickness – as his eyes told me that he wanted to take me in his arms. He waited, holding me only with his eyes. But we both knew that I must take the first step of this difficult journey into freedom without farewells.

I bent to pick up a suitcase.

"No! Leave those for me, Maxie. Just bring your coat and hat, and lock the door."

So we went out of my flat and down to the car. And we were separate. The fever ebbed and left me cold and empty. This was how it had to be. Soon I would be gone – far from here, far from him.

I caught the five o'clock plane for Johannesburg on a calm summer's evening. The Consadines would meet me there and set me on my way next morning.

Mummie and Jamie came to D. F. Malan Airport to see me off, and, at the last, Simon and Aunt Kate joined them at the barrier – too late for more than a word, a smile and a last quick embrace. But Simon didn't touch me. It was Jamie who swung me off my feet in one of his great boyish hugs.

"Come back soon," he whispered. "Come back to me!"

The other passengers had straggled across the runway to the plane. I was the last. I didn't look back. Simon hadn't even touched my hand, but I knew that he could feel me in his arms, because we had loved each other. I did not then know whether that love was over or whether it would one day reawaken.

The air hostess checked me into the plane.

"Miss Lamotte: Yes, over there by the window. Number eleven. Fasten your seat-belt, please."

I took my seat and looked down to make some sign to Mummie and the others, but the wing blocked my view.

The steps were trundled away and the door slammed. There was a roar and a shudder, the forward lumbering run, the slow turn into the wind; off again, faster now; up with the quiet drumming of flight and the wheels folding away into the belly of the silver bird. I looked down at the lonely dragon-fly shadow, cut adrift and cast loose to flit alone over the wattle-clothed Flats. It moved over the locations of Nyanga and Langa, over Rocky's little house and the bleak Bachelors' Quarters, and the place on the road where my father had been stoned and burned to death by men who did not even know his name. It climbed the jagged Drakenstein Range and headed north, away from the sea and the Gansbaai coast.

Away over there the amber evening light would be falling upon a small white farmhouse under a wooded hill, on sheep in the heatherlands and cattle under the willows, on the thatch of a cool clean shed where a white heifer stood with her calf.

My father had found freedom in a mountain stable with the white oxen of Italy. Where would I find it? Perhaps it existed only in the heart. Perhaps one day I would hang Rima's pictures in the living-room of a white farmhouse, and look at them with tranquil eyes.

That day I would be free.

CAPE OF GOOD HOPE
1961